HOW TO FIND

FAIRIES

ISBN: 9798432686930

Table of contents

Introduction

Setting the Stage for the Exploration of the World of Fairies

In the very heart of lush and ancient forests, where the canopy of leaves above parts just enough to reveal a mesmerizing tapestry of twinkling stars in the inky night sky, and where the gentle caresses of the wind carry hushed whispers that seem to emanate from the very depths of nature itself, there exists a realm unlike any other—a realm shrouded in an aura of enchantment and untamed beauty. This is a world that lies hidden from the casual observer, a world inhabited by creatures of boundless wonder and whimsy, a world where the extraordinary becomes ordinary—the realm of fairies.

Titania. My Oberon! what visions have I seen!
Methought I was enamour'd of an ass.
Oberon. There lies your love. *Act IV. Scene 1.*

As we prepare to embark on this extraordinary journey into the captivating world of fairies, let us take a moment to conjure the atmosphere, to conjure the very essence of this mystical realm. Close your eyes, if you will, and let your imagination be the compass that guides you. Picture yourself at the edge of an ancient woodland, where the trees stand tall and proud, their gnarled branches reaching out like welcoming arms, inviting you to step into their sacred domain.

The air is thick with the heady scent of earth and flora, carrying hints of wildflowers and dew-kissed grass. Each step you take is cushioned by a carpet of velvety moss and fallen leaves, releasing a faint, melodic rustle as you move forward. The world around you seems to shimmer with an otherworldly light, and the sounds of nature blend into a soothing symphony—the soft babbling of a hidden brook, the occasional chirping of crickets, and the distant call of an owl, echoing through the woods.

Above, the celestial canvas is alive with stars, each one a tiny beacon in the vast expanse of the cosmos, and the moon, a pale, silvery disk, bathes the forest in its gentle glow. It's a night where time itself appears to stand still, where the boundaries between reality and fantasy blur, and the unseen wonders of the natural world come to life.

Now, as we stand at the threshold of this enchanted realm, let us collectively open our minds to the possibility that, just beyond the next gnarled tree trunk or behind the cascading waterfall, we may catch our first glimpse of the ethereal and magical beings that have long danced at the edges of our collective imagination—the fairies. With our hearts open and our senses attuned, we prepare to venture deeper into the enchanting world that has beckoned to us since time immemorial, ready to discover the secrets, stories, and enchantments that await us within.

My Personal Motivation and Connection to the Subject

Allow me to illuminate the personal wellspring of motivation that fuels this expedition into the labyrinthine tapestry of fairy folklore and legend. From the earliest chapters of my life, I have been inexorably drawn to the enchanting realm of fairies, a connection that has remained unwavering throughout my journey into adulthood. This deep affinity for the fairy world has been, and continues to be, a source of inspiration that sustains me.

It was during my formative years that I initially encountered the ethereal allure of fairies, a fascination that was not merely ephemeral but rather a lifelong calling. My earliest recollections are suffused with the entrancing tales shared by my grandmother, who spun vivid narratives of fairies, their luminous presence gracing the twilight hours. These stories, more than mere anecdotes, became integral threads interwoven within the fabric of my being, stimulating a ceaseless curiosity to comprehend these enigmatic beings and the realms they inhabit.

Thus, this undertaking transcends the boundaries of a mere scholarly endeavor or whimsical flight of fancy; it is, instead, a labor of devotion. A manifestation of the abiding fascination that fairies have kindled within my soul, as well as within the hearts of countless others. It signifies a journey embarked upon to unlock the mysteries of a world that exists at the juncture of reality and fantasy—a world that has enthralled humanity for centuries. However, it is imperative to emphasize that this narrative is not confined solely to my connection and experiences; rather, it extends an open-hearted invitation to you, dear reader, to traverse the threshold into this realm of enchantment. Together, we will traverse the diverse dimensions of fairy existence, decipher the myths and legends that have been seamlessly woven into the rich tapestry of our cultural heritage, and explore the intricate classifications that defy simplistic categorization.

In the course of our exploration, we will scrutinize how the duality of good and malevolent fairies has left indelible marks on our collective moral compass. We will venture into the kaleidoscopic world of fae, from the most renowned and beloved to the lesser-known and regionally nuanced. Along this voyage, we shall uncover the ancient methodologies for communicating with fairies, unveil the secrets of their discovery, and illuminate their profound interconnectedness with the natural world. The tales of personal encounters, leaving enduring imprints on the lives of those who attest to the magic, will be rendered with both the reverence of believers and the scrutiny of rational inquiry. Our final chapters will contemplate the contemporary beliefs and practices surrounding fairies, shedding light on how these ethereal beings continue to influence our world in an era of rapid technological advancement and global interconnectedness. Additionally, we shall underscore the indispensable need to safeguard fairy folklore and traditions, ensuring that the essence of enchantment perseveres for generations to come.

Chapter 1
The Nature of Fairies

1A. Cultural Significance

Fairies in Different Cultures

The captivating realm of fairies holds an enduring fascination for the human imagination, transcending geographical boundaries and cultural divides. In this comprehensive and enchanting exploration, we embark on a captivating global journey, delving deep into the multifaceted manifestations of fairies that grace the tapestry of cultures and societies around the world. Each unique culture we encounter weaves its own distinct interpretation into the rich fabric of fairy lore, bestowing upon these mystical beings profound and varied symbolic meanings.

From the playful and mischievous Puck, a beloved character in Shakespeare's immortal classic "A Midsummer Night's Dream," to the ethereal and benevolent Sidhe of Irish folklore, fairies have assumed an astonishing array of forms and roles throughout history. We shall venture into the depths of literature, art, and even religion, embarking on a quest to unravel the intricate threads of their influence and significance within these realms. In doing so, we aim to uncover how these enchanting entities have etched themselves indelibly into the cultural narratives of diverse societies across time and space.

By donning the lenses of different cultures, we aspire to attain a deeper and more profound understanding of the enduring and profound impact that fairies have had on the human imagination. These magical creatures, in their countless forms and interpretations, have left an indelible mark on the collective consciousness of humanity. They beckon us to explore the ever-enticing realm of the fantastical, where the boundaries of reality blur and the extraordinary becomes ordinary. Through this exploration, we seek not only to appreciate the remarkable diversity of fairy folklore, but also to acknowledge the universal fascination that binds cultures together through the enchantment of these mystical beings.

In essence, this odyssey through the world of fairies is an invitation to uncover the hidden secrets of our shared human history, where imagination, magic, and cultural exchange intertwine. It is a journey that celebrates the power of storytelling, creativity, and the timeless allure of the mystical, reminding us that the enchantment of fairies knows no bounds and continues to captivate hearts and minds across the globe.

1B. Origins of Belief

Historical Context and Early Beliefs in Fairies

Fairies, those enchanting and elusive beings, have a rich history steeped in mythology, folklore, and the collective human imagination. To truly understand the evolution of fairy beliefs, we must embark on a journey through time, exploring the historical contexts and early beliefs that laid the foundation for these captivating creatures' enduring presence in our cultural tapestry. The origins of fairy beliefs can be traced back to ancient civilizations. In the mists of history, cultures across the world harbored beliefs in supernatural entities akin to fairies. These beings often occupied an intermediary realm between humans and gods, bridging the gap between the mundane and the mystical.

The Celtic Connection

The Celtic connection to fairy folklore is a pivotal aspect of understanding the historical roots and early beliefs in fairies. Within the rich tapestry of Celtic mythology, we find a wealth of influences that have contributed significantly to the development of fairy beliefs, particularly in the British Isles and Ireland. At the heart of the Celtic influence on fairy lore are the Tuatha Dé Danann, a race of supernatural beings often described as god-like in Celtic mythology. These beings inhabited ancient Ireland and were considered the precursors to modern fairies. The Tuatha Dé Danann possessed an array of magical abilities, and they played pivotal roles in shaping the landscape, culture, and history of Ireland.

These divine beings were associated with nature, magic, and the Otherworld, a mystical realm that existed parallel to the mortal world. It was believed that the Tuatha Dé Danann retreated to this Otherworld after the arrival of the Milesians, the mortal ancestors of the Irish people. In this retreat, they transformed into the Aos Sí, a term often used to describe fairies in Ireland. The Aos Sí continued to interact with humans, both benevolently and capriciously, much like their divine predecessors. The Tuatha Dé Danann and the Aos Sí were closely associated with specific geographical features, particularly the fairy mounds or "sidhe" (pronounced 'shee') scattered throughout Ireland. These mounds were considered entrances to the Otherworld and were often revered and approached with caution by the local population. They were believed to be inhabited by fairies or supernatural beings.

The term "Sidhe" also refers to the fairies themselves, and they were seen as guardians of these mounds. These beings could bestow blessings or curses upon those who interacted with them, and many traditions revolved around showing respect and deference to the Sidhe to avoid their wrath. Beyond the divine origins of the Tuatha Dé Danann, Celtic folklore is replete with tales of fairies and their interactions with humans. These narratives often portrayed fairies as ethereal, elusive beings who dwelled in the natural world but remained hidden from human eyes. They were known for their enchanting music, which could lure mortals into their realm for what seemed like hours but could be mere minutes in the human world. Moreover, the concept of the "changeling" is deeply rooted in Celtic folklore. It was believed that fairies could steal human infants and replace them with their own kind. This belief gave rise to numerous superstitions and rituals aimed at protecting infants from such a fate.

The Celtic connection to fairy lore offers a profound glimpse into the early beliefs surrounding these mystical beings. The Tuatha Dé Danann's transformation into the Aos Sí, the reverence for fairy mounds, and the rich tapestry of folklore that weaves together their interactions with humanity all contribute to a cultural heritage that continues to enchant and captivate the human imagination. This Celtic influence laid the foundation for the development of fairy beliefs in the British Isles and beyond, shaping the enduring fascination with fairies that persists to this day.

Medieval Europe: The Emergence of Fairies

The medieval period in Europe marked a significant turning point in the development of fairy beliefs. During this era, fairies began to emerge as distinct and recognizable supernatural beings in the popular imagination. Their portrayal in literature, folklore, and everyday life reflected the evolving societal and cultural dynamics of medieval Europe. Medieval Europe was a tapestry of diverse cultures, each with its own rich tapestry of folklore and superstitions. These folk traditions played a pivotal role in shaping early fairy beliefs. In many cases, fairies were viewed as elemental spirits, closely tied to the natural world. They inhabited ancient forests, meadows, and secluded glens, existing in parallel to human society.

The medieval Christian Church held considerable sway over the beliefs and practices of the population. As Christianity spread across Europe, it sought to integrate indigenous beliefs into its religious framework. Fairies, with their ethereal and often ambiguous nature, posed a challenge to Christian orthodoxy. The Church interpreted fairies as either fallen angels or as remnants of pagan deities, attempting to reconcile their existence with Christian doctrine. Medieval literature played a crucial role in popularizing fairy beliefs. Stories such as "Sir Orfeo," a Middle English romance, featured encounters with fairy-like beings in enchanted forests. These narratives often blurred the lines between the supernatural and the mundane, weaving tales of human-fairy interactions filled with wonder and danger.

The poetry of Geoffrey Chaucer, notably "The Wife of Bath's Tale" from "The Canterbury Tales," introduced readers to fairies like Queen Titania, known for her beauty and capricious nature. Chaucer's work, characterized by its complex characters and moral themes, showcased how fairies could be both enchanting and morally ambiguous. During the medieval period, fairies began to take on certain defining attributes that persist in modern depictions. They were often portrayed as diminutive beings, possessing magical powers and an otherworldly allure. The concept of "elfin" beauty, with fair features and ethereal grace, became associated with these creatures.

Medieval writers frequently used fairy folklore to convey moral lessons and allegorical meanings. Fairies were sometimes portrayed as testing the virtue of humans, offering rewards to the pure-hearted and punishments to the wicked. This allegorical use of fairies reflected the moralistic ethos of the time. Medieval Europeans believed in the very real possibility of interacting with fairies. Legends abounded of people being lured into fairy rings or abducted by fairies to their hidden realms. To avoid such encounters, individuals employed various protective rituals, such as carrying iron or reciting prayers. The emergence of fairies in medieval Europe marked a crucial point in their development as distinct entities. They evolved from ancient, nature-bound spirits to creatures that inhabited the twilight realm between the mystical and the mundane. This transformation set the stage for the rich and diverse fairy folklore that would continue to evolve in the centuries to come.

In summary, the medieval period in Europe witnessed the emergence of fairies as a unique and captivating aspect of folklore and mythology. As these beings transitioned from ancient spirits to the enchanting creatures of medieval literature, they became deeply entwined with the cultural and religious dynamics of the time, setting the stage for their enduring presence in the collective imagination.

The Interplay of Folk Beliefs and Christianity

The interplay between folk beliefs in fairies and the rise of Christianity during the medieval period was a complex and often contentious relationship. As Christianity spread across Europe, it encountered well-established pagan traditions, including beliefs in supernatural beings like fairies. This encounter gave rise to a fascinating dynamic of adaptation, assimilation, and tension between the two belief systems.

From the perspective of the Church during the medieval and early modern eras, the existence of fairies presented a formidable challenge to the established Christian worldview. These enigmatic beings, with their otherworldly attributes and mysterious powers, raised eyebrows and suspicions within the ranks of the Church. Fairies, often shrouded in an aura of skepticism and caution, were perceived as potentially contradictory to the tenets of Christianity, challenging its spiritual authority.
Fairies as Fallen Angels: Theological Interpretations One intriguing theological interpretation that emerged from the Christian perspective posited that fairies were, in essence, fallen angels. According to this belief, these ethereal creatures had once resided in the celestial realms as angels, basking in the divine presence. However, due to their acts of pride or disobedience, they had incurred the wrath of the Almighty and were subsequently cast down from heaven. Now dwelling in the earthly realm, fairies found themselves in a state of liminality, neither entirely benevolent nor irredeemably malevolent.
This theological viewpoint offered Christianity a means to integrate fairies into its cosmology, albeit in a manner that underscored their morally ambiguous nature. These beings existed in a state of suspension, hovering between the divine and the profane. Much like the angels from whom they were believed to have fallen, fairies were often depicted as capricious and unpredictable in their actions.
Attempts to Suppress Belief: The Clash of Worldviews Throughout history, the Church made concerted efforts to suppress belief in fairies, especially when such beliefs ran afoul of Christian

doctrine. Clergy members were adamant in discouraging pagan rituals and offerings made to fairies, deeming these practices as idolatrous and incompatible with the monotheistic principles of Christianity.
However, the Church's endeavors to suppress faith in fairies did not always yield the desired results. The allure of these mystical beings, intertwined with their connection to the natural world, persevered among the populace. While the Church could condemn the rituals and traditions associated with fairies, it found itself facing a formidable challenge in eradicating the deeply ingrained belief in these ethereal creatures.
In essence, the encounter between Christian faith and the world of fairies exemplifies the intricate interplay between established religious institutions and the enduring enchantment of folklore. Fairies, whether perceived as fallen angels or as custodians of nature, have etched an indelible mark on the cultural fabric of humanity. Their existence, viewed skeptically by some and revered by others, continues to beckon us to ponder the boundaries of belief, the enigmas of the supernatural, and the perpetual tension between the domains of faith and folklore.

The interplay between folk beliefs in fairies and Christianity during the medieval period illustrates the complexity of cultural adaptation and the enduring power of traditional beliefs. While the Church attempted to assert its authority and suppress pagan practices, it could not completely erase the deeply ingrained belief in fairies. Instead, these beliefs evolved, merged, and adapted, resulting in a fascinating fusion of folklore and religion that continues to shape our understanding of fairies and their place in history.

Cross-Cultural Influences

Fairies, those ethereal and enchanting beings, are not confined to the folklore of a single culture or region. Instead, they manifest in various forms across the globe, revealing the fascinating interplay of human imagination and the universal human fascination with the mystical. In this chapter, we will embark on a journey across continents and delve into the rich tapestry of fairy-like beings from diverse cultures.

In Japan, the equivalent of fairies can be found in the "yosei" and various "kami" (spirits or deities). The yosei are graceful, supernatural beings closely associated with nature and the elements. They often inhabit secluded groves, serene lakes, or misty mountains. While the yosei share similarities with Western fairies in their beauty and connection to nature, they possess a unique cultural flavor.
Shrines dedicated to kami, such as those found in Shintoism, demonstrate the reverence for nature and the supernatural in Japanese culture. These kami can be akin to fairies in their roles as protectors of forests, rivers, and other natural features. The interplay between human and kami, as well as their presence in everyday life, showcases the deep-rooted belief in the coexistence of the human and spirit worlds.

African folklore teems with a myriad of supernatural beings, some of which bear resemblance to fairies. For instance, in North African and Middle Eastern traditions, we encounter the "djinn," powerful spirits capable of both malevolence and benevolence. Djinn often inhabit remote, secluded places, and their capricious nature is reminiscent of the mischievous fairies in Western folklore.

In other African cultures, various "lesser spirits" exist. These spirits are believed to inhabit natural features such as trees, rivers, and rocks. They are regarded with reverence and respect, much like fairies in European traditions. The belief in these spirits underscores the deep connection between African cultures and their natural surroundings.

The indigenous peoples of North America and other regions have their own pantheon of supernatural beings. These beings are often closely linked to nature and the environment. For example, among the Cherokee Nation, "Little People" are considered diminutive, mischievous beings dwelling in the woods. They are believed to bring both good and bad fortune, much like fairies in European folklore.

Similarly, in the mythology of the Ainu people of Japan, the "kamuy" are divine spirits inhabiting natural elements. These spirits bear similarities to fairies in their close association with the natural world.

In the heart of the Amazon rainforest, indigenous cultures believe in "jaguar spirits" and "water spirits." These supernatural entities are thought to inhabit the lush, untamed landscape of the Amazon basin. Their connection to the flora and fauna of the rainforest mirrors the relationship between fairies and nature in other traditions.

Conclusion

Despite the geographical and cultural diversity, certain commonalities emerge among these fairy-like beings from around the world. Many of them are associated with natural features, embodying the spirit of their respective environments. Additionally, they often play a dual role, capable of both benevolence and mischief, mirroring the complex nature of fairies in Western folklore.

The exploration of fairy-like beings from different cultures reveals the remarkable universality of human imagination and the human need to connect with the supernatural. These cross-cultural influences demonstrate that, regardless of geography, humans have consistently sought to bridge the gap between the ordinary and the extraordinary through the enchanting realm of beings akin to fairies. The historical context and early beliefs surrounding fairies provide a foundation for the intricate tapestry of folklore and mythology that weaves together the diverse threads of fairy lore. From their ancient origins to their medieval interpretations, the beliefs in fairies have evolved and adapted to changing times and cultural influences. As we delve deeper into the world of fairies in the following chapters, we will witness how these beliefs continued to flourish and transform over the centuries, leaving an indelible mark on the human imagination.

Chapter 2
Folklore and Legends

2A. Ancient Legends

Examination of Ancient Texts and Stories Featuring Fairies

Our journey into the enchanting world of fairies continues as we delve into the examination of ancient texts and stories that have contributed to the rich tapestry of fairy folklore. These narratives, often shrouded in the mists of time, offer us invaluable insights into the cultural, historical, and spiritual significance of these mystical beings. As we traverse the annals of literature and legend, we will encounter a diverse array of fairy-like entities and their captivating narratives, each serving as a testament to the enduring fascination with these elusive creatures.

The Ancient Roots of Fairy Folklore

To grasp the full extent of the enchantment surrounding fairies, it is essential to embark on a journey back in time and explore the ancient origins of fairy folklore. These early manifestations of mystical beings, while distinct from the modern concept of fairies, laid the groundwork for the captivating stories and beliefs that would later evolve.

1. Nymphs of Ancient Greece:

Our odyssey begins in the heart of Ancient Greece, a realm steeped in mythology and folklore. Here, we encounter the nymphs, ethereal and exquisite female spirits closely intertwined with the natural world. Nymphs inhabited a multitude of domains, ranging from lush forests and meandering rivers to towering mountains and crystalline springs. These captivating beings embodied the very essence of nature's beauty and vitality and played an instrumental role in shaping the Greek understanding of the natural world.

Nymphs, much like the fairies of later European folklore, were renowned for their capricious nature. They could take on the roles of benevolent protectors of the environment, bestowing blessings upon those who paid homage to their domains. Conversely, they could also embody mischievous and elusive qualities, enticing travelers deeper into the wilderness. The nymphs' profound connection to nature and their pivotal role within the mythological tapestry of Greece foreshadowed the later association of fairies with the natural world.

2. Celtic Tuatha Dé Danann:

Shifting our focus to the ancient Celtic lands, we encounter the Tuatha Dé Danann, a supernatural race often referred to as "the people of the hills" or "the fairy folk." These mystical entities inhabited the verdant hills and enigmatic landscapes of ancient Ireland, leaving an indelible mark on Celtic mythology.

The Tuatha Dé Danann represented far more than mere fairies; they were revered as deities possessing extraordinary powers. Their influence extended over a wide array of aspects of life, including agriculture, craftsmanship, magic, and warfare. In many ways, the Tuatha Dé Danann served as the guardians of Celtic lands, with their presence believed to bring either blessings or curses upon those who crossed their paths.

These ancient Celtic narratives formed a solid foundation for the subsequent development of fairy folklore in Ireland and the broader Celtic world. The reverence for these mystical beings and their profound connections to both the natural and supernatural realms set the stage for the enduring fascination with fairies in Celtic culture.

3. Cross-Cultural Parallels:

It is crucial to acknowledge that, while the specific characteristics of these ancient beings may differ from the modern conception of fairies, there exist intriguing cross-cultural parallels. The nymphs of Greece and the Tuatha Dé Danann of Ireland exemplify humanity's timeless fascination with the mystical and the unseen forces that shape our world. These early narratives serve as a testament to our intrinsic inclination to personify nature and attribute it with agency, weaving stories of supernatural beings to elucidate the profound mysteries of existence.

The Role of Fairies in Folklore and Superstition

In our expedition through the captivating world of fairies, we must pause to examine the profound role that these ethereal beings have played in folklore and superstition throughout the course of history. Fairies have consistently transcended the realm of whimsical characters in stories, profoundly interweaving themselves into the cultural fabric of diverse regions, shaping beliefs, traditions, and even daily practices.

1. Belief in Fairies:

The belief in fairies, often referred to as the "fairy faith," held a prominent place in folk belief across numerous parts of Europe, particularly during the medieval and early modern periods. People genuinely embraced the notion that fairies were genuine, supernatural entities coexisting with humans within the natural world. These beliefs, while subject to regional variations, shared certain common themes and characteristics.

2. The Enigmatic World of Fairy Rings:

One of the most enduring and captivating aspects of fairy folklore is the phenomenon of "fairy rings." These circular patterns of mushrooms found in fields and forests have long been associated with the presence of fairies. Fairy rings, often described as portals to the fairy realm, have fascinated and mystified generations of storytellers and folklore enthusiasts alike. They remain an enchanting testament to the enduring allure of fairies and their enigmatic connections to the natural world.

Our exploration into ancient legends and the profound role of fairies in folklore and superstition has provided us with a deeper understanding of the enduring fascination with these mystical beings. These narratives, rooted in the mists of time, continue to captivate our imagination and remind us of the timeless allure of the mystical and the enchanting world of fairies.be the result of fairies dancing in a ring during their nocturnal revelries. Stepping into a fairy ring, it was thought, could have dire consequences or lead to being transported to the fairy realm. These mysterious circles not only fueled superstition but also influenced agricultural practices, as farmers avoided disturbing fairy rings out of fear of angering the fairies and inviting misfortune upon their crops.

3. Changelings and Abductions

A particularly poignant aspect of fairy folklore involved changelings, infants believed to have been swapped by fairies for human babies. It was thought that fairies would abduct healthy human infants and replace them with changelings—often sickly or deformed fairy children. This belief arose from attempts to explain unexplained illnesses or developmental disorders in children. Desperate parents would resort to various rituals, such as passing their child through fire or iron, to drive away the changeling and hopefully have their real child returned.

4. Protective Measures

To coexist with the sometimes unpredictable and capricious fairies, people developed numerous protective measures and charms. Iron was considered a potent deterrent against fairies, and iron objects were often placed near cribs or thresholds to ward off potential intrusions. Additionally, offerings of milk, butter, or bread were left outside one's home as appeasement to the fairies, especially during holidays like Midsummer's Eve when the veil between the worlds was believed to be thin.

5. Influence on Everyday Life

The belief in fairies influenced various aspects of daily life. People would avoid certain places in the landscape believed to be fairy territory, as well as activities such as whistling at night, which was thought to attract their attention. Even tasks like cutting down a tree or clearing a field were approached with caution, as disturbing the natural world could incur the wrath of the fairies. Such beliefs reinforced a deep respect for nature and a sense of humility in the face of the unknown.

6. Evolution of Belief

While belief in fairies has waned in many parts of the world with the advent of science and rationalism, traces of this folklore persist in modern superstitions and customs. The enduring legacy of fairy belief reminds us of the power of these enchanting begins to shape human behavior and perceptions, even in an era dominated by reason.

In this examination of the role of fairies in folklore and superstition, we come to appreciate the profound impact these mystical entities have had on the lives and imaginations of countless generations. The next chapters of our journey will continue to unravel the multifaceted nature of fairies, delving into their portrayal in art, literature, and spirituality, and exploring how these captivating beings have left an indelible mark on the human psyche.

Shakespeare's Contribution:

No examination of fairy folklore would be complete without a closer look at William Shakespeare's contributions. In "A Midsummer Night's Dream," Shakespeare introduced the mischievous Puck and the enchanting world of the fairies. We analyze the symbolism of these characters and their portrayal in the play, shedding light on Shakespeare's role in popularizing fairy lore in the English-speaking world.

William Shakespeare, often hailed as the greatest playwright in the English language, played a pivotal role in not only shaping the literary landscape but also in elevating the status of fairies within the realm of folklore and storytelling. His iconic play "A Midsummer Night's Dream" stands as a cornerstone in the resurgence of fairy folklore during the Renaissance, and its enduring influence on our perception of these enchanting beings cannot be overstated.

1. Puck and the Realm of the Fairies

Central to Shakespeare's exploration of the fairy realm is the character of Puck, also known as Robin Goodfellow. Puck serves as the mischievous and sprightly jester of the fairy court. His whimsical antics, such as transforming Bottom's head into that of an ass, are emblematic of the capricious nature often associated with fairies in medieval and Renaissance literature. Yet, beneath Puck's playful exterior lies a deeper layer of complexity. He is not merely a trickster, but also a character who embodies the enigmatic duality of the fairy world, capable of both benevolent and vexing actions.

Shakespeare's portrayal of the fairy realm as a place of enchantment, wonder, and shifting realities showcases his extraordinary ability to evoke a sense of magic on the stage. The ethereal setting of the play, the forest of Arden, becomes a space where the boundaries between reality and dreams blur, mirroring the essence of the fairy world itself. This portrayal resonates with audiences, drawing them into a realm where the fantastical and the mundane coexist in a delicate balance.

2. Symbolism and Themes

Shakespeare's exploration of fairies extends beyond mere entertainment. The presence of the fairy world in "A Midsummer Night's Dream" serves as a rich tapestry of symbolism and thematic depth. Fairies, in this context, represent the forces of nature, the unpredictable aspects of love, and the mysteries of the human psyche. Their actions, often driven by desires and emotions, mirror the tumultuous affairs of the human heart. Through Puck's meddling with love potions and the chaotic entanglements of the mortal characters, Shakespeare masterfully weaves a narrative that explores the complexities of human relationships and the transformative power of love.

Moreover, the fairy realm in the play also hints at a commentary on the blurred lines between reality and illusion, a theme that resonates with the broader Renaissance fascination with the interplay of appearance and reality. Fairies, with their shape-shifting abilities and their propensity to manipulate perception, embody this theme, inviting audiences to ponder the nature of truth and deception in their own lives.

3. Shakespearean Legacy

Shakespeare's contributions to the world of fairy folklore did not end with "A Midsummer Night's Dream." His influence extended to subsequent generations of writers, artists, and scholars who continued to draw inspiration from his portrayal of fairies. The enduring appeal of Puck and the fairy realm can be witnessed in countless adaptations, reinterpretations, and artistic representations in various media.

In essence, Shakespeare's masterful storytelling and imaginative prowess not only elevated fairies from the margins of folklore to the center stage of literary and cultural consciousness but also imbued them with a depth and complexity that continues to captivate audiences today. "A Midsummer Night's Dream" remains a testament to the enduring enchantment of fairies and their ability to evoke wonder, laughter, and introspection in those who encounter their mesmerizing world on the stage.

Ancient Texts and Modern Interpretations:

In our examination, we also explore how ancient texts and stories featuring fairies continue to inspire contemporary literature, art, and popular culture. From J.M. Barrie's "Peter Pan" to J.R.R. Tolkien's Middle-earth, fairies and fairy-like creatures have endured and evolved in the literary landscape.

Conclusion:

As we conclude this chapter, we have uncovered the intricate web of ancient texts and stories that have shaped our understanding of fairies. These narratives, spanning centuries and cultures, continue to cast their spell on our collective imagination, revealing the timeless allure of these mystical beings. In the chapters that follow, we will further unravel the multifaceted nature of fairies, exploring their role in art, religion, and the human psyche, while constantly considering the cultural contexts that have shaped their ever-evolving stories.

2B. Regional Variations

How Fairy Folklore Differs Across the World

Fairy folklore, enchanting and diverse, weaves intricate narratives that reflect the cultural, geographical, and historical tapestries of the world. As we delve into the captivating realm of fairies, we find that these mystical beings are not confined to a singular interpretation but manifest themselves in an array of forms and tales across different corners of the globe. This chapter embarks on a journey across continents and cultures, unveiling the rich tapestry of fairy folklore that distinguishes one society from another.

1. European Enchantment

Europe, with its diverse cultures, landscapes, and histories, is a treasure trove of fairy folklore that has enchanted generations. These ethereal beings, often deeply rooted in European imagination, have manifested in various forms, embodying the essence of the continent's multifaceted identity.

A. British Isles: The Realm of Shakespearean Puck and Irish Sidhe

In the British Isles, the world of fairies is rich and storied. Shakespeare's "A Midsummer Night's Dream" introduces us to Puck, also known as Robin Goodfellow, a whimsical and mischievous sprite who personifies the playful nature of English folklore. Puck, with his shape-shifting abilities and penchant for causing mayhem, remains a beloved character in literature.

Meanwhile, Irish folklore paints a more complex picture with the Sidhe (pronounced "shee"), a race of ethereal beings who dwell in the hills and mounds of Ireland. Unlike the capricious Puck, the Sidhe can be both benevolent and vengeful, often demanding respect and reverence from those who enter their domains. They are deeply woven into the fabric of Irish mythology, representing a connection to the land and the spiritual world.

B. Northern Mysteries: The Huldra and Älvor

In the northern reaches of Europe, Scandinavian countries have their own enchanting interpretations of fairy folklore. In Norway, the huldra is a bewitching forest spirit who appears as a stunningly beautiful woman, often luring unsuspecting travelers into the depths of the woods. However, beneath her beauty lies a hidden cow's tail, a symbol of her dual nature, embodying both allure and danger.

Swedish folklore introduces the älvor, graceful and ethereal fairies who inhabit the natural landscapes. These beings are often associated with the beauty of the countryside, blending seamlessly with the enchanting forests and meadows of Sweden. Their stories reflect a reverence for the Scandinavian wilderness.

C. Continental Variations: Germanic and Slavic Fairy Folklore

On the European continent, the enchantment of fairies extends across various regions. In Germany, tales of the Lorelei, a water spirit who lures sailors to their doom with her enchanting song, speak to the mystical qualities of the Rhine River. These stories exemplify the deep connection between Germanic folklore and the country's landscapes.

In Slavic folklore, the rusalki, water nymphs or spirits, play a prominent role. These supernatural beings are often associated with lakes, rivers, and forests and are said to possess the power to either help or harm humans. The stories of rusalki reflect the intricate relationship between Slavic cultures and their natural surroundings.

D. Mediterranean Magic: Fairies in Southern Europe

Southern Europe, with its Mediterranean charm, offers its own unique take on fairy folklore. In Mediterranean cultures, particularly in Italy, stories of the "Fata" or "Fate" depict enchanting female spirits who control the destinies of humans. These beings are both captivating and enigmatic, embodying the intertwined concepts of fate and free will.

The Mediterranean island of Sicily, with its rich history of Greek and Roman influences, has its own version of fairies known as the "Morgana." These alluring beings are believed to inhabit hidden caves along the coast, and their tales reflect the island's blend of ancient mythologies.

E. Eastern European Mystique: Domovoi and Kikimora

Eastern Europe contributes to the enchantment with fairy folklore through creatures like the Domovoi, household spirits in Russian and Slavic cultures. These beings are believed to protect the home and its occupants, but can also become mischievous if neglected or offended. The Domovoi represent the close bond between the Slavic people and their dwellings.

Kikimora, another Slavic spirit, resides in the depths of the forest and is often associated with domestic tasks. Her tales reflect the importance of harmony between humans and nature in Eastern European folklore.

European enchantment is a captivating mosaic of fairy folklore, where each culture and region infuses its own unique blend of whimsy, mystery, and cultural significance into these timeless beings. The stories of fairies in Europe serve as windows into the continent's diverse landscapes, history, and the boundless human imagination.

2. Asian Enchantments

Asia, a continent steeped in ancient traditions and diverse cultures, offers a fascinating tapestry of fairy folklore that is as varied as the lands themselves. Within this vast expanse, we explore the realms of yōkai in Japan and the enigmatic huli jing in China, delving into the intricate and enchanting narratives that have captivated generations.

Yōkai: Guardians and Harbingers of the Supernatural (Japan)

Japanese folklore is a labyrinthine realm of spirits and supernatural entities, and at the heart of it lies the concept of yōkai. Yōkai are a myriad of beings, ranging from benevolent and protective to mischievous and malevolent. The term "yōkai" itself translates to "bewitching" or "attractive mystery," encapsulating the enigmatic nature of these creatures.

One iconic yōkai is the kitsune, a fox spirit that embodies both cunning and wisdom. Kitsune are known for their shape-shifting abilities, often assuming the form of beautiful women to interact with humans. They can be guardians of the home or powerful tricksters, playing pranks on unsuspecting travelers. Kitsune stories reflect complex themes of desire, transformation, and the blurred boundaries between the human and supernatural worlds.

Another notable yōkai is the tanuki, a shape-shifting raccoon dog known for its playful and mischievous nature. Tanuki are often depicted with a large belly and a flask of sake, symbolizing their love for revelry and merriment. They are considered protectors of the forest, and their tales often carry themes of environmental conservation and respect for nature.

Japanese folklore is also rich with vengeful spirits like the yurei and malevolent entities like the oni, which embody the darker aspects of human emotions and actions. These tales reflect the cultural nuances of Japan, including its reverence for nature, its historical struggles, and its fascination with the supernatural.

Huli Jing: Seductive Fox Spirits (China)

In China, the huli jing, or fox spirit, takes center stage in a unique and enduring folklore tradition. These enchanting beings are both alluring and perilous, often appearing as beautiful women to seduce men. Huli jing stories are deeply rooted in Chinese mythology and literature, their origins tracing back thousands of years.

One famous literary work, "The Investiture of the Gods" (Fengshen Yanyi), features a huli jing named Daji who uses her charms to manipulate a king, ultimately leading to his downfall. This tale reflects themes of power, desire, and the consequences of succumbing to temptation.

The huli jing are not always malevolent, though. In some stories, they are depicted as compassionate beings who seek to attain humanity through virtuous deeds. This duality in their character adds depth to the folklore and speaks to the complexities of human nature.

In addition to their appearances in literature, huli jing also find their place in Chinese art and popular culture, where they continue to captivate audiences and serve as symbols of both allure and danger.

Asian enchantments, embodied by yōkai in Japan and huli jing in China, offer a captivating glimpse into the region's rich folklore. These supernatural beings are more than mere myths; they are cultural touchstones, reflections of the values, fears, and desires of their respective societies. As we continue to explore the world's fairy folklore, we encounter a kaleidoscope of stories and characters that illuminate the profound connection between humanity and the supernatural.

3. African Mysticism

African folklore is a treasure trove of mystical beings and supernatural entities that mirror the continent's rich cultural diversity and profound spiritual beliefs. Rooted in ancient traditions and deeply ingrained in daily life, African fairy folklore is a testament to the intimate connection between humanity and the mystical forces of nature. In this exploration of African mysticism, we delve into the enchanting world of spirits, gods, and mythical creatures that shape the narratives of this vast and varied continent.

1. Yoruba Orisha: Guardians of the Divine

In the Yoruba culture of West Africa, the Orisha reign supreme. These divine entities are akin to fairies in their mystical nature, embodying distinct aspects of life, nature, and the human experience. Each Orisha possesses a unique personality, traits, and powers. Oshun, for instance, is the Orisha of rivers, love, and beauty, often depicted as a graceful and sensuous deity. In contrast, Shango, the Orisha of thunder and lightning, is a powerful and formidable force.

The Yoruba people believe that the Orisha not only govern the natural world but also play an integral role in human affairs. Ceremonies and rituals dedicated to these deities are central to Yoruba spirituality, and they serve as a bridge between the physical and spiritual realms. The Orisha are celebrated not only in religious practices but also in art, dance, and music, showcasing their enduring presence in Yoruba culture.

2. San Mantindane: Guardians of the Natural World

In the arid landscapes of Southern Africa, the San people hold a deep reverence for the natural world, and their fairy-like beings, the mantindane, reflect this connection. These tiny, spirit creatures inhabit the deserts, grasslands, and mountains of the region. They are considered the protectors of the environment, ensuring the balance and harmony of the natural world.

San folklore tells of the mantindane's interactions with humans, often illustrating the importance of respecting the land and its resources. These stories emphasize the delicate dance between humanity and nature, where the mantindane serve as reminders of the consequences of disrupting this fragile equilibrium. The San people's profound connection with the land and their unique folklore contribute to the preservation of their traditional way of life.

3. Akan Ananse: The Trickster Spider

Among the Akan people of West Africa, the folklore of Ananse, the trickster spider, takes center stage. Ananse stories are a vibrant part of Akan oral tradition, and they are often used to impart moral lessons and wisdom. Ananse is a complex character, both cunning and clever, who navigates the challenges of life in imaginative and humorous ways.

These tales featuring Ananse often involve encounters with supernatural beings, demonstrating the blurred lines between the human and spirit worlds. Ananse's wit and resourcefulness in these stories highlight the importance of intelligence and adaptability in the face of adversity. The enduring popularity of Ananse stories reveals their role as a cultural touchstone, reinforcing the Akan people's values and worldview.

4. Igbo Ala: The Earth Goddess

In Igbo culture of Nigeria, the Earth Goddess, Ala, holds a prominent place in the pantheon of deities. She is the embodiment of the earth itself and is revered as the ultimate provider of sustenance and fertility. Ala is often depicted as a maternal figure, symbolizing the nurturing aspects of nature.

The rituals and ceremonies dedicated to Ala are an integral part of Igbo spirituality, reflecting the deep respect and gratitude for the land's abundance. Ala's presence extends beyond religious practices and is woven into the fabric of Igbo society. The Igbo people see themselves as custodians of the land, entrusted with the responsibility of maintaining its well-being and ensuring a harmonious coexistence between humanity and nature.

In the tapestry of African mysticism, these examples merely scratch the surface of the diverse and intricate world of fairy folklore. Across the continent, from the vast savannas to dense jungles, from the bustling cities to remote villages, stories of supernatural beings continue to shape African cultures and offer profound insights into the spiritual and cultural landscapes of this diverse continent.

4. Indigenous Wisdom of the Americas

The Indigenous peoples of the Americas have a rich tapestry of folklore that introduces us to an enchanting world of spirits and mystical beings. These entities are deeply ingrained in the spiritual and cultural fabric of Native American and Amazonian communities, offering insights into their profound connection with the natural world.

Native American Folklore: The Kachina Spirits and Beyond

In Native American cultures, particularly among the Hopi and Pueblo tribes of the American Southwest, the kachina spirits are prominent figures. These spirits are believed to embody the essence of various aspects of the natural world, such as animals, plants, celestial bodies, and even ancestral wisdom. They are revered for their role in maintaining the balance of nature and the community's well-being.

The kachinas often take the form of elaborately crafted masks and costumes, and their presence is central to ceremonial dances and rituals. These ceremonies not only celebrate the spirits but also serve as educational tools, passing down cultural knowledge and wisdom from one generation to the next. The reverence for the kachinas reflects the Native American worldview, emphasizing the interconnectedness of all living things and the importance of maintaining harmony with nature.

Beyond the kachinas, Native American folklore is replete with other supernatural beings, such as the Thunderbirds, shape-shifters, and skinwalkers. These entities embody the spiritual and mystical dimensions of Native American cosmology, emphasizing the profound respect and spiritual connection that Indigenous peoples have with the natural world.

Amazonian Mysteries: Yacuruna and Forest Spirits

In the heart of the Amazon rainforest, Indigenous communities have their own unique folklore that revolves around enigmatic forest spirits. Among these is the yacuruna, a term used in different Amazonian regions to describe guardian spirits of the jungle's aquatic ecosystems. The yacuruna are believed to inhabit lakes, rivers, and hidden places in the rainforest. These spirits are responsible for maintaining the delicate ecological balance of their domains.

The yacuruna are often depicted as shape-shifters, capable of appearing as humans or animals, making them elusive and mysterious. Indigenous communities in the Amazon rely on these stories to teach valuable lessons about respecting and preserving the natural environment. The tales of the yacuruna emphasize the profound connection between Indigenous peoples and the Amazon rainforest, where they live in harmony with nature and rely on its resources for their survival.

Additionally, the Amazon is home to a myriad of other forest spirits and creatures, each with its unique attributes and significance. These stories are passed down orally from generation to generation, and they play a crucial role in the transmission of cultural knowledge, ecological wisdom, and a sense of belonging to the vast and intricate tapestry of the rainforest.

Indigenous wisdom of the Americas is steeped in a rich tradition of folklore that introduces us to a world inhabited by enchanting and mystical beings. The kachina spirits of the American Southwest and the yacuruna of the Amazon are just a glimpse into the vibrant cultural narratives that underscore the profound connection between Indigenous communities and the natural world. These stories not only preserve the heritage of these societies but also serve as valuable guides for sustainable living and maintaining the delicate balance of the ecosystems they call home.

5. Oceanic Wonders

The islands scattered throughout the vast expanse of the Pacific Ocean hold a treasure trove of enchanting fairy folklore, deeply rooted in the rich cultures of their indigenous peoples. These tales, passed down through generations, not only depict mystical beings but also offer profound insights into the spiritual connection between the islanders and their pristine natural surroundings.

Hawaiian Menehune: Forest Dwellers and Craftsmen

One of the most beloved figures in Hawaiian folklore is the Menehune, pint-sized beings who are believed to inhabit the lush forests and valleys of the Hawaiian Islands. These elusive creatures are renowned for their exceptional craftsmanship, often credited with the construction of ancient temples, fishponds, and other mysterious structures that dot the Hawaiian landscape.

The Menehune are more than just whimsical characters; they embody the Hawaiian reverence for nature and its resources. Their legends stress the importance of respecting the land and its bounty, teaching that harmony with the environment is the key to abundance. These tales serve as a reminder of the deep connection between the Hawaiian people and the islands that sustain them.

Maori Taniwha: Guardians of Waters

Across the ocean in New Zealand, the indigenous Maori people share their own mystical tales, with the Taniwha taking center stage. These aquatic spirits are believed to inhabit lakes, rivers, and coastal waters. Taniwha are not merely supernatural entities; they are guardians of the waterways and protectors of the land.

The Maori relationship with the Taniwha reflects their deep connection to the land and its natural features. In Maori culture, the land, sea, and sky are seen as living entities, and the Taniwha serve as emissaries between the human world and the realm of the spirits. Their stories underscore the importance of respecting these waterways and the creatures that dwell within them, emphasizing the need for balance and harmony.

Interconnectedness of Island Cultures

What makes the fairy folklore of the Pacific Islands even more intriguing is the interconnectedness between the various island cultures. Despite vast distances between these islands, there are striking similarities in the stories and mythologies. This is a testament to the shared ancestral heritage of many Pacific Islanders and their common bond with the natural world.

For example, the concept of guardian spirits or protective entities that dwell in natural features like waterways and forests is a recurring theme across multiple island cultures. This shared belief underscores the universal human connection with the environment and the desire to live in harmony with it.

The fairy folklore of the Pacific Islands provides us with a captivating glimpse into the spiritual and cultural richness of these island nations. These stories not only entertain but also educate, offering valuable lessons about the importance of stewardship and respect for the environment. As we continue to explore the enchanting world of fairy folklore, we are reminded that the mystical beings that inhabit our tales often serve as bridges between the human and natural realms, fostering a profound sense of unity and reverence for the wonders of the world.

6. South American Legends

South America, with its diverse landscapes, cultures, and traditions, boasts a tapestry of enchanting fairy folklore that reflects the region's rich history and deep connection to the natural world. In this segment, we will embark on a journey through the captivating legends of South American fairies, each narrative offering a unique glimpse into the complex relationship between humanity and nature on this vast and wondrous continent.

1. Curupira: Guardians of the Amazon

Nestled within the dense jungles of the Amazon Basin, the curupira emerges as a central figure in Brazilian folklore. This mischievous forest spirit possesses flaming red hair and backward-facing feet, a clever disguise that confuses and deters would-be intruders into the rainforest's depths. While the curupira may be playful in its tricks, it serves a vital role as a protector of the rainforest's delicate ecosystems. Indigenous tribes and local communities often tell tales of their encounters with the curupira, emphasizing the need to respect and preserve the natural world.

2. Apus: Guardians of the Andes

The Andes Mountains that stretch across several South American countries are home to the Quechua and Aymara peoples, who hold a deep reverence for the towering peaks and valleys that shape their lives. Within this majestic landscape, the apus are revered mountain spirits. These guardian beings are believed to inhabit the highest summits, overseeing the well-being of the surrounding communities. In return for their protection, rituals and offerings are made to honor the apus, ensuring harmony between humans and the formidable forces of nature.

3. Chaneques: Forest Spirits of Mexico

Moving northward to Mexico, the indigenous Nahua people have their own fairy-like beings known as chaneques. These forest spirits, often depicted as small, playful children, are protectors of the natural world. They inhabit the lush forests and are said to guide and assist those who respect the environment. However, those who harm the forests or show disrespect may fall victim to the chaneques' pranks and tricks.

4. Nymphs of the Andean Lakes

Peru's Andean lakes, renowned for their breathtaking beauty and serene landscapes, are said to be inhabited by aquatic nymphs. These enchanting beings, known as "ninfas" or "yacurunas," are believed to be ethereal guardians of the waterways. Their stories emphasize the importance of preserving these pristine environments, reminding the local communities of the delicate balance between human activity and the protection of the natural world.

5. Duendes: The Enigmatic Forest Dwellers

Throughout various regions of South America, legends of the duendes, or forest dwarves, abound. These diminutive beings are thought to reside deep within the forests, often helping or hindering travelers depending on their intentions. Duendes, with their whimsical personalities and mysterious ways, symbolize the enchantment and unpredictability of the wilderness. They serve as a reminder of the need to approach the natural world with both caution and respect.

In South America, fairy folklore transcends mere tales of whimsy; it embodies a profound connection to the environment, a respect for the land and its resources, and an acknowledgment of the mystical forces that shape the continent's diverse cultures. These legends remind us of the intricate relationship between humanity and nature, inspiring reverence for the enchanting landscapes and the enchanting beings that inhabit them. As we continue to explore the rich tapestry of South American fairy folklore, we discover a world where the boundaries between the natural and supernatural blur, inviting us to embrace the wonder and magic of this captivating continent.

Chapter 3
Classifications of Fairies

3A. Taxonomy of Fairies

Different Categorizations and Classifications of Fairies

In our quest to explore the captivating world of fairies, we turn our attention to the intricate web of categorizations and classifications that have emerged over centuries to help us understand the diverse array of these mystical beings. Fairies, known by a myriad of names and appearing in countless forms, defy easy categorization, yet the human imagination has endeavored to make sense of their multifaceted nature. This chapter delves deep into the various systems and typologies used to classify fairies across different cultures and time periods. Fairies, as they are known, differ significantly from one culture to another. In this section, we'll explore how regional and geographical factors have led to distinct categorizations of fairies:

1. Celtic Realms:

The Celtic cultures, known for their deep connection to the mystical and the natural world, have given rise to some of the most intricate and diverse categorizations of fairies. In this section, we embark on a journey into the heart of Celtic folklore to explore the rich classifications of these enchanting beings.

A. Sidhe - The Fairy Folk of Ireland:

Origins and Attributes:

The Irish Sidhe, often pronounced as "shee" or "shee-uh," are perhaps the most iconic of Celtic fairies. They are believed to be the remnants of the Tuatha Dé Danann, a supernatural race in Irish mythology, driven underground after their defeat by the Milesians, the ancestors of the modern Irish.

Distinctive Types:
Within these courts, numerous distinctive types of Sidhe fairies exist. These include:

Within the mystical realm of the Sidhe, one encounters the Leannán Sí, captivating fairies known for their unparalleled allure. These ethereal beings are often the muses of poets and artists, their beauty serving as a wellspring of inspiration for the creative soul. Yet, their beguiling charm is not without its treacherous side. The Leannán Sí possess capricious hearts and a hunger that extends beyond the ordinary. They have been known to consume not just the hearts of their lovers but also their creativity, a Faustian exchange for artistic brilliance.
Aos Sí (The People of the Mounds): Keepers of Subterranean Realms
Beneath the verdant hills and ancient mounds of Ireland, the Aos Sí, the People of the Mounds, reside. These enigmatic fairy folk guard the entrances to their underground realms, where time flows differently, and magic dwells in abundance. At times, they extend their benevolence to humans, offering gifts, protection, and guidance. Yet, woe betides those who disturb their sacred abodes, for the Aos Sí can be vengeful guardians, unleashing their wrath upon interlopers.
Banshees: Harbingers of Fate
In the moonlit hours of the Irish night, the mournful wail of the Banshee echoes through the land. These spectral figures are often categorized as female spirits or fairies and are harbingers of fate, their eerie cries foretelling the imminent death of a family member. Their presence is both a warning and a lament, a reminder of the fragility of human existence.
Distinct Roles and Attributes: The Tapestry of the Sidhe

The Sidhe are a diverse tapestry of beings, each type with its unique attributes and roles. Some serve as protectors of the land, guarding its natural wonders. Others don the mantle of tricksters, weaving riddles and illusions to test the character of passing mortals. Still, some take on the mantle of guides, leading the way to the enigmatic Otherworld, where dreams and reality intertwine.
Interaction with Humans: The Dance of Mortals and Fairies
The interaction between mortals and the Sidhe is a recurrent theme in Celtic folklore. These encounters can take various forms, from amicable meetings, where humans receive gifts of otherworldly beauty, to tests of character that challenge the virtues of courage and kindness. Yet, not all interactions are benign; some tales tell of abductions, enchantments, or the mischief wrought by fairy folk upon unsuspecting humans.

Festivals and Offerings: Honoring the Sidhe
Celtic traditions include festivals and rituals dedicated to appeasing the Sidhe, ensuring their goodwill and protection. Samhain, the precursor to Halloween, and Bealtaine, the celebration of May Day, are times when the veil between worlds thins, and offerings of milk, honey, or other sustenance are left to honor the fairies and secure their blessings.
Adaptation in Modern Culture: The Ever-Evolving Sidhe
The legacy of the Sidhe endures, not confined to the annals of history but woven into the very fabric of Irish culture. These mystical beings continue to inspire contemporary writers, artists, and filmmakers. In the hands of modern storytellers, the Sidhe take on new forms and interpretations, shaping the evolving narrative of Ireland's cultural heritage and captivating audiences with their

timeless allure. Whether as the subjects of novels, the muses of painters, or the enchanting characters of cinema, the Sidhe remain an integral part of the ever-evolving Irish creative landscape.

The categorizations of fairies within Celtic realms, particularly the Irish Sidhe, offer a glimpse into the intricate world of these mythical beings. Their rich hierarchy, distinctive types, and multifaceted roles continue to captivate the imagination, illustrating how folklore and tradition can breathe life into the fantastical, transcending time and enchanting generations of storytellers and dreamers.

2. Scandinavian Folklore:

- Scandinavian folklore is rich with tales of fairies, and one of the most intriguing and enigmatic groups of fairies to emerge from this region are the Hulder. These forest-dwelling beings, also known as "Huldrefolk" or "Skogsfru," have captured the imaginations of generations with their alluring beauty, complex personalities, and deep connection to the natural world.

Appearance and Characteristics:

- Hulders are often described as stunningly beautiful, captivating anyone who encounters them. They are typically depicted as women with long, flowing hair, fair skin, and a bewitching aura that draws people in. However, their true nature is shrouded in mystery, for Hulders possess a unique quality: they have hollow backsides, resembling a hollow tree trunk or the bark of a tree. To conceal this peculiar feature, Hulders usually wear long, flowing gowns or cowls that cover their backs, allowing them to appear as ordinary humans.

The Light and Dark Hulders:

Within Scandinavian folklore, Hulders are sometimes categorized into two distinct groups: Light Hulders and Dark Hulders. These classifications are not based on morality but rather on their disposition and interactions with humans:

1. Light Hulders:

Light Hulders are often associated with benevolence and kindness. They are known to assist lost travelers, protect animals in the forest, and provide guidance to those in need. Encounters with Light Hulders are generally positive, and they are believed to bring good fortune to those who approach them with respect.
2. Dark Hulders:
In contrast, Dark Hulders exhibit more mischievous and capricious behavior in their interactions with humans. They may lead wanderers astray in the woods, play tricks, or even abduct those

who displease them. Dark Hulders are known to be less forgiving and more inclined to seek revenge if offended.
Role in Nature:
Hulders are profoundly connected to the natural world, especially forests and mountains. They are often regarded as guardians of these wilderness areas and are believed to possess the ability to command the creatures of the woods. In certain legends, they are associated with the spirits of trees and are thought to protect ancient groves.
Human Interaction:
Interacting with Hulders is a nuanced affair. While they can be friendly and helpful, they are also easily offended by disrespectful or impolite behavior. To gain their favor, one must show reverence for nature, leave offerings at sacred sites, or simply be courteous when traversing their domain. Those who disrespect Hulders might find themselves subjected to pranks or worse.
Modern Interpretations:
The allure of Hulders continues to influence modern Scandinavian culture. They make appearances in literature, art, and even contemporary folklore, often symbolizing the wild, untamed aspects of nature and emphasizing the importance of maintaining a harmonious relationship with the environment. Additionally, they serve as a reminder of the mysterious and unpredictable elements of the natural world that continue to captivate and mystify us.
In conclusion, the Hulder of Scandinavian folklore represents a unique and captivating category of fairies. Their beauty, connection to nature, and dual nature as both benevolent and mischievous beings have secured their enduring place in the rich tapestry of folklore from the Nordic lands. These enigmatic creatures serve as a reminder of the intricate relationship between humans and the natural world, where respect and harmony are essential for coexisting with the mystical inhabitants of the wilderness.

3. English and Scottish Folklore:

In the rich tapestry of English and Scottish folklore, a distinctive category of fairies emerges—Brownies and Household Fairies. These enchanting beings, deeply woven into the cultural fabric of the British Isles, play unique roles in the everyday lives of those they encounter. In this section, we will delve into the captivating realm of these household fairies, exploring their origins, characteristics, and the various subtypes that populate the folklore of these regions.

Origins and Characteristics: Brownies and Household Fairies are renowned for their diligent and benevolent nature. Unlike the mischievous and capricious fairies found in other traditions, these fairies are considered domestic protectors who perform chores and tasks in exchange for small offerings. They are known for their loyalty and attachment to a specific household or farm, where they take on the role of a guardian spirit.

The Brownie:

The Brownie, a beloved figure in Scottish folklore, is perhaps the most famous of these household fairies. They are typically depicted as small, haggard, and wrinkled creatures, often dressed in rags or brown clothing, from which their name derives. Despite their unassuming appearance, Brownies are characterized by their tireless work ethic and their commitment to helping the families they serve. They perform tasks such as sweeping, cleaning, and tending to livestock, all while remaining unseen or shrouded in invisibility.

Subtypes and Regional Variations:

Within the realm of Brownies and Household Fairies, there exist regional variations and subtypes, each with its own unique attributes and preferences. Some of these variations include:

Hearth Brownies:

- These fairies are particularly fond of the hearth and fireplace. They are known to take offense if the hearth is not kept clean and fires are not tended properly. In return for a well-maintained hearth, they ensure the family's home remains warm and welcoming.

Farm Brownies:

- Farm Brownies, as the name suggests, are more closely associated with agricultural tasks. They assist with planting, harvesting, and tending to crops and animals. A well-treated Farm Brownie is believed to bring prosperity to the farm.

Bogles and Boggarts:

While not as benevolent as Brownies, Bogles and Boggarts are part of the household fairy tradition in northern England and Scotland. They are mischievous rather than malicious, and are known for playing tricks on unsuspecting residents.

- Offerings and Etiquette: Household fairies, including Brownies, are known to be particular about offerings and displays of gratitude. It is customary to leave out a small dish of milk, cream, or honey for them as a token of appreciation. Failure to do so might result in the Brownie departing or even causing minor disturbances in the household.
- Interaction with Humans: Brownies and Household Fairies are generally shy and reclusive, preferring to work in the shadows or under the cover of darkness. They are most active at night and typically only reveal themselves to those they trust completely. If a human attempts to thank or reward them directly, they may take offense and vanish forever, so it is essential to show gratitude indirectly.
- Legacy and Endurance: The enduring appeal of Brownies and Household Fairies in English and Scottish folklore reflects the deep connection between the people of these regions and the mystical world that resides alongside their own. These fairies continue to inspire stories, traditions, and even modern adaptations in literature and media,

demonstrating that their legacy endures, and the charm of these domestic protectors continues to captivate the hearts and imaginations of those who encounter them.

3B. Elemental Beings

Fairies Associated with Natural Elements like Water, Air, Earth, and Fire
Fairies have often been associated with the natural elements, reflecting their connection to the natural world. This section explores the elemental categorizations of fairies:

1. Water Fairies:

Water fairies, known for their ethereal beauty and connection to aquatic environments, have been a source of fascination and inspiration in folklore, mythology, and literature throughout the ages. These enchanting beings are intimately tied to the world's lakes, rivers, oceans, and other bodies of water, and their classifications often depend on their dwelling place and unique attributes.

A. Nymphs: The Nurturers of Waterways

Nymphs, perhaps the most renowned of water fairies, are prevalent in Greek and Roman mythology. They are classified into various types, each associated with specific water sources:

- Naiads: These freshwater nymphs inhabit springs, rivers, and fountains. Each Naiad is believed to be a guardian spirit of her specific water source, and she is often depicted as a beautiful maiden, sometimes seen bathing in her spring.
- Oceanids: Oceanids, on the other hand, are nymphs of saltwater bodies, including the vast ocean itself. They are associated with the primal forces of the sea and are portrayed as daughters of Oceanus and Tethys, ancient sea deities.
- Nereids: Nereids are sea nymphs who dwell in the Mediterranean Sea. They are known for their grace and often accompany sea gods like Poseidon. Each Nereid has her own role in the sea's ecology and mythology.

B. Water Fairies Beyond the Mediterranean

While nymphs are the most famous water fairies in classical mythology, similar beings can be found in various cultures worldwide:

- Kelpies (Scotland): Kelpies are shape-shifting water spirits that often appear as horses near lochs and rivers. They lure unsuspecting travelers into the water, where they are drowned or devoured.

- Mami Wata (West Africa): Mami Wata is a water deity celebrated in West and Central African folklore. She is often depicted as a beautiful woman with a lower body resembling a serpent. Mami Wata is associated with both fertility and danger.
- Selkies (Ireland and Scotland): Selkies are seal-like creatures that can shed their skins to become human. When in human form, they may interact with and even marry humans, but always retain a deep connection to the sea.

C. Guardians and Enchantresses

Water fairies often serve as protectors of their respective domains, ensuring the health and vitality of the aquatic ecosystems they inhabit. They are believed to have the power to bless or curse those who come into contact with their waters. Additionally, they are often seen as enchantresses who can lure humans with their beauty and melodious voices, leading them into the depths of the water, never to return.

D. Cultural Significance

The classification of water fairies is a testament to humanity's deep connection with water and the vital role it plays in our lives. These beings personify the captivating and sometimes treacherous nature of water, reflecting both its life-giving properties and its potential for danger. In many cultures, offerings and rituals are made to appease water fairies and ensure safe passage on waterways.

E. Contemporary and Literary Influence

Water fairies continue to be a source of inspiration in contemporary literature, art, and popular culture. Their mysterious allure and connection to the natural world make them compelling characters in fantasy novels, movies, and even video games. Their ability to embody the beauty and unpredictability of water ensures that these mythical beings will remain a timeless and captivating aspect of human folklore and creativity.

2. Earth Fairies:

Earth fairies, often associated with the elemental realm of the earth, are enchanting beings deeply connected to the underground world. Within this category, two prominent groups of earth fairies stand out: gnomes and dwarves. These subterranean creatures have carved a unique niche in folklore and mythology, each with its distinct characteristics, roles, and regional variations.

A. Gnomes: The Guardians of Gardens and Greenery

Gnomes, also known as earth elementals, are celebrated as guardians of the natural world, particularly in gardens and forests. These diminutive beings are characterized by their affinity for earth and their harmonious relationship with plant life. Here, we delve into the world of gnomes, exploring their roles, attributes, and regional interpretation.

1. *Roles and Attributes:*

In the quiet corners of gardens and the hidden realms of the natural world, gnomes emerge as enigmatic and timeless beings, embodying both the wisdom of the ages and an intimate connection to the Earth's mysteries. While they often appear as diminutive, bearded figures draped in earthy hues, gnomes are far more than meets the eye.

The Earth's Guardians: Gnomes take on the profound role of guardians of gardens and greenery. These pint-sized custodians are believed to possess an innate ability to nurture and protect plants, ensuring their growth and vitality. With their wrinkled faces and long, flowing beards, gnomes bear the marks of agelessness, signifying their timeless wisdom and the enduring secrets they hold.

Whisperers of Nature: In the intricate tapestry of the natural world, gnomes are thought to be nature's communicators. They form intricate bonds with the flora and fauna of their domains, fostering a harmonious and balanced ecosystem. These benevolent beings are said to possess a unique ability to converse with plants and animals, fostering mutual understanding and unity within their enchanted realms.

Shape-Shifters of the Earth: Among the most intriguing aspects of gnome lore is the notion that these creatures can shape-shift, seamlessly blending with their surroundings. Some tales suggest that they can transform into animals, allowing them to move unnoticed through the forests and meadows. Others believe that gnomes can meld with the very elements themselves, becoming one with rocks, trees, or even the bubbling streams that course through their domains. This extraordinary gift enables them to observe the world from hidden vantage points and protect their cherished natural spaces.
Regional Variations: Gnomes Around the World

As we embark on a journey through the rich tapestry of global folklore, we encounter gnomes in diverse cultural manifestations, each contributing its unique essence to the captivating world of gnome lore.

Germanic Garden Guardians: Within the enchanting gardens of Germany and its neighboring lands, gnomes assume the delightful role known as "Gartenzwerge," or garden gnomes. These whimsical creatures are renowned for their vibrant attire and cheerful disposition as they diligently tend to the gardens. Adored for their contribution to the vitality of botanical wonders, they grace gardens with their lively presence.

Slavic Hearth Spirits: Across the tapestry of Slavic traditions, gnome-like entities known as "Domovoi" emerge as cherished household spirits. These beings find their abode at the very heart of homes—the hearth—and are revered as protectors of family dwellings. Their remarkable adaptability is evident as they seamlessly transition from being guardians of the garden to becoming caretakers of the home. In their multifaceted role, they ensure the well-being and harmony of the household, embodying the enduring essence of gnome-like beings across diverse settings.

In the narratives and lore surrounding gnomes, we catch a glimpse of humanity's timeless fascination with these enchanting creatures. They symbolize the intrinsic bond between humanity and the natural world, offering wisdom, protection, and a touch of magic to those who acknowledge their presence. Whether nestled in the gardens of Germany or diligently tending to the hearths of Slavic homes, gnomes remain a source of wonder, curiosity, and a profound appreciation for the mystical connections that bind us to the concealed realms of the Earth.

2. Regional Variations:

- Dwarves appear in various forms across cultures, from the Norse "Dvergar" to the Celtic "Daurad" and the Persian "Divs." Each culture imparts its unique characteristics to these earthy beings.
- The Nordic dwarves, known for their roles in crafting the treasures of the gods, are often referenced in the Poetic Edda and Prose Edda, two significant texts in Norse mythology.
- In Tolkien's Middle-earth, dwarves play a central role as skilled craftsmen and warriors, adding a rich layer to the lore of these subterranean entities.

In summary, earth fairies, including gnomes and dwarves, constitute a captivating category of mystical beings deeply rooted in the earth's fertile soil and subterranean realms. Their roles as guardians, craftsmen, and stewards of nature reflect the diverse ways in which human cultures have engaged with the natural world. Whether tending to gardens or forging legendary treasures, these earth fairies continue to inspire our imaginations and remind us of the profound connection between humanity and the Earth.

3. Air and Fire Fairies:

In the ethereal realm of elemental fairies, two distinct categories emerge: Air Fairies, known as Sylphs, and Fire Fairies, referred to as Salamanders. These enchanting beings are intimately connected to the elements they represent, embodying the very essence of air and fire. Let us delve deeper into the captivating world of these elemental fairies:

Sylphs - The Airy Enchantments:

Air, the invisible yet omnipresent element, gives rise to the delicate and ephemeral Sylphs. These ethereal fairies are often associated with the skies, winds, and the breath of life itself.

Embracing the Enchantment of Fairy Lore

As we conclude our mesmerizing journey through the captivating world of fairy lore, we find ourselves at the intersection of history, culture, nature, and imagination. This exploration has not only unraveled the timeless mysteries that surround these mystical beings but has also revealed the profound impact they continue to exert on our lives and the world around us.

Interplay of Sylphs and Salamanders:

In the intricate dance of elemental forces, Sylphs and Salamanders often find themselves in a harmonious yet contrasting relationship. While Sylphs seek to extinguish the flames that Salamanders embody, the two elemental fairies coexist in a delicate balance, representing the eternal cycle of creation and destruction.

Symbolism and Elemental Magic

Within the mystical realm of fairies, the interplay of air and fire holds profound symbolic significance, echoing the duality of existence itself. Here, we delve into the symbolism behind these elemental forces, where destruction ushers in renewal, and opposing energies unite to maintain the delicate equilibrium of the natural world.

The dance of air and fire illustrates the intricate balance necessary for harmony in both the material and spiritual realms. This chapter explores how practitioners of elemental magic invoke Sylphs and Salamanders to tap into the potent energies of air and fire, viewing these elemental beings as powerful allies who bestow unique abilities upon those who seek their assistance. It is believed that by harmonizing these elements, one can attain enlightenment and transformation across physical and metaphysical planes.

In the Tapestry of Fairy Folklore

In the rich tapestry of fairy folklore, Sylphs and Salamanders emerge as captivating embodiments of the intangible elements of air and fire. These ethereal beings, with their distinctive appearances, powers, and roles in folklore, illuminate the profound connection between elemental forces and the human experience. By exploring their essence, we gain insights into the intricate dance between the seen and the unseen, the tangible and the ephemeral, within the wondrous world of fairies.

Chapter 2: Fairy Folk Roles: The Enchanting Household Fairies

In the vast spectrum of fairy roles, from benevolent protectors to mischievous tricksters, few hold as cherished a place in the hearts of humans as household fairies. These enchanting beings are intimately woven into the fabric of daily life, becoming integral to the well-being of the homes they inhabit. In this chapter, we embark on a deep exploration of household fairies, unraveling their characteristics, regional variations, and the unique roles they play in households around the world.

Characteristics and Attributes

Household fairies are renowned for their diminutive stature, often standing no taller than a few feet. Their small size allows them to move effortlessly through the nooks and crannies of a household, making them expert housekeepers. These endearing beings are typically depicted with delicate and attractive features, adorned in tiny, intricate garments that reflect their status as house guardians. Unlike some of their mischievous fairy counterparts, household fairies are generally benevolent and helpful. They willingly take on domestic chores, such as cleaning, tidying, and even babysitting, while the household sleeps. To ensure their goodwill, it is customary in many cultures to leave out offerings, including milk, bread, honey, or small trinkets as tokens of appreciation.

Regional Variations

Household fairies take on diverse forms and names in different regions, each with its unique attributes and customs. These regional variations offer a glimpse into the rich tapestry of human-fairy interactions:

Brownies (Scotland and England): Brownies are among the most famous household fairies. Often depicted as short, brown-skinned beings with a penchant for tidying and completing chores in the dead of night, Brownies are loyal and diligent helpers if acknowledged and appreciated. However, they can become mischievous if slighted.

Domovoi (Russia): In Russian folklore, Domovoi are guardian spirits of the home. These small, bearded creatures are believed to inhabit the stove. Domovoi protect the household and its inhabitants but can bring misfortune if displeased.

Tomte (Scandinavia): Tomte, or Nisse, are household fairies from Scandinavian folklore. They are often depicted as elderly men with long white beards, wearing traditional red caps. Tomte oversee the welfare of the farm and its animals, and it is customary to leave them offerings of porridge on Christmas Eve.

Hobs (Northern England): Hobs are known for their helpful nature in northern English folklore. They are often associated with farmhouses and have a distinct liking for the hearth. Providing them with a cozy space by the fire ensures their continued assistance.

Household Fairy Customs

The presence of household fairies brings forth specific customs and traditions meant to appease and maintain their goodwill. These customs often revolve around politeness, respect, and the expression of gratitude:

Leaving Out Offerings: To ensure the continued help of household fairies, it is customary in many cultures to leave out offerings of food or small gifts. This gesture acknowledges their presence and expresses gratitude for their assistance.

Politeness: Interactions with household fairies are governed by politeness and respect. It is considered essential not to offend or upset these beings, as they can easily switch from helpful to mischievous if provoked.

Concealing Their Actions: Household fairies prefer to work in secret, so it's best not to observe them at their tasks. They may take offense if their activities are witnessed.

Observing Customs: Different cultures have various customs and rituals associated with household fairies, such as setting aside a special place for them, making small sacrifices, or observing specific holidays.

The Endearing Legacy of Household Fairies

Household fairies have left an endearing and lasting legacy in folklore, symbolizing the harmony between humans and the natural world. They remind us of the importance of showing gratitude and respect for the unseen forces that bless our homes with order and protection. Even in the modern age, the spirit of household fairies lives on, inspiring stories, traditions, and acts of kindness in households around the world, fostering a sense of connection between the human realm and the enchanting world of the unseen.

Nature Guardians: Elemental Spirits and Their Enchanted Realms

In the heart of the natural world, where the elements dance and converge, a realm of enchantment beckons. Within this captivating tapestry, elemental spirits, guardians of the Earth's most fundamental forces, weave their ethereal tales. This chapter delves deep into the ancient and contemporary lore of these elemental spirits, exploring their unique roles in shaping the natural world and captivating the human imagination.

I. The Airy Sylphs - Whisperers of the Wind

Among the wisps of clouds and the currents of the breeze, the sylphs soar, their presence as elusive as the very air they command. These airy spirits are revered as guardians of the skies, the winds, and the ethereal realm.

In mythology and folklore, sylphs are often associated with the gentle zephyrs and tempestuous gales that sweep across the heavens. Their graceful forms and ever-changing nature embody the mercurial qualities of the wind itself. In some traditions, sylphs are believed to influence weather patterns, their whims shaping the destinies of sailors and farmers alike.

II. The Nereids - Oceanic Nymphs of the Deep

In the watery depths of the world's oceans, the Nereids hold court. These sea nymphs are both guardians and companions of the deep, their ethereal presence embodied in the endless waves and the mysteries of the sea.

In the ancient tales of Greek mythology, the Nereids are celebrated as the daughters of Nereus, the old man of the sea. Riding on the backs of dolphins and guiding sailors through treacherous waters, these graceful nymphs are revered as protectors of the sea and its creatures. Their songs are said to enchant sailors, luring them into the depths with promises of maritime adventures.

III. The Earthbound Gnomes - Keepers of Hidden Treasures

Beneath the surface of the Earth, within the labyrinthine depths of caves and tunnels, the gnomes reign. These small, bearded guardians are the custodians of the Earth's treasures, and they watch over its precious gems, minerals, and natural resources.

Gnomes, with their diminutive stature and often cheerful demeanor, are guardians of the Earth's hidden riches. In European folklore, they are believed to dwell deep underground, where they safeguard precious gems and minerals. Though they may appear playful, they are fierce protectors of their domain and can be both benevolent and mischievous.

IV. Regional Variations:

a. Native American Nature Spirits:

Within the diverse tapestry of Native American cultures, myriad nature guardian spirits emerge, each deeply rooted in the traditions and beliefs of distinct tribes. For instance, the Navajo people honor Yé'iitsoh, a guardian spirit associated with the immense power of mountains and the Earth itself. These spirits play pivotal roles in tribal cosmology, shaping the narratives and rituals of indigenous communities.

b. African Ancestral Spirits:

Across the vast and diverse expanse of Africa, ancestral spirits are often regarded as nature guardians. These spirits are believed to inhabit various natural elements, from rivers and rocks to forests and mountains. Communities maintain a profound reverence for these spirits, expressing their respect through sacred rituals and offerings that ensure harmony with the natural world.

V. Modern Interpretations:

a. Contemporary Nature Spirits:

In the modern era, the concept of nature guardians has found renewed purpose within environmental and conservation movements. As humanity grapples with pressing ecological challenges, some individuals invoke the idea of nature spirits to foster a profound sense of responsibility and stewardship toward the Earth and its elements. The notion of nature guardians serves as a poignant reminder of our interconnectedness with the environment.

b. Fairy Conservation Efforts:

In select regions, particularly throughout Europe, passionate efforts have been initiated to safeguard the habitats of plants and trees associated with fairy lore. These endeavors reflect a deep-rooted desire to honor the cultural significance of these nature guardians. Conservationists and folklorists alike have united in their dedication to preserving the mystical realms where fairies and their elemental kin continue to thrive.

As we navigate the enchanting realm of elemental guardians, we are reminded that the natural world is not merely a backdrop to human existence; it is a living tapestry, woven with the threads of wind, water, earth, and fire, and guarded by ethereal beings whose presence transcends time and culture. These elemental spirits beckon us to embrace our roles as stewards of the Earth, to honor the delicate balance of nature, and to celebrate the enduring enchantment of the elements that surround us.

The realm of Nature Guardians within fairy folklore highlights humanity's enduring connection to the natural world. These fairies serve as a reminder of the interdependence between humans and their environment. Through stories, rituals, and beliefs, cultures around the world have celebrated the beauty and sanctity of nature, ensuring that the legacy of these enchanting nature guardians lives on in the collective consciousness of humanity. Whether as protectors of ancient trees or spirits of the wind and waters, these fairies embody our deep-rooted reverence for the Earth and its myriad wonders.

3. Tricksters: Unraveling the Enigma

Within the diverse spectrum of fairy classifications, few are as captivating and enigmatic as the tricksters. These whimsical, mischievous, and at times capricious fairies have carved a distinctive niche within folklore, often straddling the line between light-hearted jesters and cunning troublemakers. In this section, we embark on an exploration of the enthralling world of fairy tricksters, uncovering their unique characteristics, their pivotal role in cultural narratives, and the classifications that have emerged to delineate their multifaceted personalities.

i. Fairy Tricksters in Folklore and Literature

Fairy tricksters, sometimes known as pranksters or jesters, are ubiquitous figures in the folklore and literature of numerous cultures. They embody the unpredictable and whimsical aspects of the fairy realm, making them both beloved and feared characters in stories and legends.

Puck, the Merry Prankster:

Among the most iconic trickster fairies stands Puck, who gained fame in William Shakespeare's "A Midsummer Night's Dream." Puck, also known as Robin Goodfellow, is a shape-shifting and mischievous spirit who revels in creating confusion among the characters. His capricious nature and penchant for playing pranks add a whimsical element to the play's comedic proceedings.

Brownies and Hobgoblins:

In English and Scottish folklore, brownies and hobgoblins often find classification as trickster fairies. While they can be helpful around the house, they are also known to engage in playful tricks, such as moving objects, hiding belongings, or creating unusual noises. Their actions are rarely malevolent but serve as a reminder of their mercurial nature.

Imps and Sprites:

Imps and sprites, diminutive trickster fairies found in various cultures, are known for their affinity for pranks. From stealing socks to causing household chaos, these mischievous beings delight in their antics. While their actions are typically harmless, they can be vexing for humans.

ii. Classifications of Fairy Tricksters

Within the realm of fairy tricksters, intriguing subcategories exist, each possessing distinct traits and tendencies. These classifications aid in differentiating between the types of pranks they play and the level of mischief they engage in:

1. Playful Pucks:

- Pucks, like Shakespeare's portrayal, are often considered the archetypal tricksters. They revel in creating confusion, mischief, and humorous chaos. They may change their forms, lead travelers astray, or concoct love potions to bewilder mortals.

2. House-Haunting Hobgoblins:

- Hobgoblins are typically found in homes, where they alternate between helpful chores and perplexing tricks. Their playful antics can range from tidying up a messy room to rearranging furniture overnight.

3. Prankish Imps:

- Imps are known for their relentless pranks, sometimes bordering on the malicious. They enjoy causing discomfort and vexation to humans, such as tangling hair, hiding keys, or creating eerie noises in the night.

iii. The Symbolism of Fairy Tricksters

Fairy tricksters, despite their penchant for mischief, hold a special place in folklore and storytelling. They represent the capricious and unpredictable aspects of the natural world, serving as a reminder that not everything can be controlled or explained. Their playful antics often carry deeper symbolism:

Embracing Chaos:

- Fairy tricksters challenge the human desire for order and predictability. Their actions invite us to embrace chaos, spontaneity, and the unexpected in our lives.

Blurring Boundaries:

- Trickster fairies blur the boundaries between reality and the supernatural. They challenge our perceptions of what is possible and open our minds to the mysteries of the unseen world.

Humor and Resilience:

- Through their pranks, trickster fairies teach us the value of humor and resilience in the face of adversity. They remind us not to take ourselves too seriously and to find joy in life's unexpected twists and turns.

In conclusion, fairy tricksters represent a captivating and complex aspect of fairy folklore. Their playful yet unpredictable nature adds depth and richness to the world of fairies, reminding us that the mystical realm is not always what it seems. Whether through the enduring legacy of Puck or the mischievous antics of brownies and imps, these trickster fairies continue to captivate our imaginations, inviting us to embrace the enchanting unpredictability of the fairy realm and the world around us.

3D. Fairy Hierarchies: Understanding the Seelie and Unseelie Courts

In certain traditions and mythologies, fairies are organized into intricate hierarchical systems, reflecting the complexities of the fairy realm. This section delves into the fascinating hierarchies that exist within the fairy world, shedding light on the distinctive Seelie and Unseelie Courts—a classification system that offers profound insights into the rich tapestry of fairy beliefs, particularly in the folklore and mythology of Scotland and Ireland.

1. Seelie and Unseelie Courts: Guardians and Tricksters

The concept of the Seelie and Unseelie Courts is deeply ingrained in the folklore of Scotland and Ireland, serving as a captivating categorization of fairies based on their nature, behavior, and intentions towards humans. This division provides a nuanced glimpse into the diverse world of fairy beings within these regions.

The Seelie Court: Guardians of Goodwill

The term "Seelie" finds its origins in the Scots word "seel," meaning "blessed" or "good." Fairies associated with the Seelie Court are generally regarded as benevolent, friendly, and inclined to assist or interact with humans in a positive and harmonious manner. This court embodies a realm of goodwill, characterized by:

Origins of Benevolence: The Seelie Court's benevolent nature has deep roots in folklore and history. Over time, these radiant and protective fairies have evolved into guardians and benefactors, epitomizing their role as protectors of those who approach them with reverence and respect.

Favorable Actions: Members of the Seelie Court are renowned for their fair and compassionate dealings with humans. Unlike their counterparts in the Unseelie Court, they are more inclined to engage in acts of kindness, healing, and protection. Their benevolent actions extend to those who approach them with courtesy and reverence, and their gifts often bestow blessings and good fortune upon the recipients.

Courteous Interaction: Interacting with Seelie fairies involves the art of politeness and respect. Humans are advised to approach these mystical beings with utmost courtesy, recognizing their status as guardians of the natural world and benefactors to those in need. Proper manners and gratitude are seen as pathways to forging positive interactions and garnering the goodwill of these enchanted entities.

Celebrations and Festivals: Certain days and festivals hold a special place in the hearts of the Seelie Court, serving as occasions when their presence is believed to be more active and accessible to humans. Festivals such as Beltane and Midsummer's Eve are steeped in tradition, where fairies are celebrated, and humans seek their favor and guidance.

Examples of the Seelie Court: Within the Seelie Court, a diverse array of benevolent fairies assumes distinct roles in their interactions with humans. The beloved Brownie, known for its helpful nature in completing household chores under the cover of night, exemplifies the Seelie Court's commitment to aiding humanity. Another cherished member is the Leanan Sidhe, a beautiful and gentle fairy who serves as a muse and lover to artists, inspiring creativity and devotion.

In essence, the Seelie Court and its benevolent fairies stand as beacons of goodwill and protection in the mystical world of fairies. Their actions, rooted in kindness and courtesy, serve as a reminder of the harmonious relationship that can exist between humanity and the supernatural. As we continue our exploration of the realm of fairies, let us carry with us the knowledge that benevolence and protection are ever-present, awaiting those who approach with respect and gratitude.

The Unseelie Court:

In contrast, the term "Unseelie" is derived from the Scots word "unseely," meaning "unblessed" or "evil." Fairies associated with the Unseelie Court are perceived as malevolent or capricious, often causing harm or mischief to humans. Key characteristics of the Unseelie Court include:

Malevolence: Unseelie fairies are known for their unpredictable and sometimes malicious behavior. They may play pranks, cause illness, or lead humans astray.
Dangerous Encounters: Interactions with members of the Unseelie Court can be perilous. It is believed that humans should avoid crossing their paths or intruding upon their territories, especially at night.
Aversion to Iron: Iron is thought to repel Unseelie fairies, and people would often carry iron objects or place them near entrances to protect themselves from malevolent encounters.
Nighttime Activity: Unseelie fairies are believed to be more active at night, making nighttime journeys particularly risky in regions where these fairies are prevalent.
Examples: Notorious members of the Unseelie Court include the Redcap, a malevolent fairy who stains his hat with the blood of his victims, and the fearsome Bean Sidhe (Banshee), an omen of death.

Gray Areas and Complexity:

While the Seelie and Unseelie Courts provide a broad classification system for fairies, it's important to note that not all fairies neatly fit into these categories. Some fairies may exhibit traits from both courts, and their behavior can vary depending on circumstances and the individuals involved. This complexity adds depth to the folklore and reflects the nuanced relationship between humans and fairies in these cultures.

In essence, the Seelie and Unseelie Courts offer a fascinating glimpse into the world of fairy beliefs, where the line between benevolence and malevolence is often blurred, and human interactions with these enchanting beings are characterized by a delicate balance of respect and caution.

2. Fairy Monarchs:

Within the intricate hierarchy of the fairy realm, there exists a fascinating category known as Fairy Monarchs. These regal and often enigmatic beings reign over their fellow fairies and occupy a special place in the folklore and mythology of various cultures. The concept of Fairy Monarchs is particularly prominent in English and Welsh folklore, where these rulers of the fairy kingdom are depicted with unique attributes, powers, and mythological significance.

A. English Folklore:

In English folklore, Fairy Monarchs are commonly associated with the world of the Fae. Two prominent figures in this realm are King Oberon and Queen Titania. These names might ring a bell for those familiar with William Shakespeare's timeless play, "A Midsummer Night's Dream." Shakespeare drew inspiration from existing folklore when he introduced Oberon and Titania as the King and Queen of the Fairies.

King Oberon: King Oberon, also known as Auberon or Alberon, is a central figure in English fairy lore. He is often depicted as a powerful and benevolent monarch who presides over the fairy kingdom. Oberon is known for his wisdom, magical prowess, and his role in mediating disputes among fairies. He is also associated with the concept of love and romance, playing a key role in the tangled love affairs of the play's mortal characters.

Queen Titania: Titania, the Queen of the Fairies, is Oberon's counterpart and is equally influential. She is known for her beauty, grace, and a strong-willed nature. In "A Midsummer Night's Dream," Titania becomes embroiled in a conflict with Oberon, leading to comical and fantastical events that underscore her authority and presence within the fairy realm.

B. Welsh Folklore:

In Welsh mythology, a similar concept of fairy monarchy exists, although the names and characteristics of these fairy rulers may vary. The Welsh often refer to them as "Tylwyth Teg," which translates to "the Fair Folk." Within the Tylwyth Teg, there are figures known as Fairy Kings and Queens, although these titles may not be as firmly established as in English folklore.

Fairy Kings and Queens: In Welsh tales, Fairy Kings and Queens govern the Tylwyth Teg, leading their fairy subjects in their enchanted domains. These rulers are often depicted as majestic and mysterious figures, embodying the magic and wonder of the Welsh countryside. They are associated with ancient mounds, enchanted forests, and hidden valleys where the Tylwyth Teg are said to dwell.

C. Characteristics and Powers:

Fairy Monarchs, regardless of their specific names or cultural origins, share certain characteristics and powers:

Magical Authority: Fairy Monarchs possess immense magical powers, allowing them to control and manipulate the natural world. They can influence the weather, shape-shift, and cast enchantments over both fairy and human realms.

Wisdom and Guidance: Fairy Monarchs are revered for their wisdom and are often sought after for guidance and counsel. They play essential roles in the moral and ethical guidance of their fairy subjects.

Influence on Mortals: Fairy Monarchs sometimes interact with humans, often drawing them into the enchanting world of the fairies. They may bestow blessings or challenges upon mortals, and their actions can have far-reaching consequences in the lives of those they encounter.

D. Legacy and Modern Influence:

The concept of Fairy Monarchs has left an indelible mark on literature, art, and popular culture. Shakespeare's portrayal of King Oberon and Queen Titania has been adapted and reimagined in numerous theatrical productions, films, and novels. Moreover, contemporary fantasy literature and media continue to draw inspiration from the regal and otherworldly nature of Fairy Monarchs, perpetuating their enduring appeal.

In summary, Fairy Monarchs stand as majestic and central figures within the intricate tapestry of fairy folklore. Their influence extends far beyond the pages of ancient myths and legends, continuing to captivate the human imagination and reminding us of the enduring fascination with the magical realms of fairydom.

Chapter 3D: Cultural Syncretism

In an era characterized by globalization, cultures have frequently merged and exchanged ideas. This section explores instances of syncretism where fairies from different cultural backgrounds blend and influence one another.

1. The Fairy Pantheon:

In the modern age of globalized culture and literature, the concept of a "Fairy Pantheon" has emerged as a captivating testament to the fusion and cross-pollination of fairy lore from various corners of the world. This phenomenon, often seen in contemporary fantasy literature and media, exemplifies how the enchanting realm of fairies transcends geographical boundaries and cultural confines, weaving together a tapestry of mythical beings that resonate with audiences worldwide.

I. An Intercontinental Gathering of Fairy Folk

Within the framework of the Fairy Pantheon, fairies from diverse cultural backgrounds come together in an eclectic and harmonious assembly. This multicultural mélange features an array of fairies, each bearing the unique characteristics and attributes of their respective origins:

1. Celtic Fairies:

Sidhe and Tuatha Dé Danann: From Irish and Scottish mythology, the Sidhe, often referred to as the "Aes Sidhe" or "People of the Mounds," join forces with the Tuatha Dé Danann, the divine race of Irish mythology. These fairies, once divided by Celtic legend, now coexist harmoniously in the pantheon.

2. Nordic Fairies:

Elves and Light Hulders: The elegant and ethereal elves of Norse mythology find common ground with the Light Hulders of Norwegian folklore, forming a collective presence within the pantheon.

3. English and Welsh Fairies:

Brownies and Tylwyth Teg: The helpful household spirits known as Brownies from English and Scottish traditions align with the Tylwyth Teg, the fairy folk of Wales, to bring their domestic magic to the Fairy Pantheon.

II. Bridging East and West

The Fairy Pantheon does not limit its membership to Western traditions alone. It welcomes a harmonious blend of East and West, demonstrating the global appeal of these magical beings:

1. Japanese Yokai:

Tengu and Kitsune: From the rich tapestry of Japanese folklore, Tengu, the avian spirits, and Kitsune, the shape-shifting foxes, find themselves intertwined with fairies from other cultures, infusing their unique brand of enchantment into the pantheon.

2. Arabian Jinn:

Marid and Ifrit: Arabian jinn, including the powerful Marid and the fiery Ifrit, contribute their elemental magic to the Pantheon, creating an intriguing fusion of Middle Eastern and Western mythologies.

III. Fairy Diversity and Unity

The Fairy Pantheon celebrates the incredible diversity of fairy folklore while emphasizing the universal themes that unite these mystical beings. Despite their varied origins, fairies within the pantheon often share common attributes such as a connection to nature, shape-shifting abilities, and a penchant for both mischief and benevolence.

IV. Modern Literary and Cinematic Expressions

The concept of the Fairy Pantheon has found fertile ground in contemporary literature and popular media. Authors, filmmakers, and artists have embraced this fusion of fairy traditions to craft compelling narratives that resonate with audiences worldwide. Works like Neil Gaiman's "American Gods" and Holly Black's "The Folk of the Air" series illustrate the enduring allure of the Fairy Pantheon in modern storytelling.

V. A Testament to Cultural Exchange

The emergence of the Fairy Pantheon serves as a testament to the rich history of cultural exchange and the enduring power of mythical beings to captivate the human imagination. It embodies the idea that, in the interconnected world of today, the allure of fairies knows no borders. Instead, it thrives on the ability of these enchanting beings to transcend cultural confines, bringing together a diverse array of legends, stories, and traditions into one harmonious celebration of the fantastical.

In conclusion, the Fairy Pantheon stands as a testament to the enduring enchantment of fairies, showcasing how these mythical beings continue to evolve and captivate the hearts and minds of people from all walks of life, fostering a sense of unity in the shared wonder and fascination they inspire.

2. Global Fairy Phenomena:

In regions where cultures have historically intermingled, such as the British Isles and other areas with rich and diverse histories, we witness the fascinating phenomenon of global fairy syncretism. Here, the categorization and classification of fairies become a captivating tapestry of shared beliefs, cross-cultural exchanges, and a testament to the enduring nature of these enchanting beings in the human imagination.

The British Isles: A Mosaic of Fairy Diversity

The British Isles serve as a prime example of a region where different cultures have contributed to the diverse landscape of fairy folklore. Over the centuries, waves of Celts, Romans, Vikings, Normans, and others have left their mark on the region, each bringing their own beliefs and mythologies. As a result, the fairies of the British Isles are not confined to a single tradition but represent a rich mosaic of influences.

Within this multifaceted world of British fairy folklore, we find fairies hailing from various origins:

Celtic Fairies: The indigenous Celtic traditions have contributed significantly to British fairy folklore. The Tuatha Dé Danann of Irish mythology, for example, merged with local beliefs to create beings like the Sidhe. The Sidhe, in turn, found their place within the broader landscape of British fairy folklore.

Norse Influence: Viking settlers in the British Isles brought with them their own beliefs in supernatural beings. These Northern influences blended with local lore to create entities like the Huldrefolk in Scotland and the Hulders in Norway.

Christian Syncretism: With the spread of Christianity, fairies often became associated with angels or demons. This syncretism resulted in hybrid beings like the Fairy Queen, who embodies both pagan and Christian elements.

Cross-Cultural Exchanges: Trade and cultural exchanges between the British Isles and other regions introduced foreign concepts and fairy types. For instance, Silkies, selkies or seal folk, have origins in Scandinavian and Scottish folklore but found a place in the shared fairylore of the British Isles.

Modern Literature and Media: The Globalization of Fairies

In the modern era, literature and media have played a significant role in the globalization of fairy phenomena. Writers, artists, and filmmakers from diverse backgrounds draw upon a vast array of fairy classifications, creating new interpretations and amalgamations of these beings. This phenomenon transcends geographical boundaries and connects cultures through the universal appeal of fairies.

For instance, J.R.R. Tolkien's creation of Elves in "The Lord of the Rings" drew inspiration from various mythologies, blending elements of Celtic, Norse, and Germanic fairy traditions. These Elves, with their distinct hierarchies and characteristics, have become iconic figures in fantasy literature.

Similarly, the Harry Potter series by J.K. Rowling incorporates a wide range of magical creatures, including house-elves and pixies, each with its unique attributes drawn from global folklore. Rowling's portrayal of house-elves, in particular, raises questions about the treatment of magical beings, reflecting broader societal discussions on social justice.

In the realm of film and television, fairies have transcended borders in works such as the animated series "Winx Club," which merges European fairy traditions with contemporary themes and settings.

A Shared World of Enchantment

The global fairy phenomenon demonstrates how cultures have converged and collaborated in shaping the world of fairies. Whether through historical interactions, cross-cultural exchanges, or the creative endeavors of storytellers, fairies have become a bridge that connects societies and fosters a sense of shared enchantment. This phenomenon not only enriches the tapestry of fairy folklore but also reminds us of the universal human desire to explore the mystical and embrace the extraordinary, transcending cultural boundaries to celebrate the enduring allure of these timeless beings.

Chapter 4
Myths and Legends

In our enchanting journey through the captivating world of fairies, we now embark on an exploration of grand myths that have intricately woven narratives around these enchanting beings. Across diverse cultures and epochs, fairies have held central roles in myths and legends, symbolizing themes of magic, transformation, and the interplay between the mortal and the mystical. In this chapter, we delve into some of the most iconic and enduring myths featuring fairies, unraveling their significance and cultural resonance.

I. The Legend of the Tuatha Dé Danann: Ireland's Divine Ancestors

The Tuatha Dé Danann, often referred to as the Children of Danu, occupy a prominent place in Irish mythology, representing a captivating fusion of divine beings and fairies. Their legend is a cornerstone of Celtic folklore, embodying the rich tapestry of Ireland's ancient past and the intricate interplay between the mortal realm and the mystical Otherworld.

1. Divine Ancestry:

The Tuatha Dé Danann are believed to trace their lineage back to the goddess Danu, a maternal figure intricately associated with fertility, abundance, and the very essence of the land itself. Their divine heritage firmly ties them to the Irish landscape, reinforcing their status as otherworldly beings deeply intertwined with the natural world.

2. Arrival in Ireland:

Legend has it that the Tuatha Dé Danann arrived in Ireland aboard a magnificent fleet of magical ships. They were perceived as an invincible people, possessing extraordinary talents and profound knowledge. However, their arrival coincided with the presence of the Fir Bolg, the indigenous people of Ireland, leading to a series of conflicts for control of the land.

3. Battles and Alliances:

The Tuatha Dé Danann engaged in several epic battles to assert their dominance over Ireland. Their most renowned confrontation was the Battle of Mag Tuired (Moytura), a mythic clash against the Fir Bolg and later, the Fomorians, another supernatural group often depicted as sea deities.

These battles transcended mere physical conflicts, symbolizing the struggle between the old order and the new, with the Tuatha Dé Danann embodying the forces of light and prosperity against the chaos and darkness.

4. Retreat to the Otherworld:

Despite their victories, the Tuatha Dé Danann eventually withdrew from the mortal world, retreating to the Otherworld, often associated with the realm of fairies. This transition poignantly reflects the fluid boundaries between the worlds and the cyclical nature of life and death as perceived in Celtic beliefs.

5. Guardians of the Land:

Even in their withdrawal, the Tuatha Dé Danann maintained a profound connection to Ireland. They became guardians of the land, dwelling in sidhe (fairy mounds) and hills, where they continued to exert influence over human affairs. These hills, such as the renowned Sidhe of Brú na Bóinne (Newgrange), were perceived as portals to the Otherworld.

6. Symbolism and Themes:

The legend of the Tuatha Dé Danann encapsulates several enduring themes found in Irish mythology:

Cyclical Nature: The cyclical theme of divine beings withdrawing and returning to the Otherworld mirrors the cycles of life, death, and rebirth ingrained in Celtic belief.
Fertility and Prosperity: Their connection to the land and the fertility goddess Danu underscores the profound significance of the natural world in Celtic culture and the aspiration for abundance.
Interplay Between Mortal and Divine: The Tuatha Dé Danann function as intermediaries between the mortal and divine realms, underscoring the permeable boundaries between these worlds.
Mythic Struggles: Their confrontations with other supernatural beings illuminate the moral and ethical choices faced by both gods and humans in the relentless pursuit of power and dominion.
Living Myths of Ireland:

The legend of the Tuatha Dé Danann transcends being a mere relic of the past; it is a living myth that continues to mold Ireland's cultural identity. The profound connection between these divine ancestors and fairies illustrates the enduring influence of the mystical in Irish folklore. It serves as a reminder that the realm of the Tuatha Dé Danann is one where the lines between myth and reality blur, where the past and present are intricately interwoven, and where the enchantment of the Otherworld beckons through the age.

The Arthurian legend, a rich tapestry of medieval tales, introduces us to two iconic and enigmatic figures whose roles are pivotal in the life of King Arthur and the mythology surrounding him: Morgana Le Fay and the Lady of the Lake. These characters are deeply intertwined with the Arthurian narrative and offer unique insights into the intersection of magic, destiny, and the human condition.

Morgana Le Fay: The Enigmatic Sorceress

Morgana Le Fay, also known as Morgan Le Fay or Morgaine, stands as one of the most complex and enduring characters in Arthurian legend. She is often depicted as Arthur's half-sister, the daughter of Arthur's mother, Igraine, and the sorcerer Gorlois. Morgana is both a powerful enchantress and a controversial figure, and her motives and actions vary across different versions of the legend.

Morgana's Character Traits and Ambiguity: Morgana's character is a study in ambiguity and contradiction. She possesses exceptional magical abilities, which she employs for both benevolent and malevolent purposes. In some renditions of the legend, she is portrayed as a healer and protector of the land, while in others, she is a conniving villainess. This duality adds depth to her character, making her a fascinating and multifaceted figure.

Rivalry with Merlin: A recurring theme in Morgana's narrative is her complex relationship with Merlin, the legendary wizard of Arthurian lore. Their rivalry showcases the tension between her magical prowess and Merlin's wisdom, and they often engage in magical duels, each trying to outwit the other.

Role in Arthurian Quests: Morgana frequently appears as an obstacle in Arthurian quests and adventures. She is known for her ability to shape-shift and deceive, making her a formidable adversary. Her actions often contribute to the challenges faced by Arthur and his knights.

The Lady of the Lake: Guardian of Excalibur

The Lady of the Lake is another enigmatic figure within the Arthurian legend, often associated with mystical bodies of water, particularly lakes and pools. She serves as the guardian of powerful magical artifacts, most notably the sword Excalibur.

Bestowing Excalibur: One of the most iconic moments in Arthurian mythology is when the Lady of the Lake presents Excalibur, the legendary sword, to Arthur. This act symbolizes her role as a bestower of destiny and the embodiment of the mystical connection between the natural world and the Arthurian realm.

The Mysterious Nature of the Lady: The Lady of the Lake is often depicted as a beautiful and ethereal figure, a water nymph or fairy-like being. Her supernatural attributes blur the line between the human and the mystical, reflecting the pervasive theme of magical intercession in Arthurian stories.

Symbolism and Themes: The Lady of the Lake represents themes of fate, the power of objects, and the relationship between Arthur and the land. She is both a guide and a keeper of secrets, reminding us of the mystical forces at play in the Arthurian world.

The Mystical Threads in the Arthurian Tapestry

In the Arthurian legend, the characters of Morgana Le Fay and the Lady of the Lake add layers of intrigue, magic, and complexity to the narrative. They embody timeless themes of power, destiny, and the blurred boundaries between the human and supernatural realms. Morgana's multifaceted nature and the Lady of the Lake's mysterious influence reflect the enduring fascination with the mystical and the timeless appeal of the Arthurian legend, where fairy-like figures are instrumental in shaping the destiny of Camelot and the legacy of King Arthur. Their stories continue to captivate audiences, reminding us of the enduring allure of the Arthurian world and its timeless connection to the realm of fairies and enchantment.

IV. Scandinavian Lore: The Hidden World of the Hulder

Deep within the heart of the dense Scandinavian forests, concealed from the prying eyes of mortals, lies a world brimming with enchantment and mystery. This world belongs to the Hulderfolk, or simply the Hulders, captivating beings deeply ingrained in the folklore and mythology of the Scandinavian countries. Their myths and legends offer a unique and intriguing glimpse into the world of fairies, one that is both alluring and cautionary.

The Allure of the Hulders

Hulders are often described as exceptionally beautiful, possessing fair complexions, long flowing hair, and captivating eyes. They exude an otherworldly charm that can easily ensnare the hearts of mortals, rendering them susceptible to the enchantments of these mysterious beings. Their beauty and allure are central to the myths surrounding them, and it is said that a mere glimpse of a Hulder can leave a person spellbound.

Seduction and Transformation

One of the most prominent themes in Hulder mythology revolves around their interactions with humans, particularly the seduction of young men. Hulder women are known to appear as stunning, human-like females, often luring unsuspecting men into their world. These encounters can lead to passionate affairs or even marriage. However, the consequences of such unions can be both beguiling and perilous.

In some tales, it is revealed that the Hulder woman is not what she seems. She may possess a cow's tail hidden beneath her clothing, a sign of her true identity. Discovering this tail can have dire consequences, ranging from angering the Hulder to breaking the enchantment. In other versions of the story, the Hulder reveals her true form when she feels betrayed, resulting in the disappearance of her mortal lover.

3. The Hidden Hulder Home

The Hulders are believed to reside deep within the remote forests, and their homes are often depicted as hidden caves or subterranean dwellings. These hidden abodes are shrouded in secrecy and magic, making them invisible to mortal eyes. In some tales, humans stumble upon these hidden homes and are welcomed with feasts and merriment, but they are also bound by an unspoken rule to never disclose their location to others.

4. Guardians of Nature

Beyond their interactions with humans, the Hulders are often associated with nature. They are believed to protect the forests, animals, and plants, and their presence is seen as a symbol of the untamed wilderness. In some tales, they are described as benevolent forest spirits, aiding lost travelers and guiding them safely out of the woods. However, these guardians of nature are not to be trifled with, as they can quickly turn into vengeful entities if their realm is threatened.

5. Hulder Music and Dance

Hulders are known for their love of music and dance. It is said that they hold elaborate gatherings in their hidden homes, where they engage in mesmerizing dances and play enchanting melodies on their instruments. Mortals who accidentally stumble upon these festivities may find themselves irresistibly drawn to join in the revelry, often losing track of time and emerging from the encounter with hazy memories.

The Enigmatic Hulders

The Hulders of Scandinavian folklore offer a captivating and complex portrayal of fairies in their hidden world. Their beauty, seduction, and connection to nature make them intriguing figures in the rich tapestry of fairy mythology. The tales of Hulders serve as cautionary stories, reminding us of the enchanting yet perilous nature of the mystical world. They beckon us to venture deeper into the forests and explore the hidden realms of the Hulders, where the boundary between the ordinary and the extraordinary blurs, and the mysteries of the enchanted woods await those who dare to seek them.

V. Japanese Yōkai: The Kitsune and Tengu

The Arthurian legend, a rich tapestry of medieval tales, introduces us to two iconic and enigmatic figures whose roles are pivotal in the life of King Arthur and the mythology surrounding him: Morgana Le Fay and the Lady of the Lake. These characters are deeply intertwined with the Arthurian narrative and offer unique insights into the intersection of magic, destiny, and the human condition.

Morgana Le Fay: The Enigmatic Sorceress

Morgana Le Fay, also known as Morgan Le Fay or Morgaine, stands as one of the most complex and enduring characters in Arthurian legend. She is often depicted as Arthur's half-sister, the daughter of Arthur's mother, Igraine, and the sorcerer Gorlois. Morgana is both a powerful enchantress and a controversial figure, and her motives and actions vary across different versions of the legend.

Morgana's Character Traits and Ambiguity: Morgana's character is a study in ambiguity and contradiction. She possesses exceptional magical abilities, which she employs for both benevolent and malevolent purposes. In some renditions of the legend, she is portrayed as a healer and protector of the land, while in others, she is a conniving villainess. This duality adds depth to her character, making her a fascinating and multifaceted figure.

Rivalry with Merlin: A recurring theme in Morgana's narrative is her complex relationship with Merlin, the legendary wizard of Arthurian lore. Their rivalry showcases the tension between her magical prowess and Merlin's wisdom, and they often engage in magical duels, each trying to outwit the other.

Role in Arthurian Quests: Morgana frequently appears as an obstacle in Arthurian quests and adventures. She is known for her ability to shape-shift and deceive, making her a formidable adversary. Her actions often contribute to the challenges faced by Arthur and his knights.

The Lady of the Lake: Guardian of Excalibur

The Lady of the Lake is another enigmatic figure within the Arthurian legend, often associated with mystical bodies of water, particularly lakes and pools. She serves as the guardian of powerful magical artifacts, most notably the sword Excalibur.

Bestowing Excalibur: One of the most iconic moments in Arthurian mythology is when the Lady of the Lake presents Excalibur, the legendary sword, to Arthur. This act symbolizes her role as a bestower of destiny and the embodiment of the mystical connection between the natural world and the Arthurian realm.

The Mysterious Nature of the Lady: The Lady of the Lake is often depicted as a beautiful and ethereal figure, a water nymph or fairy-like being. Her supernatural attributes blur the line between the human and the mystical, reflecting the pervasive theme of magical intercession in Arthurian stories.

Symbolism and Themes: The Lady of the Lake represents themes of fate, the power of objects, and the relationship between Arthur and the land. She is both a guide and a keeper of secrets, reminding us of the mystical forces at play in the Arthurian world.

The Mystical Threads in the Arthurian Tapestry

In the Arthurian legend, the characters of Morgana Le Fay and the Lady of the Lake add layers of intrigue, magic, and complexity to the narrative. They embody timeless themes of power, destiny, and the blurred boundaries between the human and supernatural realms. Morgana's multifaceted nature and the Lady of the Lake's mysterious influence reflect the enduring fascination with the mystical and the timeless appeal of the Arthurian legend, where fairy-like figures are instrumental in shaping the destiny of Camelot and the legacy of King Arthur. Their stories continue to captivate audiences, reminding us of the enduring allure of the Arthurian world and its timeless connection to the realm of fairies and enchantment.

IV. Scandinavian Lore: The Hidden World of the Hulder

Deep within the heart of the dense Scandinavian forests, concealed from the prying eyes of mortals, lies a world brimming with enchantment and mystery. This world belongs to the Hulderfolk, or simply the Hulders, captivating beings deeply ingrained in the folklore and mythology of the Scandinavian countries. Their myths and legends offer a unique and intriguing glimpse into the world of fairies, one that is both alluring and cautionary.

The Allure of the Hulders

Hulders are often described as exceptionally beautiful, possessing fair complexions, long flowing hair, and captivating eyes. They exude an otherworldly charm that can easily ensnare the hearts of mortals, rendering them susceptible to the enchantments of these mysterious beings. Their beauty and allure are central to the myths surrounding them, and it is said that a mere glimpse of a Hulder can leave a person spellbound.

Seduction and Transformation

One of the most prominent themes in Hulder mythology revolves around their interactions with humans, particularly the seduction of young men. Hulder women are known to appear as stunning, human-like females, often luring unsuspecting men into their world. These encounters can lead to passionate affairs or even marriage. However, the consequences of such unions can be both beguiling and perilous.

In some tales, it is revealed that the Hulder woman is not what she seems. She may possess a cow's tail hidden beneath her clothing, a sign of her true identity. Discovering this tail can have dire consequences, ranging from angering the Hulder to breaking the enchantment. In other versions of the story, the Hulder reveals her true form when she feels betrayed, resulting in the disappearance of her mortal lover.

1. The Sidhe: Guardians of the Fairy Mounds

The Sidhe are believed to inhabit ancient burial mounds and hills, known as fairy mounds or síde (singular: síd). These mounds are scattered across the Irish and Scottish landscapes, and they serve as entrances to the hidden world of the Sidhe. The Sidhe are renowned for their ethereal beauty, often described as fair of face with radiant, ageless features. They possess supernatural powers, including the ability to heal, enchant, or curse, depending on their disposition.

2. The Land of Promise: A Realm Beyond Mortal Reach

At the heart of Celtic mythology lies the tantalizing concept of the Land of Promise, an Otherworldly realm where the Sidhe reside. This realm is often depicted as a place of eternal beauty, where time stands still, and the land flourishes in perpetual youth. The Land of Promise is a place where sorrow and aging are unknown, and its allure beckons mortals to venture forth, often with dire consequences.

3. Mortals and the Land of Promise: A Tempting Destiny

Celtic myths frequently feature mortals who are drawn into the world of the Sidhe and the Land of Promise. These tales explore the complex relationship between humanity and the Otherworld, where the desire for eternal happiness and the promise of unending youth often lead mortals astray. The most famous of these stories is that of Oisín, the son of the legendary Irish hero Fionn mac Cumhaill.

4. Oisín and Niamh of the Golden Hair: A Tragic Love Story

The story of Oisín and Niamh is a poignant narrative that encapsulates the allure and tragedy of the Land of Promise. Oisín, a great warrior and poet, encounters the fairy princess Niamh of the Golden Hair. She invites him to her Otherworldly realm, where he enjoys timeless happiness and love. However, Oisín eventually longs to return to the mortal world to visit his family and homeland. Niamh reluctantly grants his wish but warns him not to touch the ground when he returns.

Upon reaching Ireland, Oisín discovers that centuries have passed, and his beloved family and friends are long gone. As he dismounts his magical steed, he ages instantly, crumbling into an old man. This tragic tale highlights the bittersweet nature of the Land of Promise, where the pursuit of eternal happiness ultimately leads to the loss of the mortal world.

5. Themes and Symbolism

The myth of the Sidhe and the Land of Promise encapsulates several profound themes:

- The Eternal Temptation: The Land of Promise symbolizes the eternal human desire for happiness, youth, and immortality. It serves as a metaphor for the allure of the unknown and the consequences of pursuing perfection at the expense of reality.
- The Passage of Time: The contrasting experiences of time in the Land of Promise and the mortal world underscore the inevitability of aging and the transience of human existence.
- The Boundary Between Worlds: The fairy mounds represent the threshold between the mortal realm and the Otherworld. They serve as a reminder that the mystical and the mundane are intertwined, and crossing the boundary can have profound consequences.

The Enchantment of the Sidhe and the Land of Promise

The myths surrounding the Sidhe and the Land of Promise in Celtic folklore continue to captivate audiences with their timeless allure. These tales evoke a sense of wonder and contemplation about the human condition, mortality, and the pursuit of the extraordinary. The Sidhe and their hidden realm stand as testaments to the enduring power of folklore to convey universal truths and inspire a sense of magic and enchantment in the hearts of those who venture into their mystical world.

In these grand myths involving fairies, we encounter a rich tapestry of themes and motifs that have transcended time and culture. Fairies serve as conduits between the ordinary and the extraordinary, embodying the human fascination with the supernatural and the desire to explore the boundaries of reality. These myths, whether in the verdant hills of Ireland, the mystical realms of King Arthur, or the enchanting forests of Scandinavia, reflect the enduring allure of fairies and their ability to captivate our imaginations, offering us glimpses into the wondrous and magical. They remind us that the world of fairies is not confined to a single culture but is a universal wellspring of wonder, magic, and eternal fascination.

4B. Modern Interpretations

How Fairy Myths Continue to Influence Modern Literature, Film, and Art

As we navigate the enchanting world of fairies, it becomes evident that these mythical beings are not confined to ancient lore or historical contexts. Instead, they persistently shape and influence contemporary creative endeavors across various mediums, including literature, film, and art. In this chapter, we explore how fairy myths continue to hold sway over modern imagination, breathing life into new narratives and sparking artistic innovation.

I. Literary Magic: Contemporary Fairy Literature

Modern literature remains an enchanting realm where fairy myths find vibrant expression. Authors draw inspiration from traditional fairy tales, folklore, and mythologies to create captivating narratives that resonate with readers of all ages.

J.K. Rowling's "Harry Potter" Series: Rowling's wizarding world is teeming with magical creatures, including house-elves, hippogriffs, and the mischievous Cornish Pixies. The portrayal of house-elves, akin to traditional household fairies, raises important questions about freedom and servitude, underscoring the enduring relevance of fairy themes.

Philip Pullman's "His Dark Materials" Trilogy: In this epic series, the concept of daemons, animal companions reflecting the soul, bears striking resemblance to the idea of spirit animals or familiar spirits associated with fairy traditions. Pullman's exploration of the connection between humans and daemons is a modern take on age-old themes of companionship and identity.

Holly Black's "The Folk of the Air" Series: Black's books feature the world of the Folk, which includes both traditional fairies and more contemporary interpretations. The series explores the complexities of power, politics, and morality in the realm of the Folk.

II. Cinematic Enchantment: Fairy Myths on the Silver Screen

Film has become a powerful medium for translating fairy myths into visual storytelling, offering audiences a chance to immerse themselves in magical worlds and fantastical narratives.

Disney's Animated Classics: Disney's adaptations of classic fairy tales like "Cinderella," "Sleeping Beauty," and "The Little Mermaid" have introduced generations to fairy-tale characters and settings. These films reinterpret traditional stories with modern sensibilities, often emphasizing themes of love, hope, and resilience.

Guillermo del Toro's "Pan's Labyrinth": Del Toro's dark fantasy masterpiece blends Spanish folklore with the enchantment of the fairy realm. The film's eerie and captivating portrayal of a young girl's journey through a mythical labyrinth mirrors traditional fairy-tale motifs, while also exploring themes of innocence and brutality.

Studio Ghibli's "Spirited Away": This iconic anime film directed by Hayao Miyazaki transports viewers to a magical bathhouse inhabited by an array of fantastical creatures, some reminiscent of traditional Japanese Yōkai. "Spirited Away" explores themes of identity, environmentalism, and the resilience of the human spirit.

III. Artistic Alchemy: Fairies in Contemporary Art

The allure of fairies has not been lost on contemporary artists, who continue to draw inspiration from these enchanting beings. Artistic expressions of fairy myths can be found in various forms, from traditional paintings to digital art and sculptures.

Brian Froud's Fantasy Art: Brian Froud, renowned for his illustrations in "Faeries" and "Good Faeries/Bad Faeries," has had a profound influence on contemporary fairy art. His detailed and imaginative portrayals of fairies and fae creatures have inspired generations of artists.

Contemporary Fairy Sculptures: Artists like Wendy Froud and Nene Thomas create exquisite fairy sculptures that capture the essence of these mystical beings. These three-dimensional works of art bring fairies to life in a tangible and captivating way.
Digital and Concept Art: The digital age has ushered in new possibilities for artists to explore the world of fairies. Concept artists working in video games, animation, and digital media often infuse their creations with elements of traditional fairy myths, creating visually stunning and immersive worlds.

IV. Reimagining Gender and Identity

Modern interpretations of fairy myths frequently challenge traditional gender roles and identities. Contemporary authors and artists explore non-binary and LGBTQ+ themes through fairy characters, highlighting the adaptability and relevance of fairy narratives in addressing evolving societal norms.
Neil Gaiman's "Stardust": Gaiman's novel, adapted into a film, features a gender-fluid character named Yvaine, a fallen star who takes on a human form. This character embodies themes of transformation, identity, and love in a way that resonates with modern audiences.
Queer Fairy Art: LGBTQ+ artists have embraced fairy motifs to explore themes of identity, transformation, and love. These works challenge conventional narratives and offer new perspectives on the fluidity of identity within the enchanting realm of fairies.

Conclusion: A Timeless Well of Inspiration

Fairy myths have proven to be a timeless well of inspiration for contemporary creators across literature, film, and art. Their enduring appeal lies in their ability to adapt and evolve, offering new interpretations that reflect the changing dynamics of society and culture. As we continue to explore the multifaceted world of fairies in the modern age, it becomes clear that these mythical beings will forever remain a source of wonder, magic, and artistic innovation, perpetually captivating the human imagination.

Chapter 5
The Good and The Bad Fairies

In the captivating realm of fairies, where enchantment and mysticism reign, one of the most intriguing aspects is the stark contrast between benevolent and malevolent fairies. As we delve deeper into the captivating world of these mystical beings, this chapter unveils the fascinating dichotomy that characterizes them, exploring the distinctive traits, motives, and cultural nuances that differentiate fairies as either benevolent protectors or mischievous tricksters.

A MOONLIGHT DISCOVERY.

I. The Benevolent Guardians

In the realm of fairy folklore, the benevolent guardians stand as luminous figures, often revered for their protective and nurturing roles. These ethereal beings, brimming with goodwill, embody the brighter side of the mystical world, offering assistance, guidance, and blessings to those who encounter them. This section delves deep into the endearing characteristics, roles, and cultural significance of these enchanting benevolent fairies.

1. Protectors of Hearth and Home: The Brownies

Among the most beloved of household fairies, the Brownies are celebrated for their unwavering helpfulness. They undertake chores in the dead of night, completing tasks that might otherwise be arduous for the household inhabitants.

Traits and Attributes:

Helpful Nature: The Brownies, perhaps one of the most beloved of household fairies, are celebrated for their unwavering helpfulness. They undertake chores in the dead of night, completing tasks that might otherwise be arduous for the household inhabitants.
Homely Appearance: Often described as small, brown-clad figures with wrinkled faces and twinkling eyes, Brownies embody a sense of coziness and domesticity.
Conditional Friendship: Brownies do not demand payment for their services but appreciate small offerings left out for them, such as a saucer of milk or a bit of honey.
Roles and Significance:

Home Guardians: Brownies are the quintessential home guardians. They take up residence in a household, and their presence is said to bring good fortune and protection. They defend the home against malevolent spirits or misfortune, ensuring a sense of security for the family.
Symbol of Household Harmony: The Brownies symbolize the harmony that can exist between humans and the supernatural. Their tales reinforce the importance of respecting and coexisting with the unseen forces that inhabit the domestic sphere.

Cultural Variations: While they are known as Brownies in English and Scottish folklore, similar beings appear in different cultures under various names, such as Hobgoblins and Nisse in Nordic traditions, reflecting the universal appeal of benevolent household guardians.
2. Nature's Caretakers: Tree Spirits and Nymphs

Benevolent tree spirits and nymphs are deeply intertwined with the ecosystems they inhabit. They are known for their ethereal beauty, often described as radiant and graceful.

Traits and Attributes:

Connected to the Natural World: Benevolent tree spirits and nymphs are deeply intertwined with the ecosystems they inhabit. They are known for their ethereal beauty, often described as radiant and graceful.
Elemental Guardians: These fairies personify the earth's vitality and are often associated with specific types of trees or natural features. Dryads, for example, are nymphs of oak trees, while Naiads inhabit freshwater sources.
Roles and Significance:

Forest and Waterside Protection: Tree spirits and nymphs are the gentle sentinels of the natural world, guarding forests, rivers, and lakes from harm. Their presence ensures the flourishing of flora and fauna.
Symbol of Environmental Stewardship: These benevolent fairies symbolize the importance of environmental conservation and the interconnectedness of all living beings. Stories about their protection highlight the value of respecting and preserving the natural world.
Romantic and Artistic Inspiration: The beauty of tree spirits and nymphs has inspired countless poets, artists, and writers, emphasizing their enduring allure in human culture.
3. Fairy Godmothers: Granters of Wishes and Miracles

Fairy Godmothers possess extraordinary magical abilities and are often portrayed as wise and benevolent figures. They can transform the lives of those they aid through the bestowal of gifts, blessings, and guidance.

Traits and Attributes:

Magical Benefactors: Fairy Godmothers possess extraordinary magical abilities and are often portrayed as wise and benevolent figures.
Transformational Powers: They can transform the lives of those they aid through the bestowal of gifts, blessings, and guidance.
Mentors and Guides: Fairy Godmothers often serve as mentors or guides to protagonists in fairy tales, offering invaluable support and counsel.
Roles and Significance:

Agents of Transformation: Fairy Godmothers play a crucial role in the transformation of ordinary individuals into heroes and heroines. They empower the powerless and elevate the downtrodden.

Symbol of Hope: These benevolent fairies represent hope and the possibility of positive change even in the face of adversity. Their interventions inspire optimism and resilience.
Cross-Cultural Archetype: The concept of the Fairy Godmother is a cross-cultural archetype that transcends geographical boundaries, appearing in various forms in folklore and literature around the world.
In the intricate tapestry of benevolent guardians, these fairies serve as symbols of protection, guidance, and kindness. Their enduring presence in folklore and literature reflects humanity's eternal desire for benevolence and the belief in the power of goodness to prevail. Through the ages, these luminous figures have illuminated the darkest corners of our collective imagination, reminding us of the innate goodness that resides within the mystical world and within ourselves.

II. Malevolent Mischief-Makers

In the enigmatic world of fairies, the malevolent mischief-makers stand as intriguing and often unsettling figures. These fairies, known for their mischievous and sometimes downright malicious behavior, embody the darker side of fairy folklore. In this section, we will delve deep into the characteristics, actions, and cultural significance of these malevolent fairies, exploring the realms of tricksters, tormentors, and nightmarish beings that haunt the human imagination.

1. Tricksters and Pranksters:

Among the malevolent fairies, tricksters and pranksters reign supreme. They derive immense pleasure from playing pranks, causing chaos, and bewildering unsuspecting humans. Some notable examples include:

Pucks (or Pookas): Often featured in English and Irish folklore, Pucks are notorious tricksters. They may lead travelers astray, transform into various shapes to confound witnesses, and generally revel in causing confusion and mild havoc.

Imps: Imps, found in various forms in European folklore, are known for their playful but sometimes malicious antics. They may steal small items, make strange noises, and create general disturbances.

Lutins and Kobolds: *

Chapter 5A: The Light and Dark - Distinguishing Benevolent and Malevolent Fairies

In the captivating realm of fairies, where enchantment and mysticism reign, one of the most intriguing aspects is the stark contrast between benevolent and malevolent fairies. As we delve deeper into the captivating world of these mystical beings, this chapter unveils the fascinating dichotomy that characterizes them, exploring the distinctive traits, motives, and cultural nuances that differentiate fairies as either benevolent protectors or mischievous tricksters.

I. The Benevolent Guardians

In the realm of fairy folklore, the benevolent guardians stand as luminous figures, often revered for their protective and nurturing roles. These ethereal beings, brimming with goodwill, embody the brighter side of the mystical world, offering assistance, guidance, and blessings to those who encounter them. This section delves deep into the endearing characteristics, roles, and cultural significance of these enchanting benevolent fairies.

1. Protectors of Hearth and Home: The Brownies

Among the most beloved of household fairies, the Brownies are celebrated for their unwavering helpfulness. They undertake chores in the dead of night, completing tasks that might otherwise be arduous for the household inhabitants.

Traits and Attributes:

Helpful Nature: The Brownies, perhaps one of the most beloved of household fairies, are celebrated for their unwavering helpfulness. They undertake chores in the dead of night, completing tasks that might otherwise be arduous for the household inhabitants.
Homely Appearance: Often described as small, brown-clad figures with wrinkled faces and twinkling eyes, Brownies embody a sense of coziness and domesticity.
Conditional Friendship: Brownies do not demand payment for their services but appreciate small offerings left out for them, such as a saucer of milk or a bit of honey.
Roles and Significance:

Home Guardians: Brownies are the quintessential home guardians. They take up residence in a household, and their presence is said to bring good fortune and protection. They defend the home against malevolent spirits or misfortune, ensuring a sense of security for the family.
Symbol of Household Harmony: The Brownies symbolize the harmony that can exist between humans and the supernatural. Their tales reinforce the importance of respecting and coexisting with the unseen forces that inhabit the domestic sphere.
Cultural Variations: While they are known as Brownies in English and Scottish folklore, similar beings appear in different cultures under various names, such as Hobgoblins and Nisse in Nordic traditions, reflecting the universal appeal of benevolent household guardians.

2. Nature's Caretakers: Tree Spirits and Nymphs

Benevolent tree spirits and nymphs are deeply intertwined with the ecosystems they inhabit. They are known for their ethereal beauty, often described as radiant and graceful.

Traits and Attributes:

Connected to the Natural World: Benevolent tree spirits and nymphs are deeply intertwined with the ecosystems they inhabit. They are known for their ethereal beauty, often described as radiant and graceful.
Elemental Guardians: These fairies personify the earth's vitality and are often associated with specific types of trees or natural features. Dryads, for example, are nymphs of oak trees, while Naiads inhabit freshwater sources.
Roles and Significance:

Forest and Waterside Protection: Tree spirits and nymphs are the gentle sentinels of the natural world, guarding forests, rivers, and lakes from harm. Their presence ensures the flourishing of flora and fauna.
Symbol of Environmental Stewardship: These benevolent fairies symbolize the importance of environmental conservation and the interconnectedness of all living beings. Stories about their protection highlight the value of respecting and preserving the natural world.
Romantic and Artistic Inspiration: The beauty of tree spirits and nymphs has inspired countless poets, artists, and writers, emphasizing their enduring allure in human culture.
3. Fairy Godmothers: Granters of Wishes and Miracles

Fairy Godmothers possess extraordinary magical abilities and are often portrayed as wise and benevolent figures. They can transform the lives of those they aid through the bestowal of gifts, blessings, and guidance.

Traits and Attributes:

Magical Benefactors: Fairy Godmothers possess extraordinary magical abilities and are often portrayed as wise and benevolent figures.
Transformational Powers: They can transform the lives of those they aid through the bestowal of gifts, blessings, and guidance.
Mentors and Guides: Fairy Godmothers often serve as mentors or guides to protagonists in fairy tales, offering invaluable support and counsel.
Roles and Significance:

Agents of Transformation: Fairy Godmothers play a crucial role in the transformation of ordinary individuals into heroes and heroines. They empower the powerless and elevate the downtrodden.
Symbol of Hope: These benevolent fairies represent hope and the possibility of positive change even in the face of adversity. Their interventions inspire optimism and resilience.
Cross-Cultural Archetype: The concept of the Fairy Godmother is a cross-cultural archetype that transcends geographical boundaries, appearing in various forms in folklore and literature around the world.
In the intricate tapestry of benevolent guardians, these fairies serve as symbols of protection, guidance, and kindness. Their enduring presence in folklore and literature reflects humanity's eternal desire for benevolence and the belief in the power of goodness to prevail. Through the ages, these luminous figures have illuminated the darkest corners

of our collective imagination, reminding us of the innate goodness that resides within the mystical world and within ourselves.

II. Malevolent Mischief-Makers

In the enigmatic world of fairies, the malevolent mischief-makers stand as intriguing and often unsettling figures. These fairies, known for their mischievous and sometimes downright malicious behavior, embody the darker side of fairy folklore. In this section, we will delve deep into the characteristics, actions, and cultural significance of these malevolent fairies, exploring the realms of tricksters, tormentors, and nightmarish beings that haunt the human imagination.

1. Tricksters and Pranksters:

Among the malevolent fairies, tricksters and pranksters reign supreme. They derive immense pleasure from playing pranks, causing chaos, and bewildering unsuspecting humans. Some notable examples include:

Pucks (or Pookas): Often featured in English and Irish folklore, Pucks are notorious tricksters. They may lead travelers astray, transform into various shapes to confound witnesses, and generally revel in causing confusion and mild havoc.

Imps: Imps, found in various forms in European folklore, are known for their playful but sometimes malicious antics. They may steal small items, make strange noises, and create general disturbances.

Lutins and Kobolds: In French and German folklore, respectively, Lutins and Kobolds are mischievous household spirits that play tricks on residents. They may hide objects, tangle hair, or make loud noises.

III. Cultural Influences and Interpretations

The perception and interpretation of fairies as benevolent or malevolent entities are profoundly influenced by cultural and regional factors, giving rise to a rich tapestry of beliefs and practices. This section delves into the cultural nuances and historical influences that have shaped the complex nature of fairies in various societies.

1. Celtic Variations: Seelie and Unseelie Courts

In Scottish and Irish folklore, fairies are categorized into the Seelie and Unseelie Courts, exemplifying the intricate and dual nature of these supernatural beings:

- Seelie Court (Benevolent): The Seelie Court is associated with benevolent fairies who are generally considered friendly towards humans. They might offer assistance, protection, or guidance, especially to those who respect their traditions and territories. However, even within the Seelie Court, there can be capricious individuals who may act unpredictably.

- Unseelie Court (Malevolent): The Unseelie Court comprises malevolent fairies who often engage in mischief, pranks, and even harmful actions towards humans. These fairies are regarded with caution and fear, as they may cause misfortune or chaos if provoked.

The Seelie and Unseelie Courts illustrate the complex interplay of benevolence and malevolence within Celtic fairy folklore, emphasizing the importance of appeasing and respecting these supernatural entities to ensure their favor.

2. Christian Influence: Angelic and Demonic Associations

The Christianization of Europe had a profound impact on how fairies were perceived. They were sometimes likened to angels or demons, highlighting their dual nature as both protectors and tricksters:

- Angel Associations: Some fairies were considered angelic beings or messengers of divine will, particularly in regions where Christian beliefs intertwined with traditional folklore. This association aligned with their role as benevolent protectors and guides.
- Demon Associations: In contrast, malevolent fairies were often likened to demons or evil spirits. They were seen as entities to be feared and exorcised, reflecting the more sinister aspects of their nature.

The Christian influence on fairy interpretations added a layer of moral and religious complexity to their characterizations, reinforcing the notion that fairies straddle the boundary between good and evil.

3. Offerings and Propitiation: Honoring Fairies

Many cultures developed rituals and offerings to appease or seek the favor of fairies, reflecting the belief in a fine line between benevolence and malevolence:

- Food Offerings: In numerous traditions, offerings of food and drink were made to fairies to gain their favor and ensure protection. This practice symbolized reciprocity and respect for the supernatural world.
- Taboos and Superstitions: Specific taboos and superstitions developed around fairies, such as avoiding certain actions or places on particular days to avoid their wrath. These practices aimed to maintain harmony and prevent malevolent encounters.
- Gift Exchanges: In some cultures, it was customary to leave gifts for fairies, which might include milk, honey, or small trinkets. In return, fairies were expected to bestow blessings or avoid causing harm.

These rituals and offerings illustrate the importance of maintaining a balanced relationship with fairies, recognizing their dual nature and the need to appease them to ensure their benevolent influence.

4. Folk Tales and Legends: Shaping Cultural Interpretations

Folk tales, legends, and oral traditions played a significant role in shaping cultural interpretations of fairies. These stories often portrayed fairies as complex characters, blurring the lines between benevolence and malevolence:

- Moral Lessons: Fairy tales frequently used fairies to convey moral lessons. Benevolent fairies rewarded kindness and virtue, while malevolent fairies punished arrogance or cruelty, emphasizing the consequences of one's actions.
- Cultural Values: The portrayal of fairies in folklore reflected cultural values and societal norms. In some tales, fairies represented the capriciousness of nature, while in others, they embodied the resilience and resourcefulness of the human spirit.
- Historical Context: The historical context of a region often influenced fairy narratives. During times of adversity, malevolent fairies might take on more sinister roles, reflecting the challenges faced by communities.

The stories passed down through generations served not only as entertainment, but also as a means of transmitting cultural wisdom and preserving the delicate balance between humanity and the mystical realm of fairies. The interpretation of fairies as benevolent or malevolent entities is deeply rooted in the cultural and historical context of each society. The intricate nuances of these interpretations reflect humanity's ongoing fascination with the supernatural and its enduring quest to understand the mysteries of the unseen world. The complex nature of fairies continues to shape our collective imagination and offers a glimpse into the intricate relationship between humans and the mystical beings that inhabit the borderlands of our reality.

IV. Blurring the Lines: Complex Fairy Characters

In the realm of fairy folklore and modern literature, the boundary between benevolent and malevolent fairies often blurs, giving rise to complex and multifaceted characters that challenge our perceptions of these supernatural beings. This section delves into the fascinating world of such intricate fairy figures, exploring their motivations, characteristics, and the nuanced roles they play in our stories and imaginations.

1. Tinkering with Morality: Tinker Bell and Ambiguity

One of the most iconic examples of a complex fairy character is Tinker Bell, created by J.M. Barrie in his timeless work "Peter Pan." Tinker Bell is a tiny and fiery fairy known for her unwavering loyalty to Peter Pan, the boy who never grows up. Yet, her character is far from one-dimensional.

- Loyalty and Love: Tinker Bell's loyalty to Peter is unwavering, and she exhibits genuine affection for him. Her dedication to keeping him safe and helping him in his adventures is evident throughout the story.
- Jealousy and Vengefulness: Tinker Bell's character takes an interesting turn when she becomes jealous of Wendy, a human girl who enters Neverland. This jealousy leads her to

make decisions that endanger Wendy's life, demonstrating her capacity for less-than-benevolent actions.

Tinker Bell's character embodies the complexity of fairies. Her unwavering loyalty to Peter Pan represents the protective and caring nature often associated with benevolent fairies, while her jealousy and vengefulness highlight the potential for darker impulses. Her character illustrates that fairies, like humans, can harbor both positive and negative emotions, defying easy categorization.

2. Nuanced Motivations: The Tooth Fairy's Transactional Nature

The Tooth Fairy is a widely recognized figure in modern folklore, especially in Western cultures. This character collects children's lost teeth in exchange for money or gifts, creating a unique and transactional relationship with humans.

- Benevolence through Tradition: The Tooth Fairy is generally perceived as benevolent because she rewards children for a natural and sometimes uncomfortable occurrence (losing teeth). This tradition serves to comfort children and make the experience more positive.
- Transactional Motives: However, the Tooth Fairy's actions are not purely altruistic. The exchange of teeth for rewards introduces a transactional aspect, blurring the lines between pure benevolence and an implied quid pro quo.

The Tooth Fairy's character underscores how fairies can be both benevolent and motivated by transactions, reflecting the nuanced relationships we often have with the supernatural. It also highlights the role of tradition in shaping our understanding of fairy characters, as these rituals are passed down through generations.

3. Reinterpreting Classic Fairies: A Modern Twist

In contemporary literature and media, authors and creators frequently reimagine classic fairy characters with modern twists, infusing them with new complexities:

- Antiheroes and Redeemable Villains: Some authors explore the inner struggles of fairies who may have malevolent tendencies but possess the potential for redemption. These characters challenge the traditional notion of fairies as either purely good or evil.
- Cultural Reinterpretations: Modern adaptations often draw inspiration from various cultural traditions, creating hybrid fairy characters that embody diverse attributes and beliefs. These reinterpretations reflect our evolving understanding of fairy folklore in a globalized world.

- Moral Ambiguity: Many contemporary fairy characters grapple with moral dilemmas and ethical choices, blurring the lines between benevolence and malevolence. These characters serve as mirrors of our own complex human nature.

The blurring of lines between benevolent and malevolent fairy characters mirrors the evolving nature of our relationship with the supernatural. These intricate figures challenge our preconceptions, reminding us that fairies, like humans, are capable of a wide range of emotions and actions. They reflect the multifaceted nature of our own psyche and serve as conduits for exploring the complexities of morality, loyalty, and the ever-shifting boundaries between good and evil. As our stories and interpretations of fairies continue to evolve, they invite us to ponder the mysteries of the enchanted world and the enduring allure of these enigmatic beings.

The duality inherent in the world of fairies, where benevolence and malevolence coexist, transcends mere folklore to mirror the complex tapestry of human existence. As we delve deeper into this intriguing facet of fairy mythology, we uncover a treasure trove of wisdom and guidance that transcends cultural boundaries.

Embracing the Balance:

In the realm of fairies, where benevolence and malevolence coexist, we encounter a timeless lesson about the equilibrium of life. Just as these mystical beings embody both light and shadow, humans, too, experience moments of joy and sorrow, success and failure. The benevolent fairies remind us to cherish the moments of grace and compassion, while the malevolent ones caution us to remain vigilant and resilient in the face of adversity.

The Complexity of Morality:

Fairies, especially those depicted with complex personalities, challenge our perceptions of right and wrong. Characters like Tinker Bell or the Fairy Godmother blur the lines of morality, prompting us to acknowledge the shades of gray in our own actions and choices. They teach us that individuals, like fairies, are multifaceted, capable of both kindness and folly.

Lessons in Resilience:

Malevolent fairies, with their propensity for mischief and trickery, remind us of the importance of resilience and adaptability in navigating life's challenges. Just as humans encounter obstacles and setbacks, fairies' malevolent acts symbolize the unpredictability of fate. We learn to persevere and develop inner strength in the face of adversity, much like the protagonists in fairy tales who outwit malevolent fairies.

Cultivating Empathy:

Benevolent fairies, known for their compassion and assistance, inspire us to cultivate empathy and kindness towards others. The Fairy Godmother, for instance, exemplifies the transformative power of selflessness and generosity. Her actions teach us that even small acts of kindness can have a profound impact on the lives of others.

Finding Harmony in Dualities:

The coexistence of benevolent and malevolent fairies reflects the inherent dualities in the human experience. Just as day and night, light and darkness are integral parts of our world, fairies remind us that embracing these dualities can lead to personal growth and understanding. By acknowledging the complexities of life, we learn to find harmony amidst the contrasts.

Respecting Nature and the Unknown:

Fairies' connections to nature and the mystical realms offer a lesson in respecting the natural world and embracing the mysteries beyond our understanding. Tree spirits, for example, emphasize our interconnectedness with nature and the importance of nurturing the environment. Fairies teach us to appreciate the beauty and wonder of the world around us, while respecting its mysteries.

The Power of Belief:

Fairies thrive on belief, and their existence is often contingent on human faith. This dynamic underscores the significance of belief in shaping our realities. Just as fairies come to life through the belief of storytellers and dreamers, our beliefs and perceptions have the power to shape our experiences and influence our destinies.

Conclusion: Navigating Life's Enchanting Paradoxes

The captivating world of benevolent and malevolent fairies invites us to explore the intricate balance between light and shadow, benevolence and malevolence, joy and sorrow. Through their stories, we glean timeless lessons about resilience, empathy, adaptability, and the profound impact of belief.

As we navigate the dualities of life, the enduring allure of fairies serves as a reminder that embracing these paradoxes can lead to personal growth and a deeper understanding of our own existence. These enchanting beings beckon us to cherish the moments of grace, to persevere in the face of adversity, and to cultivate kindness and empathy in our interactions with others. They encourage us to appreciate the beauty of nature, respect the mysteries of the unknown, and harness the power of belief to shape our own realities.

Ultimately, the lessons derived from the realm of fairies extend far beyond folklore, offering profound insights into the complexities of the human journey. In their tales, we find wisdom that guides us through life's enchanting paradoxes, encouraging us to embrace both the light and the shadow as we continue to navigate the wondrous and ever-enticing realm of existence.

Fairy tales have long held a cherished place in the world of literature, captivating audiences of all ages with their enchanting narratives and timeless characters. Beyond their entertainment value, these tales serve as vessels for conveying profound ethical and moral lessons. In this chapter, we embark on a comprehensive exploration of the rich tapestry of moral teachings woven into these ageless stories. We will examine the ways in which fairy tales illuminate essential aspects of human nature, ethics, and morality.

I. The Power of Storytelling and Allegory

Fairy tales, often presented in the form of allegory and symbolism, transcend cultural boundaries to communicate universal truths and ethical principles:

1. Allegorical Elements:

Fairy tales employ fantastical elements, such as talking animals, magical objects, and otherworldly creatures, to symbolize real-world concepts and dilemmas. For instance, Cinderella's glass slipper represents the idea that true identity cannot remain hidden forever.

2. Cultural Universality:

These stories resonate across cultures because they tap into shared human experiences and dilemmas, making them powerful tools for conveying ethical lessons that span the globe.
II. Virtues and Vices in Fairy Tales

Fairy tales often present characters embodying virtues and vices, providing valuable lessons about the consequences of one's actions:

1. Virtuous Characters:

Characters like Cinderella, Snow White, and Belle from "Beauty and the Beast" exemplify virtues such as kindness, humility, and courage. Their stories emphasize the rewards of these qualities and inspire readers to cultivate them.
2. Vicious Antagonists:

Wicked stepmothers, evil witches, and conniving villains serve as cautionary examples of the consequences of greed, jealousy, and cruelty. Fairy tales illustrate the moral downfall that accompanies these vices.

III. Resilience and Resourcefulness

Fairy tales often feature protagonists who face adversity with resilience and resourcefulness, teaching valuable life lessons:

1. Perseverance and Resilience:

Characters like Hansel and Gretel or Little Red Riding Hood demonstrate the importance of resilience in the face of danger. Their stories encourage readers to confront challenges with determination.

IV. Transformation and Redemption

Fairy tales frequently explore the themes of transformation and redemption, underscoring the potential for growth and change:

1. Transformation:

Characters like the Beast in "Beauty and the Beast" and the Frog Prince undergo profound transformations, emphasizing that appearances can be deceiving, and individuals have the capacity for change.

2. Redemption:

Some fairy tales, such as "The Little Mermaid," delve into the concept of redemption through selflessness and sacrifice, highlighting the transformative power of genuine love and altruism.

V. Lessons in Empathy and Compassion

Many fairy tales emphasize the importance of empathy and compassion towards others:

1. Helping Those in Need:

Characters like the Good Samaritan in "The Golden Goose" or the shoemaker's elves in "The Elves and the Shoemaker" demonstrate the value of extending a helping hand to those less fortunate.

2. Understanding Different Perspectives:

Fairy tales often explore the consequences of misunderstanding and prejudice, encouraging readers to seek understanding and empathy when encountering people from different backgrounds.

Through these moral lessons, fairy tales not only entertain but also guide readers on a journey of self-reflection and personal growth. They remind us of the timeless values and virtues that transcend cultures and generations, offering wisdom that continues to resonate in our complex and ever-changing world.

2. Problem-Solving Skills:

- Fairy tales often involve characters solving puzzles or overcoming obstacles, encouraging readers to think critically and creatively in challenging situations.

IV. Consequences of Choices

Fairy tales frequently highlight the concept of cause and effect, emphasizing the repercussions of one's choices:

1. Decision-Making:

- In tales like "The Three Little Pigs," choices made by characters directly impact their outcomes. This underscores the importance of making wise decisions and considering the consequences.

2. Responsibility:

- Characters often face consequences for their actions, whether positive or negative. These tales teach the significance of taking responsibility for one's choices.

V. The Role of Morality and Justice

Fairy tales frequently explore themes of morality and justice, illustrating that good deeds are rewarded while wrongdoing is punished:

1. Justice Prevails:

- Fairy tales often depict the triumph of justice, where wrongdoers receive their comeuppance. This reinforces the belief that fairness and morality should prevail in society.

2. Rewards for Virtue:

- Characters who exhibit virtues like kindness and selflessness are often rewarded. These tales convey the idea that living a moral life leads to positive outcomes.

VI. Cultural Variations and Adaptations

While many moral lessons in fairy tales are universal, cultural variations and adaptations add depth and diversity to the ethical messages conveyed:

1. Cultural Nuances:

- Different cultures infuse their fairy tales with unique moral lessons that reflect their values, traditions, and societal norms.

2. Contemporary Relevance:

- Fairy tales continue to evolve and adapt to contemporary contexts, addressing new ethical and moral dilemmas relevant to modern society.

Conclusion: The Timeless Relevance of Fairy Tales

As we traverse the intricate landscape of moral lessons in fairy tales, we discover that these timeless stories hold a mirror to our own moral compass. The enduring appeal of fairy tales lies not only in their enchanting narratives, but also in their capacity to guide us through the complex terrain of human ethics and morality. By exploring the virtues and vices of their characters, the consequences of their choices, and the triumph of justice, fairy tales invite us to reflect on our own values and actions, reminding us that the wisdom of these ageless stories continues to illuminate the path towards a more ethical and virtuous existence.

Chapter 6
Species of Fae

A Detailed Look at Various Common Fairy Species

In the vast tapestry of folklore and myth, the realm of fairies stands as one of the most enchanting and captivating domains. Within this mystical world, a cornucopia of species thrives, each with its own intricate tapestry of attributes, unique habitats, and intriguing behaviors. In this chapter, we embark on a spellbinding journey, a journey that will take us deep into the heart of some of the most cherished and renowned fairy species. This exploration will unveil the secrets of these ethereal beings, providing us with a profound insight into the astounding diversity that populates the fairy kingdom. We encounter the ever-mischievous pixies, celebrated denizens of British folklore. These pint-sized tricksters are known far and wide for their playful antics, often causing mirthful mayhem wherever they go. With their delicate wings and tiny stature, they flit about like iridescent fireflies, weaving their enchantments with an impish glee. Pixies hold a special place in the hearts of many, often becoming synonymous with the whimsical spirit of fairyland.

Moving across the rolling hills of Ireland, we come upon the Sidhe, a fairy species that exudes an otherworldly grace and ethereal beauty. These enchanting beings are believed to dwell in hidden realms, far removed from the mundane world of humans. Their presence is felt in the whispering winds and the shimmering moonlight, where they are said to convene in glittering courts beneath ancient hawthorn trees. Sidhe, with their luminous presence, have long captivated the imaginations of storytellers and dreamers, embodying the enchantment of Celtic folklore. But our journey doesn't end there. The world of common fairy species is teeming with diversity. Consider the Brownies, gentle and benevolent household fairies of Scottish and English lore. These diminutive creatures, known for their diligent work and penchant for tidiness, often help humans in secret, taking care of domestic chores while homeowners sleep. Their acts of kindness go unnoticed but are indispensable, serving as a reminder that benevolence often hides in the shadows.

Delving into the rich tapestry of fairy species, we find the Dwarves, not to be confused with the towering figures of fantasy literature. These sturdy and skilled artisans of the fairy realm are renowned for their craftsmanship, crafting intricate jewelry, weapons, and magical items hidden away in subterranean realms. Their dedication to their craft is matched only by their fondness for gems and precious metals, making them the ultimate miners and metalworkers of the fairy kingdom. As we journey through the realms of common fairy species, it becomes evident that each one possesses a unique identity and set of characteristics that sets them apart. The pixies' playful nature, the Sidhe's ethereal elegance, the Brownies' hidden benevolence, and the Dwarves' craftsmanship are just a glimpse into the multifaceted world of fairies.

Banshee

1A. Species Introduction

The Banshee, often referred to as the "Wailing Woman" or "Bean Sidhe" in Irish folklore, is a fascinating and eerie species of fairy known for its haunting cries and association with death. The Banshee is a unique and distinctive type of fairy, setting it apart from the more common fairy tales and legends.
Banshees are primarily found in Irish and Celtic mythology, where they are believed to be spirits or fairies that serve as harbingers of death. Unlike many other fairies, Banshees are not associated with beauty or enchantment, but are rather symbols of sorrow and foreboding. Their presence is both dreaded and respected in Irish culture.

1B. Unique Characteristics

The most prominent characteristic of a Banshee is her heartrending wail, which is said to be heard before a death in the family of those who encounter her. This mournful cry is often described as both beautiful and chilling, filling those who hear it with a sense of impending doom. The wail is a unique ability that distinguishes the Banshee from other fairies.
Banshees are typically depicted as ghostly, ethereal women, often dressed in flowing white or gray robes. They have long, tangled hair that frames their pale faces, which are marked by an expression of eternal sadness. Their eyes are usually red from continuous weeping.
Unlike some fairies, Banshees are not believed to interact directly with humans or engage in everyday activities. They exist solely as omens, appearing on moonlit nights near the homes of those whose deaths they foretell. While they are often feared, they are also treated with a degree of reverence, as they are seen as messengers from the spirit world.
The lore and legends surrounding Banshees are deeply rooted in Celtic culture, and their eerie presence has left an indelible mark on Irish folklore. In the following chapters, we will delve into their general appearance, their unique role as omens of death, the cultural significance of their mournful cries, and the historical accounts of encounters with these enigmatic spirits.

2. General Appearance

2A. Detailed Physical Description

The Banshee's physical appearance is hauntingly memorable. She is often depicted as a tall, ethereal woman with a ghostly pallor. Her long, flowing hair is wild and unkempt, cascading like dark waterfalls around her figure. The Banshee's eyes, deeply sorrowful and bloodshot from ceaseless weeping, radiate a mournful intensity that lingers in the memory of those who witness her.

Her attire consists of long, flowing robes, usually in shades of white or gray. These robes seem to billow and flutter even in the absence of wind, adding to her spectral and otherworldly appearance. Her feet barely touch the ground as she moves, gliding rather than walking, leaving a trail of cold mist in her wake.

2B. Distinctive Clothing and Accessories

The Banshee's attire is deliberately designed to enhance her ethereal and ominous presence. Her robes, often tattered and torn, evoke a sense of decay and melancholy. Some accounts even describe her garments as shrouds or burial cloths, symbolizing her connection to death and the afterlife.

In her bony, pale fingers, the Banshee may carry a symbol of death or sorrow, such as a withered rose or a silver comb. These items hold significance in Celtic symbolism and further emphasize her role as a harbinger of death.

The eerie combination of her ghostly appearance and her heartrending wail makes the Banshee one of the most distinctive and unsettling figures in fairy folklore. Her appearance alone is enough to strike fear into the hearts of those who encounter her, as they know that her presence heralds an impending tragedy.

3. Sexes

3A. Description of Male and Female Banshees

In Irish folklore, Banshees are almost exclusively depicted as female entities. These female Banshees are often referred to as "Bean Sidhe," which translates to "woman of the fairy mound." They are the primary bearers of the ominous wail and are associated with foretelling deaths within specific families.

Male Banshees, on the other hand, are rarely mentioned in traditional folklore. The focus is predominantly on the female Banshees, who are believed to have the unique ability to keen or wail before a death occurs. This ability is passed down through generations within specific families, often acting as a familial protector or forewarner.

3B. Differences in Appearance or Behavior Between the Sexes

Since male Banshees are not commonly depicted in Irish folklore, there is limited information available about their appearance or behavior. Female Banshees, on the other hand, are described as ghostly women with long, flowing hair, pale skin, and eyes reddened from weeping. Their primary role is to wail mournfully to announce a death in the family they are bound to.

It is worth noting that the absence of male Banshees in traditional folklore contributes to the idea that the Banshee is a predominantly female figure associated with the realm of death and sorrow.

4. Lore and Legends

4A. Cultural and Historical References to Banshees

Banshees have left an indelible mark on Irish and Celtic culture through the ages. Their presence is deeply woven into the fabric of folklore, and their haunting wails have reverberated through the annals of history. These mournful spirits are often considered one of the most iconic and ominous figures in Celtic mythology.
In Irish and Celtic mythology and literature, Banshees are frequently mentioned as foretellers of death. Families who believe they have a Banshee watching over them consider it a solemn honor and a mark of their heritage. The Banshee's keening cry is regarded as a mournful yet essential part of the death process.

4B. Stories, Myths, and Folklore Associated with Banshees

Countless stories and legends feature the Banshee as a central figure. One well-known legend recounts how the Banshee, often appearing as a spectral woman in white, would wail outside the homes of those about to experience a death in their family. Her cry was said to be so chilling and mournful that it sent shivers down the spines of anyone who heard it, instantly recognizing it as an omen of impending doom.
Another common belief is that Banshees are ancestral spirits, tied to particular families and clans. They are thought to be deeply connected to the bloodlines they watch over, appearing to mourn the death of a family member who is about to pass away.
Throughout Irish literature and folklore, Banshees serve as both ominous warnings and reminders of the ephemeral nature of life. Their stories have been passed down through generations, cementing their place as a symbol of death and the afterlife.

5. Habitat and Natural Environment

5A. Information about the Natural Habitats They Prefer

Banshees are ethereal beings deeply connected to the spirit world, and as such, they do not have physical habitats in the same way that terrestrial creatures do. They are not bound by earthly constraints, and their appearances are not tied to a specific location.
However, in Irish and Celtic folklore, the Banshee is often associated with particular families and bloodlines. In this context, her presence is linked to the homes and ancestral lands of these families. She is believed to appear near the residences of those she is destined to warn of impending death, making the family's dwelling her de facto habitat.

5B. Environmental Factors Affecting Their Choice of Residence

The choice of residence for a Banshee is not influenced by environmental factors in the traditional sense. Instead, her connection to a specific family is the defining factor in her choice of where to appear. Her presence is tied to the family's history and lineage, as well as their ancestral lands. While Banshees are not bound by physical geography or environmental conditions, their connection to specific families and locations is deeply ingrained in Irish and Celtic traditions. Their role as harbingers of death is intimately tied to the homes and territories of the families they watch over.

6. Lifestyle and Social Structure

6A. Insights into Their Societal Structure and Hierarchy

Banshees do not have a structured society or hierarchy in the traditional sense, as they are primarily solitary beings with a specific familial duty. Each Banshee is linked to a particular family, serving as a guardian or harbinger of death for that bloodline. Their role is deeply personal and ancestral.

These ethereal beings are not known to interact with other Banshees, and there is no evidence of organized Banshee communities. Instead, they exist as individual spirits bound to the fate of the family they are associated with.

6B. Daily Routines, Occupations, and Communal Activities

The daily routines and occupations of Banshees are shrouded in mystery, as they are primarily known for their role in foretelling death. They do not engage in communal activities, gatherings, or daily rituals that are observable to humans. Their existence revolves around their solitary task of appearing before the impending death of a family member.

In the absence of a structured daily life, Banshees are enigmatic and elusive entities that emerge from the spirit world when their presence is needed. Their lives, as understood by humans, are intertwined with the destinies of the families they watch over.

7. Diet and Food Sources

7A. What Do They Eat? Are They Herbivores, Carnivores, or Omnivores?

Banshees, as supernatural beings deeply connected to the spirit world and death, do not possess physical bodies, and thus, they do not have biological needs for sustenance. Unlike many other creatures from folklore or mythology, Banshees are not associated with eating or drinking.

In the realm of Irish and Celtic mythology, the Banshee's existence transcends the physical world, and her primary purpose is to serve as a herald of death. Therefore, they are not defined by their dietary habits, as is often the case with earthly creatures.

7B. Special Dietary Preferences or Rituals

Due to their ethereal and otherworldly nature, Banshees do not have special dietary preferences or rituals related to food. Instead, their presence and actions are intimately tied to their role as omens of death within specific families. The very essence of a Banshee is concerned with the spiritual and metaphysical, rather than the physical realm.
The lack of physical needs or preferences in Banshees sets them apart from many other mythical beings, further emphasizing their unique connection to death, mourning, and the afterlife.

8. Communication and Language

8A. How Do They Communicate with Each Other?

Banshees, as solitary and otherworldly beings, do not have a traditional need for interpersonal communication among themselves. Their existence is primarily centered on their role as harbingers of death for specific families, and their communication is directed towards the living, not other Banshees.
While there is no record of Banshees communicating with one another, their presence is often described as ethereal and haunting. Their most prominent form of communication is the mournful wail that they emit when a death is imminent. This wail is their unique method of conveying their message and serving as an omen to the family they watch over.

8B. Any Unique Languages or Gestures Used

Banshees are not known to use distinct languages or gestures, as they do not engage in conventional communication. Their primary mode of expression is their wail, which is universally recognized as a foreboding and ominous sound.
The wail of a Banshee is considered a language unto itself, a chilling and mournful cry that sends a clear and haunting message to those who hear it. It transcends language barriers and is understood by all as an omen of impending death. In this way, the wail serves as a unique form of communication that is deeply embedded in the lore and traditions of Irish and Celtic culture.

9. Reproduction and Life Cycle

9A. The Fairy's Life Stages from Birth to Death

Banshees exist as spectral and ethereal beings, and as such, they do not undergo typical life stages or biological reproduction. Their existence is not bound by the cycle of birth, life, and death in the same way as physical creatures. Instead, they are believed to be ancestral spirits or fairies with a specific purpose.
The concept of birth and death as understood by humans does not apply to Banshees. They are ageless and do not experience the natural progression of life. Instead, their existence centers around their role as omens of death, and they are linked to the families they watch over for generations.

9B. Mating Rituals and Reproduction Process

Banshees are not known to engage in mating rituals or reproduction processes. Their connection to specific families is not based on procreation or family ties in the traditional sense. Instead, they are bound to these families through ancestral or spiritual connections.
The absence of reproductive processes and family structures distinguishes Banshees from many other mythical beings and creatures in folklore. Their existence revolves solely around their role as foretellers of death and the spiritual link they share with the families they protect or warn.

10. Magic Abilities and Powers

10A. A More Detailed Breakdown of Their Magical Abilities

Banshees are believed to possess several powerful and otherworldly abilities, often rooted in their connection to the spirit world and the realm of death. While these abilities may vary in different accounts and folklore, some common magical attributes associated with Banshees include:

- Foretelling Death: The primary and most renowned power of Banshees is their ability to foretell death. They emit a mournful wail or keen when a death is imminent in the family they watch over. This power makes them potent harbingers of sorrow and loss.
- Invisibility: Banshees are often described as ethereal and elusive beings, capable of appearing and disappearing at will. They can remain hidden from human sight until they choose to reveal themselves.
- Shapeshifting: In some legends, Banshees are said to have the ability to change their appearance, allowing them to take on different forms to carry out their mysterious tasks.
- Cursing or Blessing: Depending on the context of their appearance, Banshees may be seen as both ominous and protective. Some tales suggest that they can either curse a family with impending doom or offer a blessing of protection and guidance.

10B. Specific Spells or Powers Unique to This Species

Banshees do not typically engage in spellcasting or the use of specific magical spells in the same way that wizards or witches might. Their power lies in their connection to the spirit world and their ability to serve as omens of death.
The wail of a Banshee is often considered their most potent and unique power. It is a supernatural cry that can be heard by those it is meant for, serving as an unmistakable warning or announcement of an impending death in a specific family. This ability is distinctive to Banshees and is central to their role in Irish and Celtic mythology.

11. Interactions with Humans

11A. Historical Encounters with Humans, Both Positive and Negative

Historically, encounters with Banshees have been marked by a mix of awe, fear, and respect. When a Banshee appeared to a family, it was often perceived as a forewarning of an impending death, a solemn and sorrowful event that could have both positive and negative connotations.
Positive interactions often occurred when a Banshee was seen as a protective spirit watching over a family's well-being. In such cases, her appearance was a blessing, offering guidance and foretelling the impending death as a means of emotional preparation.
Negative interactions were characterized by fear and dread, as the Banshee's wail signaled an impending tragedy or loss. Her mournful cries were a haunting reminder of the inevitability of death, and could evoke deep sorrow and anxiety within those who heard them.

11B. Any Legends of Fairy-Human Friendships or Conflicts

Unlike many other fairy beings in mythology, Banshees are not known for forming friendships or conflicts with humans in the traditional sense. Their interactions are primarily tied to their role as harbingers of death and their connection to specific families.
Banshees do not engage in playful or mischievous behavior, as some fairies do. Instead, they maintain a solemn and mysterious presence, appearing only when their unique duty calls for it. Their interactions with humans are typically brief and emotionally charged, centered around the anticipation of death.

12. Country of Origin

12A. The Geographic Regions or Countries Where This Fairy Species Is Commonly Found

Banshees are most commonly associated with Irish and Celtic mythology, and their presence is deeply ingrained in the folklore of Ireland and Celtic nations. These haunting spirits have their origins in the rich tapestry of Celtic culture and history.
In Ireland, in particular, the belief in Banshees remains strong to this day. Families with Irish heritage may hold onto stories and traditions associated with these spirits, especially those who believe they have a Banshee connected to their bloodline.
Celtic nations such as Scotland, Wales, and parts of Brittany also share a connection to Banshee lore, although the specific details and characteristics of these spirits may vary across regions. Nevertheless, the theme of a mournful spirit foretelling death remains a common thread in Celtic folklore.

12B. Cultural Significance in Those Areas

Banshees hold significant cultural and historical importance in the regions where they are commonly found. They are seen as both symbols of ancestry and reminders of the transient nature of life.

In Ireland, the Banshee is often viewed as a guardian spirit of certain families, appearing as a protector and guide in times of need. Her presence underscores the deep sense of family and heritage within Irish culture.
Banshees also feature prominently in Celtic literature and art, where their haunting cries and spectral appearances serve as powerful symbols of mortality and the afterlife. Their stories continue to be shared and celebrated as an integral part of Celtic identity.

13. Where to Find Them

13A. Specific Locations, Forests, or Landscapes Where They Are Often Sighted

Banshees are not typically found in specific physical locations or landscapes, in the same way that terrestrial creatures inhabit certain habitats. Instead, their presence is intimately tied to the families they watch over and their ancestral homes.
When a Banshee appears, it is usually near the residence of the family she is associated with. She is often sighted outside the homes of those about to experience a death within their family, especially on moonlit nights or evenings with atmospheric conditions conducive to her eerie presence.
While Banshees are not tied to specific geographic regions or landscapes, they are commonly associated with the cultural and historical heritage of Ireland and Celtic nations, where their legends have thrived.

13B. Best Times of Day or Year for Sightings

Sightings of Banshees are not limited to particular times of day or seasons. However, their appearances often occur during the nighttime or under the moon's silvery glow, adding to the mystique and eeriness of their presence.
Traditionally, the wailing cry of a Banshee is heard before dawn or during the darkest hours of the night. These haunting cries are said to pierce the silence of the night, serving as an unmistakable omen to those who hear them.

14. How to See Them

14A. Practical Tips for Encountering Them

Encountering a Banshee is not something that can be sought out or provoked, as their appearances are deeply connected to specific families and events. However, some practical tips and advice for those interested in the lore of Banshees include:

> Learn Your Family's Heritage: If you have Irish or Celtic ancestry, delve into your family's history and folklore to see if there are any stories or traditions related to a Banshee watching over your bloodline.
>
> Respect Ancestral Homes: Paying respects to ancestral homes and traditions can create an atmosphere that acknowledges the importance of familial connections and ancestral spirits, including the possibility of a Banshee presence.

Study Local Folklore: Familiarize yourself with local legends and folklore related to Banshees in the regions associated with their presence, such as Ireland, Scotland, and Wales.
Listen to Oral Histories: Talk to older family members or community members who may have stories or accounts of encounters with Banshees within your family or region.

14B. Rituals, Offerings, or Behaviors That May Attract Them

Banshees are not typically attracted by rituals, offerings, or specific behaviors, as their appearances are spontaneous and related to their role as harbingers of death. However, it is essential to approach any interactions or inquiries with respect for the cultural and historical significance of Banshees in Irish and Celtic traditions.
Attempting to summon or attract a Banshee is not a recommended practice, as it can be considered disrespectful and may not yield the desired results. Instead, a reverence for the stories and traditions associated with Banshees is a more appropriate approach.

15. Protection and Etiquette

15A. Guidance on How to Respect and Protect Fairies and Their Habitats

Respecting Banshees and their role as omens of death is of utmost importance in Irish and Celtic traditions. Here are some general guidelines for respecting and protecting these enigmatic spirits:

Respect Ancestral Customs: Acknowledge the ancestral customs and traditions of your family or community, as they may hold the key to understanding and respecting Banshees.
Maintain Family Ancestry: Preserve and honor your family's ancestry, as Banshees are often associated with specific bloodlines. Show respect for your ancestors and their traditions.
Protect Natural Spaces: Banshees are often linked to natural landscapes near ancestral homes. Preserve and protect these natural spaces to maintain the spiritual connections associated with these spirits.
Exercise Discretion: If you believe you have encountered a Banshee or experienced her cry, exercise discretion and respect for the emotional significance of such an event.

15B. Superstitions or Taboos Related to Interacting with Them

Interacting with Banshees is generally discouraged, as their appearances are connected to sorrow and foreboding. There are few superstitions or taboos associated with interacting with them, but it is crucial to approach any potential encounters with reverence and caution:

Do Not Seek Them Out: Attempting to summon or seek out a Banshee is not recommended, as it can be perceived as disrespectful or intrusive.
Maintain Respectful Distance: If you believe you have encountered a Banshee, maintain a respectful distance and do not attempt to engage or communicate with her.
Listen and Reflect: If you hear the wail of a Banshee, listen and reflect on its significance within your family or cultural context. It is a somber and poignant moment.

16. Art and Representation

16A. Explore How This Fairy Species Has Been Portrayed in Art, Literature, and Media

Banshees have left an enduring mark on various forms of artistic expression, literature, and media, often captivating audiences with their eerie and haunting presence. Here are some ways Banshees have been portrayed:

Literature: Banshees have featured prominently in Irish and Celtic literature, where their mournful cries and spectral appearances are woven into tales of mystery and foreboding. They often serve as symbols of impending doom or the supernatural.

Visual Arts: In visual arts, Banshees are depicted as ghostly and ethereal figures, with long, flowing hair and flowing robes. These artworks capture the haunting beauty and melancholy essence of these spirits.

Music: Some musical compositions, particularly in traditional Irish and Celtic music, draw inspiration from the concept of the Banshee. Their mournful wail may be evoked through musical compositions that convey a sense of sorrow and foreboding.

Literary Works: Banshees have appeared in both classical and contemporary literature, adding depth to stories and novels with their role as harbingers of death.

Film and Television: In film and television, Banshees have made appearances in various genres, from horror to fantasy. Their presence often introduces an element of supernatural mystery and impending tragedy.

16B. Iconic Artists or Authors Who Have Featured Them

Several iconic artists and authors have contributed to the enduring representation of Banshees in various forms of media:

William Butler Yeats: The renowned Irish poet and playwright featured Banshees in his literary works, such as "The Celtic Twilight." His writings explored the rich folklore and mythology of Ireland, including the role of Banshees.

Edmund Dulac: The celebrated French-born illustrator created hauntingly beautiful depictions of Banshees in his fairy tale illustrations, capturing their ethereal and enigmatic qualities.

Contemporary Authors: Modern authors like Neil Gaiman and Patricia Briggs have incorporated Banshees into their fantasy and paranormal novels, introducing these spirits to new generations of readers.

17. Modern Beliefs and Practices

17A. Contemporary Beliefs and Practices Related to These Fairies

In contemporary times, the belief in Banshees has evolved but remains deeply rooted in Irish and Celtic culture. While many view them as legendary figures from the past, others continue to hold a belief in their existence as ancestral spirits.
Some modern beliefs and practices related to Banshees include:

- Cultural Preservation: Banshees are celebrated and preserved as important cultural symbols in Ireland and Celtic nations. They are often featured in cultural festivals, storytelling, and art, keeping their legacy alive.
- Interest in Heritage: People with Irish or Celtic heritage may maintain a connection to Banshee lore as a way of honoring their ancestry and cultural roots.
- Spiritual Connection: Some individuals view Banshees as spiritual or ancestral guardians, maintaining a reverence for their role as protectors or omens.
-

17B. Current Festivals or Gatherings Dedicated to Them

While there may not be specific festivals or gatherings dedicated solely to Banshees, their presence is often felt in broader cultural and folklore events in Ireland and Celtic regions. These events celebrate the rich tapestry of mythological beings, including Banshees, that are part of the cultural heritage.
One example is the celebration of Samhain, the Celtic festival marking the end of the harvest season and the beginning of winter. During Samhain, there is a focus on honoring ancestral spirits and acknowledging the thinning of the veil between the living and the dead, creating an atmosphere in which the presence of Banshees and other spirits is acknowledged.

18. Conservation Efforts

18A. Discuss Any Conservation Initiatives Aimed at Preserving Their Habitats

Conservation efforts related to Banshees primarily focus on preserving the cultural and historical significance of these spirits, rather than physical habitats. These initiatives aim to ensure that the rich folklore and traditions associated with Banshees are passed down through generations and continue to be celebrated. Some conservation measures include:

- Oral Tradition Preservation: Efforts are made to record and document oral traditions, stories, and folklore related to Banshees. This includes interviewing elders and community members who may have unique insights and accounts.
- Cultural Festivals: Cultural festivals and events that celebrate Banshees and other mythical beings are organized to keep these traditions alive. These gatherings help ensure that Banshees remain a vital part of Irish and Celtic culture.
- Education and Outreach: Educational programs and outreach efforts are designed to engage younger generations in the appreciation and understanding of Banshees. This includes school curricula and museum exhibits.
- Artistic Expression: Supporting artists and writers who draw inspiration from Banshees in their creative works helps maintain the spirit's presence in contemporary culture.

18B. Threats They May Face and Steps to Mitigate Them

Banshees themselves do not face physical threats, as they are otherworldly beings. However, the preservation of Banshee lore and traditions can face challenges in the modern world:

- Cultural Erosion: As societies evolve, there is a risk of cultural erosion, where traditional beliefs and practices may fade away over time. Conservation efforts aim to combat this erosion by emphasizing the importance of Banshees in cultural heritage.
- Loss of Oral Traditions: Oral traditions are vulnerable to being lost if not passed down through generations. Recording and documenting these traditions help safeguard their continuity.
- Changing Belief Systems: As belief systems change, the significance of Banshees may diminish for some individuals. Efforts to educate and engage the public help counteract this trend.
- Commercialization: There is a risk of commercial exploitation of Banshee imagery and stories. Conservation efforts seek to strike a balance between preserving the spirit's cultural importance and preventing inappropriate commercialization.

19. Additional Folklore

19A. Lesser-Known Stories or Beliefs Associated with This Fairy Species

While the core concept of the Banshee as a wailing spirit foretelling death is well-known, there are lesser-known stories and beliefs associated with these ethereal beings. Some of these include:

- Guardians of the Family: In some variations of Banshee folklore, these spirits are seen not only as omens of death but also as guardians of their associated families. They may watch over and protect family members from harm.
- Dual Nature: Some stories depict Banshees with a dual nature, where they can be both ominous and comforting. They may appear to mourn the loss of a loved one but also provide solace and guidance to the grieving.
- Transformative Powers: In certain tales, Banshees are said to have the ability to transform into various forms, allowing them to move through the mortal world undetected. This shape-shifting ability adds an additional layer of mystery to their character.
- Association with Water: In Celtic folklore, water bodies such as lakes and rivers are often linked to mystical beings. Some versions of Banshee lore tie them to watery locations, where their mournful cries are said to carry over the water.

19B. Variations in Their Portrayal Across Different Cultures

While Banshees are most commonly associated with Irish and Celtic culture, variations of similar spirits can be found in other cultures as well. These spirits may share some common themes with Banshees, but have distinct characteristics and names. Examples include:

- Bean Nighe (Scotland): The Bean Nighe is a Scottish spirit similar to the Banshee. She is often depicted as a washerwoman who is seen near water, washing the clothes of those about to die.
- Leanan Sidhe (Ireland and Scotland): The Leanan Sidhe is a fairy lover who grants artistic inspiration to mortals, but often leads them to an early death. While not a direct counterpart to the Banshee, she embodies a complex relationship with death and creativity.

- Moirai (Greece): In Greek mythology, the Moirai, also known as the Fates, control the destinies of mortals by spinning, measuring, and cutting the thread of life. While not spirits in the same sense as Banshees, they play a role in determining the length of human lives.

20. Famous Encounters

20A. Historical or Modern Accounts of Famous Individuals Encountering These Fairies

Throughout history and into the modern era, there have been accounts of famous individuals encountering Banshees. These encounters have often been profound and left a lasting impact on those who experienced them. Some notable examples include:

- The O'Brien Family of Dromoland Castle: The O'Brien family, who resided in Dromoland Castle in Ireland, claimed to have a Banshee who would wail before the death of a family member. This belief was held by several generations of the O'Brien clan.
- Lady Gregory: Augusta, Lady Gregory, a prominent Irish playwright and folklorist, documented encounters with Banshees in her work. Her writings helped preserve and popularize the stories of these spirits.
- W.B. Yeats: William Butler Yeats, the renowned Irish poet and Nobel laureate, mentioned Banshees in his poetry and essays. He contributed to the broader understanding of Banshees in the context of Irish folklore.
- Modern Encounters: In contemporary times, individuals have reported encounters with Banshees or hearing their wails before the death of a loved one. While these encounters are deeply personal, they continue to be part of the living folklore surrounding Banshees.

20B. The Impact of These Encounters on Their Lives or Work

Encounters with Banshees, whether in history or the modern era, have often had a profound impact on individuals and their creative or personal lives. Some of the ways these encounters have influenced people include:

- Inspiration for Art: Banshee encounters have inspired works of literature, poetry, music, and visual art. Many artists have drawn from the eerie and mournful aspects of these experiences.
- Cultural Preservation: Encounters with Banshees have contributed to the preservation of Irish and Celtic folklore and cultural traditions. They remind people of the importance of maintaining their heritage.
- Personal Reflection: Individuals who have encountered Banshees often reflect on mortality, the interconnectedness of life and death, and the significance of ancestral ties.
- Legacies: The stories of famous encounters with Banshees have become part of the cultural legacy of Ireland and Celtic nations. They are celebrated and shared as important elements of national identity.

Elves

Species Introduction

1A. Brief Overview of Elves

Elves, also known as the Eldar in some cultures, are a captivating and enigmatic species of fairy. These graceful beings have fascinated humans for centuries, and their existence is steeped in myth and legend. Elves are renowned for their ethereal beauty, keen intellect, and affinity for the natural world.

1B. Unique Characteristics of Elves

One of the most captivating aspects of elves is their exceptional longevity. They are often described as immortal or living for hundreds, if not thousands, of years. This extended lifespan allows them to accumulate vast knowledge and wisdom, making them formidable scholars and guardians of ancient secrets. Elves are deeply attuned to the natural world, possessing an innate connection with the forests, rivers, and mountains that surround them. They are skilled in various forms of magic, particularly nature-based and elemental magic, allowing them to influence the world around them in profound ways.
Their society is often organized into tightly-knit communities or kingdoms, hidden away in the depths of ancient forests or secluded valleys. Elves are known for their affinity for music and art, and their creations are renowned for their exquisite beauty. They are also skilled in archery and swordsmanship, making them formidable warriors when the need arises.
The complex relationship between elves and humans is a recurring theme in their mythology. Some stories depict elves as benevolent protectors of the natural world, while others portray them as aloof and distant, only revealing themselves to those they deem worthy.

2. General Appearance

2A. Detailed Physical Description

Elves possess a strikingly ethereal appearance. They are generally tall, slender, and graceful. Their skin tones vary from fair to deep, earthy shades. A defining feature of Elves is their pointed ears, which are often considered a symbol of their fairy heritage. Their eyes are vivid and can range from various shades of blue, green, or silver, often with a captivating luminescence.

2B. Clothing and Accessories

Elves are known for their exquisite fashion sense. They often wear garments made from natural materials such as silk, leaves, and flowers, seamlessly blending with their forest surroundings. Elaborate and intricate designs, often embellished with gems or embroidery, adorn their attire. Elves are also known for their intricate jewelry, including delicate circlets, necklaces, and earrings made from precious stones and metals.

3. Sexes

3A. Description of Male and Female Elves

Elves do have distinct genders, with both male and female individuals. Male Elves are known for their chiseled features and tend to have a slightly more muscular build than females. Female Elves, on the other hand, often have a more delicate and ethereal appearance, emphasizing their grace and beauty.

3B. Differences in Appearance and Behavior

While both male and female Elves share many physical characteristics, such as pointed ears and longevity, their societal roles and behaviors can differ. In some Elven cultures, males may take on roles as warriors or hunters, while females may excel in arts, music, and magic. However, these roles are not rigidly defined and can vary among different Elven communities.

4. Lore and Legends

4A. Cultural and Historical References

Elves have left an indelible mark on human culture and history. References to Elves can be found in numerous mythologies, literature, and folklore across the world. From the Norse Aesir to J.R.R. Tolkien's Middle-earth, Elves have captured the imaginations of storytellers and readers alike.

4B. Myths and Folklore

Elves have been portrayed in a myriad of ways in different cultures. In some myths, they are depicted as wise and benevolent beings, while in others, they are seen as mischievous tricksters. These tales often feature Elves as guardians of the natural world, protectors of ancient forests, or skilled craftsmen who create magical items.
As we continue our exploration of Elves, we will delve into their natural habitats, societal structures, dietary preferences, and the unique languages and communication methods they employ. Elves are a multifaceted and intriguing species, and there's much more to uncover about them.

5. Habitat and Natural Environment

5A. Preferred Natural Habitats

Elves are most commonly associated with lush and ancient forests. These mystical beings often dwell in hidden enclaves within these woods, secluded from the outside world. They are deeply connected to the natural environment and find solace in the tranquility of their forest homes.

5B. Environmental Factors Affecting Residence

Elves are highly sensitive to changes in their natural surroundings. They are known to withdraw deeper into the forests or relocate their communities when faced with environmental disruptions, such as deforestation or pollution. Their ability to adapt to these changes is a testament to their enduring connection with nature.

6. Lifestyle and Social Structure

6A. Societal Structure and Hierarchy

Elven society is often organized into hierarchical structures, with rulers or leaders at the top. These leaders may be monarchs, council elders, or revered individuals chosen for their wisdom and guidance. Beneath them, Elves are divided into different social classes, often determined by their skills, talents, or roles within the community.

6B. Daily Routines and Communal Activities

Elves lead lives deeply intertwined with nature. Their daily routines include activities such as tending to the forests, practicing arts and crafts, and engaging in communal rituals and celebrations. Music and dance are integral to their culture, and these activities often bring Elves together in joyous gatherings.

7. Diet and Food Sources

7A. Dietary Habits

Elves are primarily herbivores, with a diet centered around fruits, vegetables, nuts, and grains. They have a deep respect for the natural world and are known for harvesting their food sustainably to minimize their impact on the environment.

7B. Special Dietary Preferences or Rituals

Some Elves engage in unique dietary rituals, such as consuming certain enchanted foods or partaking in communal feasts during significant occasions. These rituals often have symbolic meanings and connect Elves to their cultural heritage.

8. Communication and Language

8A. Methods of Communication

Elves communicate through various methods, including spoken language, telepathy (in some interpretations), and non-verbal cues. Their language is often melodious and complex, with subtle nuances that convey deep meaning.

8B. Unique Languages and Gestures

Elven languages can be intricate and unique to their communities. Some Elves use specific gestures or hand signs to convey emotions or intentions, allowing for silent communication when necessary. There are several real languages that have inspired the idea of Elvish languages in literature and mythology. These languages are often associated with elves and other mythical beings. Here's a brief exploration of such languages:

1. Irish (Gaeilge): Irish is sometimes considered an inspiration for Elvish languages due to its lyrical and ancient nature. Its melodic sounds and rich history resonate with the elegance often associated with elves. In particular, the Old Irish language, with its complex grammar and poetic traditions, can be seen as a source of inspiration.
2. Welsh (Cymraeg): Welsh is another Celtic language that carries a mystic and enchanting quality, making it a fitting source of inspiration for Elvish languages. Its unique phonology and vocabulary are often likened to the speech of mythical creatures. The Welsh language has a strong literary tradition, and its use of mutations and consonant clusters adds to its otherworldly charm.
3. Finnish (Suomi): Finnish is renowned for its complex grammar and distinctive phonetics, which are reminiscent of the elegance often attributed to elves. Its agglutinative nature, with words formed by combining multiple suffixes, can be seen as a model for constructing a unique Elvish language. Finnish mythology also includes beings similar to elves, which further connect the language to this concept.
4. Hawaiian (‘Ōlelo Hawai‘i): Hawaiian, with its rhythmic syllables and soothing pronunciation, can be a source of inspiration for an Elvish language. The language's connection to nature and the islands' lush landscapes align with the close bond elves are often portrayed to have with their natural surroundings.
5. Quenya-inspired Elvish: It's worth noting that J.R.R. Tolkien's Elvish languages, especially Quenya, were heavily inspired by real languages like Finnish, Latin, and Greek. While you requested not to mention Tolkien, his work has had a profound influence on the portrayal of Elvish languages in literature and popular culture.

In summary, while there isn't a real-world Elvish language, various existing languages possess qualities that have inspired the creation of Elvish languages in fiction and mythology. These languages' melodic qualities, unique grammatical structures, and cultural contexts contribute to the ethereal and enchanting image often associated with the speech of elves.

9. Reproduction and Life Cycle

9A. Life Stages

Elves have a unique life cycle that sets them apart from humans and other creatures. They are born and grow much like humans, but do not experience the physical signs of aging as we do. Instead, they appear eternally youthful until the end of their exceptionally long lives. Elves go through stages of childhood, adolescence, and adulthood, but their maturity is marked by wisdom rather than physical aging.

9B. Mating Rituals and Reproduction

Elves hold a deep reverence for the act of procreation, which they view as a sacred bond between two individuals. Mating rituals vary among different Elven cultures, but often involve ceremonies in natural settings, such as moonlit groves or by ancient trees. The birth of an Elf child is a momentous occasion, celebrated with great joy and communal festivities.

10. Magic Abilities and Powers

10A. Magical Abilities

Elves are renowned for their proficiency in magic. Their magic is often rooted in nature, allowing them to commune with and manipulate the elements. They can heal wounds, communicate with animals, control the weather, and even shape-shift in some traditions.

10B. Unique Spells and Powers

Different Elven communities may possess unique spells or magical abilities that are passed down through generations. These abilities can range from creating illusions to invoking protection over their forests. Elves often guard these magical secrets closely.

11. Interactions with Humans

11A. Historical Encounters

Throughout history, there have been numerous accounts of humans encountering Elves. These interactions vary from tales of kindness and guidance to stories of mischievous trickery. Elves are known to appear to humans in times of need, offering wisdom or aid.

11B. Fairy-Human Relationships

Some legends speak of profound friendships and alliances between Elves and humans. These relationships are often depicted as mutually beneficial, with humans gaining knowledge and protection while Elves find worthy allies.

12. Country of Origin

12A. Geographic Regions

Elves are often associated with specific geographic regions where they are commonly found. These regions include ancient and mystical forests, secluded valleys, and remote mountain ranges. Some of the most renowned locations for Elf sightings in the hidden glades of Alfheim in Norse mythology.

12B. Cultural Significance

In the regions where Elves are believed to reside, their presence carries significant cultural and historical importance. They are often seen as guardians of these natural landscapes, and their influence can be felt in local customs, art, and folklore. Many festivals and traditions are dedicated to honoring the Elves and their connection to the land.

13. Where to Find Them

13A. Specific Locations

Finding Elves is a rare and elusive experience. They are often found deep within ancient forests, concealed by enchantments or cloaked in invisibility. Specific locations may include secluded groves, moonlit glades, or the heart of an old-growth forest.

13B. Best Times for Sightings

Elves are most likely to reveal themselves during moments of tranquility when the natural world is in harmony. Twilight and dawn are considered auspicious times for sightings, as the boundary between day and night blurs, and the veil between their world and ours becomes thinner.

14. How to See Them

14A. Practical Tips

Seeing Elves is a challenging endeavor, but there are practical steps one can take to increase the likelihood of an encounter. These may include respecting their natural habitats, practicing mindfulness, and approaching with humility and reverence.

14B. Rituals and Offerings

Some cultures believe that performing specific rituals or making offerings can attract the attention of Elves. These rituals may involve offerings of food, music, or recitations of ancient poetry. However, it's crucial to approach such practices with deep respect and sincerity.

15. Protection and Etiquette

15A. Guidance on Respect and Protection

Interacting with Elves requires a deep understanding of the natural world and a profound respect for their existence. Guidelines for protecting them include refraining from harming their habitats, not disturbing sacred groves or ancient trees, and avoiding any behavior that may be seen as disrespectful.

15B. Superstitions and Taboos

Various cultures have superstitions and taboos related to interactions with Elves. These may include refraining from speaking their names aloud, avoiding whistling in forests to prevent offending them, or never accepting food from an Elf unless offered as a sign of goodwill.

16. Art and Representation

16A. Portrayal in Art and Literature

Elves have been a popular subject in art, literature, and media for centuries. Their portrayal has varied greatly, from the ethereal and benevolent Elves of classical fantasy literature to the more enigmatic and mysterious interpretations in ancient legends. Iconic authors like J.R.R. Tolkien and artists such as Brian Froud have created timeless representations of Elves.

16B. Iconic Artists and Authors

Several artists and authors have left an indelible mark on the way we perceive Elves. J.R.R. Tolkien's Middle-earth, with its Elves of Rivendell and Lothlórien, remains a defining fantasy world. Artists like Alan Lee and John Howe have visualized these Elves, influencing the aesthetic of fantasy art.

17. Modern Beliefs and Practices

17A. Contemporary Beliefs

In modern times, beliefs in Elves have evolved. While many people consider Elves as mythical beings from folklore, there are still individuals and groups who maintain spiritual connections with them. New Age and pagan communities often incorporate the reverence of nature and the mystical aspects of Elves into their belief systems.

17B. Festivals and Gatherings

Certain festivals and gatherings celebrate the enduring fascination with Elves. These events may feature art exhibitions, music performances, and discussions about Elven lore and spirituality. They serve as opportunities for enthusiasts to connect and share their experiences.

18. Conservation Efforts

18A. Initiatives for Habitat Preservation

As natural environments face increasing threats, some conservation initiatives aim to protect the habitats associated with Elves. These efforts focus on reforestation, sustainable land management, and education to raise awareness about the importance of preserving ancient forests.

18B. Threats and Mitigation

Elves, like many other creatures, face threats from habitat destruction, pollution, and climate change. Efforts to mitigate these threats may include partnerships between conservation organizations and local communities, as well as the implementation of sustainable practices to safeguard the natural world.

19. Additional Folklore

19A. Lesser-Known Stories and Beliefs

Elves are not a uniform concept; they vary in appearance, behavior, and significance across different cultures. Exploring lesser-known stories and beliefs about Elves reveals the rich diversity of interpretations and cultural significance attached to these beings.

19B. Cultural Variations

From the Scottish "Seelie" and "Unseelie" Courts to the Scandinavian "Ljósálfar" and "Dökkálfar," Elves take on different names and characteristics in various cultures. Understanding these variations provides a deeper appreciation for the global tapestry of Elf lore.

20. Famous Encounters

20A. Historical Accounts

Throughout history, numerous famous individuals have claimed to have encountered Elves. These accounts range from poets and artists inspired by mystical experiences to explorers and scholars who documented their encounters in journals and letters.

20B. Impact on Lives and Work

The encounters with Elves have had a profound impact on the lives and work of those who claimed to have met them. These experiences often inspired art, literature, and philosophy, influencing the course of human creativity and spirituality.

Púcaí

1. Species Introduction

1A. Brief Overview of Pooka

The Pooka is a mischievous and elusive fairy creature deeply rooted in Irish folklore. Often described as a shape-shifter, the Pooka takes on various forms, including that of a horse, a goat, or even a human. This transformation ability allows it to both enchant and confound those who encounter it.
Pookas are known for their capricious nature, and their motivations can be hard to decipher. Some believe they are playful tricksters, while others consider them more malevolent entities. They have a unique connection to the nighttime and are often associated with autumn and Halloween, a time when their antics are said to be at their peak.

1B. Unique Characteristics

One of the most distinctive features of the Pooka is its shape-shifting ability. It can seamlessly transform into different creatures, making it difficult to identify.
However, in its equine form, the Pooka is often depicted as a sleek, black horse with fiery eyes. This form is the most well-known and feared, as it is said to roam the countryside, offering unwary travelers rides before subjecting them to a wild and terrifying journey.
Pookas are known to be mischievous rather than inherently evil. They enjoy playing tricks on humans and are particularly active during harvest season. They may lead people astray at night or cause chaos in farmyards. However, some stories also suggest that they can be helpful, offering valuable advice or guidance when they choose.
The Pooka's ambiguous nature is what makes it a fascinating and enduring figure in Irish folklore. Its enigmatic behavior and shape-shifting abilities keep people wary and respectful of the fairy, even as they find themselves captivated by its mysteries.

2. General Appearance

2A. Detailed Physical Description

The physical appearance of the Pooka can vary greatly depending on the form it chooses to take. In its equine form, it is often described as a sleek, jet-black horse with glistening, fiery eyes that burn like embers in the darkness. Its mane and tail flow like silk, adding to its eerie beauty. This equine manifestation is the most iconic representation of the Pooka.

When the Pooka takes on a more humanoid form, it may appear as a figure cloaked in shadow, its features obscured by darkness. In its goat form, it resembles a large, black goat with the same fiery eyes, making it equally unsettling to encounter.

Despite its different forms, the Pooka always carries an air of enchantment and mystery. Its supernatural appearance is both captivating and eerie, drawing those who dare to approach it into its web of enchantment.

2B. Distinctive Clothing or Accessories

In its humanoid form, the Pooka is often depicted as wearing tattered and ancient clothing, reminiscent of a bygone era. These garments may appear to be made of materials not found in the mortal realm, adding to the otherworldly nature of this fairy. However, it's important to note that the Pooka's appearance can change at will, and it may choose to be clothed or unclothed as it pleases.

The Pooka's choice of clothing, or lack thereof, serves to enhance its mystical and unpredictable nature, leaving those who encounter it unsure of what to expect. This ever-changing appearance contributes to the sense of wonder and unease associated with the Pooka.

3. Sexes

3A. Description of Male and Female Pookas

In the realm of Pookas, gender distinctions are rarely emphasized or documented. Pookas, with their shape-shifting abilities, often transcend traditional gender roles and appearances. They are known to assume forms that are best suited to their whims or the situation at hand. Consequently, distinguishing between male and female Pookas based on physical characteristics is seldom possible.

3B. Differences in Appearance or Behavior

While the Pooka's shape-shifting abilities make it challenging to differentiate between male and female Pookas based on physical appearance, their behavior remains a topic of intrigue. Some stories suggest that Pookas exhibit varying personalities and tendencies, regardless of gender. For instance, some encounters with Pookas depict them as playful and mischievous, leading travelers on wild chases or tricking them for amusement. Others describe Pookas as more sinister, with a malevolent streak that can lead to accidents or harm. These differences in behavior may be attributed to individual temperament rather than gender distinctions.

In essence, the fluid nature of the Pooka, both in terms of form and behavior, keeps its gender a secondary concern in the rich tapestry of Pooka lore. What truly captivates and mystifies observers is the Pooka's capacity for transformation and its unpredictable nature, regardless of gender.

4. Lore and Legends

4A. Cultural and Historical References

The Pooka holds a prominent place in Irish folklore and has been a subject of fascination for generations. Its origins are deeply rooted in Celtic mythology and pre-Christian beliefs. In Celtic culture, the Pooka was considered a supernatural entity that embodied the mysteries of the natural world.
Throughout Irish history, the Pooka has been referenced in various forms of literature, oral traditions, and artistic representations. It has appeared in poems, plays, and stories, often as a symbol of the uncanny and the unpredictable forces of nature.

4B. Stories, Myths, and Folklore

Countless tales and legends surround the Pooka, reflecting its dual nature as a trickster and an enigmatic presence. One well-known story tells of the Pooka appearing as a horse and offering rides to unsuspecting travelers. Once mounted, the Pooka takes them on a wild and chaotic journey, leaving them disoriented and exhausted.
In other accounts, the Pooka is depicted as both a malevolent and benevolent figure. Some stories describe it causing harm to humans and livestock, while others depict it providing guidance or valuable advice when approached with respect.
The Pooka's association with the harvest season and Halloween is particularly significant in Irish folklore. It is believed that during this time, the Pooka becomes more active and its pranks more pronounced, making it a central character in the festivities and traditions of the season.
The Pooka's enduring presence in Irish culture serves as a testament to its mysterious allure and the deep connection between folklore, nature, and the supernatural in Celtic traditions.

5. Habitat and Natural Environment

5A. Natural Habitats Preferred by Pookas

Pookas are known to be elusive creatures that roam the Irish countryside, and their preferred natural habitats are varied. They are often associated with rural landscapes, particularly remote and wild areas. These can include dense forests, rolling hills, moorlands, and even coastal regions. Pookas are known to dwell in places where human influence is minimal, and the natural world is allowed to flourish undisturbed.

The darkness of night is when Pookas are most active, and they are often encountered near bodies of water, such as lakes, rivers, and streams, during these hours. Some legends suggest that they have a special affinity for standing stones, ancient ruins, and other mystical sites.

5B. Environmental Factors Affecting Residence

Environmental factors play a significant role in the Pooka's choice of residence. They are known to be especially active during the autumn harvest season, which aligns with their association with Halloween. During this time, the natural world undergoes significant changes, with crops being harvested and the days growing shorter.
The Pooka's preference for the harvest season could be linked to the abundance of food sources and the changing energies in the environment. It is believed that the Pooka's behavior is influenced by the rhythms of nature, making it more active and visible during specific times of the year.
The mysterious connection between the Pooka and its natural surroundings adds to the intrigue and complexity of this fairy species. Its elusive nature and ties to the changing seasons have contributed to the enduring fascination with the Pooka in Irish folklore.

6. Lifestyle and Social Structure

6A. Societal Structure and Hierarchy

The Pooka, as a solitary and enigmatic creature, does not adhere to a structured societal hierarchy or community. Unlike some other fairy species, Pookas are known to be independent and self-reliant. They do not form organized groups or societies like the Seelie or Unseelie courts found in other fairy lore.
Each Pooka is believed to lead a solitary existence, shaping their behavior based on individual temperament and whims. This independence is reflected in their tendency to act as free spirits, following their own desires and instincts without allegiance to a higher authority or communal structure.

6B. Daily Routines, Occupations, and Communal Activities

The daily routines of Pookas are shrouded in mystery, as they are known for their capricious and unpredictable nature. Their activities are often intertwined with their tricks and pranks on humans, making it challenging to discern a consistent routine or occupation.
While some tales describe Pookas as active during the night, especially around harvest season, others suggest that they may appear at any time. Their primary occupation seems to be mischief-making and playing tricks on humans. In some cases, they may provide guidance or offer help, but such actions are typically unpredictable and rarely follow a pattern.
Overall, the Pooka's lifestyle is characterized by its enigmatic and independent nature. Its actions are driven by a sense of playfulness and an affinity for disrupting the ordinary, making it a challenging creature to pin down in terms of daily routines or communal activities.

7. Diet and Food Sources

7A. What Do They Eat?

The dietary habits of Pookas are a subject of intrigue and mystery. While they are known to be shape-shifters and pranksters, their actual consumption of food is not well-documented in folklore. Some stories suggest that Pookas may indulge in natural foods found in their preferred habitats, such as wild berries, grains, and roots. However, these details are often overshadowed by their playful and enigmatic behavior.

7B. Special Dietary Preferences or Rituals

There are no specific dietary preferences or rituals associated with Pookas in traditional folklore. Their primary interactions with humans tend to revolve around tricks, enchantments, or mysterious journeys rather than shared meals or offerings. Pookas are more commonly linked to the harvest season and Halloween festivities, where their activities focus on pranks rather than feasting.

The enigmatic nature of Pookas extends to their dietary habits, which remain largely unexplored in the realms of folklore and legend. This mystery adds to the intrigue and complexity surrounding these shape-shifting fairies.

8. Communication and Language

8A. How Do They Communicate with Each Other?

The modes of communication among Pookas are shrouded in mystery, and little is known about their interactions with one another. As solitary beings, Pookas do not appear to rely on complex verbal or written language to convey messages or information within their kind. Instead, they seem to possess a deep and instinctual understanding of their surroundings and the natural world.

Pookas are believed to communicate with each other through non-verbal means, such as body language, gestures, and perhaps even telepathic or empathic connections. Their connection to the mystical and supernatural aspects of the world may allow them to share thoughts and intentions in ways that elude human comprehension.

8B. Any Unique Languages or Gestures Used

There is no evidence to suggest that Pookas have developed unique languages or gestures specific to their kind. Their ability to shape-shift, and their enigmatic nature, may render the need for complex linguistic communication unnecessary.

It is worth noting that when Pookas interact with humans, they often do so in a non-verbal, symbolic manner. Their actions and pranks are intended to convey messages, emotions, or lessons, but these are typically left open to interpretation, adding to the sense of mystery that surrounds them.

The Pooka's unconventional means of communication are a testament to its otherworldly nature, reinforcing its status as a being that exists on the periphery of human understanding.

9. Reproduction and Life Cycle

9A. The Fairy's Life Stages from Birth to Death

The life cycle of a Pooka is a subject of great mystique, and it is not extensively detailed in folklore. Pookas are believed to be ageless, immortal beings, and as such, they do not undergo the traditional life stages of birth, growth, and death as humans do. Instead, they exist in a perpetual state of existence, transcending the boundaries of time and mortality.
While Pookas do not age or perish in the same way humans do, they may undergo transformations and changes in their appearance and behavior, depending on their whims and circumstances. Their enigmatic nature ensures that they remain elusive and unpredictable throughout their existence.

9B. Mating Rituals and Reproduction Process

The matter of Pooka reproduction is rarely explored in fairy folklore. Unlike some other fairy species, Pookas do not appear to have well-defined mating rituals or a documented process for bringing new Pookas into existence. Their solitary nature and lack of organized communities may contribute to the absence of information regarding their reproductive practices.
Pookas are known for their shape-shifting abilities, and it is possible that their appearance or form may change to reflect the season or their desires, but this is not directly linked to reproduction. Their capacity to transform, and their enigmatic existence contribute to the enduring sense of mystery that surrounds the Pooka, including its reproductive aspects.
The Pooka's timeless and ageless nature, combined with its lack of documented reproductive practices, only deepens the fascination and enigma that surround this elusive fairy species.

10. Magic Abilities and Powers

10A. A More Detailed Breakdown of Their Magical Abilities

The Pooka is renowned for its magical abilities, which are central to its identity as a fairy creature. While the specifics of its magical powers are often left open to interpretation, certain abilities are commonly associated with the Pooka:

> Shape-Shifting: The most iconic power of the Pooka is its ability to change its form at will. It can transform into various creatures, with its equine form being the most famous. This shape-shifting allows it to bewilder and enchant those who encounter it.
> Illusions: Pookas are adept at creating illusions, often using them to play tricks on humans. They can make themselves appear and disappear at will, manipulate their surroundings, or create fantastical scenes that challenge human perception.

Night Vision: Pookas are creatures of the night, and they possess the ability to see clearly in the darkest of environments. This night vision aids them in their nocturnal activities and adds to their aura of mystery.
Teleportation: Some stories suggest that Pookas have the power to teleport or move instantaneously from one place to another. This ability enhances their reputation for appearing and disappearing mysteriously.

10B. Specific Spells or Powers Unique to This Species

The Pooka's magical abilities are often fluid and adaptable, allowing it to employ them creatively depending on its whims or intentions. While there are no specific spells associated with Pookas, their shape-shifting and illusion-casting abilities are highly distinctive. These powers enable them to interact with the mortal realm in ways that are both enchanting and confounding, further contributing to their reputation as mischievous and enigmatic fairy creatures.
The Pooka's magic, deeply intertwined with its shape-shifting nature, plays a central role in its interactions with humans and the natural world. Its abilities are a testament to the allure and fascination surrounding this fairy species.

11. Interactions with Humans

11A. Historical Encounters with Humans

Throughout history, the Pooka has had a complex and often ambiguous relationship with humans. Accounts of encounters with Pookas vary widely, reflecting the creature's capricious and enigmatic nature. Some interactions with humans are characterized by playful tricks and harmless pranks, while others take a more unsettling turn.
Many stories depict Pookas offering rides to travelers on dark, moonless nights. These rides often lead to wild and disorienting journeys, with the rider eventually deposited back where they began, exhausted and bewildered. Such encounters emphasize the Pooka's reputation as a shape-shifter with a mischievous streak.

11B. Legends of Fairy-Human Friendships or Conflicts

Pookas are known to be elusive and unpredictable, making it challenging to establish long-lasting friendships or conflicts with humans. However, some legends suggest that individuals who approach Pookas with respect and humility may find themselves in the favor of these enigmatic creatures.
Conversely, Pookas are also known for causing mischief and mayhem, which can lead to conflicts and misunderstandings with humans. In these tales, the Pooka's tricks and pranks may result in accidents or chaos, leaving humans to grapple with the consequences.
The dynamic between Pookas and humans is marked by uncertainty and complexity. Their interactions serve as a reminder of the mystical and unpredictable nature of the fairy realm, where encounters with these shape-shifting beings can evoke wonder, fear, or both.

12. Country of Origin

12A. Geographic Regions or Countries

The Pooka is deeply rooted in Irish folklore and is primarily associated with the island of Ireland. Ireland's lush and ancient landscapes, steeped in mythology and mysticism, provide an ideal backdrop for the Pooka's enigmatic presence. Stories of Pookas have been passed down through generations in Ireland, making it an integral part of the country's cultural heritage.

12B. Cultural Significance in Ireland

In Ireland, the Pooka holds a unique place in the pantheon of fairy creatures. It is not only a figure of folklore but also an emblem of the mysterious and unpredictable forces of nature. Its association with the harvest season and Halloween festivities adds to its cultural significance, as these occasions are celebrated with reverence for the Pooka's mischievous and enchanting presence.
The Pooka's enduring presence in Irish culture serves as a reminder of the deep connection between the natural world, mythology, and the supernatural. It has become an iconic symbol of Ireland's rich folklore tradition, captivating both locals and visitors with its mystique and allure.

13. Where to Find Them

13A. Specific Locations, Forests, or Landscapes

The Pooka is known to be a creature of the Irish countryside, and encounters with it typically occur in remote and rural areas. Specific locations where Pookas are often reported include:

- Forests: Dense and ancient woodlands, such as the Black Forest in County Kerry, are believed to be favored habitats for Pookas. These mystical forests provide ample cover for the shape-shifting fairy to conceal itself.
- Moors and Hills: Remote moorlands and rolling hills, common in the Irish landscape, are also associated with Pooka sightings. These open spaces offer a canvas for the Pooka's nocturnal antics.
- Lakes and Rivers: Bodies of water, such as lakes, rivers, and streams, are frequently linked to Pooka encounters, particularly during the darkness of night.

13B. Best Times of Day or Year for Sightings

Pookas are most active during the nighttime, especially during the autumn months when the harvest season is in full swing. The period leading up to Halloween is often considered the prime time for Pooka encounters, as their pranks and tricks are believed to peak during this season. The darkness of night adds to the mystique and uncertainty surrounding their appearances.
It is important to note that Pookas are known to be unpredictable, and sightings may occur at any time of the year. However, for those seeking to increase their chances of encountering a Pooka, venturing into the countryside during the harvest season and around Halloween may provide a greater opportunity to witness their shape-shifting and mischievous activities.

14. How to See Them

14A. Practical Tips and Advice for Encountering Pookas

Encountering a Pooka is a rare and mystical experience, as these shape-shifting fairies are known for their elusive nature. While there are no guarantees of sighting a Pooka, here are some practical tips and advice that may increase the chances:

- Visit Remote Areas: Venture into the Irish countryside, especially in regions known for Pooka sightings, such as ancient forests, moors, and hills. Remote and less-visited locations offer a better chance of encountering this elusive fairy.
- Nighttime Exploration: Pookas are most active at night, so consider nighttime outings, especially around the harvest season and Halloween. Be prepared for the darkness and bring appropriate lighting equipment.
- Quiet Observation: When in potential Pooka habitats, practice quiet observation. Listen for unusual sounds or movements, and be patient. Pookas are known for their cunning and may reveal themselves when least expected.

14B. Rituals, Offerings, or Behaviors That May Attract Them

Traditional beliefs suggest that Pookas may be enticed or appeased through certain rituals or offerings:

- Leave Out Food: Some legends suggest that leaving out offerings of food or milk in natural settings, such as near ancient stones or by the water's edge, may attract the attention of a Pooka. However, this approach should be undertaken with respect and caution.
- Meditation and Reverence: Engage in moments of meditation or quiet reflection while in natural settings. Show reverence for the land and the unseen forces of the natural world. Pookas are believed to be sensitive to such energies.
- Speak Politely: If one encounters a Pooka, it is advised to speak politely and respectfully. Address it as "Mr." or "Mrs. Pooka" and avoid causing offense or alarm.

It is essential to approach any attempts to see or interact with Pookas with reverence for the natural world and an understanding of their unpredictable nature. While encounters with these shape-shifters are rare, they can be profoundly mysterious and enchanting when they occur.

15. Protection and Etiquette

15A. Guidance on How to Respect and Protect Pookas and Their Habitats

Respecting Pookas and their habitats is essential, as they are powerful and enigmatic beings deeply connected to the natural world. Here are some guidelines on how to interact with them respectfully and protect their environments:

- Leave No Trace: When venturing into Pooka habitats, practice "Leave No Trace" principles by minimizing your impact on the environment. Avoid littering, damaging vegetation, or disrupting the natural surroundings.
- Respect Natural Sites: If you come across ancient stones, ruins, or other mystical sites that are associated with Pookas, treat them with reverence. Avoid disturbing or vandalizing these locations.
- Offerings with Respect: If you choose to leave offerings of food or milk to attract Pookas, do so with respect and an understanding of the traditions surrounding such practices. Use natural, biodegradable materials, and ensure that your offerings do not harm the environment.

15B. Superstitions or Taboos Related to Interacting with Them

Interacting with Pookas requires a degree of caution, as they are known to be unpredictable and may have capricious tendencies. Some superstitions and taboos related to Pookas include:

- Avoid Offending Them: It is advisable to avoid causing offense or harm to Pookas through disrespectful behavior, loud noises, or actions that disrupt their surroundings. Pookas may respond unpredictably to perceived disrespect.
- Never Ride a Pooka: In Irish folklore, riding a Pooka, especially in its equine form, is considered a perilous endeavor. Pookas are known to lead riders on wild, dangerous journeys, and such encounters can have dire consequences.
- Be Cautious in Interactions: If you encounter a Pooka, approach with caution and respect. Address it politely and avoid making demands or assuming that you can control it. Maintain an attitude of reverence and humility.

By adhering to these guidelines and being mindful of the potential consequences of interactions with Pookas, individuals can navigate the mystical and unpredictable nature of these fairy beings while showing respect for the natural world they inhabit.

16. Art and Representation

16A. How Pookas Have Been Portrayed in Art, Literature, and Media

Pookas have left a lasting impression on various forms of artistic expression, from literature to visual arts and beyond. Their shape-shifting nature and mysterious allure have made them captivating subjects for artists and writers:

- Literature: Pookas have appeared in numerous works of Irish literature and folklore. Writers like W.B. Yeats, Lady Gregory, and Padraic Colum have featured them in their stories, adding to the enduring fascination with these fairy creatures.
- Visual Arts: Pookas have been depicted in various forms in visual arts, including paintings, illustrations, and sculptures. Their shape-shifting abilities and eerie beauty have made them compelling subjects for artists seeking to capture the mystique of Irish folklore.
- Film and Media: Pookas have made appearances in films and television shows that draw upon Irish folklore and mythology. Their ability to transform, and their enigmatic nature, make them intriguing characters in fantasy and supernatural genres.

16B. Iconic Artists or Authors Who Have Featured Them

Several iconic artists and authors have contributed to the enduring representation of Pookas in art and literature:

- W.B. Yeats: The renowned Irish poet and playwright W.B. Yeats featured Pookas in his works, including "The Celtic Twilight." His writings helped solidify the Pooka's place in Irish folklore and cultural identity.
- Lady Gregory: Lady Augusta Gregory, a prominent figure in the Irish Literary Revival, included Pookas in her collections of folklore and plays. Her contributions to Irish literature preserved and popularized Pooka stories.
- Brian Froud: Brian Froud, a celebrated fantasy artist, is known for his intricate and imaginative depictions of mythical creatures, including Pookas. His illustrations have added depth and detail to the Pooka's visual representation.

Pookas continue to inspire and captivate artists and creators across different mediums, ensuring their enduring presence in the world of art and imagination.

17. Modern Beliefs and Practices

17A. Contemporary Beliefs and Practices Related to Pookas

In modern times, beliefs and practices related to Pookas have evolved, reflecting a continued fascination with these enigmatic fairy beings. Some contemporary beliefs and practices include:

- Cultural Celebrations: Pookas are still celebrated in cultural festivals and events in Ireland, particularly around Halloween. These celebrations often include storytelling, music, and art that pay homage to the Pooka's mischievous and mysterious nature.
- Artistic Interpretations: Pookas remain popular subjects in contemporary art, literature, and media. Artists and writers continue to draw inspiration from their shape-shifting abilities and captivating allure, adding new layers to their portrayal.
- New Age and Spiritual Perspectives: Some individuals within the New Age and spiritual communities view Pookas as mystical and elemental beings connected to the natural world. They may incorporate Pooka imagery or symbolism into their practices and beliefs.

17B. Current Festivals or Gatherings Dedicated to Them

While there may not be specific festivals exclusively dedicated to Pookas, their presence is often woven into broader cultural and folklore celebrations, particularly in Ireland. Halloween, known as Samhain in Celtic traditions, is a time when Pookas are believed to be most active, and their influence is acknowledged in various ways:

- Samhain Festivals: Samhain festivals in Ireland often feature storytelling sessions that include tales of Pookas and other supernatural beings. These events celebrate the connection between the natural and supernatural worlds.
- Arts and Crafts Exhibitions: Artisans and crafters may create Pooka-themed artwork and crafts for sale at festivals and gatherings, allowing attendees to immerse themselves in the world of these captivating fairies.

- Costume and Mask-Making: Participants in Halloween and Samhain celebrations often create costumes and masks inspired by Pookas and other mythical creatures, embracing the playful and mysterious spirit of the season.

Contemporary beliefs and practices related to Pookas continue to evolve, celebrating the enduring mystique and charm of these shape-shifting fairies within the context of modern culture and spirituality.

18. Conservation Efforts

18A. Conservation Initiatives Aimed at Preserving Their Habitats

While Pookas are mythical creatures, there is a growing awareness of the importance of preserving the natural environments that are associated with them in folklore. Conservation efforts focused on protecting these habitats include:

- Preservation of Ancient Sites: Conservation organizations work to protect ancient stone circles, standing stones, and ruins that are often linked to Pookas and other fairy beings. This helps maintain the cultural and historical significance of these sites.
- Woodland Conservation: Efforts are made to preserve and restore ancient woodlands and forests that are believed to be favored habitats for Pookas. These initiatives aim to safeguard biodiversity and maintain the mystical qualities of these landscapes.
- Environmental Education: Some organizations and initiatives incorporate Pooka folklore into environmental education programs. By connecting folklore with conservation, they raise awareness about the importance of preserving natural habitats.

18B. Threats They May Face and Steps to Mitigate Them

While Pookas themselves are not subject to environmental threats, their association with specific natural environments highlights the need to protect these landscapes. Threats to the habitats linked to Pookas include:

- Habitat Destruction: Urbanization, deforestation, and land development pose a threat to the natural landscapes where Pookas are said to reside. Conservation efforts aim to mitigate these threats by advocating for sustainable land use and habitat preservation.
- Cultural Preservation: The loss of cultural traditions and folklore can indirectly impact Pookas by eroding the connection between mythical beings and their natural habitats. Conservationists and cultural advocates work to preserve and promote these stories and traditions.
- Climate Change: Environmental changes, including shifts in weather patterns and rising temperatures, can affect the ecosystems associated with Pookas. Conservation efforts focus on addressing climate change and its impact on these habitats.

By combining environmental conservation with the preservation of cultural traditions and folklore, efforts are made to honor the connections between mythical creatures like Pookas and the natural world, ensuring that these stories and landscapes continue to inspire wonder and appreciation.

19. Additional Folklore

19A. Lesser-Known Stories or Beliefs Associated with Pookas

While the Pooka is well-known in Irish folklore, there are lesser-known stories and beliefs that provide additional layers to their mysterious nature. These lesser-known aspects of Pooka folklore include:

- Pooka as Protectors: In some local traditions, Pookas are seen as protectors of the natural world, guarding ancient sites, stone circles, and sacred groves. They are believed to keep these places safe from harm and desecration.
- Pooka Transformations: Beyond their famous equine forms, Pookas are said to be capable of transforming into a wide range of creatures, from black dogs to birds and even human-like figures. These transformations add to their aura of unpredictability.
- Pooka Riddles: Pookas are known for their love of riddles and puzzles. In some stories, they challenge travelers with riddles, offering rewards to those who solve them correctly and pranks to those who fail.

19B. Variations in Their Portrayal Across Different Cultures

While the Pooka is primarily associated with Irish folklore, variations of similar shape-shifting fairy beings exist in the folklore of other cultures. These variations often share the theme of mysterious, trickster spirits:

- Kelpies in Scottish Folklore: Kelpies are water spirits in Scottish folklore that often appear as shape-shifting horses. They are known for luring unsuspecting travelers into the water.
- Selkies in Nordic Folklore: Selkies are mythical beings in Nordic folklore that can transform from seals into human form. Like Pookas, they are enigmatic and associated with the sea.
- Púca in Welsh Folklore: The Púca is a fairy creature in Welsh folklore with similarities to the Pooka. It can take various forms, often appearing as a horse or other animals, and enjoys playing tricks on humans.

These variations highlight the universality of the theme of shape-shifting, mysterious fairy beings in folklore and the enduring fascination with such creatures across different cultures.

20. Famous Encounters

20A. Historical or Modern Accounts of Famous Individuals Encountering Pookas

While encounters with Pookas are often personal and elusive, there are historical and modern accounts of famous individuals who are said to have crossed paths with these enigmatic fairy beings. Some of these encounters include:

- Lady Wilde: Lady Jane Wilde, an Irish poet and folklorist, documented various fairy legends in Ireland, including stories of Pookas. Her writings helped preserve and popularize Pooka folklore.

- Walter Starkie: Walter Starkie, an Irish writer and scholar, documented his experiences with Pookas in his book "Raggle-Taggle." He recounted a journey during which he encountered these shape-shifting beings in rural Ireland.
- Contemporary Encounters: While less common, contemporary accounts of Pooka encounters occasionally surface, often from individuals exploring remote areas of the Irish countryside. These encounters continue to contribute to the enduring mystique of Pookas.

20B. The Impact of These Encounters on Their Lives or Work

Famous encounters with Pookas have left a lasting impact on the lives and work of individuals involved. These encounters often serve as a source of inspiration, fascination, or curiosity, leading to contributions to folklore and literature:

- Literary Contributions: Many individuals who have encountered Pookas have gone on to write about their experiences, contributing to the rich body of Pooka folklore and adding depth to the cultural understanding of these beings.
- Artistic Expression: Encounters with Pookas have inspired artists and creators to incorporate these mystical beings into their art, literature, and other creative endeavors.
- Cultural Preservation: Famous encounters with Pookas contribute to the preservation of Irish folklore and cultural traditions, ensuring that these stories continue to be shared and celebrated.

The enduring allure of Pookas and the impact of encounters with them on famous individuals underscore the profound and lasting impression that these shape-shifting fairies leave on those who cross their paths.

Trow

1A. Species Introduction

The Trow, often referred to as Trolds or Trows in different regions, are a fascinating and lesser-known species of fairy that originate from the folklore of the Shetland Islands and Orkney Islands in Scotland. These diminutive beings are shrouded in mystery and are known for their reclusive nature and distinctive characteristics that set them apart from other fairies.
Trows are typically described as small, stocky creatures, standing about three to four feet tall. They possess a robust build, with strong limbs and weathered skin, reflecting their affinity for the rugged landscapes of the northern isles. Their faces are often wrinkled, and they have bushy eyebrows that almost meet in the middle, giving them a distinctive appearance.

1B. Unique Characteristics

One of the most distinguishing features of trows is their unique approach to clothing. They are often depicted wearing gray or brown attire made from natural materials like rough wool or animal hides. Trows are known for their preference for earthy, muted colors that help them blend seamlessly into their rocky and heather-covered surroundings.
Trows are creatures of the night, typically shunning the daylight hours. They are often active during the twilight or under the cover of darkness, which has led to their reputation as nocturnal beings. This preference for darkness has also earned them a reputation as mischievous tricksters.
In the realm of folklore, trows are known for their connection to the subterranean world. They are said to dwell in hidden underground chambers or mounds known as "trowie knowes." These dwellings are often hidden from human sight and serve as both their homes and places of protection from the outside world.
Trows are believed to have magical abilities, although these powers can vary depending on the specific legends and stories. Some tales suggest that they have the ability to shape-shift into other forms, while others emphasize their skills in enchantment and illusion, often using these talents to play tricks on unsuspecting humans.
Their interactions with humans are often portrayed as complex, ranging from benevolent to mischievous to malevolent, depending on the circumstances and the individuals involved. Trows are known to be particularly protective of their territories and can become aggressive if they feel threatened.

2. General Appearance

Trows are a unique and distinct species of fairy when it comes to their general appearance. Their physical characteristics reflect their close association with the rugged landscapes of the Shetland and Orkney Islands. Here, we delve into the details of their appearance, including their size, coloration, and notable features.

2A. Size and Build

Trows are typically small in stature, standing around three to four feet tall. This diminutive size allows them to navigate the rocky terrain and concealed underground chambers of their island homes with ease. Despite their small stature, they possess a stocky and robust build, suggesting physical strength and resilience.

2B. Coloration and Features

Trows' physical features are adapted to their natural surroundings. Their skin is often described as weathered and tough, reflecting exposure to the elements. They tend to have wrinkled faces, with bushy eyebrows that almost meet in the middle, giving them a distinctive and somewhat grizzled appearance.
Their attire further emphasizes their connection to the earth and their environment. Trows are known for wearing clothing made from natural materials, such as rough wool or animal hides. The colors of their clothing are typically earthy and muted, like shades of gray and brown, allowing them to blend seamlessly into the rocky and heather-covered landscapes.
In some depictions, trows may wear simple accessories like leather belts or boots, but their overall appearance remains practical and unadorned. Their attire serves both functional and camouflaging purposes, enabling them to move stealthily and avoid detection by humans or other creatures.
Trows' unique physical characteristics, attire, and rugged appearance contribute to their mystique and distinguish them from other fairy species. These traits are not only integral to their folklore but also reflect their adaptation to the harsh and isolated environments of the Shetland and Orkney Islands.

3. Sexes

Trows, the enigmatic fairies of the Shetland and Orkney Islands, exhibit distinct characteristics that are believed to differentiate between the sexes. In this section, we explore the descriptions of male and female trows and any differences in their appearance or behavior.

3A. Male Trows

Male trows are often portrayed as slightly larger and more robust than their female counterparts. They share the same stocky build and weathered features common to trows, but may have a slightly more imposing presence. Male trows are typically depicted as guardians of their underground homes and are responsible for protecting their territories.

In some folklore, male trows are described as having a gruff and sometimes menacing demeanor, especially when defending their dwellings from intruders. They are known to be strong and agile, often using their physical prowess to patrol the rocky landscapes of the islands.

3B. Female Trows

Female trows are generally characterized as being of similar size to male trows, with the same distinctive features. However, there is often a difference in their roles and behavior within trow society. Female trows are frequently associated with nurturing and caring for trow children and maintaining the household.
In some legends, female trows are depicted as kinder and more approachable than their male counterparts, although they can also be protective of their homes and loved ones. They are known for their resourcefulness and adaptability, particularly when it comes to managing their underground dwellings and providing for their families.
It's important to note that while there may be distinctions between male and female trows in folklore, the specifics can vary depending on the source and regional variations. Trow mythology is rich and diverse, and the roles and characteristics of male and female trows may differ in different tales and interpretations. These distinctions, however, add depth and complexity to the overall portrayal of trows in the folklore of the Shetland and Orkney Islands.

4. Lore and Legends

Trows, the mysterious fairies of the Shetland and Orkney Islands, have a rich tapestry of lore and legends associated with them. These stories have been passed down through generations and contribute to the enduring fascination with these elusive beings. In this section, we delve into the cultural and historical references to trows, as well as the captivating myths and folklore that surround them.

4A. Cultural and Historical References

Trows have left an indelible mark on the cultural and historical fabric of the Shetland and Orkney Islands. They are woven into the oral traditions, customs, and beliefs of the people who call these islands home. References to trows can be found in the following aspects of island culture:

- Language: Trows have influenced the local dialects and languages spoken in the islands. Words and phrases related to trows are often used in everyday conversation, reflecting their enduring presence in the linguistic heritage of the region.
- Festivals and Celebrations: Trow-related themes and symbols may be incorporated into local festivals and celebrations. These events serve as opportunities to celebrate and commemorate the relationship between islanders and the fairy realm.
- Art and Crafts: Trows often feature prominently in the art and crafts of the islands. Paintings, sculptures, and other forms of artistic expression may depict trows and their underground dwellings.

4B. Stories, Myths, and Folklore

The tales of trows are both enchanting and varied, reflecting the complex nature of these fairy beings. Throughout the centuries, stories and myths have emerged, offering insights into the lives, habits, and interactions of trows. Some of the common themes in trow folklore include:

- Trowie Knowes: These are the underground dwellings of trows, hidden from human sight. Legends often describe the entrances to these dwellings as hidden in plain sight, appearing as simple mounds or hillocks. Stories about human encounters with trows within these knowes are prevalent.
- Trow Visits: Many stories revolve around trows visiting human households during the night. These nocturnal visits may involve acts of mischief, such as rearranging household items or stealing food. However, trows can also be helpful, performing chores or assisting with tasks.
- Trow Marriages: Some legends tell of trow-human marriages, often initiated by a trow's fascination with a human. These unions may lead to unique challenges and adventures, as humans enter the secretive world of the trows.
- Trow Music and Dance: Trows are known for their love of music and dance. They are said to have their own mesmerizing tunes and dances, which they sometimes share with humans. These enchanting experiences are central to many trow tales.

The lore and legends of trows continue to captivate the imagination, providing a window into the mystical and sometimes mischievous world of these fairy beings. These stories, passed down through generations, contribute to the enduring fascination with trows in the Shetland and Orkney Islands.

5. Habitat and Natural Environment

Trows, the elusive fairies of the Shetland and Orkney Islands, have a deep connection with their natural environment, which plays a crucial role in shaping their identity and way of life. In this section, we explore the natural habitats they prefer, as well as the environmental factors that influence their choice of residence.

5A. Natural Habitats

Trows are intimately linked to the landscapes of the Shetland and Orkney Islands. They are known to inhabit specific environments that reflect their rugged and secluded nature. Common natural habitats associated with trows include:

- Rural Landscapes: Trows are often found in remote and rural areas, away from the hustle and bustle of human settlements. They prefer the tranquility and isolation of the countryside, where they can maintain their hidden existence.
- Rocky Terrain: Trows are particularly fond of rocky landscapes, where they can carve out their underground homes within natural crevices and caves. These rocky formations provide shelter and protection from the elements.
- Heather-Covered Moors: Heather-covered moors and hillsides are also favored habitats for trows. These areas offer ample hiding spots and a source of food, as heather is known to attract small game and insects.

- Coastal Regions: Some trow legends describe their dwellings near the coast, where they have access to the sea's resources, such as fish and seaweed. Coastal environments offer a diverse range of food sources and materials for trows.

5B. Environmental Factors

Several environmental factors influence the choice of residence and lifestyle of trows:

- Isolation: Trows thrive in isolated areas, away from human settlements. The remoteness of their habitats ensures their privacy and minimizes interactions with humans.
- Terrain Features: The rocky terrain of the islands provides natural nooks and crannies for trows to establish their underground homes, known as "trowie knowes." These dwellings are concealed from prying eyes and offer protection from the harsh island weather.
- Seasonal Changes: Trows are known to be active during the twilight hours or at night. Their preference for darkness is influenced by the extended periods of daylight in the northern isles during the summer months.
- Resources: Trows rely on the natural resources of their environments for sustenance. They are known to forage for food, such as small game, berries, and plants, and may also engage in fishing or gathering along the coast.

Understanding the natural habitats and environmental factors that trows are associated with provides valuable insights into their lifestyle and adaptability. These connections to the land and its resources are integral to their folklore and way of life in the Shetland and Orkney Islands.

6. Lifestyle and Social Structure

Trows, the secretive fairies of the Shetland and Orkney Islands, have a unique lifestyle and social structure that distinguishes them from other fairy species. In this section, we delve into the intricate details of their societal organization, daily routines, occupations, and communal activities.

6A. Societal Structure and Hierarchy

Trow society is often depicted as close-knit and organized, with a well-defined hierarchy. While the specifics of their social structure can vary in different legends and tales, some common elements include:

- Clans or Communities: Trows are known to live in clan-like groups or communities, often residing within the same trowie knowe (underground dwelling). These communities are typically led by a prominent figure, such as a chieftain or elder trow.
- Hierarchy of Roles: Within a trow community, various roles and responsibilities are assigned based on age, experience, and abilities. The elder trows often hold positions of authority and leadership, guiding the community's decisions and actions.
- Family Units: Trows are believed to form familial bonds, with family units residing together within their underground homes. These units may include parents, children, and extended family members.

6B. Daily Routines and Occupations

Trow daily life is characterized by a blend of practical activities, magical pursuits, and communal interactions. Some of the key aspects of their daily routines and occupations include:

- Nocturnal Habits: Trows are predominantly active during the night or twilight hours. They use this time for various activities, including foraging for food, tending to their underground dwellings, and engaging in social gatherings.
- Hunting and Gathering: Trows are known to forage for food in their natural habitats, hunting small game, collecting berries and plants, and fishing along the coast. Their resourcefulness allows them to sustain themselves in their secluded environments.
- Craftsmanship: Trows are skilled craftsmen and craftswomen. They are known for their ability to create intricate and beautiful items, often using materials found in their natural surroundings. Trow-made objects may include jewelry, clothing, and household items.
- Music and Dance: Music and dance are integral to trow culture. They are said to have their own mesmerizing tunes and dances, which they enjoy during communal gatherings. These activities serve both as entertainment and as a means of bonding within the trow community.
- Magic and Enchantment: Trows are believed to possess magical abilities, which they use for various purposes, including protection, mischief, and illusion. Their magical talents are woven into their daily lives and interactions with the world.

Understanding the intricacies of trow society, their roles within their communities, and their daily activities provides a deeper appreciation for their way of life in the secluded and mystical landscapes of the Shetland and Orkney Islands.

7. Diet and Food Sources

Trows, the fairy inhabitants of the Shetland and Orkney Islands, have unique dietary preferences and rituals that reflect their deep connection to the natural world. In this section, we explore what trows eat, their foraging habits, and any special dietary customs.

7A. Dietary Preferences

Trows are resourceful beings, known for their ability to adapt to their surroundings and find sustenance in the rugged landscapes of their island homes. Their dietary preferences include:

- Foraging: Trows are skilled foragers, relying on the abundance of the natural world for their food. They are known to gather a variety of edibles, such as berries, nuts, and wild plants, which they find in the moors and forests of the islands.
- Small Game: Trows may hunt small game, such as rabbits, birds, or other creatures that inhabit the islands. Their keen senses and agility make them proficient hunters, ensuring a steady supply of protein in their diet.
- Seafood: Coastal-dwelling trows may have a preference for seafood, including fish, shellfish, and seaweed. The proximity of the sea provides them with an additional source of nourishment.

- Dietary Variety: Trows are known for their adaptability when it comes to food. They are not limited to a single type of cuisine and have a diverse diet based on the seasonal availability of resources in their environment.

7B. Special Dietary Rituals

Trows have certain dietary rituals and customs that are integral to their way of life:

- Food Sharing: Trow communities often engage in communal meals, where food is shared among family members and neighbors. These gatherings strengthen social bonds and reinforce the sense of community among trows.
- Harvest Celebrations: Trows may celebrate the changing seasons with special harvest festivals. These events mark the abundance of food in their environment and may involve music, dance, and rituals to express gratitude to the natural world.
- Offerings: Some trow legends suggest that leaving small offerings of food, such as berries or nuts, in designated locations can be a way to appease or honor these fairy beings. This practice reflects the reverence that trows have for the land and its resources.

Trows' dietary preferences and rituals are closely tied to their connection with the natural world and their ability to thrive in the challenging environments of the Shetland and Orkney Islands. These customs highlight the importance of sustenance and community within trow society.

8. Communication and Language

Communication is a fundamental aspect of trow culture and social interaction within their secluded communities. In this section, we explore how trows communicate with each other and any unique languages or gestures they employ.

8A. Modes of Communication

Trows employ various modes of communication to convey their thoughts, emotions, and intentions:

- Verbal Communication: Trows are believed to have their own language or dialect, which is distinct from human languages. The specifics of the trow language can vary among different legends and stories, but it is often described as melodic and enchanting, with subtle nuances that convey meaning.
- Non-Verbal Communication: Trows are known for their expressive body language and gestures. Their communication may involve facial expressions, hand movements, and postures, all of which play a crucial role in conveying messages and emotions.
- Telepathic Abilities: In some trow legends, it is suggested that these fairies possess telepathic abilities, allowing them to communicate silently with one another. This telepathic connection can transcend language barriers and is a form of secret communication within their communities.

8B. Symbols and Markings

Trows may also use symbols and markings as a means of communication or to convey messages to other trows or even humans:

- Symbols in Nature: Trows are known to create patterns or symbols using rocks, stones, or natural materials in their environments. These markings may serve as territorial boundaries, warnings, or even invitations.
- Carvings and Artifacts: Trows are skilled craftsmen, and they may inscribe symbols or patterns onto objects they create, such as jewelry or tools. These markings may hold cultural or personal significance.
- Graffiti: In legends involving trow-human interactions, trows may leave graffiti or symbols as a form of communication or as a means of marking their presence.

The combination of verbal, non-verbal, and symbolic communication methods enhances the richness of trow culture and enables them to interact effectively within their communities and with the natural world around them. These forms of expression contribute to the air of enchantment that surrounds trow society.

9. Reproduction and Life Cycle

The life cycle and reproduction of trows, the mystical fairies of the Shetland and Orkney Islands, are subjects of enduring fascination and mystery. In this section, we explore the stages of a trows life from birth to death, as well as the rituals and customs associated with their reproduction.

9A. Life Stages

Trows, like many other fairy species, are believed to go through distinct life stages:

- Birth: The birth of a trow is often shrouded in secrecy and mysticism. Legends suggest that trow infants are born in hidden underground chambers, known as trowie knowes, and are cared for by their parents and extended family.
- Childhood: Trow childhood is a time of growth and learning. Young trows are taught the customs, traditions, and skills necessary for survival in their secluded communities. They often live within family units and receive guidance from elder trows.
- Adulthood: As trows reach adulthood, they take on roles within their communities, contributing to the welfare of their clan or family. They may engage in activities such as foraging, crafting, and maintaining their underground dwellings.
- Elderhood: Elder trows hold positions of authority and wisdom within their communities. They provide guidance and leadership, ensuring the well-being and harmony of the trow society. Elder trows often play a central role in decision-making and conflict resolution.

9B. Mating Rituals and Reproduction

Trows are known to engage in mating rituals and reproduce, though the specifics can vary among different legends and stories:

- Courtship: Courtship among trows may involve rituals that emphasize their connection to the natural world. These rituals may include dances, songs, and offerings of natural materials as expressions of affection.
- Family Units: Trow families are believed to form through the union of male and female trows. The birth of trow children is a significant event within trow communities, celebrated with gatherings and feasts.
- Child Naming: The naming of trow children is a special occasion. Names are chosen with care and significance, often reflecting elements of the natural world or trow heritage.
- Immortality: Trows are often portrayed as ageless or having exceptionally long lifespans, leading to the belief that they do not experience aging in the same way humans do. Their immortality is tied to their unique status as fairy beings.

The life cycle and reproductive customs of trows add depth to their folklore, highlighting their connection to the land and their secluded way of life. These aspects of trow culture underscore the enduring fascination with these enigmatic fairy beings.

10. Magic Abilities and Powers

Trows, the reclusive fairies of the Shetland and Orkney Islands, are known for their mystical abilities and powers that set them apart from both humans and other fairy species. In this section, we explore the magical prowess of trows, including a detailed breakdown of their abilities and unique spells or powers.

10A. Magical Abilities

Trows are believed to possess a wide range of magical abilities, some of which include:

- Shape-Shifting: Trows are often associated with the ability to change their forms, allowing them to assume different appearances or sizes. This shape-shifting ability can be used for various purposes, such as concealment or mischief.
- Invisibility: Trows are known to be skilled at rendering themselves invisible to human eyes. This power helps them move stealthily and avoid detection when interacting with humans or traversing the human world.
- Illusion and Glamour: Trows can create powerful illusions and glamours, which can deceive or enchant those who encounter them. These illusions can range from disguising their underground dwellings to creating captivating visual displays.
- Elemental Manipulation: Trows often demonstrate a deep connection to the elements, including earth, water, and wind. They may have the ability to control or influence these elements, using them for practical purposes or as displays of their power.

10B. Unique Spells and Powers

Trows are known for their distinct spells and powers, some of which are unique to their species:

- Weather Control: In certain legends, trows are believed to have control over the weather, particularly the ability to summon storms or mist. This power is often associated with their connection to the natural world.

- Dream Manipulation: Trows may possess the ability to enter and manipulate the dreams of humans or other beings. This power can be used for communication, guidance, or mischief.
- Blessings and Curses: Trows can bestow blessings or curses upon individuals, affecting their lives in profound ways. These blessings and curses are often tied to trow interactions with humans.
- Healing Magic: Trows are sometimes depicted as skilled healers, using their magical abilities to mend injuries or ailments. Their healing powers are believed to be connected to their deep understanding of the natural world's medicinal properties.

The magical abilities and powers of trows are central to their folklore and contribute to their aura of mystery and enchantment. These abilities are woven into the fabric of their culture and interactions with the human world, making trows truly unique among fairy beings.

11. Interactions with Humans

The interactions between trows, the secretive fairies of the Shetland and Orkney Islands, and humans have been a recurring theme in folklore and legends. In this section, we explore the historical encounters between trows and humans, both positive and negative, and delve into stories of fairy-human friendships and conflicts.

11A. Historical Encounters

Trows have left their mark on the human history and culture of the Shetland and Orkney Islands. Historical encounters often include:

- Nighttime Visits: Trows are predominantly nocturnal, and their nighttime activities occasionally bring them into contact with humans. Tales describe trow visits to human households, where they may engage in activities like moving household items or participating in communal gatherings.
- Friendships: Some legends depict harmonious relationships between humans and trows. These friendships are marked by mutual respect and trust, with humans and trows occasionally helping each other in times of need.
- Conflict and Mischief: Trow-human interactions aren't always peaceful. Stories abound of trows playing tricks on humans, leading to various forms of mischief. These tricks can range from harmless pranks to more vexing actions.

11B. Legends of Friendship and Conflict

Trow-human relationships have been a source of inspiration for numerous legends and tales. Some notable themes include:

- Rescue Stories: In these tales, humans find themselves in dire situations, only to be saved by trows who come to their aid. These stories emphasize the protective nature of some trows towards humans they care for.
- Trow Bargains: Trow-human bargains are a common theme, where individuals strike deals or make promises with trows. Fulfilling these bargains often leads to rewards, while breaking them can result in consequences.

- Kidnappings and Abductions: Some legends recount stories of humans being abducted or lured into the trow world. These tales typically involve daring rescue missions or intricate plots to free captives from trow captivity.
- Cautions and Warnings: Folklore often includes cautions about trow encounters. Humans are advised to tread carefully when dealing with these fairy beings, as misunderstandings or perceived slights can lead to conflicts.

The interactions between trows and humans reflect the complexities of their coexistence in the folklore of the Shetland and Orkney Islands. These stories, whether portraying friendship or conflict, showcase the enduring fascination with the enigmatic trow-human relationship.

12. Country of Origin

The origins of trows, the mystical fairies of the Shetland and Orkney Islands, are deeply intertwined with the geography and cultural history of these remote northern isles. In this section, we explore the geographic regions and countries where trows are commonly found, as well as their cultural significance within these areas.

12A. Geographic Regions

Trows are primarily associated with the Shetland and Orkney Islands, which are situated off the northern coast of Scotland. These islands, characterized by their rugged terrain, coastal landscapes, and rich natural beauty, serve as the ancestral homeland of the trows.

- Shetland Islands: Trows have a particularly strong presence in the Shetland Islands, where many legends and stories about these fairy beings originate. The islands' isolation and unique landscapes contribute to the mystique of trows.
- Orkney Islands: Trows are also a part of the folklore and cultural heritage of the Orkney Islands, which share a similar natural environment and cultural history with the Shetlands. The tales of trows in Orkney add depth to the broader narrative of these fairy beings.

12B. Cultural Significance

Trows hold a significant place in the cultural history of the Shetland and Orkney Islands:

- Oral Tradition: Trow folklore has been passed down through generations in these island communities. Stories, legends, and cautionary tales featuring trows have played a vital role in preserving the oral traditions of the islands.
- Cultural Identity: Trows are an integral part of the cultural identity of the Shetland and Orkney Islanders. They serve as symbols of the islands' unique heritage and their enduring connection to the natural world.
- Festivals and Celebrations: Trows are sometimes celebrated in local festivals and gatherings, where islanders come together to honor their cultural heritage and the mystical beings that inhabit their landscapes.

The Shetland and Orkney Islands provide the backdrop for the rich tapestry of trow folklore, and their cultural significance is deeply rooted in the traditions and beliefs of these island communities. Understanding the country of origin sheds light on the unique place trows hold in the hearts and history of the people of these remote northern isles.

13. Where to Find Them

Locating trows, the elusive fairies of the Shetland and Orkney Islands, is a quest that has fascinated many. In this section, we explore specific locations, forests, or landscapes where trows are often sighted, as well as the best times of day or year for potential sightings.

13A. Specific Locations

Trows are believed to inhabit specific places within the Shetland and Orkney Islands. These locations are often associated with their underground dwellings, known as "trowie knowes," which serve as both homes and sanctuaries. Common trow habitats include:

- Rocky Outcrops: Trows are frequently found in rocky and hilly areas, where they can create concealed entrances to their underground dwellings. These natural formations provide them with shelter and protection.
- Heather-Covered Moors: Heather-covered moors and hillsides are favored by trows for their foraging activities. The dense vegetation and natural cover offer opportunities for sightings.
- Coastal Regions: Some trow legends describe their dwellings near the coast, where they have access to the sea's resources. Coastal landscapes provide diverse environments for potential encounters.

13B. Timing and Seasons

Trows are primarily nocturnal beings, and their activities are often associated with specific times of day or year:

- Twilight and Night: Trows are most active during the twilight hours or at night. These periods of darkness provide cover for their movements and interactions within their communities.
- Seasonal Variations: The timing of potential trow sightings can vary with the seasons. Summer nights in the northern isles have extended daylight, while winter offers longer hours of darkness for those seeking trows.
- Special Occasions: In some trow legends, certain festivals or celebrations may provide opportunities for humans to encounter these fairies. These occasions often involve rituals, music, and gatherings that bridge the divide between the human and trow worlds.

Trow sightings are the stuff of legend and mystery, with stories often emphasizing the need for respect, caution, and a deep connection to the natural world to increase the chances of encountering these elusive beings. Understanding where and when trows are likely to be found adds depth to the quest to glimpse these mystical fairies.

14. How to See Them

Glimpsing trows, the elusive fairies of the Shetland and Orkney Islands, is a pursuit that has intrigued adventurers and storytellers alike. In this section, we explore practical tips and advice for increasing the chances of encountering trows, as well as rituals, offerings, or behaviors that may attract these enigmatic beings.

14A. Practical Tips for Sighting Trows

While trows are known for their secrecy, there are practical measures one can take to increase the likelihood of a sighting:

- Explore Remote Locations: Venture into the remote and rural areas of the Shetland and Orkney Islands, where trows are believed to dwell. These areas often provide the best opportunities for encounters.
- Visit Trowie Knowes: Keep an eye out for mounds or hillocks in the landscape, as these may conceal the entrances to trowie knowes, the underground dwellings of trows. Approach such locations with respect and caution.
- Observe During Twilight: Trows are predominantly active during twilight and nighttime hours. If you seek a sighting, consider venturing out during these times when they are more likely to be active.
- Practice Discretion: Trows are known to be shy and secretive. Move quietly and respectfully in their environments to avoid startling them.

14B. Rituals and Offerings

In trow folklore, certain rituals, offerings, or behaviors are believed to attract or appease these fairy beings:

- Leave Offerings: Some legends suggest that leaving small offerings of food or natural materials, such as berries or nuts, near trowie knowes or in specific locations may invite trows to interact with humans.
- Respect Boundaries: Trows are known to be protective of their territories. Avoid intruding into their dwellings or engaging in activities that may be perceived as invasive.
- Participate in Festivals: Attend local festivals or celebrations that have trow-related themes, as these events may provide opportunities for interactions with trows in a celebratory and communal setting.

- Maintain a Connection to Nature: Trows have a deep connection to the natural world. Engage in activities that foster a connection to the land and its rhythms, as this may align you more closely with the trow way of life.

Trow sightings are rare and often shrouded in mystery, but those who approach the quest with respect, reverence for nature, and an understanding of trow folklore may find themselves on a fascinating and enchanting journey to glimpse these mystical fairies.

15. Protection and Etiquette

Respecting and protecting the world of trows, the secretive fairies of the Shetland and Orkney Islands, is essential for anyone seeking to interact with them. In this section, we explore guidance on how to respect and safeguard trows and their habitats, as well as superstitions or taboos related to interacting with them.

15A. Respecting Trows and Their Homes

- Maintain Distance: Trows value their privacy and seclusion. It's important to maintain a respectful distance from their dwellings, known as trowie knowes, and avoid entering them without permission.
- Leave No Trace: When exploring trow habitats, adhere to the principle of "leave no trace." Avoid littering, disturbing natural features, or disrupting the environment in any way.
- Do Not Take: Resist the temptation to take souvenirs or artifacts from trow locations. Removing items from these areas can be seen as disrespectful and may lead to misfortune.

15B. Superstitions and Taboos

- Whistling at Night: In some trow legends, it is believed that whistling at night can attract trows, as they are drawn to certain sounds. Be mindful of your surroundings and refrain from making loud or startling noises during nocturnal visits to trow habitats.
- Offerings and Respect: As mentioned in the previous section, leaving offerings of food or natural materials near trowie knowes is a common practice. However, these offerings should be left with respect and genuine intent, rather than as a means to manipulate or exploit trows.
- Respect Trow Boundaries: Trows are known to be territorial, and crossing their boundaries without permission can lead to conflicts or misunderstandings. It's essential to be aware of the boundaries and entrances to trow dwellings and avoid trespassing.

Respecting trow customs, protecting their habitats, and adhering to local superstitions and taboos are essential for fostering positive interactions with these fairy beings. Approaching trows with reverence and care is not only a sign of respect, but also a way to preserve the enchantment of their world.

16. Art and Representation

Trows, the mysterious fairies of the Shetland and Orkney Islands, have been subjects of artistic representation and inspiration in various forms of media. In this section, we explore how this fairy species has been portrayed in art, literature, and media, as well as iconic artists or authors who have featured them.

16A. Artistic Representations

- Visual Arts: Trows have been depicted in paintings, illustrations, and sculptures that capture their unique appearance, magical abilities, and interactions with the natural world. Artists often draw upon trow folklore to create enchanting and evocative artworks.
- Sculptures and Statues: Some sculptures and statues in the Shetland and Orkney Islands incorporate trow imagery as a tribute to the islands' folklore and cultural heritage. These installations celebrate the enduring presence of trows in the local identity.

16B. Literary Works and Media

- Folklore and Legends: Trow folklore has been a wellspring of inspiration for local storytellers and authors. These tales, passed down through generations, continue to be shared in written form, preserving the rich oral tradition of trow stories.
- Literature: Trows have made appearances in both regional and international literature. Authors have woven trow characters and themes into novels, short stories, and poetry, often exploring the intersections between the human and trow worlds.
- Film and Television: Trows have occasionally been featured in film and television productions, with stories that draw upon their mystical abilities and interactions with humans. These portrayals contribute to the enduring fascination with trows beyond the written word.

16C. Iconic Artists and Authors

- George Mackay Brown: The renowned Orkney writer George Mackay Brown incorporated trow folklore and themes into his poetry and prose. His works, deeply rooted in the landscapes and traditions of Orkney, have contributed to the enduring allure of trows.
- Walter Traill Dennison: Walter Traill Dennison, a Shetland poet and folklorist, collected and preserved trow folklore in his writings. His contributions have helped ensure that trow stories remain an integral part of Shetland's cultural heritage.
- Contemporary Artists: Contemporary artists from the Shetland and Orkney Islands continue to draw upon trow mythology in their creative endeavors. Their works reflect the ongoing fascination with these enigmatic fairy beings.

The artistic representation of trows serves as a means of keeping their folklore alive and celebrating their enduring presence in the cultural and creative landscapes of the Shetland and

Orkney Islands. These artistic interpretations offer glimpses into the world of trows and contribute to their enduring mystique.

17. Modern Beliefs and Practices

While trow folklore is deeply rooted in the past, modern beliefs and practices related to these fairy beings continue to evolve. In this section, we explore contemporary beliefs and practices connected to trows, as well as any current festivals or gatherings dedicated to them.

17A. Contemporary Beliefs

- Continued Folklore: Trow folklore remains a cherished part of the cultural heritage of the Shetland and Orkney Islands. Islanders continue to share stories, legends, and experiences related to trows, passing them down to younger generations.
- Environmental Conservation: Modern beliefs often emphasize the importance of protecting the natural habitats associated with trows. Conservation efforts aim to safeguard the landscapes that trows are believed to inhabit.

17B. Festivals and Gatherings

- Trowie Nights: Some local festivals or gatherings may include elements related to trows. "Trowie Nights" or similar events celebrate trow folklore, featuring storytelling, music, and performances that pay homage to these fairy beings.
- Cultural Celebrations: Regional cultural festivals in the Shetland and Orkney Islands occasionally incorporate trow-related themes as a way of honoring the islands' rich traditions and folklore.

While modern beliefs and practices related to trows may have evolved, the enduring fascination with these fairy beings and their significance in the cultural identity of the Shetland and Orkney Islanders continue to be celebrated and cherished. Trows remain a living part of the islands' cultural fabric.

18. Conservation Efforts

Conservation efforts aimed at preserving the habitats of trows, the enigmatic fairies of the Shetland and Orkney Islands, are crucial for maintaining the unique ecosystems associated with these fairy beings. In this section, we discuss conservation initiatives, potential threats faced by trow habitats, and steps to mitigate these threats.

18A. Conservation Initiatives

- Habitat Preservation: Conservationists and local authorities work together to protect the natural habitats, including rocky outcrops, moors, and coastal areas, where trows are believed to reside. This includes designating certain areas as protected zones.

- Educational Programs: Conservation organizations often run educational programs to raise awareness about trows and their habitats. These programs may include guided tours, lectures, and interactive exhibits, fostering a sense of stewardship among the public.
- Monitoring and Research: Ongoing research efforts focus on studying the flora and fauna of trow habitats. Understanding these ecosystems better allows for informed conservation decisions and helps identify potential threats.

18B. Threats and Mitigation

- Human Development: Urbanization and land development pose significant threats to trow habitats. Conservation efforts seek to strike a balance between development and habitat preservation, emphasizing responsible planning and construction practices.
- Environmental Pollution: Pollution from various sources, such as agriculture and industry, can negatively impact the ecosystems inhabited by trows. Conservationists work to reduce pollution and maintain water and air quality in these areas.
- Invasive Species: The introduction of invasive plant or animal species can disrupt the delicate balance of trow habitats. Conservation initiatives include measures to control and mitigate the impact of invasive species.
- Climate Change: Climate change can alter the landscapes and habitats that trows depend on. Conservation efforts aim to address the effects of climate change and adapt to the shifting conditions in these regions.

The conservation of trow habitats not only safeguards the unique ecosystems associated with these fairy beings but also contributes to the broader goal of preserving the natural beauty and biodiversity of the Shetland and Orkney Islands. Balancing the protection of trow habitats with the needs of human communities is a complex endeavor, but it is essential for the long-term well-being of these mystical landscapes.

19. Additional Folklore

Beyond the well-known tales and legends, trows, the secretive fairies of the Shetland and Orkney Islands, have inspired lesser-known stories and beliefs across different cultures. In this section, we delve into these lesser-known aspects of trow folklore and explore variations in their portrayal.

19A. Lesser-Known Stories and Beliefs

- International Variations: While trow folklore is most closely associated with the Shetland and Orkney Islands, similar fairy beings with shared characteristics are found in other parts of the world. These international counterparts often share common themes of seclusion and connection to the land.
- Trow Encounters: In some lesser-known stories, travelers and adventurers who venture into the trow domains may encounter these fairy beings unexpectedly. These encounters can be both enchanting and perplexing.

- Trow Myths in Literature: Trow-inspired stories and themes have made their way into works of fiction and literature beyond the islands. Writers and authors from diverse backgrounds have drawn upon trow mythology to craft their narratives.

19B. Variations in Portrayal

- Physical Attributes: While trows are generally depicted as small in stature with distinctive appearances, variations in their physical attributes exist in different stories. These variations may reflect regional differences in trow folklore.
- Character Traits: The character traits and behaviors attributed to trows can vary widely in folklore. Some stories portray them as mischievous tricksters, while others depict them as wise and protective beings.
- Trow Societies: The societal structures and hierarchies of trows can differ in various tales. Some legends emphasize tight-knit family units, while others suggest complex communities with leaders and elders.
- Cultural Influences: The portrayal of trows may be influenced by the cultural contexts in which they are depicted. Trow folklore may intersect with other local legends and beliefs, creating unique hybrid stories.

Exploring lesser-known stories, beliefs, and variations in the portrayal of trows adds depth to the rich tapestry of their folklore. These diverse narratives reflect the enduring fascination with these enigmatic fairy beings across different cultures and regions.

20. Famous Encounters

Throughout history, there have been accounts of famous individuals encountering trows, the secretive fairies of the Shetland and Orkney Islands. In this section, we explore historical or modern accounts of these encounters and the impact of such interactions on the lives or work of those involved.

20A. Historical Accounts

- Walter Traill Dennison: Walter Traill Dennison, a Shetland poet and folklorist, is known for his contributions to the preservation of trow folklore. His encounters with trows, as recounted in his writings, played a significant role in his dedication to collecting and documenting local legends.
- George Mackay Brown: The renowned Orkney writer George Mackay Brown drew inspiration from trow encounters in his poetry and prose. These experiences influenced his creative work and contributed to the enduring presence of trows in Orkney literature.

20B. Modern Accounts

- Contemporary Witnesses: There have been sporadic reports of trow sightings in the Shetland and Orkney Islands by contemporary witnesses. These encounters often generate local interest and discussion, adding to the ongoing fascination with these fairy beings.

- Artistic Inspirations: Modern artists, writers, and filmmakers continue to draw upon trow folklore and the legacy of famous encounters. Trows serve as a wellspring of inspiration for creative works that explore the mystical and mysterious.
- Cultural Celebrations: Some contemporary festivals or gatherings in the Shetland and Orkney Islands incorporate trow-related themes and reenactments of famous encounters. These events celebrate the enduring legacy of trow folklore in the islands' cultural identity.

The accounts of famous encounters with trows serve as a testament to the enduring allure of these fairy beings and their impact on the cultural, artistic, and literary heritage of the Shetland and Orkney Islands. These encounters continue to captivate the imagination and inspire new generations to explore the enchanting world of trows.

Brownie

1. Species Introduction

1A. Brief Overview of Brownies

Brownies are diminutive and reclusive fairy beings known for their helpful nature and strong ties to human households. Unlike some other fairy species, brownies are primarily benevolent and are often associated with domestic chores and protection of their chosen households. These small, elf-like creatures have a distinct appearance and personality that sets them apart from other fairies.

Brownies are typically about 12 to 18 inches in height, with earthy-toned skin that ranges from tan to deep brown. Their clothing consists of simple, rustic garments made from leaves, moss, and other natural materials. They are often seen wearing pointed caps and carrying tiny tools or utensils, which they use for their chores.

1B. Unique Characteristics of Brownies

Brownies are renowned for their unwavering commitment to aiding the families they adopt as their own. They are highly industrious and carry out domestic tasks in the dead of night, working tirelessly to ensure the household is in order by the time the sun rises. Some common chores they undertake include cleaning, mending, and even tending to the family's livestock.
One of the most unique features of brownies is their shy and elusive nature. They are typically invisible, only revealing themselves to those they trust or to children, who are more sensitive to their presence. Brownies are known for their strong aversion to being seen, and any attempt to catch sight of them might lead to their departure from the household.
Despite their desire for anonymity, brownies can be fiercely loyal to the families they serve. They expect no payment or gratitude for their work, but they do appreciate small offerings of food or milk left out for them. If a brownie feels unappreciated or slighted, they might choose to abandon their household, leaving it in disarray.

2. General Appearance

2A. Detailed Physical Description of Brownies

Brownies, though small in stature, possess distinctive physical characteristics that set them apart from other fairy species. These diminutive beings stand at an average height of 12 to 18 inches, making them easily distinguishable in a world populated by fairies of various sizes and shapes. Their most noticeable feature is their earthy-toned skin, which ranges from light tan to deep brown. This skin tone allows them to blend seamlessly with the natural world, making them difficult to spot by casual observers. Brownies have a lithe and wiry build, which aids in their agility and ability to navigate the intricate terrain of human households.
Their eyes, despite their diminutive size, are particularly expressive. Brownies' eyes often shimmer with a mischievous or playful glint when they are at ease, but they can turn stern and watchful if they sense a threat to their adopted household. Their hair is typically a shade darker than their skin, and it tends to be unruly, adding to their impish appearance.

2B. Clothing and Accessories of Brownies

Brownies are known for their simple yet practical attire, reflecting their nature as diligent and hardworking domestic fairies. They fashion their garments from natural materials readily available in the environment, such as leaves, moss, and tiny scraps of fabric they might find in the household.
The most iconic piece of clothing worn by brownies is their pointed cap, often resembling a miniature version of a wizard's hat. These caps serve both decorative and practical purposes, providing protection from the elements and an additional layer of camouflage when they need to blend into their surroundings.
Brownies are often seen carrying tiny tools and utensils on their belts or in pouches they craft from leaves. These miniature tools help them perform their household chores efficiently. They are known to use thimble-sized buckets for carrying water and sewing needles made from twigs to mend torn clothing.

3. Sexes

3A. Description of Male and Female Brownies

Brownies do not conform to traditional human notions of gender, and distinguishing between male and female brownies is a challenging task. Unlike some other fairy species, brownies are generally considered to be asexual beings with no distinct male or female counterparts. Their diminutive size, similar physical characteristics, and attire make it nearly impossible to differentiate them based on appearance alone.

3B. Behavior and Roles within the Household

Instead of being defined by gender, brownies are characterized by their roles and behavior within the households they adopt. They are known for their strong work ethic and dedication to domestic tasks, and this devotion transcends gender-based distinctions. Regardless of whether they are perceived as male or female, brownies fulfill the same responsibilities within their adopted homes. Brownies are often observed carrying out chores such as sweeping, dusting, repairing household items, and even assisting with cooking and caring for animals. Their dedication to these tasks is

unwavering, and they take great pride in their ability to maintain a well-kept and harmonious household environment.
Their interactions with humans are guided by their sense of duty rather than gender-based expectations. They avoid direct contact with humans and prefer to work discreetly in the shadows, ensuring that their presence remains unnoticed. This anonymity allows them to carry out their tasks without disruption while safeguarding their own privacy.

4. Lore and Legends

4A. Cultural and Historical References

Brownies have left an indelible mark on folklore and legends across various cultures. These benevolent household fairies have been celebrated for their helpful nature, and their presence has been woven into the tapestry of human storytelling for centuries. Different cultures have unique names and interpretations for brownies, but the essence of their character remains consistent.
In Scottish folklore, brownies are known as "bogles" or "boggarts." They are seen as guardian spirits of households, diligently performing chores in exchange for small gifts of food. In other parts of Europe, they are referred to as "hobs" or "domovoi," and they play similar roles as protectors and maintainers of domestic harmony.

4B. Stories, Myths, and Folklore Associated with Brownies

Countless stories and myths celebrate the endearing and hardworking nature of brownies. These tales often emphasize the importance of showing gratitude and respect to these fairy housekeepers. One famous story tells of a farmer who left out a special coat for the brownie, who had been helping with farm chores. In return, the brownie presented the farmer with a magical cloak that granted wishes.
Another well-known legend speaks of a family that moved to a new home and accidentally brought their loyal brownie with them. When they discovered the brownie, they realized they had unknowingly transported their helpful guardian spirit, leading to the brownie's departure. This story emphasizes the importance of maintaining goodwill and respect between brownies and humans.
The rich tapestry of brownie folklore includes stories of their interactions with humans, both heartwarming and cautionary. They are often portrayed as gentle beings who respond positively to kindness and generosity, reinforcing the belief that treating brownies with respect can lead to a harmonious coexistence.

5. Habitat and Natural Environment

5A. Natural Habitats Preferred by Brownies

Brownies, despite their preference for human households, have distinct natural habitats where they are believed to originate and occasionally retreat to. These habitats are often found in close proximity to human settlements and typically include:

- Forests: Brownies are commonly associated with wooded areas, especially those that border human villages or farms. Within these forests, they seek shelter in gnarled tree roots, small caves, or hidden burrows.
- Meadows and Fields: Brownies also have an affinity for open spaces like meadows and fields. They may create hidden underground burrows or construct tiny shelters from natural materials to remain close to the crops and livestock they oversee.
- Streams and Rivers: Some tales suggest that brownies have been known to dwell near water sources. They are said to enjoy the soothing sounds of flowing water and may build tiny homes within the roots of riverside trees.

5B. Environmental Factors Affecting Residence

The choice of residence for brownies is influenced by several environmental factors that align with their secretive and elusive nature:

- Proximity to Humans: Brownies tend to inhabit areas where they can easily access human households. This proximity allows them to fulfill their roles as domestic caretakers and guardians.
- Hidden Nooks and Crannies: Brownies seek out secluded and concealed spaces within their chosen habitats, ensuring they remain hidden from prying eyes. They are experts at blending into their surroundings, making them virtually invisible to casual observers.
- Natural Materials: Brownies craft their shelters from natural materials like leaves, moss, and twigs. These materials help them maintain their camouflage and integrate seamlessly into their chosen environments.

6. Lifestyle and Social Structure

6A. Insights into Brownie Societal Structure and Hierarchy

Brownies, while primarily solitary beings, do exhibit a certain level of societal structure and hierarchy within their small communities. Brownie communities are typically limited to a single household or a closely-knit group of neighboring households. They work together in a coordinated manner to fulfill their domestic duties.
Within these communities, there may be an informal leader or elder brownie who oversees the tasks and ensures that everyone is contributing effectively. This elder brownie is often the most experienced and knowledgeable member of the group. While there is no formal hierarchy, the elder's wisdom and guidance are respected by others.

6B. Daily Routines, Occupations, and Communal Activities

Brownies are renowned for their diligent work ethic and their commitment to maintaining the households they serve. Their daily routines revolve around various domestic tasks, including:

- Cleaning: Brownies are meticulous cleaners and take it upon themselves to ensure that the home is spotless by the time the family awakens. They scrub, sweep, and dust with incredible precision.
- Repairing: Brownies are skilled craftsmen, adept at fixing broken items and mending torn clothing. They use their miniature tools to complete these tasks efficiently.
- Animal Care: Some brownies take on the responsibility of caring for the family's livestock. They ensure that animals are well-fed and comfortable.
- Cooking Assistance: In households where brownies are particularly attached, they may assist with meal preparation by gathering ingredients or stirring pots.

Despite their dedication to their chores, brownies remain reclusive during daylight hours, avoiding direct contact with humans. They conduct their work silently and discreetly, often working through the night to complete their tasks before dawn.
Brownie communities may also engage in occasional communal activities, such as celebrating important milestones or seasonal festivals. These gatherings provide an opportunity for brownies to socialize and strengthen their bonds.

7. Diet and Food Sources

7A. Brownies' Dietary Habits

Brownies, though primarily known for their dedication to domestic chores, do have dietary needs that are integral to their well-being. While their diet is modest, it is important to understand what sustains these diligent fairy beings.
Brownies are primarily herbivores, and their diet consists of plant-based foods. They have a particular fondness for foods found within the households they inhabit. Some common dietary items include:

- Grains: Brownies may consume small quantities of grains like oats, barley, or wheat. They often gather these grains from the family's pantry.
- Fruits and Vegetables: Brownies are known to enjoy fresh fruits and vegetables, which they might pick from gardens or orchards. Apples, berries, and leafy greens are among their favorites.
- Dairy Products: Some brownies have been known to partake in dairy products such as milk, cheese, and butter, which they collect from the family's dairy stores.

7B. Special Dietary Preferences and Rituals

Brownies are not extravagant in their dietary preferences and are generally content with modest offerings. However, there are some special dietary rituals and practices associated with these domestic fairies:

- Food Offerings: To express gratitude for the brownies' assistance and to ensure their continued presence, some households leave out small offerings of food or drink. These

offerings are often placed in a quiet, out-of-the-way corner of the home where the brownies can access them discreetly.
- Milk and Honey: Brownies are particularly fond of milk and honey. These offerings are believed to be especially pleasing to them, and they are often left out as tokens of appreciation.
- Harvest Celebrations: In some traditions, families celebrate harvest festivals and leave out a portion of the season's first harvest for the brownies. This is a gesture of goodwill and gratitude for their assistance in tending to the crops.

Understanding the dietary preferences and rituals of brownies is essential not only for fostering a harmonious relationship with these fairy beings, but also for appreciating the role they play in maintaining the household's well-being. In the upcoming chapters, we will explore their modes of communication, their magical abilities, and their interactions with humans in more detail.

8. Communication and Language

8A. How Brownies Communicate with Each Other

Brownies have developed a unique and intricate system of communication that allows them to work together harmoniously within their communities. This system relies on non-verbal cues, gestures, and even telepathic communication, making it largely imperceptible to humans.
- Telepathic Bonds: Brownies are believed to share a telepathic connection with one another. This mental link enables them to coordinate their activities and convey messages silently and instantly. It's through this telepathic bond that they orchestrate their nightly chores without spoken words.
- Gestures: Brownies often use subtle hand gestures and movements to convey information. For instance, they may signal to one another to coordinate their cleaning efforts or indicate the need for assistance with a particular task.

8B. Brownies' Interaction with Humans

While brownies communicate seamlessly among themselves, they are extremely cautious when it comes to interacting with humans. Their primary goal is to remain unnoticed, and they avoid direct communication or contact with the human occupants of the household. Instead, they rely on their diligent work to convey their presence and appreciation.
Brownies may occasionally leave small tokens or signs of their gratitude, such as neatly repaired items or exceptionally clean spaces. These acts of service serve as a form of communication, indicating their continued willingness to assist and maintain the household. However, they do not engage in verbal or written communication with humans, as maintaining their anonymity is paramount to their existence.

9. Reproduction and Life Cycle

9A. The Fairy's Life Stages from Birth to Death

Brownies have a unique life cycle that sets them apart from many other fairy species. They are believed to come into existence through a process akin to spontaneous generation rather than traditional reproduction.

- Emergence: Brownies are said to spontaneously emerge from natural elements and earthy materials, often taking form in a secluded and magical place within their chosen habitat. This emergence is not tied to mating or childbirth but rather seems to be a manifestation of the fairy's intrinsic connection to the environment.
- Immortality: Brownies are considered immortal beings in many traditions. They do not age in the same way humans do, and they can potentially live for centuries, carrying out their duties within the households they adopt.
- Transition: When a brownie's time in a particular household or community comes to an end, they are believed to transition to a different form or state rather than experiencing death. Some tales suggest that they return to the natural world, merging with the elements from which they originated.

9B. Mating Rituals and Reproduction Process

Brownies, as mentioned earlier, are not typically associated with traditional reproduction or mating rituals. Their emergence is independent of such processes, and they do not engage in romantic or sexual relationships.
Instead, brownies focus their energies on their domestic duties and maintaining their close-knit communities. Their immortal nature and unique method of coming into existence allow them to concentrate on their roles as household caretakers without the distractions of procreation.
This absence of reproductive rituals and the absence of gender distinctions in brownie society highlight their exceptional focus on their responsibilities and the unique nature of their existence as domestic fairies.

10. Magic Abilities and Powers

10A. Detailed Breakdown of Brownies' Magical Abilities

Brownies possess a range of magical abilities that make them unique among fairy species. While their powers are not as overtly dramatic as those of some other fairies, they are deeply connected to their roles as domestic caretakers and guardians. Some of their notable magical abilities include:

- Invisibility: Brownies are masters of invisibility, allowing them to move about undetected by humans. This magical cloak of invisibility is crucial to their work, as it enables them to perform their chores discreetly during the night.
- Teleportation: Brownies are known for their ability to quickly and silently move from one part of the household to another, making it appear as if they are in multiple places at once. This power allows them to efficiently complete their tasks.
- Telekinesis: Brownies can manipulate small objects using their telekinetic abilities. They can mend torn clothing, arrange items neatly, and perform intricate tasks with precision.

- Nature Affinity: Brownies have a deep connection with the natural world and can influence the growth and well-being of plants and animals in their care. They are often credited with ensuring healthy crops and contented livestock.

10B. Specific Spells or Powers Unique to Brownies

While brownies share some magical abilities with other fairies, they have certain powers unique to their role as household caretakers:

- Household Blessings: Brownies are believed to bring blessings and good fortune to the households they serve. Their presence is thought to protect the family from misfortune and negative energy.
- Ward against Harm: Brownies are known to ward off harmful spirits or entities that might seek to harm the household. Their protective presence ensures the safety and well-being of the family.
- Healing Touch: In some traditions, brownies are thought to possess healing powers. They can provide comfort and relief to those who are unwell or injured, often working discreetly to aid the family's health.

Understanding these magical abilities and powers sheds light on the significance of brownies within the households they adopt. These powers are a testament to their dedication to maintaining a harmonious and well-protected environment for their human companions.

11. Interactions with Humans

11A. Historical Encounters with Humans

Brownies have a long and intricate history of interactions with humans, characterized by their dedication to maintaining households and their desire to remain hidden. Throughout history, humans have reported various encounters and experiences with brownies, both positive and negative.

Positive Interactions:

- Many tales celebrate the positive relationships between brownies and the families they serve. Brownies are known to be diligent and dedicated domestic caretakers, often ensuring that homes are well-maintained and harmonious.
- Families that recognize the presence of brownies in their homes often leave out small offerings of food or gifts as tokens of appreciation. These gestures of goodwill strengthen the bond between humans and brownies.

Negative Interactions:

- Brownies are notoriously shy and averse to being seen by humans. If a human attempts to catch sight of them or directly engage with them, the brownies may choose to depart from the household, leaving their duties unfulfilled.

- In some cases, brownies have been known to play pranks or engage in mischief when they feel unappreciated or disrespected. These tricks can range from mild inconveniences to more disruptive behavior.

11B. Legends of Brownie-Human Friendships and Conflicts

Legends and stories that depict brownie-human interactions are rich and varied. These tales often highlight the importance of treating brownies with respect and gratitude.
Friendships:

- Some legends tell of enduring friendships between brownies and humans. These friendships are built on trust, kindness, and mutual respect. In these stories, brownies may offer guidance and protection to their human friends.

Conflicts:

- Conflicts between brownies and humans typically arise when the brownies' work goes unacknowledged or when they feel slighted. Legends warn against mistreating or disrespecting these elusive beings, as it can lead to disturbances in the household.

Understanding the delicate balance of interactions between brownies and humans is crucial for those who seek to coexist peacefully with these helpful domestic fairies. In the following chapters, we will explore more practical aspects of encountering brownies, their country of origin, and where to find them in various landscapes.

12. Country of Origin

12A. Geographic Regions of Common Brownie Presence

Brownies are often associated with specific geographic regions where they are commonly believed to reside. While they are known to adapt to various habitats, their presence is most frequently reported in the following areas:

- Scotland: Brownies are deeply woven into Scottish folklore and are often referred to as "bogles" or "boggarts." Scottish brownies are celebrated as household protectors and helpful spirits.
- England: In English folklore, brownies are known for their diligent household chores. They are called "hobs" or "hobgoblins" in some regions, and their presence is cherished.
- Scandinavia: In Scandinavian countries, brownies are similar to the "tomte" or "nisse," known for assisting with farm work and protecting the homestead.
- Ireland: In Irish folklore, brownies are called "clurichauns" and are known for their affinity for drink and mischief. While their behavior differs from the classic brownie, they are still associated with the household.

12B. Cultural Significance in These Areas

In the regions where brownies are commonly found, they hold significant cultural and folkloric importance. They are celebrated as helpful and benevolent beings who contribute to the

well-being of households. Their presence is often intertwined with local customs and traditions, including the leaving of offerings and celebrating festivals in their honor.
Understanding the cultural significance of brownies in these regions provides valuable insight into the respect and reverence with which they are treated. It also sheds light on the enduring folklore and stories that continue to celebrate their roles as domestic caretakers and protectors of human homes.

13. Where to Find Them

13A. Specific Locations for Brownie Sightings

While brownies are known for their ability to adapt to various environments, there are specific locations where they are often sighted or believed to be more prevalent:

- Homes and Farms: Brownies are most commonly associated with human households, where they tirelessly perform their domestic duties. Families that leave offerings or express gratitude are more likely to experience the presence of brownies.
- Wooded Areas: Brownies are often linked to forested regions, where they may establish hidden homes among the trees or in small, concealed burrows. Woodlands near human settlements are prime locations for brownie activity.
- Fields and Gardens: Brownies may also inhabit meadows, fields, and gardens, especially those in proximity to homes. They have been known to aid in the care of crops and garden plants.
- Near Water Sources: Some legends suggest that brownies are drawn to riversides and streams, where they may take up residence among the roots of trees. The soothing sound of flowing water seems to appeal to them.

13B. Best Times for Sightings

Brownies are most active during the nighttime, typically beginning their chores after dusk and finishing before dawn. This nocturnal behavior aligns with their desire to remain unseen by humans. Therefore, the best times for potential sightings are late evening and early morning.
It's important to note that brownies are exceptionally shy and prefer to remain invisible. Any attempt to directly observe them may result in their departure from the area. They are more likely to reveal themselves to children, who are often more receptive to their presence.

14. How to See Them

14A. Practical Tips for Encountering Brownies

Seeing a brownie is a rare and elusive experience, as they are masters of remaining hidden from human sight. However, for those who wish to increase their chances of encountering these enigmatic beings, there are several practical tips to consider:

- Create an Inviting Environment: Make your home or garden a welcoming place for brownies by keeping it clean, well-maintained, and harmonious. This may attract their attention and encourage them to visit.
- Leave Offerings: Brownies appreciate small offerings of food, milk, or other tokens of gratitude. Place these offerings in a quiet, out-of-the-way spot within your home or garden, where they can access them discreetly.
- Respect Their Privacy: Brownies are extremely shy and will avoid contact with humans. To see them, it's essential to be patient, respectful, and unintrusive. Avoid trying to capture or photograph them, as this will likely drive them away.
- Observe at Night: Brownies are nocturnal beings, and the best time to observe them is during the late evening or early morning hours. Stay quiet and still while watching for any signs of their presence.

14B. Rituals, Offerings, and Behaviors

There are various rituals, offerings, and behaviors associated with trying to see brownies:

- Offer Milk and Honey: Milk and honey are believed to be particularly pleasing to brownies. Leaving out a small dish of these offerings may attract their attention.
- Express Gratitude: Vocalize your appreciation for any assistance you believe brownies have provided. A simple "thank you" can go a long way in fostering a positive relationship.
- Avoid Disruption: Brownies are most likely to reveal themselves when they feel their presence is respected and unthreatened. Avoid any disruptive behavior that might startle or upset them.
- Involve Children: Brownies are sometimes more inclined to reveal themselves to children who are sensitive to their presence. Encourage children to maintain a respectful and open-minded attitude.

While there are no guarantees when it comes to seeing brownies, following these tips and rituals can create a more inviting atmosphere and increase the likelihood of an encounter with these elusive domestic fairies. In the chapters ahead, we will explore the importance of protecting brownies and adhering to etiquette when interacting with them. We will also delve into their representation in art and literature.

15. Protection and Etiquette

15A. Guidance on Respecting and Protecting Brownies

Respecting and protecting brownies is essential for maintaining a harmonious relationship with these elusive domestic fairies. Here are some key guidelines to follow:

- Respect Their Privacy: Brownies are shy and value their anonymity. Avoid attempting to capture, photograph, or directly interact with them, as this can cause them to depart from the household.
- Maintain a Clean Environment: Keeping your home or garden clean and well-maintained is a way to show respect for brownies. They are more likely to frequent spaces that are orderly and harmonious.
- Offer Tokens of Gratitude: Leaving small offerings of food, milk, or other gifts in a quiet corner of your home or garden is a gesture of appreciation for the brownies' assistance. This can help strengthen the bond between humans and brownies.
- Avoid Disturbing Their Work: If you suspect brownies are assisting with household chores, avoid interrupting or disturbing their work. Acknowledge their contributions with gratitude.

15B. Superstitions and Taboos

In some traditions and superstitions, there are specific taboos associated with brownies:

- Naming Them: It is considered taboo to attempt to name a brownie, as it is believed to give power over them and could lead to their departure.
- Misusing Their Services: Taking advantage of a brownie's helpful nature without showing appreciation or offering gratitude is considered disrespectful and may result in their departure.
- Attempting to Bind Them: Some legends caution against trying to bind or control brownies through magical means, as this can lead to negative consequences.

Following these guidelines and respecting the superstitions and taboos associated with brownies is essential for those who wish to maintain a positive and harmonious relationship with these benevolent domestic fairies. In the upcoming chapters, we will explore how brownies are portrayed in art, literature, and media, as well as contemporary beliefs and practices related to these elusive beings. We will also discuss conservation efforts aimed at preserving their habitats and the threats they may face.

16. Art and Representation

16A. How Brownies Are Portrayed in Art, Literature, and Media

Brownies have been a source of inspiration in various forms of artistic expression, including:

- Literature: Brownies have appeared in numerous books, stories, and poems, where they are often depicted as diligent and helpful household spirits. Some famous literary works that feature brownies include "The Brownie of Bodsbeck" by James Hogg and "The Brownies" by Juliana Horatia Ewing.
- Art: Artists have created illustrations and paintings depicting brownies in their domestic roles. These artworks often capture the whimsical and mischievous nature of these elusive fairies.
- Folklore Collections: Brownies are commonly featured in folklore collections from regions where they are believed to be present. These collections compile stories, legends, and accounts of brownie encounters, preserving their cultural significance.

- Children's Literature: Brownies have become beloved characters in children's literature, often appearing in tales that emphasize the importance of kindness and gratitude. These stories help introduce young readers to the world of fairies.

16B. Iconic Artists and Authors

Several artists and authors have contributed significantly to the portrayal of brownies in art and literature:

- Palmer Cox: Palmer Cox, a Canadian illustrator and author, is perhaps best known for his series of children's books featuring the "Brownies." His whimsical illustrations and stories introduced brownies to a wide audience and popularized their image in the late 19th and early 20th centuries.
- J.K. Rowling: In the world of contemporary literature, J.K. Rowling's "Harry Potter" series includes house-elves called "house-elves," some of whom share characteristics with traditional brownies. These creatures serve as domestic helpers, similar to brownies in folklore.

Understanding how brownies have been portrayed in art and literature provides insight into their enduring cultural significance and the ways in which their benevolent and hardworking nature has been celebrated over the centuries. In the chapters ahead, we will explore modern beliefs and practices related to brownies, including festivals and gatherings dedicated to them, as well as conservation efforts aimed at preserving their habitats.

17. Modern Beliefs and Practices

17A. Contemporary Beliefs Related to Brownies

While belief in brownies as actual supernatural beings has waned in modern times, they continue to hold a place in the realm of folklore and cultural traditions. Some modern beliefs and practices associated with brownies include:

- Folklore Preservation: Folklore enthusiasts and scholars work to preserve the stories and legends related to brownies. These efforts ensure that the cultural significance of brownies is not forgotten.
- Household Rituals: In some regions, especially where brownie folklore is strong, households may engage in traditional rituals or customs to honor and show respect to brownies. These rituals often involve leaving offerings or keeping the home tidy.

17B. Current Festivals and Gatherings

While there are no widespread festivals dedicated solely to brownies, their presence and influence can be found in various celebrations of folklore, fairies, and domestic spirits. These gatherings often include elements related to brownies:

- Fairy Festivals: Many regions host fairy-themed festivals that celebrate a wide range of fairy beings, including brownies. These events often feature storytelling, art, music, and activities related to fairy folklore.

- Local Traditions: In some areas where brownie legends are particularly strong, local communities may organize small gatherings or events to acknowledge the role of brownies in their folklore and traditions.

Understanding how brownies are acknowledged and celebrated in modern times helps us appreciate their enduring cultural significance and the ways in which they continue to be a part of the collective imagination. In the upcoming chapters, we will delve into conservation efforts aimed at preserving the habitats of brownies and the potential threats they may face in the contemporary world. Additionally, we will explore lesser-known stories and folklore associated with these enigmatic domestic fairies.

18. Conservation Efforts

18A. Initiatives Aimed at Preserving Brownie Habitats

Conservation efforts related to brownies are primarily focused on preserving their natural habitats and the ecosystems they inhabit. These initiatives are driven by a desire to protect not only brownies but also the broader biodiversity of these areas. Key elements of these conservation efforts include:

- Habitat Preservation: Conservationists work to protect the woodlands, meadows, and other natural areas where brownies are believed to reside. This involves establishing nature reserves, implementing land-use policies that prioritize conservation, and raising awareness about the importance of these habitats.
- Ecosystem Health: Efforts to maintain the overall health of ecosystems benefit brownies indirectly. This includes managing invasive species, reducing pollution, and restoring damaged habitats to create thriving environments for brownies and other wildlife.

18B. Potential Threats to Brownies

While brownies are primarily mythical beings, the potential threats to their folklore and cultural significance include:

- Fading Traditions: As belief in brownies and other domestic fairies wanes, there is a risk that the stories and traditions associated with them may be forgotten over time.
- Loss of Habitats: Human activities such as deforestation, urban development, and agricultural expansion can lead to the destruction or fragmentation of brownie habitats. This loss of natural spaces may impact the survival of these mythical beings in folklore.

Conservation efforts related to brownies are not aimed at protecting an actual species, but rather preserving the cultural heritage and folklore associated with these domestic fairies. By safeguarding the environments and traditions linked to brownies, enthusiasts hope to ensure that their stories continue to be passed down through generations.

19. Additional Folklore

19A. Lesser-Known Stories and Beliefs

In addition to the more well-known aspects of brownie folklore, there exist lesser-known stories, beliefs, and variations that provide a richer tapestry of these elusive domestic fairies:

- Regional Variations: Different regions have their own variations of brownies, with unique names, characteristics, and behaviors. Exploring these regional differences reveals the diverse nature of brownie folklore.
- Mischief and Pranks: While brownies are generally seen as helpful, some stories depict them as mischievous tricksters who enjoy playing pranks on humans. These tales highlight the multifaceted nature of brownie folklore.
- Transformation Abilities: In certain traditions, brownies are believed to possess the power of transformation, allowing them to take on various forms, from small animals to household objects. This shape-shifting ability adds an intriguing layer to their legends.

*****19B. Variations in Portrayal Across Different Cultures**

Brownies, or beings similar to them, appear in the folklore of various cultures, each with its own unique spin on these domestic fairies:

- Scotland: In Scotland, brownies are known as "bogles" or "boggarts" and are often associated with specific locations, such as bogs and marshes. They are celebrated as protective spirits of the household.
- England: English brownies, also known as "hobs" or "hobgoblins," are known for their dedication to household chores. They are often depicted as small, bearded creatures who are friendly if treated with respect.
- Scandinavia: In Scandinavian folklore, beings similar to brownies are called "tomte" or "nisse." These creatures are known for assisting with farm work and protecting the homestead. They are often portrayed with red hats.
- Ireland: In Irish folklore, brownies are known as "clurichauns" and are associated with mischief and drink. These beings are different in behavior from the classic brownie but share a connection to the household.

Understanding these lesser-known stories and cultural variations enriches our understanding of brownie folklore and the diverse ways in which these elusive domestic fairies have been imagined and celebrated across different cultures and regions. In the final chapter, we will explore famous encounters with brownies and the impact of these encounters on the lives and work of those who claimed to have met them.

20. Famous Encounters

20A. Historical and Modern Accounts of Famous Encounters

Throughout history, there have been accounts of individuals claiming to have encountered brownies, which have often had a profound impact on their lives and work. These encounters have been a source of inspiration, wonder, and curiosity. Here are a few notable instances:

- Robert Burns: The famous Scottish poet Robert Burns claimed to have had a personal encounter with a brownie at the Burns family farm in Ayrshire. This encounter is said to have inspired his poem "The Brownie of Bodsbeck," celebrating the diligent household spirit.

- Palmer Cox: The Canadian illustrator and author Palmer Cox, known for his "Brownies" series of books, drew inspiration from folklore and his own imagination. His portrayal of brownies introduced these domestic fairies to a wide audience and contributed significantly to their enduring popularity.
- Modern Folklorists: In modern times, folklorists and enthusiasts continue to document encounters and stories related to brownies. These accounts help preserve the cultural significance and enduring fascination with brownies.

20B. The Impact of Brownie Encounters

Encounters with brownies have often left a lasting impact on those who claim to have met them. This impact may manifest in various ways:

- Artistic Inspiration: Many individuals who have encountered brownies, whether in dreams, visions, or folklore, have drawn upon these experiences for artistic inspiration. Paintings, stories, and poems have been created to capture the essence of these encounters.
- Preservation of Folklore: Brownie encounters contribute to the preservation of folklore and cultural traditions. They reinforce the belief in the existence of these elusive domestic fairies and serve as a reminder of their enduring significance.
- Personal Belief: For some, encounters with brownies have solidified their personal belief in the existence of supernatural beings. These experiences can be deeply meaningful and shape their worldview.

The accounts of famous encounters with brownies serve as a testament to the enduring allure and impact of these elusive domestic fairies. While belief in brownies may have evolved over time, their place in folklore and cultural traditions remains significant.
These enchanting domestic fairies continue to captivate the imagination and inspire wonder in those who seek to understand and appreciate their elusive presence.

Leprechaun

1. Species Introduction

1A. Brief Overview of the Leprechaun

Leprechauns, often associated with Irish folklore, are a distinct and iconic fairy species. These mischievous creatures are known for their small stature and their crafty, solitary nature. Leprechauns are typically male fairies, and they are known for their elusive and secretive behavior.
Leprechauns are commonly depicted as small beings, standing at around two feet in height. They have ruddy, weathered faces and often sport long, white beards. Their clothing is a crucial element of their identity, featuring green coats, buckled shoes, and tall hats, which are usually red or green. This distinctive attire has become emblematic of leprechaun folklore.

1B. Unique Characteristics of Leprechauns

Leprechauns are renowned for their skilled craftsmanship, particularly in the creation of shoes.
Legend has it that they spend much of their time cobbling and repairing shoes for other fairies. Their craftsmanship is impeccable, and they take great pride in their work.
These fairies are known for their keen wit and cleverness. They are skilled tricksters who enjoy playing pranks on humans and other creatures. However, they are also solitary beings who prefer their own company and the quiet solitude of the Irish countryside.
Leprechauns are the keepers of a legendary pot of gold, which is said to be hidden at the end of a rainbow. This pot of gold is their most prized possession, and they are fiercely protective of it. Capturing a leprechaun and compelling them to reveal the location of their pot of gold is a common theme in leprechaun legends.
In Irish folklore, leprechauns are deeply tied to the culture and traditions of the Emerald Isle. Their presence is often associated with good fortune, but their tricks and riddles can confound those who encounter them.

2. General Appearance

2A. Detailed Physical Description

Leprechauns are diminutive creatures, standing at only about two feet in height, making them one of the smallest known fairy species. Their small stature allows them to easily hide amidst the lush Irish countryside. They have wrinkled, weathered faces that often reflect the wisdom of their many years.

Their most recognizable feature is their attire. Leprechauns are often seen wearing green coats, sometimes with tails, and their coats are adorned with brass buttons. Beneath their coats, they wear waistcoats and white shirts, adding to their dapper appearance. Their pants, often knee-length, are typically of a contrasting color, and they wear stockings and buckled shoes, which they are famous for repairing with great skill.

2B. Distinctive Clothing and Accessories

The most iconic accessory of a leprechaun is undoubtedly their hat. These fairies don tall, pointed hats that come in shades of red or green, sometimes adorned with buckles or bands. These hats are symbolic of their fairy status and are often seen as a sign of their magical abilities.
In addition to their hats, leprechauns may carry a shillelagh, a traditional Irish walking stick, which they use for both defense and to help them navigate the uneven terrain of the Irish countryside. The shillelagh is often ornately carved and serves as both a practical tool and a symbol of their Irish heritage.
Leprechauns also have a penchant for pocket watches, which they use to keep track of time, as they are known to be punctual beings. These watches are often finely crafted and can be another item of pride for a leprechaun.
The distinctive clothing and accessories of leprechauns are not only an essential part of their identity but also a reflection of their meticulous craftsmanship and attention to detail. These elements contribute to their charming and whimsical appearance, making them a beloved figure in Irish folklore and beyond.

3. Sexes

3A. Description of Male Leprechauns

Leprechauns are traditionally considered to be male fairies, and this is evident in their appearance and behavior. Male leprechauns are the most commonly encountered and discussed in Irish folklore. They are typically depicted as elderly, with white beards and weathered faces that reflect their wisdom and agelessness.

3B. Behavior and Traits of Female Leprechauns

In traditional Irish folklore, there is limited mention of female leprechauns. These creatures are primarily portrayed as solitary beings, and there is little documentation or lore surrounding their female counterparts. The focus of leprechaun legends is predominantly on the male leprechauns, who are known for their craftsmanship, trickery, and guardianship of the pot of gold.
The scarcity of information about female leprechauns suggests that they may not play as prominent a role in leprechaun mythology as their male counterparts. It's essential to note that folklore can evolve over time, so contemporary interpretations of leprechauns may differ in this regard.

4. Lore and Legends

4A. Cultural and Historical References

Leprechauns hold a special place in Irish folklore and culture. Their origin can be traced back to ancient Celtic mythology, where they were known as "luchorpán," meaning "small body." Over time, their name evolved into "leprechaun," and they became one of the most recognizable figures in Irish folklore.

These mischievous fairies are often associated with good luck and are believed to bring fortune to those who encounter them. However, their cunning nature means that they may also play tricks on unsuspecting individuals. Leprechaun legends have become deeply ingrained in Irish traditions and celebrations, especially around St. Patrick's Day.

4B. Stories, Myths, and Folklore

Leprechaun folklore is rich and diverse, with numerous stories and legends passed down through generations. One of the most famous tales involves the leprechaun's pot of gold. According to legend, if you capture a leprechaun and keep your eyes on him, he will be compelled to reveal the location of his hidden pot of gold. However, if you look away for even a moment, the leprechaun will vanish, taking his secret with him.

Another common theme in leprechaun stories is their association with cobbling. Leprechauns are renowned shoemakers, and it's said that if you hear the tap-tap-tapping of a cobbler's hammer in the distance, a leprechaun may be nearby, hard at work.

These stories and myths have contributed to the enduring allure of leprechauns. They are not only figures of folklore, but also symbols of Ireland itself, representing the country's rich storytelling tradition and deep connection to the mystical and magical.

5. Habitat and Natural Environment

5A. Natural Habitats

Leprechauns are strongly associated with the rolling green hills, meadows, and lush countryside of Ireland. They are believed to make their homes in secluded areas, often deep within dense forests or beside burbling streams. These serene, untouched landscapes provide them with the solitude they cherish.

The proximity of their habitats to natural elements like forests, rivers, and hidden glens is a common theme in leprechaun lore. These enchanting locations not only offer them a sense of sanctuary but also provide inspiration for their craft work.

5B. Environmental Factors Influencing Their Residences

Leprechauns are highly attuned to their surroundings, and their choice of residence is influenced by several environmental factors. They prefer areas with a rich diversity of plant life, as it allows them to gather materials for their shoe making endeavors and create their signature garments. The presence of clear, clean water sources is also crucial to leprechauns, as they use these streams to wash their clothes and to quench their thirst after a hard day's work. Additionally, these

sparkling streams are often depicted as the source of the elusive rainbows that lead to their hidden pots of gold.
Their habitat choices reflect their connection to nature, as leprechauns are deeply intertwined with the Irish landscape. As we continue to explore their world, we'll delve into their societal structure, daily routines, and the communal activities that occupy their time in these idyllic natural settings.

6. Lifestyle and Social Structure

6A. Insights into Leprechaun Society

Leprechauns are known for their solitary nature, and their society is often depicted as individualistic. They typically live alone, and their homes are hidden away in remote corners of the Irish countryside. Despite their solitary lifestyles, there are occasional references to leprechaun communities or gatherings, especially during significant events or celebrations in the fairy world.

6B. Daily Routines, Occupations, and Communal Activities

A significant portion of a leprechaun's daily life revolves around their craft, which is cobblering or shoemaking. These fairies are meticulous in their work, and they take immense pride in the quality of the shoes they create. Their dedication to craftsmanship is reflected in the intricate designs and expertly crafted footwear they produce.
When not engaged in their shoemaking endeavors, leprechauns are often depicted enjoying the tranquility of the Irish countryside. They are known to be lovers of nature, and they spend time admiring the beauty of the landscape, tending to their gardens, and occasionally playing musical instruments or singing.
Despite their preference for solitude, leprechauns are not entirely reclusive. They are known to interact with other fairy beings, such as elves, gnomes, and even humans, during specific occasions or celebrations within the fairy realm. These gatherings provide opportunities for socializing, sharing stories, and participating in communal activities.
The interplay between their solitary lifestyles and occasional communal interactions adds depth to the enigmatic world of leprechauns. As we continue our exploration, we will uncover more about their dietary preferences, communication methods, and the unique languages or gestures they use to connect with one another.

7. Diet and Food Sources

7A. Leprechaun Dietary Habits

Leprechauns are known for their simple and practical dietary preferences. Their diet primarily consists of natural foods found in the Irish countryside. They are considered omnivores, meaning they consume both plant and animal-based foods, adapting to the availability of resources in their environment.
Common components of a leprechaun's diet include wild berries, nuts, mushrooms, and various greens gathered from the forest floor. These foraged foods provide them with essential nutrients to sustain their small but active frames.

Occasionally, leprechauns may include small game, such as rabbits or birds, in their diet. They are known for their skill in hunting these creatures when they seek a change from their vegetarian fare.

7B. Special Dietary Preferences or Rituals

One distinctive aspect of leprechaun lore is their connection to food and drink. Leprechauns are often depicted enjoying hearty Irish meals, including stews, potatoes, and traditional dishes like Colcannon. They have a fondness for Irish whiskey, which they may enjoy in moderation during festive gatherings.
Leprechauns are known for their hospitality, and they may invite humans to partake in their feasts during chance encounters. However, there is an unwritten rule in leprechaun etiquette: accepting food or drink from a leprechaun may result in a binding obligation or a cleverly crafted riddle.
These dietary customs and preferences add depth to their portrayal in folklore, showcasing their connection to Irish culture and traditions. In the upcoming sections of our exploration, we will delve into their unique communication methods, magical abilities, and interactions with humans throughout history.

8. Communication and Language

8A. How Leprechauns Communicate

Leprechauns, like many fairy species, possess a unique form of communication that extends beyond spoken words. They often use non-verbal cues, including subtle gestures and expressions, to convey their thoughts and feelings. This silent communication is especially useful for maintaining their secrecy and hiding from humans or other beings when necessary.
Additionally, leprechauns are known for their musical talents. They may communicate through songs, melodies, or even playful tunes on traditional Irish instruments like the fiddle, flute, or tin whistle. Music is an integral part of their culture, and it helps them connect with one another during gatherings and celebrations.

8B. Unique Languages or Gestures

While leprechauns may not have a distinct language of their own, they are skilled in understanding the languages of other fairies and beings in the fairy realm. They can also communicate with animals, plants, and the elements of nature, enhancing their connection to the natural world.
Gestures play a crucial role in their communication, and certain hand movements, nods, or even eye contact can convey specific meanings. Leprechauns are known for their ability to communicate complex ideas with minimal words, making them adept at keeping secrets and sharing information discreetly.
Their silent and musical modes of communication are deeply woven into their culture and lifestyle, enriching the mysterious and enchanting nature of leprechauns. In the upcoming sections, we will

explore their life stages, reproduction, and the magical abilities that set them apart from other fairy species.

9. Reproduction and Life Cycle

9A. The Life Stages of Leprechauns

Leprechauns, like many fairy beings, undergo a unique life cycle. They are believed to be ageless and do not experience the same stages of life as humans do. Instead, they are thought to be eternal, maintaining their youthful appearance throughout their existence. This agelessness contributes to their air of wisdom and timelessness.
In leprechaun folklore, there is no clear distinction between youth and old age. However, they may accumulate knowledge and skills over time, making the older leprechauns especially adept in their craft and magical abilities.

9B. Mating Rituals and Reproduction

The topic of leprechaun reproduction is rarely explored in traditional Irish folklore. Leprechauns are primarily solitary creatures, and their focus is often on their craft and solitary pursuits rather than on family or reproduction.
Some versions of leprechaun lore suggest that they are born from the natural elements of the Irish countryside or are created through magical means. Others maintain that leprechauns may reproduce, but the details of their mating rituals and family life remain shrouded in mystery.
The lack of emphasis on reproduction in leprechaun legends underscores their focus on individualism and craftsmanship. As we proceed with our exploration, we will delve into their magical abilities and powers, shedding light on the unique spells and talents that make leprechauns stand out in the realm of fairies.

10. Magic Abilities and Powers

10A. Overview of Leprechaun Magic Abilities

Leprechauns are renowned for their magical abilities, which set them apart as extraordinary beings in the fairy realm. Their magic is deeply rooted in Irish folklore and plays a significant role in their tales. These magical talents encompass a wide range of abilities, making them versatile and captivating figures.
One of the most notable magical powers of leprechauns is their ability to vanish or become invisible at will. This power allows them to evade detection and hide from humans or other beings when they wish to maintain their secrecy.

Another common magical ability is their skill in creating and manipulating illusions. Leprechauns are known for their ability to conjure convincing illusions, often used to play pranks or lead curious individuals astray.

10B. Specific Spells or Powers Unique to Leprechauns

Leprechauns are also known for their mastery of enchantments, particularly related to their pots of gold. It's believed that these pots are enchanted to be much larger on the inside than they appear on the outside, allowing them to hold vast amounts of treasure.
In some legends, leprechauns possess the power of foresight, which allows them to see into the future. This ability is often associated with their knowledge of impending rainbows, which can lead humans to their hidden pots of gold.
Their magical abilities extend to matters of luck and fortune. Leprechauns are thought to have the power to bestow good fortune upon those they favor or play tricks on those who displease them. This ability is a significant reason for their association with luck and good fortune in Irish culture.
The magical prowess of leprechauns adds an enchanting and mystical dimension to their character. As we delve further into their lore, we will explore their interactions with humans, both positive and negative, and the historical encounters that have shaped their reputation over time.

11. Interactions with Humans

11A. Historical Encounters with Humans

Throughout history, leprechauns have been a source of fascination and intrigue for humans. These interactions often vary in nature, ranging from joyful encounters to mischievous escapades. Leprechaun legends frequently revolve around their interactions with humans, making them a prominent figure in Irish folklore.
Positive encounters with leprechauns typically involve humans stumbling upon them in the Irish countryside. In such cases, leprechauns may offer guidance, share their wisdom, or even grant a bit of their good luck to those they favor. These encounters are considered a stroke of good fortune and are often cherished as memorable experiences.

11B. Legends of Leprechaun-Human Relationships

While leprechauns are known for their benevolence, they are equally famous for their trickster nature. There are numerous tales of humans attempting to capture leprechauns to compel them to reveal the location of their hidden pots of gold. In these stories, leprechauns often use their magic and cleverness to escape capture, leaving the would-be treasure hunters empty-handed.
Some legends depict humans forming friendships with leprechauns, forging bonds that transcend the fairy-human divide. These friendships are based on mutual respect and shared experiences in the Irish countryside, where humans show kindness and respect toward the leprechaun inhabitants.
The complex dynamics between leprechauns and humans have contributed to their enduring popularity in folklore. In the subsequent sections of our exploration, we will delve into the

geographic regions where leprechauns are commonly found and their cultural significance in those areas, shedding light on their place in Irish heritage and tradition.

12. Country of Origin

12A. Geographic Regions Associated with Leprechauns

Leprechauns are intrinsically linked to the Emerald Isle, Ireland. Their presence is deeply ingrained in Irish folklore and culture. The lush and picturesque landscapes of Ireland serve as the backdrop for countless leprechaun stories and legends.
Within Ireland, leprechaun sightings and tales are often associated with specific regions. Counties like Cork, Kerry, and Tipperary are known for their rich leprechaun lore, and these areas have become hotspots for those hoping to catch a glimpse of these elusive fairies.

12B. Cultural Significance in Ireland

Leprechauns hold a unique place in Irish culture and traditions. They are regarded as a symbol of Ireland itself and are often used as a playful representation of the country's identity. The image of the leprechaun, complete with its green attire and mischievous demeanor, is widely recognized and associated with Ireland worldwide.
Leprechauns play a significant role in Irish celebrations and festivals, with St. Patrick's Day being the most notable example. During this holiday, leprechaun imagery, along with shamrocks and green decorations, adorns cities and towns across Ireland and the world, celebrating Irish heritage and folklore.
Their cultural significance extends beyond holidays, as leprechauns are woven into the fabric of Irish storytelling. They embody the rich tradition of storytelling in Ireland, where tales of these clever fairies have been passed down through generations, captivating young and old alike.

13. Where to Find Them

13A. Specific Locations Frequented by Leprechauns

Leprechauns are elusive creatures, and their specific hiding spots are closely guarded secrets. However, there are certain regions and landscapes in Ireland that are believed to be more favorable for leprechaun sightings.

- Forests and Woodlands: Leprechauns are often associated with dense forests, where they can blend seamlessly with the natural surroundings. Areas like the Slieve Bloom Mountains in County Laois and Killarney National Park in County Kerry are known for their leprechaun folklore.

- Hidden Glens and Valleys: Secluded glens and valleys, especially those nestled among rolling hills and mountains, are considered ideal habitats for leprechauns. Glenmalure in County Wicklow and the Black Valley in County Kerry are examples of such places.
- Bubbling Streams and Waterfalls: Leprechauns are known to frequent clear, clean streams and waterfalls. The sound of trickling water provides them with a soothing backdrop for their daily activities. Locations like Torc Waterfall in County Kerry and Glencar Waterfall in County Leitrim have their share of leprechaun legends.

13B. Best Times for Leprechaun Sightings

Leprechauns are most commonly associated with twilight, particularly during sunrise and sunset. These transitional periods between night and day are believed to be when they are most active and more likely to be seen.

It's essential to note that leprechauns are elusive by nature, and encounters with them are rare. The best approach to increase the chances of seeing a leprechaun is to visit areas with a strong leprechaun folklore tradition and keep a keen eye out during the magical moments of twilight.

14. How to See Them

14A. Practical Tips for Leprechaun Encounters

While leprechauns are known for their secretive nature, there are some practical tips that enthusiasts and curious individuals can follow to increase their chances of encountering these elusive fairies:

- Visit Leprechaun Hotspots: Explore regions in Ireland with a strong leprechaun folklore tradition, such as County Kerry, County Cork, and the Slieve Bloom Mountains. These areas are more likely to have reported leprechaun sightings.
- Dusk and Dawn: Leprechauns are traditionally believed to be most active during twilight, especially around sunrise and sunset. Plan your visits to potential leprechaun habitats during these magical hours.
- Quiet Observations: Leprechauns are easily startled, so patience and quiet observation are key. Find a secluded spot, stay still, and keep your eyes and ears open for any signs of movement or distant laughter, as leprechauns are known for their jovial nature.

14B. Rituals, Offerings, and Behaviors

Connecting with leprechauns may involve engaging in respectful rituals and behaviors that align with their folklore:

- Leave Small Offerings: Some people leave small offerings, such as a shiny coin or a piece of polished shoe leather, in areas known for leprechaun activity. This gesture is a sign of respect and may be appreciated by these fairies.
- Practice Kindness: Leprechauns are more likely to reveal themselves to those who show kindness and respect for the natural world. Treat the environment with care and respect, and you may earn their favor.

- Play Traditional Irish Music: As lovers of music, leprechauns are said to be drawn to the sound of traditional Irish instruments like the fiddle or tin whistle. Playing such music during your visit to potential leprechaun habitats may pique their curiosity.
- Seek the Rainbow's End: The legend of the pot of gold at the end of the rainbow is closely associated with leprechauns. If you spot a rainbow, follow its path to see if it leads to a leprechaun's hidden treasure.

While encountering a leprechaun remains a rare and magical experience, following these tips and showing respect for their folklore and traditions can make your journey to find them an enchanting adventure. In the subsequent sections of our exploration, we will delve into the importance of protecting and respecting leprechauns and their habitats, as well as the superstitions and taboos related to interacting with them.

15. Protection and Etiquette

15A. How to Respect and Protect Leprechauns

Respecting and protecting leprechauns and their habitats is essential to ensure the continued harmony between humans and these elusive fairies:

- Leave No Trace: When visiting potential leprechaun habitats, follow the "Leave No Trace" principles. Avoid littering, damaging plants, or disturbing the environment. Treat the natural world with care and respect.
- Offer Kind Gestures: If you encounter a leprechaun or a location associated with them, offer a kind gesture, such as a friendly greeting or a small gift. This shows respect for their traditions and may lead to positive interactions.
- Avoid Capturing Them: Leprechauns are fiercely independent and value their freedom. Attempting to capture or harm them is discouraged in folklore and should be avoided.

15B. Superstitions and Taboos Related to Leprechauns

Interacting with leprechauns carries certain superstitions and taboos, which are important to acknowledge:

- Never Steal Their Gold: Attempting to steal a leprechaun's pot of gold is considered bad luck. Leprechauns are protective of their treasures, and such actions may result in misfortune.
- Respect Their Privacy: Leprechauns are known for their solitary nature. Avoid intruding on their homes or spaces, as it is seen as disrespectful and may lead to negative encounters.
- Do Not Offend Them: Leprechauns have a playful but sometimes mischievous nature. Avoid offending them or insulting their craft, as they may respond with tricks or pranks.

By adhering to these principles of respect and following the folklore's superstitions and taboos, individuals can engage with the world of leprechauns while fostering a sense of harmony and mutual understanding. In the following sections of our exploration, we will uncover the ways in which leprechauns have been represented in art, literature, and media, as well as the iconic artists and authors who have featured them.

16. Art and Representation

16A. Portrayals in Art and Literature

Leprechauns have been a recurring subject in art and literature, capturing the imagination of artists and authors alike. Their distinctive appearance and folklore have inspired countless visual and literary works.
In art, leprechauns are often depicted wearing their signature green coats, tall hats, and buckled shoes. Artists have portrayed them in whimsical and playful scenes, showcasing their craftsmanship and mischievous antics. These representations often evoke the enchanting nature of leprechaun folklore.

16B. Iconic Artists and Authors

Several renowned artists and authors have contributed to the enduring popularity of leprechauns:

- W.B. Yeats: The celebrated Irish poet and playwright William Butler Yeats explored themes of Irish folklore and mythology in his works. His poetry, such as "The Stolen Child," features references to fairies and leprechauns, highlighting their significance in Irish culture.
- John Tenniel: The English illustrator John Tenniel is famous for his illustrations of Lewis Carroll's "Alice's Adventures in Wonderland." His detailed and imaginative depictions of leprechauns in Carroll's works have become iconic in the realm of fantasy literature.
- Darby O'Gill and the Little People: This 1959 Disney film, inspired by H.T. Kavanagh's stories, brought leprechauns to a wider international audience. The film's portrayal of leprechaun life in an Irish village continues to be cherished by audiences of all ages.

The artistic and literary representations of leprechauns have contributed to their enduring appeal and recognition in popular culture. As we move forward in our exploration, we will delve into contemporary beliefs and practices related to these fairies, exploring how leprechauns are celebrated and honored in modern times.

17. Modern Beliefs and Practices

17A. Contemporary Beliefs and Practices

In modern times, the fascination with leprechauns remains strong, and they continue to be a source of intrigue and celebration. Some contemporary beliefs and practices related to leprechauns include:

- St. Patrick's Day: Leprechauns have become iconic symbols of St. Patrick's Day celebrations worldwide. Parades, parties, and events often feature leprechaun imagery, along with traditional Irish symbols like shamrocks and green attire.

- Leprechaun-themed Merchandise: Leprechaun-themed merchandise, including clothing, decorations, and collectibles, is popular during St. Patrick's Day and throughout the year. These items often depict playful leprechauns and their iconic attributes.
- Leprechaun Hunts: Some enthusiasts organize leprechaun hunts or events, inviting participants to explore areas associated with leprechaun lore in the hopes of spotting these elusive fairies.
- Fairy Festivals: Various fairy-themed festivals and gatherings celebrate leprechauns along with other fairy beings. These events often include storytelling, music, and art that showcase the magical world of leprechauns.

17B. Current Festivals and Gatherings

- Several festivals and gatherings dedicated to leprechauns and fairy folklore take place in Ireland and other parts of the world. These events provide opportunities for people to immerse themselves in leprechaun culture and traditions.
- The National Leprechaun Museum (Dublin, Ireland): This museum in Dublin offers an immersive experience into the world of leprechauns and other Irish folklore creatures. Visitors can explore interactive exhibits and learn about the rich traditions surrounding these fairies.
- Leprechaun Days (Minnesota, USA): Leprechaun Days is an annual festival in the United States that celebrates Irish heritage and includes leprechaun-themed activities, parades, and entertainment.
- Fairy and Leprechaun Museum (Belfast, Northern Ireland): This museum in Belfast explores the world of fairies and leprechauns through exhibitions, storytelling, and interactive displays.

Contemporary beliefs and practices related to leprechauns highlight their enduring popularity and the way they continue to be celebrated as a whimsical and cherished part of Irish culture and folklore. In the subsequent sections of our exploration, we will turn our attention to efforts aimed at conserving the natural environments associated with leprechauns and addressing any threats they may face.

18. Conservation Efforts

18A. Initiatives to Preserve Leprechaun Habitats

While leprechauns are creatures of folklore and fantasy, the natural environments associated with them are real and valuable. Conservation efforts aimed at preserving these habitats are crucial for maintaining the rich biodiversity of the Irish countryside.

- Protected Areas: Some regions known for leprechaun folklore are designated as protected areas, ensuring the preservation of their unique landscapes. These areas often receive conservation attention to safeguard the flora and fauna they support.
- Environmental Education: Environmental organizations and schools in Ireland often include leprechaun folklore as part of their educational programs. This approach fosters a sense of responsibility and respect for the natural world and its mythical inhabitants.

18B. Threats to Leprechaun Environments

While leprechauns themselves are not threatened by human activities, the environments associated with them face certain challenges:

- Habitat Degradation: Urbanization, deforestation, and agriculture can lead to habitat loss and degradation, impacting the natural landscapes where leprechauns are believed to reside.
- Pollution: Pollution from various sources, including industrial activities and littering, can harm the waterways and plant life that leprechauns depend on for their sustenance and enjoyment.
- Climate Change: Changing weather patterns and climate conditions may disrupt the delicate ecosystems associated with leprechaun habitats, affecting the availability of resources.

Conservation efforts strive to address these threats and ensure the preservation of Ireland's natural beauty, including the enchanting landscapes where leprechauns are imagined to dwell. In the following sections of our exploration, we will uncover additional folklore and lesser-known stories associated with leprechauns, as well as variations in their portrayal across different cultures.

19. Additional Folklore

19A. Lesser-Known Stories and Beliefs

Beyond the well-known tales of leprechaun pots of gold and their shoe making skills, there exist lesser-known stories and beliefs surrounding these elusive fairies. Some of these include:

- Leprechaun Music: Leprechauns are said to be skilled musicians, playing enchanting melodies on their instruments. It's believed that hearing their music can lead humans into the heart of their hidden realms.
- The Leprechaun's Library: In some folklore, leprechauns are depicted as keepers of ancient and magical books. These tomes are said to hold the secrets of the fairy world and are only accessible to those granted permission.
- Leprechaun Guardians: In certain tales, leprechauns are portrayed as guardians of sacred or mystical sites in Ireland. They are believed to protect these places from harm and intrusion.

19B. Variations in Portrayal Across Cultures

While leprechauns are most commonly associated with Irish folklore, variations of similar beings exist in cultures around the world. These beings often share attributes with leprechauns, such as small stature and mischievous tendencies. For example:

- Brownies (Scotland): Similar to leprechauns, brownies are house fairies known for performing helpful tasks in exchange for small offerings. They are known for their love of cleanliness and order.
- Tomte (Sweden): The tomte is a small, bearded creature often associated with protecting farms and homesteads. They appreciate offerings of porridge and have been depicted as guardians of the household.
- Kobolds (Germany): Kobolds are creatures of Germanic folklore known for their association with mines and underground spaces. They can be helpful or mischievous, depending on how they are treated.

These variations highlight the universality of folklore themes and the presence of small, elusive beings in the mythology of different cultures.

20. Famous Encounters

20A. Historical or Modern Accounts

Throughout history, there have been accounts of famous individuals encountering leprechauns. These encounters often left a lasting impression and sometimes influenced the course of their lives or work.

- Thomas Johnson Westropp (1860-1922): This Irish archaeologist and folklorist documented numerous leprechaun encounters in his research. His detailed accounts contributed to the preservation of leprechaun folklore and Irish fairy traditions.
- P.W. Joyce (1827-1914): The renowned Irish historian and writer included accounts of leprechaun sightings in his work on Irish folklore and legends. His contributions helped to solidify the place of leprechauns in Irish cultural heritage.

20B. Impact on Lives and Work

Encounters with leprechauns often had a profound impact on those who experienced them. These experiences inspired individuals to delve deeper into Irish folklore, culture, and history.

- Artistic Creations: Some encounters inspired artists and writers to create works that celebrated leprechauns and Irish mythology. Paintings, poems, and stories continue to be influenced by these magical beings.
- Preservation of Folklore: Those who encountered leprechauns often became passionate advocates for the preservation of Irish folklore and traditions. Their contributions helped ensure that the stories of leprechauns and other fairies endured.

These famous encounters highlight the enduring allure of leprechauns and their significance in Irish culture and heritage. As we conclude our exploration, we have journeyed through the enchanting world of leprechauns, uncovering their characteristics, folklore, cultural significance, and the various ways in which they continue to captivate the human imagination.

Gnomes

1. Species Introduction

1A. Brief Overview of Gnomes

Gnomes, often portrayed as small, earthy creatures, are a unique and intriguing species of fairies. They are known for their strong connection to the earth and their affinity for the natural world, especially the world beneath our feet. These diminutive beings have captured the human imagination for generations with their mysterious and reclusive way of life.
Gnomes are typically depicted as small in stature, standing only a foot or so tall. Their skin tends to have earthy tones, reflecting their close association with the soil and plants. Their features are often weathered, as they spend much of their lives in the underground, tending to their subterranean homes and gardens.

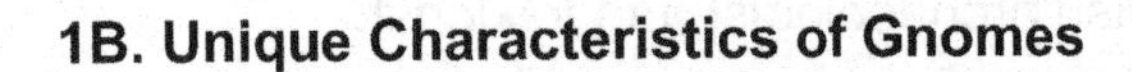

1B. Unique Characteristics of Gnomes

Gnomes possess several distinctive characteristics that set them apart from other fairy species:

- Earthly Guardians: Gnomes are considered the caretakers of the earth, responsible for maintaining the health and balance of underground ecosystems. They are experts in gardening, particularly in cultivating mushrooms, mosses, and other subterranean flora.
- Mining Expertise: Gnomes are skilled miners, known for their ability to locate valuable underground resources like gemstones and minerals. Their knowledge of the earth's depths is unparalleled.
- Loyal and Reclusive: Gnomes are generally introverted and prefer to live in small, tight-knit communities underground. They are wary of human interference and tend to keep to themselves.
- Night Dwellers: Gnomes are often nocturnal, coming out at night to tend to their gardens and explore the underground world. This nocturnal behavior is partly due to their aversion to sunlight, which they find harsh.
- Love for Music: Gnomes are known for their love of music and often play instruments like tiny violins, flutes, and drums. Their melodies are said to be enchanting and can bring a sense of peace to those who hear them.

2. General Appearance

2A. Detailed Physical Description

Gnomes possess a distinctive physical appearance that reflects their close association with the earth and underground realms. Here's a closer look at their physical attributes:

- Size: Gnomes are relatively small, typically standing around 12 to 18 inches tall, making them one of the shorter fairy species. Their diminutive stature allows them to navigate easily through the intricate tunnels and caves of their underground homes.
- Skin and Features: Gnomes have earthy complexions, ranging from deep brown to pale, mossy green. Their skin often appears weathered, resembling the texture of tree bark, which aids in camouflaging them amid rocks and foliage. Their facial features are characterized by prominent cheekbones and expressive, almond-shaped eyes.
- Hair: Gnomes' hair varies in color, mirroring the natural hues found in the underground world. It can be shades of brown, green, or even gray, often resembling the texture of lichen or moss. Gnomes take pride in their hair and often adorn it with small natural ornaments like leaves or pebbles.
- Clothing and Accessories: Gnomes typically wear simple, practical attire made from natural materials like leaves, twigs, and moss. Their clothing blends seamlessly with their environment, making them nearly invisible to human observers. They may wear small hats, often resembling toadstools or acorns, as a signature accessory.

2B. Distinctive Clothing and Accessories

Gnomes' attire and accessories are not just a matter of practicality but also reflect their connection to the natural world:

- Leafy Attire: Gnomes fashion their clothing from leaves and plant fibers, which they skillfully weave into garments. These outfits are not only functional, but also help gnomes blend into their forested or underground surroundings.
- Headwear: Gnomes are known for their charming hats, which can range from pointy caps resembling mushrooms to acorn-shaped headgear. These hats are often adorned with small trinkets, leaves, or tiny bells, adding a touch of whimsy to their appearance.
- Tool Belts: Gnomes frequently wear tiny belts with small pouches to carry their gardening tools, which are essential for maintaining their underground gardens. These belts are crafted from natural materials like woven vines or braided roots.

Gnomes' unique appearance and clothing reflect their harmonious existence with the natural world, showcasing their resourcefulness and their ability to adapt to their subterranean homes.

3. Sexes

3A. Description of Male and Female Gnomes

Within the world of gnomes, the concept of sexes is somewhat distinct from human understanding. Gnomes do have distinct male and female counterparts, but their differences go beyond the physical.

- Male Gnomes: Male gnomes are typically characterized by slightly stockier builds compared to their female counterparts. They have broader shoulders and often sport more rugged, weathered appearances, which result from their physical labor in the underground world. Male gnomes are known for their strength and endurance, qualities that serve them well in their roles as miners and protectors of gnome communities.
- Female Gnomes: Female gnomes, on the other hand, tend to have more delicate features and slightly slimmer builds. Their nimble fingers make them exceptionally skilled gardeners and caretakers of the underground ecosystems. They are also revered for their wisdom and often hold positions of leadership within gnome communities.

3B. Differences in Appearance and Behavior

While physical differences exist between male and female gnomes, it's their roles and behaviors that truly set them apart:

- Male Roles: Male gnomes are typically responsible for excavation, mining, and defending gnome communities from potential threats. They are known to venture deeper into the earth in search of valuable minerals and resources, showcasing their bravery and resilience.
- Female Roles: Female gnomes excel in horticulture, tending to the intricate underground gardens that sustain their communities. They possess an innate connection to plant life and are regarded as the primary caregivers of the gnome world. Female gnomes also serve as the keepers of traditional gnome wisdom and lore, passing down knowledge through generations.

It's important to note that gnomes, regardless of their sex, have deep respect for the roles each plays within their society. Their complementary abilities and responsibilities ensure the well-being and harmony of gnome communities. As we move forward in our exploration of gnomes, we will uncover more about their lore and legends, their habitats, and their unique lifestyles.

4. Lore and Legends

4A. Cultural and Historical References to Gnomes

Throughout history, gnomes have been an integral part of folklore and mythology in various cultures around the world. Their presence in stories and legends has helped shape our perception of these earthbound fairies. Here, we explore some of the cultural and historical references to gnomes:

- Medieval Europe: Gnomes were often mentioned in medieval European folklore, where they were believed to be guardians of the earth's treasures. They were associated with hidden underground realms and were said to assist miners by revealing valuable minerals and gems.
- Germanic Traditions: Germanic folklore introduced the concept of "gnomus," which referred to subterranean creatures with magical abilities. These beings were seen as protectors of nature and the hidden riches of the earth.
- Swiss and Alpine Folklore: In Swiss and Alpine traditions, gnomes were known as "Heinzelmännchen" and were credited with performing household chores and helping with farm work. These helpful gnomes were believed to be active during the night, completing tasks while humans slept.
- Scandinavian Myths: Norse mythology included beings known as "dvergar" or dwarves, who shared some similarities with gnomes. Dwarves were skilled craftsmen who resided underground and were known for creating powerful artifacts.

4B. Stories, Myths, and Folklore Associated with Gnomes

Gnomes have been featured in countless stories, myths, and folklore, each contributing to their rich tapestry of legends:

- The Garden Gnome: Perhaps the most iconic representation of gnomes in modern times, the garden gnome is believed to have originated in Germany in the 19th century. These small figurines, often seen in gardens, are thought to bring good luck and protect plants.
- "The Gnome King's Treasure" (German Folklore): This classic German folktale tells the story of a kind-hearted gnome king who rewards a poor woodcutter for sparing his life. The woodcutter is granted access to the gnome king's underground treasure trove.
- "The Gnome's Garden" (Scandinavian Folklore): In this story, a young girl encounters a gnome who invites her to visit his underground garden, a place of incredible beauty and magic. The girl learns valuable lessons about the importance of caring for the natural world.
- "Snow White and the Seven Dwarfs" (Grimm Brothers): Although not explicitly gnomes, the seven dwarfs in this famous fairy tale share many characteristics with gnomes, such as their love for mining and living underground.

Gnomes' presence in cultural narratives and legends has evolved over time, reflecting the changing beliefs and values of different societies. As we delve deeper into the world of gnomes, we'll explore their habitats, lifestyles, and dietary preferences, shedding more light on these fascinating earthbound fairies.

5. Habitat and Natural Environment

5A. Natural Habitats Preferred by Gnomes

Gnomes are intimately connected to the earth, and their choice of habitat reflects this deep bond. They prefer to dwell in underground realms, often hidden away from the hustle and bustle of the human world. Here's a closer look at the natural habitats gnomes call home:

- Subterranean Dwellings: Gnomes are renowned for their intricate underground homes, which can vary from simple burrows to elaborate tunnel systems. These dwellings provide them with protection from the elements and a sense of security.
- Forest Clearings: Some gnomes establish their homes in secluded clearings within dense forests. These clearings are carefully tended, serving as miniature sanctuaries filled with lush greenery, mushrooms, and small ponds.
- Rocky Outcroppings: Gnomes with a penchant for mining and rock craft often settle near rocky outcroppings or cliffsides. These locations provide them with access to valuable minerals and gemstones.
- Garden Sanctuaries: A subset of gnomes, known as garden gnomes, may reside in human gardens. While these gnomes have adapted to urban settings, they still maintain a deep connection to the natural world, often caring for the plants and animals in the garden.

5B. Environmental Factors Affecting Gnome Residences

Several environmental factors influence the selection of gnome habitats and contribute to their distinctive way of life:

- Earthen Harmony: Gnomes are drawn to locations where the earth is rich and fertile. They have a profound connection to the soil, which sustains their underground gardens and provides a sense of rootedness.
- Solitude and Seclusion: Gnomes value solitude and seclusion, seeking habitats away from the noise and disruptions of the human world. This isolation allows them to focus on their tasks and maintain the sanctity of their underground communities.
- Natural Abundance: Gnomes are highly attuned to the abundance of resources in their chosen habitats. Whether it's fertile soil for gardening or hidden mineral deposits for mining, the availability of these resources plays a crucial role in their selection of homes.
- Nighttime Preference: Many gnomes are nocturnal, venturing out at night to tend to their gardens and explore the underground world. Their habitats provide the darkness and tranquility they prefer during their active hours.

Gnome habitats are a reflection of their deep connection to the earth and their dedication to nurturing the natural world. As we continue our exploration, we'll delve into their unique lifestyle, including their societal structure, daily routines, and communal activities, offering a more comprehensive understanding of these earthbound fairies.

6. Lifestyle and Social Structure

6A. Insights into Gnome Societal Structure and Hierarchy

Gnome society is characterized by its tight-knit and communal nature. While individual gnome communities may have variations in their structures, some common elements provide insights into their way of life:

- Community Bonds: Gnome communities are often composed of extended families or clans. These clans work together to maintain their underground homes and gardens, fostering a strong sense of unity and cooperation.
- Elders and Leaders: Gnomes typically respect the wisdom of their elders and often have leaders within their communities. These leaders, often chosen for their experience and knowledge, guide the community and make important decisions.
- Caretakers and Specialists: Within gnome communities, individuals may have specialized roles. Some are dedicated gardeners, ensuring the health of their underground gardens, while others are skilled miners responsible for extracting valuable resources. These roles contribute to the overall well-being of the community.

6B. Daily Routines, Occupations, and Communal Activities

Gnomes lead simple yet fulfilling lives, deeply connected to the tasks that sustain their communities and the natural world. Here's a glimpse into their daily routines and activities:

- Gardening: Gardening is at the heart of gnome life. Gnomes tend to their underground gardens with care, cultivating a wide variety of plants, including mushrooms, mosses, and unique subterranean flora. These gardens provide both sustenance and beauty.
- Mining and Crafting: Gnomes with a talent for mining delve deep into the earth in search of valuable minerals and gemstones. They use these resources to craft intricate jewelry, tools, and decorative items, often showcasing their craftsmanship in their underground homes.
- Communal Gatherings: Gnome communities often gather for communal meals, celebrations, and storytelling sessions. These gatherings strengthen their bonds and allow them to share knowledge and experiences.
- Nighttime Activities: Many gnomes are nocturnal, venturing out at night to explore the underground world, socialize with fellow gnomes, and play music. Their nighttime activities often include sharing tales of their adventures.
- Education and Passing Down Knowledge: Gnomes place great importance on the passing down of knowledge from one generation to the next. Elders and experienced members of the community mentor the younger gnomes, ensuring that their traditions and wisdom endure.

Gnomes' lifestyle emphasizes their deep connection to the natural world, their sense of community, and their dedication to nurturing the earth. As we continue our exploration of gnomes, we'll delve into their dietary preferences, communication methods, and their unique reproduction and life cycle. These aspects offer a more comprehensive understanding of these earthbound fairies.

7. Diet and Food Sources

7A. What Gnomes Eat

Gnomes maintain a diet deeply rooted in the natural world and their underground habitats. Their culinary preferences are a reflection of their close relationship with the earth. Here's an overview of what gnomes eat:

- Subterranean Delicacies: Gnomes have a unique affinity for subterranean delicacies, including various types of mushrooms, tubers, and root vegetables. They often cultivate these plants in their underground gardens, ensuring a steady supply of fresh, nourishing food.
- Herbs and Greens: Gnomes value herbs and leafy greens, which they incorporate into their meals for flavor and nutrition. These ingredients are also key elements of their gardening efforts.
- Mineral Supplements: Gnomes recognize the importance of minerals in their diet, and they often consume small quantities of gemstone dust and crystal fragments. These minerals are believed to provide them with energy and vitality.

7B. Special Dietary Preferences and Rituals

Gnomes' dietary preferences are not limited to taste; they are deeply intertwined with their way of life:

- Gardening Rituals: Gnomes approach gardening as both a source of sustenance and a sacred ritual. They carefully tend to their underground gardens, offering prayers and songs to the earth as they cultivate their crops.
- Seasonal Variations: Gnomes adapt their diets to the changing seasons. During colder months, when fresh produce is scarce, they rely on preserved foods from their gardens and underground storage facilities.
- Symbiosis with Nature: Gnomes view their relationship with the natural world as symbiotic. They believe that by caring for the earth and its flora, they, in turn, receive the nourishment and energy needed to thrive.

Gnomes' dietary choices are a testament to their commitment to maintaining the balance of their underground ecosystems and their respect for the earth's bounty. As we continue our exploration, we will uncover more about their unique methods of communication, including languages and gestures, and delve into their intriguing reproduction and life cycle, shedding more light on these fascinating earthbound fairies.

8. Communication and Language

8A. How Gnomes Communicate with Each Other

Gnomes possess a rich and intricate system of communication that allows them to interact with one another, share knowledge, and maintain the harmony of their underground communities. Here's an insight into how gnomes communicate:

- Gnome Language: Gnomes have their own unique language, known as "Gnomic." This language consists of melodic, lilting sounds and intricate gestures. It is highly expressive and allows gnomes to convey subtle nuances of emotion and meaning.
- Songs and Music: Music is an integral part of gnome communication. Gnomes often communicate through songs, using melodies and rhythms to convey messages and stories. Musical instruments like tiny violins, flutes, and drums are commonly used.
- Signs and Symbols: Gnomes utilize a system of signs and symbols made from natural materials like leaves, twigs, and stones. These symbols are often used to mark important locations, convey warnings, or indicate directions within their underground habitats.

8B. Unique Languages and Gestures

Gnome communication extends beyond spoken language:

- Non-Verbal Gestures: Gnomes use a variety of non-verbal gestures to express themselves. Hand movements, facial expressions, and body language play crucial roles in conveying their thoughts and emotions.
- Gnome Songs: Gnome songs are not only a means of communication but also a form of artistic expression. Each song may tell a story, share knowledge, or celebrate important events within the community.
- Nature's Whisper: Gnomes are known for their ability to communicate with the natural world. They can understand the language of plants and animals, allowing them to forge deeper connections with their surroundings.
- Elemental Connection: Some gnomes have a special bond with the elements, such as earth, water, fire, or air. This connection enables them to communicate with and manipulate these elemental forces, further enhancing their abilities.

Gnome communication is a rich tapestry of spoken word, music, gestures, and a deep connection to the natural world. This intricate system allows them to navigate their underground realms, share stories, and preserve their cultural heritage. As we delve deeper into the gnome world, we'll explore their unique reproduction and life cycle, shedding more light on these earthbound fairies.

9. Reproduction and Life Cycle

9A. The Gnome's Life Stages from Birth to Death

The life of a gnome is a fascinating journey, marked by distinct stages of development and growth. Here's a closer look at the life cycle of gnomes:

- Infancy: Gnome infants, known as "seedlings," are born from carefully nurtured garden beds within their underground homes. They emerge as small, sprightly beings and are tenderly cared for by their parents and the community. Gnome seedlings are curious and eager to explore their surroundings.
- Childhood: As gnome seedlings grow, they become increasingly involved in the daily life of the community. They learn the art of gardening, mining, and craftsmanship from their elders. Childhood is a time of playful exploration, learning, and bonding with fellow gnomes.
- Adulthood: Gnomes reach adulthood around the age of 50 to 100 years, depending on their individual growth rates. At this stage, they assume more significant roles within the community, taking on responsibilities such as tending to gardens, participating in mining expeditions, and contributing to communal activities.
- Elderhood: Gnomes enter the elder stage at around 500 years of age. Elders play vital roles in preserving the wisdom and traditions of their community. They are revered for their knowledge and often serve as leaders and mentors to younger gnomes.
- Passing On: Gnomes live for several centuries, but eventually, they return to the earth they cherish. When a gnome reaches the end of their life, their body is returned to the soil, where it nourishes the underground ecosystem. Gnomes believe in the cyclical nature of life and death, viewing the earth as a continuous source of renewal.

9B. Mating Rituals and Reproduction Process

Gnome reproduction is a carefully orchestrated process, ensuring the continuation of their species and the health of their communities:

- Mating Rituals: Gnomes engage in elaborate courtship rituals, often involving music, dance, and the exchange of symbolic gifts. These rituals serve to strengthen bonds between potential mates and foster compatibility.
- Garden Blessing: Gnome reproduction is intricately tied to their gardens. Mating pairs plant a special seed in their garden, invoking blessings from the earth. The seed eventually produces a gnome seedling.
- Parental Care: Gnome parents provide dedicated care to their offspring, teaching them essential skills and values. The entire community contributes to the upbringing of gnome seedlings, ensuring they grow up well-rounded and connected to their cultural heritage.

Gnome reproduction is a sacred process deeply rooted in their connection to the earth and their commitment to preserving their way of life. As we continue our exploration of gnomes, we will delve into their magical abilities and powers, their interactions with humans, and their cultural significance in the regions where they are commonly found. These aspects offer a more comprehensive understanding of these earthbound fairies.

10. Magic Abilities and Powers

10A. A Detailed Breakdown of Gnomes' Magical Abilities

Gnomes are inherently magical beings, with a deep connection to the earth and its energies. Their magical abilities are closely tied to their role as caretakers of the underground world. Here's an exploration of the magical powers and abilities possessed by gnomes:

- Geomancy: Gnomes are master geomancers, skilled in the art of manipulating the earth's energies. They can shape the terrain, creating underground tunnels and chambers with precision. Geomancy also allows them to sense disturbances in the earth, aiding in the protection of their communities.
- Plant Manipulation: Gnomes possess a profound connection to plant life, which they use to nurture their underground gardens. They can accelerate plant growth, heal with herbal remedies, and communicate with plants to understand their needs.
- Elemental Control: Some gnomes have the ability to control elemental forces associated with the earth, such as stone, metal, and minerals. They can transmute elements, shape metals with precision, and summon earth-related phenomena.
- Earth-Attuned Magic: Gnomes draw upon the energy of the earth itself for their magic. They can manipulate soil, rocks, and crystals to create barriers, camouflage, and protective wards. Gnomes also use earth-attuned magic to maintain the structural integrity of their underground homes.

10B. Specific Spells and Powers Unique to Gnomes

Gnomes' magical abilities extend to a wide range of spells and powers, including:

- Earth Healing: Gnomes can heal the earth and revitalize plant life, ensuring the health of their underground gardens. They use this power to restore balance to the natural world.
- Mystic Tunnels: Gnomes have the ability to create concealed tunnels that lead to secret locations within their underground realms. These tunnels are often used for defense and escape.
- Mineral Vision: Some gnomes possess a unique form of vision that allows them to see valuable minerals and gemstones hidden within the earth, making them expert miners.
- Plant Whisper: Gnomes can communicate with plants, understanding their needs and desires. This power allows them to create harmonious and thriving underground ecosystems.

Gnomes' magical abilities are both practical and deeply spiritual, aligning with their role as guardians of the earth and protectors of their underground communities. As we continue our exploration, we'll uncover more about their interactions with humans, including historical encounters, legends of fairy-human friendships, and the cultural significance of gnomes in regions where they are commonly found. These aspects offer a more comprehensive understanding of these earthbound fairies.

11. Interactions with Humans

11A. Historical Encounters with Humans

Throughout history, there have been sporadic but memorable interactions between gnomes and humans. These encounters have often left lasting impressions on both parties:

- Mining Mysteries: Gnomes were occasionally encountered by miners deep underground. Miners would report hearing soft music or seeing fleeting glimpses of small, gnome-like figures. These encounters were often regarded as good omens, indicating a rich vein of minerals.
- Garden Gifts: In some instances, gnomes were known to visit human gardens at night, assisting with planting and tending to crops. These helpful gestures were considered blessings from the earth and brought prosperity to the gardeners.
- Craftsmanship Exchange: Gnomes with exceptional craftsmanship skills occasionally traded their intricately crafted items with humans, forging bonds of friendship and mutual respect. These exchanges often resulted in unique and prized possessions for humans.

11B. Legends of Fairy-Human Friendships and Conflicts

Legends and folklore abound with stories of gnome interactions with humans:

- The Gnome's Gift: In one tale, a gnome gifted a struggling artist with a magical paintbrush. This brush had the power to bring paintings to life, leading to fame and prosperity for the artist.
- The Miner's Guardian: Miners in a remote village spoke of a guardian gnome who watched over them as they worked. They left offerings of food and drink to express their gratitude, believing that the gnome ensured their safety.
- Conflicts and Misunderstandings: Not all encounters were peaceful. Some stories tell of humans unknowingly disrupting gnome homes or gardens, resulting in conflicts and occasional pranks played by the gnomes in retaliation.

Gnomes' interactions with humans are often shaped by mutual respect for the earth and its treasures. While many humans view gnomes as benevolent protectors, others regard them with a mix of reverence and caution. As we proceed in our exploration, we will uncover more about the country of origin for gnomes, the specific regions where they are commonly found, and their cultural significance in those areas. These aspects offer a more comprehensive understanding of these earthbound fairies.

12. Country of Origin

12A. Geographic Regions of Gnome Origin

Gnomes are believed to originate from various geographic regions, each with its unique cultural and ecological characteristics. Here's an exploration of the potential countries of origin for gnomes:

- Germany: Germany is often associated with the origin of gnomes, particularly due to the prominence of garden gnomes in its folklore. German gnomes, known as "Gartenzwerge," are thought to have played a significant role in shaping the modern perception of gnomes as protectors of gardens and homes.
- Scandinavia: Norse mythology features beings akin to gnomes, such as dwarves and underground spirits. The forests and mountains of Scandinavia are thought to be home to gnome-like creatures with an affinity for mining and craftsmanship.
- Switzerland and the Alps: Alpine folklore includes tales of "Heinzelmännchen," small helpful creatures who assist with household chores. These beings share similarities with gnomes and are believed to reside in the Swiss Alps.
- Central and Eastern Europe: Gnome-like creatures have been a part of the folklore in many Central and Eastern European countries, such as Poland, the Czech Republic, and Hungary. These creatures are often associated with mining and hidden treasure.

12B. Cultural Significance in Origin Regions

In regions where gnomes are believed to originate, they hold cultural significance:

- Garden Decor: In Germany, garden gnomes have become iconic decorations, adorning lawns and gardens. They are seen as symbols of good luck and protection, reflecting the positive cultural significance of gnomes in the region.
- Craftsmanship Traditions: In Scandinavia, the connection between gnomes and craftsmanship is celebrated. Gnomes are often associated with the creation of exquisite jewelry, tools, and works of art.
- Domestic Help: In Swiss and Alpine regions, gnomes are seen as helpful spirits that assist with chores and farm work. Their presence symbolizes a harmonious coexistence with the natural world.
- Mining Heritage: In Central and Eastern European countries, gnomes are linked to mining traditions and the search for hidden treasures. They embody the connection between humans and the earth's resources.

Gnomes' cultural significance varies across regions, reflecting the unique characteristics and beliefs of the people who inhabit these areas. As we continue our exploration, we will uncover more about where to find gnomes, the specific locations and landscapes where they are often sighted, and the best times of day or year for sightings. These aspects offer a more comprehensive understanding of these earthbound fairies.

13. Where to Find Them

13A. Specific Locations, Forests, and Landscapes

Gnomes are known to inhabit specific locations and landscapes, where they have established hidden communities and underground realms. Here's an exploration of where you might find gnomes:

- Enchanted Forests: Gnomes are often associated with enchanted or mystical forests, where they create secluded clearings filled with vibrant plant life, mushrooms, and other flora. These forests are prime locations for gnome sightings.
- Rocky Outcroppings: Gnomes who excel in mining and crafting may establish their homes near rocky outcroppings, cliffsides, or cavern entrances. These locations provide access to valuable minerals and gemstones.
- Meadows and Glades: Some gnomes choose to dwell in meadows and glades, where they maintain miniature sanctuaries filled with wildflowers, small ponds, and carefully tended gardens. These serene settings are beloved by gnomes for their natural beauty.
- Gardens and Arboretums: Garden gnomes, a subset of the gnome population, may choose to reside in human gardens and arboretums. They live in harmony with humans and often help care for the plants and animals in these environments.

13B. Best Times for Sightings

Gnomes are elusive and tend to be most active during specific times of day or year:

- Nocturnal Activity: Many gnomes are nocturnal creatures, venturing out at night to explore the underground world, socialize with fellow gnomes, and partake in their nighttime activities.
- Twilight Hours: Gnomes are sometimes seen during the twilight hours of dawn and dusk when the transition between day and night offers them a degree of concealment.
- Spring and Summer: Gnomes are most active during the spring and summer months, when the earth teems with life, and their gardens require diligent care. These seasons offer the best opportunities for sightings.
- Harvest Time: In regions where gnomes are associated with agriculture, they may be more visible during harvest seasons, when their assistance is most needed by farmers and gardeners.

Gnome sightings are a rare and cherished experience, often requiring patience, respect for their privacy, and a deep connection to the natural world. As we continue our exploration, we will delve into practical tips and advice on how to increase the chances of encountering gnomes and the rituals, offerings, or behaviors that may attract them. These aspects offer a more comprehensive understanding of these earthbound fairies.

14. How to See Them

14A. Practical Tips and Advice for Gnome Sightings

Seeing gnomes in their natural habitat is a special and rare experience. Gnomes are elusive and often prefer to remain hidden. Here are some practical tips and advice for increasing the chances of encountering gnomes:

- Respect Their Privacy: Gnomes value their privacy and the sanctity of their underground homes. Approach their habitats with respect and gentleness, taking care not to disturb their gardens or dwellings.
- Silent Observation: Gnomes are sensitive to noise and disruptions. When attempting to see them, practice silent observation and be patient. Find a concealed spot to watch quietly, allowing the gnomes to go about their activities undisturbed.
- Nighttime Vigilance: If you suspect gnomes are active in your area, consider venturing out during the twilight hours or at night. Many gnomes are nocturnal and may be more active during these times.
- Create a Hospitable Environment: To attract gnomes to your garden or property, cultivate an environment that mimics their natural habitat. Plant a variety of native plants, maintain a small pond, and provide sheltered areas with rocks and branches.
- Offer Tokens of Respect: Gnomes appreciate offerings of food, especially small portions of fresh vegetables, nuts, and berries. Leave these offerings near their habitats as tokens of respect.

14B. Rituals, Offerings, and Behaviors That May Attract Gnomes

Gnomes are drawn to specific rituals, offerings, and behaviors:

- Gnome Songs: Gnomes are known to respond to melodic music. Play soft, lilting tunes on musical instruments, such as flutes or violins, to create an inviting atmosphere.
- Earth-Centered Rituals: Engage in earth-centered rituals, such as meditations that connect you with the earth's energies. Gnomes are attuned to these vibrations and may be more inclined to reveal themselves in response.
- Garden Blessings: Perform garden blessings or rituals that express your gratitude for the natural world. Gnomes often respond positively to these acts of reverence.
- Environmental Stewardship: Show your commitment to environmental stewardship by taking care of the land and respecting its resources. Gnomes are guardians of the earth and are more likely to reveal themselves to those who share their values.

Gnomes are beings of deep wisdom and intuition, and their appearances are not guaranteed. However, by approaching them with respect and a harmonious attitude towards nature, you may increase the likelihood of experiencing the magic of a gnome encounter. As we continue our exploration, we'll delve into the importance of protecting and respecting gnomes and their habitats, as well as superstitions or taboos related to interacting with them. These aspects offer a more comprehensive understanding of these earthbound fairies.

15. Protection and Etiquette

15A. Guidance on How to Respect and Protect Gnomes and Their Habitats

Respecting and protecting gnomes and their habitats is of paramount importance. Gnomes are caretakers of the earth, and their well-being is intertwined with the health of the natural world. Here's guidance on how to ensure the protection of gnomes:

- Respect Their Privacy: Gnomes value their privacy and the sanctity of their underground homes. Avoid disturbing their dwellings, gardens, and tunnels. Do not attempt to uncover or enter their homes without invitation.
- Leave No Trace: When visiting areas where gnomes are believed to reside, practice Leave No Trace principles. Carry out any litter or waste, and avoid leaving behind items that could disrupt their environment.
- Avoid Using Harmful Chemicals: If you have a garden or natural area where gnomes are thought to be present, refrain from using harmful pesticides or herbicides. These chemicals can harm the gnome's underground gardens and the ecosystem they nurture.
- Offerings and Tokens: If you choose to leave offerings for gnomes, ensure that these offerings are environmentally friendly and biodegradable. Fresh fruits, vegetables, or small tokens crafted from natural materials are appropriate.

15B. Superstitions or Taboos Related to Interacting with Gnomes

Gnomes have a deep-seated respect for traditions and rituals. Understanding and respecting these superstitions and taboos can help foster positive interactions with gnomes:

- Whistling Underground: Whistling or making loud noises underground is considered disrespectful and taboo when in the presence of gnomes. These sounds can disrupt their activities and disturb their peace.
- Trespassing on Their Homes: Trespassing into gnome homes or tunnels without invitation is regarded as a serious breach of their privacy. It is best to remain at a respectful distance from their dwellings.
- Disturbing Garden Offerings: If you encounter offerings left by gnomes in gardens or natural areas, avoid disturbing them. These offerings may hold special significance for the gnomes and should be left undisturbed.
- Misusing Gnome Magic: Gnome magic is powerful and deeply connected to the earth. Misusing their magic or attempting to harness it without proper understanding is considered disrespectful and may result in unintended consequences.

Respecting gnome traditions and adhering to these superstitions and taboos is a sign of reverence and understanding. It helps ensure that interactions with gnomes are harmonious and mutually beneficial. As we continue our exploration, we will delve into how gnomes are represented in art, literature, and media, as well as the iconic artists or authors who have featured them. These aspects offer a more comprehensive understanding of these earthbound fairies.

16. Art and Representation

16A. How Gnomes Are Portrayed in Art, Literature, and Media

Gnomes have left an indelible mark on human creativity, inspiring countless works of art, literature, and media. Their portrayal in these forms of expression offers a rich tapestry of their cultural significance and mystical allure:

- Visual Art: Gnomes have been depicted in paintings, illustrations, and sculptures for centuries. Their appearances in art often emphasize their connection to the earth and nature. Garden gnomes, with their characteristic red hats and white beards, have become iconic symbols in gardens around the world.
- Children's Literature: Gnomes frequently appear in children's literature as whimsical and endearing characters. They often embark on adventures, solving mysteries or helping human protagonists. Classic works like "The Secret Book of Gnomes" by Wil Huygen and Rien Poortvliet have captivated generations with their charming gnome tales.
- Fantasy Fiction: Gnomes are a staple of fantasy literature, where they are often portrayed as skilled craftsmen, miners, or magical beings. Authors like Terry Pratchett and J.R.R. Tolkien have incorporated gnomes or gnome-like creatures into their fantasy worlds, adding depth to their narratives.
- Cinema and Animation: Gnomes have made appearances in animated films and television shows, both as main characters and in supporting roles. Their portrayals range from comical and mischievous to wise and mystical, catering to diverse audience preferences.

16B. Iconic Artists and Authors Who Have Featured Gnomes

Several artists and authors have played pivotal roles in popularizing gnomes and shaping their representation:

- Rien Poortvliet: Dutch artist Rien Poortvliet's illustrated book "Gnomes" (with Wil Huygen as the author) brought gnomes to international acclaim. His detailed and lifelike depictions of gnome life in the wild resonated with audiences worldwide.
- David the Gnome: The animated television series "David the Gnome," based on the book "The Gnomes" by Wil Huygen and Rien Poortvliet, introduced gnomes to a new generation of viewers. The show's gentle and educational storytelling made it a beloved classic.
- Terry Pratchett: British author Terry Pratchett featured gnomes in his Discworld series, where they played roles ranging from bumbling inventors to noble heroes. Pratchett's wit and satire added depth to the portrayal of gnomes in fantasy literature.
- J.R.R. Tolkien: In Tolkien's legendarium, gnomes are synonymous with the dwarves, a proud and skilled race of craftsmen and warriors. Tolkien's works, particularly "The Hobbit" and "The Lord of the Rings," established enduring archetypes for gnomes in fantasy literature.

Gnomes' representation in art and literature reflects their enduring appeal as mystical and earthbound beings. As we continue our exploration, we will uncover contemporary beliefs and practices related to gnomes, including current festivals or gatherings dedicated to them. Additionally, we will explore conservation efforts aimed at preserving their habitats and the threats they may face. These aspects offer a more comprehensive understanding of these earthbound fairies.

17. Modern Beliefs and Practices

17A. Contemporary Beliefs and Practices Related to Gnomes

In modern times, beliefs and practices related to gnomes have evolved, reflecting a continued fascination with these earthbound fairies:

- Gnome Gardens: Many people maintain gnome gardens or miniature gnome villages in their own outdoor spaces as a nod to the traditional garden gnome. These whimsical displays celebrate the connection between humans and gnomes, emphasizing the importance of harmonious coexistence with the natural world.
- Nature Conservation: Gnomes have become mascots for nature conservation efforts in some regions. Organizations and individuals may adopt gnome imagery or themes to raise awareness about environmental issues and the protection of natural habitats.
- Gnome Festivals and Gatherings: Some communities host gnome-themed festivals or gatherings, where enthusiasts come together to celebrate gnome culture, art, and folklore. These events often feature gnome-themed art exhibitions, storytelling sessions, and even gnome costume contests.
- Online Communities: The internet has brought together individuals with a shared interest in gnomes. Online forums, social media groups, and websites dedicated to gnome lore, sightings, and art have flourished, fostering a global community of gnome enthusiasts.

17B. Current Festivals or Gatherings Dedicated to Gnomes

Several festivals and gatherings around the world celebrate gnomes and their cultural significance:

- International Gnome Festival (Lauchhammer, Germany): Lauchhammer hosts an annual International Gnome Festival, where visitors can enjoy gnome-themed art exhibitions, live music, and workshops. The festival also features a parade of garden gnomes through the town.
- The Gnome Reserve and Wildflower Garden (Devon, United Kingdom): This nature reserve in England is dedicated to gnomes and features over 1,000 gnomes scattered throughout the gardens. Visitors can explore the whimsical gnome world and enjoy the natural beauty of wildflowers.
- Gnome Fest (Indiana, USA): Gnome Fest is a family-friendly event in Indiana, USA, where attendees can participate in gnome costume contests, gnome-themed arts and crafts, and enjoy gnome-inspired snacks.
- Gnomeo and Juliet Festival (Stratford-upon-Avon, United Kingdom): Inspired by the animated film "Gnomeo and Juliet," this festival in Shakespeare's hometown celebrates gnomes with garden tours, gnome art exhibitions, and gnome-themed activities.

These festivals and gatherings demonstrate the enduring appeal of gnomes and their ability to bring communities together in the spirit of creativity, whimsy, and a shared love for the natural world. As we continue our exploration, we will delve into conservation efforts aimed at preserving the habitats of gnomes, the threats they may face, and lesser-known stories or beliefs associated with these earthbound fairies. These aspects offer a more comprehensive understanding of gnomes and their significance in the modern world.

18. Conservation Efforts

18A. Initiatives Aimed at Preserving Gnome Habitats

As awareness of gnome habitats and their importance in maintaining the balance of nature grows, various conservation efforts have emerged to protect these environments. Some of these initiatives include:

- Gnome Sanctuaries: Gnome sanctuaries have been established in regions where gnomes are believed to reside. These protected areas are off-limits to human interference and are managed to ensure the well-being of gnome communities.
- Habitat Restoration: Conservationists and nature enthusiasts engage in habitat restoration projects to create and maintain environments that are conducive to gnome populations. These projects often involve planting native flora and providing protected spaces for gnomes to thrive.
- Educational Programs: Educational programs and workshops are conducted to raise awareness about the importance of gnomes and their role in maintaining healthy ecosystems. These programs encourage responsible stewardship of natural habitats.
- Gnome Census: Some regions conduct periodic gnome censuses to monitor gnome populations and assess the health of their communities. This data helps inform conservation efforts and protect gnome habitats.

18B. Threats to Gnomes and Their Habitats

While gnomes are resilient beings, they face several threats to their habitats and well-being:

- Habitat Destruction: Urbanization and land development can lead to the destruction of gnome habitats, resulting in the displacement of gnome communities. Protecting their natural environments is crucial.
- Pollution: Pollution from chemicals, plastics, and other contaminants can harm the natural world, including gnome habitats. Gnomes are particularly sensitive to environmental changes, making pollution a significant threat.
- Human Disturbances: Well-meaning but uninformed humans may unknowingly disrupt gnome habitats through activities such as landscaping, construction, or recreational activities. Conservation efforts aim to mitigate these disturbances.
- Climate Change: Climate change can alter the ecosystems where gnomes reside, affecting their food sources and living conditions. Conservationists work to address climate-related challenges and ensure the resilience of gnome populations.

Efforts to protect gnome habitats not only benefit these mystical beings but also contribute to the preservation of biodiversity and the overall health of the natural world. As we continue our exploration, we will uncover lesser-known stories or beliefs associated with gnomes, as well as variations in their portrayal across different cultures. These aspects offer a more comprehensive understanding of these earthbound fairies and their enduring mystique.

19. Additional Folklore

19A. Lesser-Known Stories or Beliefs Associated with Gnomes

Gnomes are featured in a wide range of folklore and lesser-known stories from various cultures around the world. Here are a few intriguing tales and beliefs:

- The Gnome's Whisper: In some regions, it is said that gnomes have the ability to whisper secrets of the earth to those who listen carefully. These whispered insights are believed to grant wisdom and a deeper understanding of the natural world.
- The Gnome's Compass: Gnomes are thought to possess an innate sense of direction, and they can help lost travelers find their way home. In times of need, some people would seek out gnome guidance to navigate unfamiliar landscapes.
- Gnomes and the Aurora Borealis: In Nordic folklore, gnomes are believed to be the creators of the Northern Lights, also known as the Aurora Borealis. They are said to dance and sing in the skies, creating the mesmerizing light displays.
- Gnomes and Healing Crystals: Gnomes are associated with the discovery and use of healing crystals and gemstones. It is said that they have a deep understanding of the properties and energies of these stones, and they share this knowledge with those who respect the earth.

19B. Variations in Gnome Portrayal Across Different Cultures

Gnomes, known by various names, appear in the folklore of many cultures with distinct characteristics:

- German Gartenzwerge: Garden gnomes, or "Gartenzwerge," are iconic in German culture. They are typically depicted as bearded, rosy-cheeked figures wearing colorful clothing and pointed hats. These gnomes are often seen as protectors of gardens.
- Scandinavian Dwarves: In Norse mythology, dwarves are akin to gnomes and are known for their exceptional craftsmanship. These dwarves often forge powerful weapons and items for the gods.
- Slavic Domovoi: In Slavic folklore, the "Domovoi" is a household spirit akin to gnomes. They are believed to reside in homes and protect the family. Respectful gestures and offerings are made to appease them.
- Italian Folletti: Italian folklore features "Folletti," which are similar to gnomes in some aspects. They are often depicted as playful, mischievous beings who may hide household items or lead travelers astray.
- Celtic Leprechauns: Leprechauns are a type of gnome-like creature in Celtic folklore. They are known for their shoemaking skills and their penchant for hiding pots of gold at the end of rainbows.

These variations in gnome portrayal highlight the cultural diversity and rich tapestry of beliefs and stories associated with these earthbound fairies. As we conclude our exploration, we will delve into historical and modern accounts of famous individuals encountering gnomes and the impact of these encounters on their lives or work. These accounts offer a fascinating glimpse into the enduring mystique of gnomes in the human imagination.

20. Famous Encounters

20A. Historical and Modern Accounts

Throughout history, there have been accounts of famous individuals encountering gnomes, often resulting in profound experiences or creative inspiration:

- Johann Wolfgang von Goethe: The renowned German writer Goethe is said to have had a mystical encounter with gnomes during his travels in the Harz Mountains. This experience is believed to have inspired his work, including the dramatic poem "The Sorcerer's Apprentice."
- Hans Christian Andersen: The Danish author Andersen, known for his fairy tales, claimed to have met a gnome-like creature during a visit to Switzerland. This encounter is said to have inspired his story "The Traveling Companion."
- Arthur Conan Doyle: The creator of Sherlock Holmes, Sir Arthur Conan Doyle, was a believer in the supernatural. He reportedly encountered gnomes while exploring the countryside and documented his experiences in his writings.
- Modern Encounters: In recent times, there have been accounts of individuals encountering gnomes during hikes, woodland explorations, and even in their own gardens. These encounters are often shared on social media and in online forums, sparking discussions about the existence of gnomes in the modern world.

20B. The Impact of Gnome Encounters on Lives and Work

Encounters with gnomes have had a profound impact on the lives and creative work of those who experienced them:

- Creative Inspiration: Many artists, writers, and musicians have drawn inspiration from their gnome encounters. These mystical experiences have influenced their works, leading to the creation of stories, paintings, and music that celebrate gnomes and the natural world.
- Spiritual Growth: Some individuals view their gnome encounters as spiritual awakenings, deepening their connection to the earth and the mysteries of the natural world. These experiences have led to a greater appreciation for environmental conservation and stewardship.
- Personal Transformation: Gnome encounters have been described as transformative experiences, leading individuals to reevaluate their priorities and embrace a simpler, more harmonious way of life. Some have chosen to live in closer communion with nature, inspired by the wisdom of the gnomes.

Famous encounters with gnomes serve as a testament to the enduring mystique and influence of these earthbound fairies in the realm of human imagination and creativity. As we conclude our exploration, we invite readers to embrace the wonder and magic of gnome lore, fostering a deeper connection to the natural world and the mysteries it holds.

Nymphs

1. Species Introduction

1A. Brief Overview

Nymphs, often associated with Greek mythology, are a diverse group of female spirits or fairies that inhabit the natural world. They are renowned for their ethereal beauty and their close connection to nature. Nymphs are known to reside in various natural settings, from forests and rivers to mountains and meadows. Each type of nymph is often associated with a specific natural feature, and their unique characteristics set them apart from other fairy species.

1B. Unique Characteristics Nymphs are characterized by their exquisite beauty and graceful presence. They are typically depicted as young and alluring women, although their appearances can vary depending on their specific type. Some common traits include long flowing hair, radiant skin, and luminous eyes that reflect the beauty of their natural surroundings.

What distinguishes nymphs from other fairies is their strong affinity for the environment they inhabit. They are guardians and protectors of their respective domains, ensuring the vitality and balance of nature. Nymphs possess an almost ethereal connection to the plants, animals, and elements within their realm, granting them unique powers and abilities that are tied to nature itself.

2. General Appearance

2A. Detailed Physical Description

Here are some common descriptions of nymph appearances based on their respective habitats:

- Dryads: These tree nymphs are typically depicted with bark-like skin that blends seamlessly with the trees they inhabit. Their hair often resembles leaves or branches, and their eyes may have a greenish hue. Dryads' attire appears as if it's woven from elements of the forest, making them nearly indistinguishable from the trees themselves.
- Naiads: Naiads, associated with water sources like lakes and rivers, are known for their shimmering, aquatic features. Their hair glistens like flowing water, and their eyes sparkle like sun-dappled waves. Naiads often wear flowing garments that resemble the colors and textures of water, which ripple as they move.
- Oreads: Oreads, who reside in the mountains and rocky terrains, have a more rugged and earthy appearance. Their skin may have the texture of stone or rock, and their hair can

resemble the colors of minerals and gemstones. Oreads are often adorned with jewelry made from precious stones found in their mountainous homes.
- Anthousai: These flower nymphs are the embodiment of the bloom and beauty of the meadows they inhabit. Anthousai often have floral patterns on their skin, hair that mimics the colors of wildflowers, and eyes as vibrant as blossoms in spring. They may wear garments adorned with petals and leaves.

2B. Distinctive Clothing and Accessories

Nymphs are known for their attire that blends harmoniously with their natural surroundings. Their clothing and accessories are often crafted from elements found in their habitats:
- Leaves, vines, and flowers: Nymphs living in forests and meadows frequently wear garments woven from leaves, vines, and flowers. These botanical outfits change with the seasons, reflecting the cycles of nature.
- Shells and pearls: Naiads often adorn themselves with jewelry made from shells and pearls found in their aquatic homes. These treasures shimmer with a lustrous beauty that mirrors the waters they inhabit.
- Minerals and gemstones: Oreads favor jewelry and accessories crafted from the stones and minerals of their mountain abodes. These gems not only enhance their natural beauty but also serve as symbols of their connection to the earth.
- Bark and wood: Dryads' clothing and accessories are often made from the very trees they inhabit. They may wear bark-like dresses and adorn themselves with wooden jewelry carved from their forest homes.

Nymphs' attire not only reflects their environment but also serves as a means of camouflage, allowing them to blend seamlessly into their natural habitats and maintain their mystical allure.

3. Sexes

3A. Description of Male and Female Nymphs

Nymphs are primarily known for their female representation in folklore and mythology. They are often depicted as enchanting and alluring female spirits, closely tied to the natural world. In many nymph types, there is little to no mention of male counterparts. However, it's essential to note that in some variations of mythology, male counterparts, known as "satyrs" or "fauns," are mentioned, particularly in the context of forest nymphs.

3B. Differences in Appearance

In cases where male counterparts are mentioned, they contrast the female nymphs in appearance and behavior. While nymphs are graceful, ethereal, and closely connected to nature, satyrs and fauns are often depicted as more rugged and earthy beings. They possess features like goat-like legs and horns, and their behavior is sometimes characterized by revelry and mischief.
It's important to acknowledge that the presence or absence of male counterparts varies significantly across different mythologies and interpretations. In many stories, nymphs exist as

independent, female entities, embodying the enchantment of the natural world without a direct male counterpart.

4. Lore and Legends

4A. Cultural and Historical References

Nymphs have been an enduring part of cultural and historical narratives for centuries. Their presence is particularly prominent in Greek mythology, where they are described as minor deities or spirits of nature. Nymphs often played significant roles in various myths and legends, and they were believed to be associated with specific natural features.
In addition to Greek mythology, nymphs appear in the folklore and legends of other cultures around the world. Each culture has its own interpretation of these enchanting beings, attributing them unique characteristics and roles within their respective mythologies.
4B. Stories, Myths, and Folklore Nymphs are central characters in many captivating stories and myths. Some well-known examples include:

- Echo and Narcissus: In Greek mythology, the nymph Echo was punished by the goddess Hera and could only repeat the words spoken to her. She fell in love with Narcissus, a beautiful young man who rejected her advances. This tragic tale explores themes of unrequited love and transformation.
- The Nymphs of Artemis: Artemis, the Greek goddess of the hunt, had a group of nymphs known as the "Huntress Nymphs" who were her companions. They were fierce and skilled huntresses, embodying the untamed spirit of the wilderness.
- The Nymphs of Springs and Rivers: In various mythologies, nymphs were believed to inhabit specific springs, rivers, and water bodies. They were often associated with the life-giving and purifying qualities of water. Stories of their interactions with gods and mortals abound, such as the tale of Hylas and the Nymphs.
- The Dryads of the Trees: Dryads, the tree nymphs, were closely connected to the trees they inhabited. Cutting down or harming these trees was believed to bring the wrath of the dryads upon the offender. These stories emphasized the importance of respecting and preserving nature.

These are just a few examples of the rich tapestry of nymph-related myths and legends. Nymphs' roles in these stories often reflect their connection to nature, their beauty, and the significance of the natural world in human culture.

5. Habitat and Natural Environment

5A. Natural Habitats

They Prefer Nymphs are intrinsically tied to the natural world and inhabit a variety of landscapes and environments. Their choice of habitat is often linked to their specific type:

- Dryads: These tree nymphs dwell within ancient forests and groves, often taking up residence within the heart of majestic trees. They are guardians of their woodland homes and share an intimate bond with the trees themselves.

- Naiads: Naiads are water nymphs, residing in freshwater sources such as lakes, rivers, and springs. They are deeply connected to the flow of water and the life it sustains.
- Oreads: Oreads make their homes in mountainous regions, among rocky cliffs and pristine peaks. Their presence is closely associated with the rugged beauty of the mountains.
- Anthousai: These flower nymphs thrive in meadows and fields adorned with vibrant blooms. Their very essence is intertwined with the vitality and beauty of the plant life around them.

5B. Environmental Factors

Nymphs are highly sensitive to the well-being of their natural environments. They are not merely inhabitants but also protectors of their chosen habitats. Environmental factors that influence their choice of residence include:

- Purity of Water: For naiads, the purity and health of the water in their domain are paramount. Pollution or disturbances to the water source can greatly distress these nymphs.
- Forest Health: Dryads' well-being is directly tied to the health of the trees they inhabit. Deforestation and damage to the forests can lead to their decline.
- Mountain Ecosystems: Oreads rely on the stability and integrity of the mountain ecosystems, including the balance of flora and fauna.
- Meadow Blooms: Anthousai require thriving meadows with diverse and vibrant plant life. Changes in land use or excessive development can disrupt their homes.

Nymphs' roles as stewards of their natural environments are deeply ingrained in their mythology. Stories often emphasize the consequences of disrespecting or harming the land and waters they inhabit.

6. Lifestyle and Social Structure

6A. Societal Structure and Hierarchy

Nymphs are inherently tied to the natural world, and their societal structures, if they exist, are often closely aligned with their chosen habitats. While some types of nymphs, like dryads, may lead solitary lives, others exhibit social structures within their domains.

- Dryads: These tree nymphs tend to lead solitary lives, with each dryad forming a deep bond with a specific tree. Their connection to the forest is spiritual and solitary, focusing on the protection and well-being of their individual trees.
- Naiads: Naiads, residing in water sources, often form loose communities. They are known to congregate near their water bodies, sometimes with a hierarchy based on the size and importance of their domain.
- Oreads: Oreads in mountainous regions may form small, close-knit communities with shared responsibilities for guarding their rugged territories. Their bonds are forged through their connection to the mountains.

- Anthousai: Flower nymphs usually gather in meadows and fields, where their connection to the flourishing plant life creates a sense of community. They may work collectively to ensure the beauty and vitality of their meadows.

While nymphs' social structures, if present, are not as elaborate as those of some other creatures, their connections with each other and their natural surroundings are profound and harmonious.

6B. Daily Routines

The daily lives of nymphs revolve around their roles as caretakers and protectors of their natural domains. Their routines and activities include:

- Guardianship: Nymphs diligently guard and preserve their chosen habitats, ensuring their health and vitality. They are known to fend off threats and intruders to maintain the balance of nature.
- Rituals and Offerings: Nymphs often engage in rituals and ceremonies that celebrate the cycles of nature. These rituals may include offerings to the land and waters they protect.
- Interactions with Nature: Nymphs frequently commune with the natural elements around them, gaining a deep understanding of the rhythms and needs of their habitats.
- Creativity and Expression: Many nymphs are known for their artistic and creative pursuits. They may engage in activities like singing, dancing, and crafting to celebrate the beauty of their surroundings.

Nymphs' daily lives are a harmonious blend of protection, celebration, and connection with the natural world. Their interactions with their environments are integral to their existence, and their rituals and activities ensure the well-being of the places they call home.

7. Diet and Food Sources

7A. What Do They Eat?

Nymphs are intimately connected to their natural environments, and their diets are closely tied to the ecosystems they inhabit:

- Dryads: These tree nymphs do not consume conventional food like humans. Instead, they draw sustenance from the energy and life force of the trees they protect. Their connection to the trees allows them to thrive on the tree's vitality.
- Naiads: Naiads, residing in freshwater environments, primarily feed on aquatic plants and algae found in their water bodies. Some may consume small aquatic creatures, such as insects or small fish, to maintain the ecological balance.
- Oreads: Mountain nymphs may have diets that include foraged mountain vegetation and fruits. Their diets are often herbivorous, reflecting the flora of their rocky domains.
- Anthousai: Flower nymphs share a symbiotic relationship with the plant life in their meadows. They do not consume traditional food, but instead derive nourishment from the vibrant blooms and energy of the meadow.

7B. Special Dietary Preferences

Nymphs' dietary preferences and rituals are often intertwined with their roles as guardians of their natural habitats. Some nymphs may have unique dietary rituals or practices:

- Rituals of Connection: Nymphs may engage in rituals that deepen their connection to the natural elements around them. These rituals can be seen as a form of nourishment for their spirits.
- Offerings to Nature: Nymphs often make offerings to the land, waters, or plants they protect as a way of reciprocating the energy they receive from their habitats. These offerings may include symbolic items or gestures.
- Seasonal Celebrations: Nymphs may participate in seasonal celebrations that coincide with the cycles of nature. These celebrations often involve communal activities and expressions of gratitude to their environments.

Nymphs' dietary and spiritual practices reflect their deep connection to the natural world. These practices are not only essential for their well-being but also serve as acts of stewardship and reverence for the ecosystems they inhabit.

8. Communication and Language

8A. How Do They Communicate with Each Other?

Nymphs communicate with one another primarily through non-verbal means, often relying on the natural world and their inherent connection to it. Some common modes of communication include:

- Nature's Signs: Nymphs are highly attuned to the subtle cues and changes in their natural environments. They interpret the rustling of leaves, the glistening of water, and the rustling of winds as forms of communication.
- Telepathy: In some traditions, nymphs are believed to possess telepathic abilities, allowing them to exchange thoughts and emotions directly with one another and the creatures of their domains.
- Gestures: Nymphs use graceful movements, gestures, and expressions to convey their feelings and intentions. These gestures are often fluid and harmonious, reflecting their connection to nature.

8B. Any Unique Languages or Gestures

While nymphs primarily communicate through the subtle language of the natural world, some nymphs are believed to have unique languages or gestural forms of communication within their communities:

- Musical Language: Some nymphs, particularly those associated with music and song, are thought to communicate through melodious sounds and harmonious tunes. Each musical note may convey specific meanings or emotions.
- Symbolism: Nymphs might employ symbolism in their interactions, using the arrangement of natural elements like stones, leaves, or flowers to convey messages or intentions.

- Dance: Dance is a significant form of expression for nymphs. Their movements often carry deeper meanings and can tell stories or convey their emotions, rituals, and celebrations.

Nymphs' communication is deeply intertwined with their environments, and their ability to understand and interpret the natural world is an essential part of their existence. Their forms of communication are as fluid and diverse as the ecosystems they inhabit.

9. Reproduction and Life Cycle

9A. The Fairy's Life Stages from Birth to Death

The life cycles of nymphs are intrinsically tied to the natural world and the ecosystems they inhabit. While specific details can vary depending on the type of nymph, a general overview of their life stages might include:

- Birth and Emergence: Nymphs come into existence as part of the natural world, often born from the very elements of their environments. For example, tree nymphs (dryads) may emerge from the heartwood of ancient trees, while water nymphs (naiads) are linked to the birth of freshwater springs.
- Youth and Growth: During their early years, nymphs grow and mature, becoming more attuned to their surroundings. Their connection to nature deepens as they learn to protect and care for their habitats.
- Adulthood: As they reach adulthood, nymphs take on more significant roles as guardians and protectors of their domains. They may engage in rituals and responsibilities tied to their specific natural features.
- Aging and Wisdom: Nymphs are believed to age differently than humans, with some myths suggesting they become more radiant and powerful as they grow older. Their wisdom and magical abilities may also increase with age.
- Transition and Renewal: The end of a nymph's life cycle is often closely linked to the health and vitality of their habitats. When their natural environments face threats or degradation, it can lead to the decline or disappearance of the nymphs associated with them. Conversely, when ecosystems are healthy and flourishing, nymphs thrive and continue their cycle of renewal.

9B. Mating Rituals and Reproduction Process

Nymphs' reproduction processes are deeply intertwined with the natural elements of their environments:

- Asexual Reproduction: In some myths, nymphs are believed to reproduce asexually, with new nymphs emerging directly from the natural features they inhabit. This process is often seen as a reflection of the continual renewal of nature.
- Divine Connections: In certain traditions, nymphs are associated with gods or divine beings, and their offspring may result from these divine unions. These offspring, if any, may inherit traits from both their nymph parent and the divine figure.
- Transformation: In rare cases, nymphs may transform into other beings or elements upon the completion of their life cycle, ensuring that the cycle of life and nature continues.

Nymphs' life cycles and reproduction processes are deeply symbolic of the interconnectedness of life, nature, and the ecosystems they protect. Their existence is not only tied to their individual well-being but also to the health and balance of the natural world around them.

10. Magic Abilities and Powers

10A. Breakdown of Their Magical Abilities

Nymphs possess a range of magical abilities that are intimately connected to the natural elements they inhabit:

- Elemental Influence: Nymphs often have control over the natural elements within their domains. For example, water nymphs (naiads) can manipulate water, controlling currents and tides, while tree nymphs (dryads) may influence the growth and health of trees.
- Healing Powers: Some nymphs are believed to have the ability to heal both the land and its inhabitants. They can restore vitality to ailing plants, animals, or even humans who seek their aid.
- Shape-Shifting: In some traditions, nymphs have the power to change their forms, allowing them to seamlessly blend into their environments or take on different appearances for various purposes.
- Telepathy and Empathy: Nymphs are often depicted as having a deep understanding of the emotions and intentions of those who enter their domains. They can communicate telepathically and empathetically with the creatures they protect.
- Seasonal Control: Certain nymphs may have the power to influence the changing of seasons or the growth cycles of plants and flowers in their meadows or forests.

10B. Spells or Powers Unique to This Species

Nymphs' magical abilities are unique to their respective domains, and they may have specific powers associated with their roles as protectors of nature:

- Water Purification: Naiads are known for their ability to cleanse and purify water sources, ensuring the health and vitality of their aquatic domains.
- Tree Bonding: Dryads share a profound bond with the trees they inhabit, allowing them to share the tree's strength and vitality and use it for various purposes, such as protection or healing.
- Weather Control: Some mountain nymphs (oreads) are believed to have the power to influence weather patterns in their high-altitude homes, from calming storms to bringing gentle rain.
- Floral Growth: Anthousai have the power to encourage the growth and abundance of vibrant flowers and plant life in their meadows, creating breathtaking displays of color and beauty.

Nymphs' magical abilities are not only an inherent part of their identities but also essential for their roles as stewards of nature. Their powers are closely tied to the well-being and balance of their natural environments.

11. Interactions with Humans

11A. Historical Encounters

Throughout history, humans have encountered nymphs in various ways, leading to a range of interactions:

- Positive Encounters: Nymphs are often depicted as benevolent beings who aid and guide humans who respect and honor their natural domains. Humans who approach nymphs with reverence and humility may receive their blessings, such as protection, healing, or guidance.
- Negative Encounters: On the other hand, disrespectful or invasive human actions in nymphs' territories can lead to negative interactions. Nymphs may respond to these intrusions with anger or mischief, causing misfortune or difficulties for those who transgress their boundaries.

11B. Legends of Fairy-Human Friendships or Conflicts

Nymphs' interactions with humans have given rise to numerous legends and stories:

- Friendships: Some legends tell of humans who formed genuine friendships with nymphs, often through acts of kindness or assistance. These friendships often resulted in mutual support and protection.
- Conflicts: Conflicts between humans and nymphs can arise from misunderstandings or human disregard for the natural world. In these tales, humans may face challenges or trials set by nymphs to test their intentions.

Nymphs' relationships with humans are complex and often reflect humanity's connection, or lack thereof, with the natural world. These interactions have left an indelible mark on folklore and mythology.

12. Country of Origin

12A. The Geographic Regions or Countries

Nymphs are deeply rooted in various mythologies and cultural traditions, making their presence felt in different geographic regions and countries around the world:

- Greek Mythology: Nymphs are prominently featured in Greek mythology, where they are associated with specific natural features such as forests, water bodies, mountains, and meadows. Greece and its surrounding regions are rich in nymph lore.
- Roman Mythology: Roman mythology adopted many Greek traditions and incorporated nymphs into their own pantheon. Italy, as the heart of the Roman Empire, is a region with a significant nymph presence.
- Celtic Traditions: Nymph-like beings appear in Celtic mythology, often connected to mystical forests, sacred groves, and water spirits. Regions like Ireland, Scotland, and Wales have their own variations of these nature spirits.

- Slavic Folklore: Slavic folklore features beings akin to nymphs, such as the rusalka, which are water nymphs associated with lakes and rivers. These creatures are prevalent in Slavic countries like Russia and Ukraine.
- Norse Mythology: The Norse tradition includes entities resembling nymphs, like the "huldra" in Scandinavian folklore. These forest-dwelling beings are found in regions such as Norway and Sweden.
- Asian Mythologies: Various Asian cultures have their own nature spirits and beings that share similarities with nymphs. For example, Japanese mythology includes "kami" associated with natural elements.

Nymphs, or beings resembling them, have left their mark on cultures across the globe, demonstrating the universal human connection to the natural world.

12B. Cultural Significance

In regions where nymph lore is prevalent, these beings hold significant cultural and spiritual importance. They are often seen as guardians of nature and the embodiment of the beauty and vitality of the natural world. Nymphs' presence in these cultures reinforces the reverence and respect for the environment and its interconnectedness with human existence.

13. Where to Find Them

13A. Specific Locations, Forests, or Landscapes

Nymphs are elusive beings, and sightings are often tied to their natural domains:

- Dryads: To encounter dryads, one must venture into ancient forests and groves, particularly those with majestic and venerable trees. These tree nymphs are deeply rooted in the heartwood of the oldest trees.
- Naiads: Naiads can be found near freshwater sources such as lakes, rivers, and springs. They are most active near the water's edge, where they watch over their aquatic domains.
- Oreads: These mountain nymphs are often sighted in rugged, high-altitude landscapes, among rocky cliffs and pristine peaks. Their presence is most pronounced in remote and untouched mountain regions.
- Anthousai: To witness anthousai, one should explore meadows and fields during the height of spring and summer when vibrant flowers are in full bloom. These flower nymphs are most active during these seasons.

13B. Best Times of Day or Year for Sightings

Nymph sightings are often influenced by the rhythms of nature:

- Daylight Hours: Nymphs are generally more active during daylight, when the natural world around them is vibrant and alive. Early morning and late afternoon are prime times for encounters.
- Seasonal Variations: The best times to encounter nymphs may vary depending on the type and their natural domains. For example, tree nymphs (dryads) may be more active in

spring and summer when the forest is lush, while water nymphs (naiads) may be seen year-round near flowing water sources.
- Special Occasions: In some cultures, specific rituals, festivals, or celestial events are associated with increased chances of nymph encounters. These occasions may offer unique opportunities to witness these ethereal beings.

Nymph sightings are often serendipitous and require patience, respect for their habitats, and an attunement to the natural world.

14. How to See Them

14A. Practical Tips and Advice for Them

Seeing nymphs is a rare and mystical experience, but there are some tips and practices that may enhance your chances of an encounter:
- Respect Nature: The most important aspect of nymph encounters is respecting and preserving their natural habitats. Nymphs are protectors of these environments, and a respectful attitude toward nature is often a prerequisite for an encounter.
- Visit Natural Areas: To see nymphs, visit the specific natural environments associated with their types. Venture into ancient forests, approach freshwater sources, explore mountainous regions, or walk through meadows and fields during the appropriate seasons.
- Observe Quietly: Nymphs are known to be shy and sensitive to disruptions. Moving quietly and observing the natural world without disturbance can increase the likelihood of a sighting.
- Stay Patient: Nymphs are elusive and may not reveal themselves readily. Spend time in their domains, immersing yourself in the beauty of nature, and be patient in your observations.

14B. Rituals, Offerings, or Behaviors That May Attract Them

In some traditions, certain rituals, offerings, or behaviors are believed to attract nymphs:
- Offerings: Leave small offerings like flowers, clean water, or tokens of appreciation at natural altars or sacred spots within their habitats. These offerings symbolize your respect and reverence for the nymphs and their domains.
- Music and Song: Nymphs are often associated with music and song. Playing music or singing harmonious tunes that resonate with the natural world may draw them closer.
- Meditation and Connection: Engage in mindful practices that foster a deeper connection to nature. Meditation or simply being present in the moment can attune you to the rhythms of the natural world.
- Celebrate Seasonal Festivals: Some cultures have seasonal festivals dedicated to nature and its spirits. Participating in these festivals may provide opportunities to connect with nymphs.

Encounters with nymphs are often considered rare and magical, and they require a combination of reverence for nature, patience, and a deep connection to the natural world.

15. Protection and Etiquette

15A. Guidance on How to Respect and Protect Them

Respecting and protecting nymphs and their natural habitats is paramount for maintaining the balance of nature and fostering positive interactions:

- Leave No Trace: When exploring nymph habitats, follow the principles of "Leave No Trace." Avoid littering, damaging plants or trees, or disturbing the natural environment. Leave the place as you found it.
- Do Not Harm Their Domains: Avoid actions that harm the natural features associated with nymphs. This includes refraining from cutting down trees inhabited by dryads or polluting water sources where naiads dwell.
- Observe Quietly: When in the presence of nymphs, maintain a respectful distance and observe them quietly. Sudden or disruptive behavior can cause them to withdraw.
- Respect Ritual Sites: If you encounter sacred sites or altars within nymph habitats, treat them with reverence. Do not disturb or remove any offerings left by others.

15B. Superstitions or Taboos

In some cultures and traditions, specific superstitions or taboos govern interactions with nymphs:

- Offerings and Symbols: Offerings made to nymphs should be made sincerely and respectfully. It is considered bad luck to offer insincere or inappropriate gifts.
- Names: Using a nymph's true name in vain or without permission is often considered disrespectful and may lead to negative consequences.
- Cursing or Desecrating Natural Features: Cursing or desecrating the natural elements within nymph domains is believed to incur their wrath. This can result in misfortune or disturbances in one's life.
- Breaking Sacred Pacts: In some folklore, humans who break sacred pacts or agreements made with nymphs may face severe consequences or curses.

Respecting the traditions and taboos associated with nymphs is essential for maintaining harmonious relationships and ensuring positive encounters with these enchanting beings.

16. Art and Representation

16A. Portrayed in Art, Literature, and Media

Nymphs have been a popular subject in various forms of art, literature, and media, showcasing their enduring allure:

- Classical Art: In Ancient Greece and Rome, nymphs were commonly depicted in sculptures, paintings, and mosaics. These artworks celebrated their beauty and connection to nature, often capturing their graceful forms in various natural settings.
- Literary Works: Nymphs have played significant roles in classical and mythological literature. Epic poems like Homer's "The Odyssey" and Ovid's "Metamorphoses" feature nymphs as central characters in tales of love, transformation, and adventure.
- Renaissance Art: During the Renaissance period, nymphs continued to be a prominent theme in art. Renowned artists like Sandro Botticelli and Titian depicted nymphs in lush, idyllic landscapes, evoking a sense of beauty and sensuality.
- Folklore and Fairy Tales: Nymph-like beings are found in folklore and fairy tales across cultures. These stories often emphasize their connection to nature, their protective roles, and their interactions with humans.

16B. Iconic Artists or Authors Who Have Featured Them

Several artists and authors have made significant contributions to the portrayal of nymphs in art and literature:

- Claude Monet: The renowned French Impressionist painter Claude Monet painted a series of water lily pond scenes that evoke the serene beauty and tranquility often associated with water nymphs.
- John William Waterhouse: The English Pre-Raphaelite painter John William Waterhouse created several paintings featuring nymphs, including the famous "Hylas and the Nymphs," which captures the allure and danger of these beings.
- Ovid: The Roman poet Ovid's "Metamorphoses" is a classic work of literature that features numerous stories involving nymphs. His vivid descriptions and narratives have contributed to the enduring fascination with these beings.
- Hans Christian Andersen: The Danish author Hans Christian Andersen wrote fairy tales that often included water nymphs and other supernatural beings. His story "The Little Mermaid" is one of the most famous depictions of a water nymph.

Nymphs continue to be a source of inspiration for artists and authors, influencing the portrayal of these enchanting spirits in contemporary works of art and literature.

17. Modern Beliefs and Practices

17A. Contemporary Beliefs and Practices

In modern times, beliefs and practices related to nymphs have evolved, reflecting changing cultural and spiritual perspectives:

- Nature Conservation: Many people today view nymphs as symbolic representations of the importance of environmental conservation. Belief in their existence may not be literal, but rather a way to emphasize the need to protect natural habitats.
- Ecological Stewardship: Some ecological organizations and movements incorporate nymph imagery into their campaigns to raise awareness about preserving ecosystems and protecting natural resources.
- Nature Spirituality: Contemporary spiritual and pagan belief systems often incorporate the idea of nature spirits, including nymphs, as sacred beings to be honored and respected during rituals and ceremonies.
- Nature-Based Practices: Individuals who follow nature-based spiritual practices may engage in rituals and meditations that involve invoking or connecting with nymphs as guardians of specific natural elements.

17B. Current Festivals or Gatherings

While there are no widespread festivals dedicated solely to nymphs in modern times, some nature-oriented festivals and gatherings celebrate the interconnectedness of humans and the natural world:

- Earth Day: Earth Day is an annual global event that focuses on environmental protection and awareness. It often includes activities and events that emphasize the importance of preserving the planet's ecosystems, aligning with the spirit of nymphs as protectors of nature.
- Pagan and Nature Spirit Festivals: Some pagan and nature-based spirituality festivals incorporate the honoring of nature spirits, including nymphs, as part of their rituals and celebrations.
- Ecological Initiatives: Various environmental organizations and initiatives host gatherings and events that promote ecological awareness and the protection of natural habitats, echoing the principles associated with nymphs.

These contemporary beliefs and practices reflect a deepening awareness of the importance of nature and the need to maintain a harmonious relationship with the environment, even if belief in nymphs as literal beings has waned in some cultures.

18. Conservation Efforts

18A. Conservation Initiatives

While nymphs are mythical beings, conservation efforts aimed at preserving the natural habitats they are associated with are of utmost importance:

- Habitat Protection: Conservation organizations and government agencies around the world work tirelessly to protect and preserve the forests, water bodies, mountains, and meadows that are home to a rich array of wildlife, including the species that inspire nymph lore.
- Biodiversity Conservation: Efforts to conserve biodiversity encompass not only the protection of the physical environment, but also the creatures that inhabit it. By

safeguarding the ecosystems in which nymphs are believed to reside, a diverse range of flora and fauna can thrive.

- Raising Awareness: Conservationists often use the symbolism of nymphs and other nature spirits to raise awareness about the importance of ecological preservation. This includes educational campaigns and outreach to engage the public in environmental stewardship.

18B. Threats They May Face and Steps to Mitigate Them

The habitats associated with nymphs face various threats, and conservationists take steps to mitigate these challenges:

- Deforestation: The logging industry and urban development can result in deforestation, threatening the ancient forests that dryads call home. Reforestation and protected areas help combat this threat.
- Water Pollution: Naiads are particularly vulnerable to water pollution from industrial activities and runoff. Water quality regulations and cleanup efforts are crucial to safeguarding their habitats.
- Climate Change: Climate change poses a significant threat to all ecosystems, including those inhabited by nymphs. Conservationists work to mitigate climate change and its impacts on the natural world.
- Habitat Destruction: The expansion of human settlements and agriculture can lead to the destruction of meadows and mountains that are vital to nymphs. Conservation efforts focus on land-use planning and habitat restoration.

Preserving the natural environments tied to nymphs is not only essential for the mythical beings themselves, but for the entire ecosystems they represent.

19. Additional Folklore

19A. Lesser-Known Stories or Beliefs

Beyond the well-known nymph lore, there are lesser-known stories and beliefs from various cultures that shed light on different facets of these mystical beings:

- Roman Nymphs: Roman mythology had its own nymphs, such as the Camenae, who were associated with springs and wells. Their stories often intertwined with the history of Rome and its founding.
- Asian Nature Spirits: In Asian cultures, spirits similar to nymphs exist. For example, Japanese folklore features "kami" associated with natural elements like trees, mountains, and waterfalls.
- Nymph Variations: Across Europe, there are regional variations of nymphs. In Scandinavia, for instance, there are tales of forest spirits known as "skogsra" and water spirits called "sjorar."
- Nymph Hybrids: Some mythologies describe the offspring of nymphs and humans, such as satyrs (offspring of nymphs and satyrs), who are known for their wild and hedonistic behaviors.

19B. Variations in Their Portrayal Across Different Cultures

Nymphs take on diverse forms and characteristics in different cultures:

- Greek Nymphs: Greek nymphs include dryads (tree nymphs), naiads (water nymphs), oreads (mountain nymphs), and anthousai (flower nymphs). They were deeply rooted in Greek mythology and often played central roles in various stories.
- Roman Nymphs: Roman nymphs, while similar to their Greek counterparts, had their own unique attributes and stories. They were often associated with the protection of specific regions and water sources.
- Celtic Spirits: Celtic mythology featured spirits akin to nymphs, such as the "bean sidhe" or banshee, associated with the fairy mounds and natural landscapes of Ireland.
- Slavic Water Spirits: Slavic folklore includes water spirits like the rusalka, who are believed to inhabit lakes and rivers and are known for their enchanting songs.
- Norse Beings: In Norse mythology, beings like the "huldra" and "skogsra" resembled nymphs and were associated with forests and natural landscapes.

These variations reflect the rich diversity of human cultures and their unique connections to the natural world.

20. Famous Encounters

20A. Historical or Modern Encounters

Throughout history and into modern times, there have been accounts of famous individuals encountering nymphs or experiences that evoke the spirit of these mythical beings:

- Artistic Encounters: Renowned artists and writers, such as Claude Monet, John William Waterhouse, and Hans Christian Andersen, have depicted nymphs in their works, capturing the allure and mystique of these beings.
- Naturalists and Explorers: Naturalists and explorers like John Muir and David Attenborough have had profound connections with the natural world, akin to encounters with nymphs. Their work to document and protect the environment aligns with the spirit of nymph conservation.
- Environmental Activists: Modern environmental activists, such as Greta Thunberg, embody the values associated with nymphs by advocating for the protection of nature and the importance of ecological conservation.
- Literary Encounters: Contemporary literature often explores the theme of humanity's connection to nature and its mythical beings. Authors like Neil Gaiman, in his work "American Gods," weave nymph-like characters into narratives that reflect modern sensibilities.

20B. The Impact of These Encounters

Famous encounters with nymphs, whether literal or symbolic, have often had a profound impact on the lives and work of individuals:

- Inspiration: Artists and writers often draw inspiration from their encounters with nature and the mystical beings it contains, infusing their creations with a sense of wonder and beauty.
- Activism: Encounters with the natural world and its spirits have spurred individuals to become advocates for environmental preservation and ecological consciousness.
- Spiritual Connection: Some famous encounters have deepened the spiritual connection between individuals and the natural world, fostering a sense of reverence for the environment.
- Cultural Impact: Famous encounters with nymphs have contributed to the enduring allure of these beings in popular culture, ensuring their continued presence in art, literature, and media.

Famous encounters with nymphs, whether real or metaphorical, highlight the enduring significance of these mythical beings as symbols of the deep connection between humanity and the natural world.

Pixies

1. Species Introduction

1A. Brief Overview

Pixies are diminutive and mischievous fairies that have captured the imagination of many. These tiny beings, known for their playful nature and enchanting presence, are a distinct and beloved part of fairy folklore. Pixies are often associated with the British Isles and are believed to inhabit lush meadows, woodlands, and gardens.

1B. Unique Characteristics That Distinguish Them from Other Fairies

Pixies are typically quite small, standing only a few inches tall. They are characterized by their delicate and ethereal appearance, with translucent wings that allow them to flutter gracefully through the air. Their skin often has a radiant glow, and their eyes shimmer with an inner light.
Unlike some other fairy species, pixies are known for their exuberant and mischievous personalities. They enjoy playing pranks on humans and other creatures, sometimes leading travelers astray in the woods or causing minor disruptions in households. However, they are not malicious and are usually harmless in their antics.
Pixies are also renowned for their affinity for nature. They have a deep connection with the flora and fauna of their chosen habitats, often aiding in the growth of plants and flowers. Their laughter is said to sound like the tinkling of bells, and it is believed to bring good luck to those who hear it.

2. General Appearance

2A. Detailed Physical Description

Pixies are among the smallest of fairies, standing only a few inches tall, which makes them incredibly hard to spot by human eyes. Their delicate and slender bodies are often described as graceful and elfin. They have finely proportioned features, with tiny hands and feet. Their skin carries a luminescent quality, giving them an otherworldly glow. Pixies' hair can vary in color, ranging from shades of blonde to a silvery white, and it often flows in a free-spirited manner. Pixies are recognized for their distinctive wings, which are transparent and gossamer-thin. These wings enable them to fly with agility and grace. When at rest, the wings are often folded neatly against their backs, almost appearing as intricate, delicate lacework.

2B. Distinctive Clothing and Accessories

Pixies are known for their fashion sense, often wearing garments made from petals, leaves, and other natural materials. They prefer attire that blends seamlessly with their woodland surroundings, making them appear as if they are a part of the very flora they adore. Tiny flower blossoms may serve as hats, while leaves or vines may be fashioned into skirts or tunics.
In addition to their attire, pixies are fond of adorning themselves with tiny jewelry made from dewdrops, acorns, and other miniature treasures found in the forest. These accessories are not only decorative but also imbued with a touch of magic, enhancing their connection to the natural world.

3. Sexes

3A. Description of Male and Female Pixies

Pixies, like many fairy species, exhibit both male and female individuals. However, distinguishing between male and female pixies can be quite challenging for human observers due to their small size and similar physical characteristics. In fact, the primary differences between male and female pixies are often subtle and not readily noticeable to the human eye.
In the world of pixies, gender roles tend to be more fluid and less defined than in human societies. Both males and females are equally skilled in their roles within their communities and share similar characteristics, including their mischievous natures and love for nature.

3B. Differences in Appearance or Behavior Between the Sexes

While male and female pixies share many similarities, there are subtle differences in their behavior and social roles. Female pixies are often associated with nurturing and protecting the natural world, including tending to the flowers and plants that populate their habitats. They are believed to have a gentle and caring disposition.
Male pixies, on the other hand, are often seen as more adventurous and daring. They may take on roles as guardians of their communities or engage in more playful and mischievous behavior. These distinctions, however, are not rigid and can vary from one pixie community to another.
It's important to note that the concepts of gender and behavior in pixie society are not as structured as in human society, and individuals are free to express themselves in ways that feel most authentic to them.

4. Lore and Legends

4A. Cultural and Historical References

Pixies have left an indelible mark on the folklore and legends of the British Isles, particularly in areas such as Cornwall and Devon. These enchanting beings have been a part of the local cultural fabric for centuries, and their stories have been passed down through generations.
In Celtic and English folklore, pixies are often associated with the realm of the "little people." They are believed to inhabit ancient burial mounds, sacred groves, and other mystical sites. People would leave offerings to appease the pixies, seeking their favor and protection.

4B. Stories, Myths, and Folklore Associated with Pixies

Numerous tales and legends featuring pixies have been collected over the years. Some stories depict them as benevolent guardians of the natural world, assisting lost travelers and aiding in the growth of crops. Others portray them as playful tricksters, leading wanderers astray in the woods or causing minor mischief in households.
One famous legend tells of a pixie bride who was kidnapped by a mortal man, only to return to her pixie kin after being enchanted by the sound of church bells. This story illustrates the enduring theme of the elusive and ethereal nature of pixies.
Pixie lore is also intertwined with the concept of "pixie-led," where individuals claim to have been led astray by pixies, often experiencing disorientation and lost time. This phenomenon has been attributed to the mischievous nature of pixies, who may play tricks on unsuspecting humans.

5. Habitat and Natural Environment

5A. Information about the Natural Habitats

Pixies are intimately connected to the natural world and tend to make their homes in secluded and pristine environments. They are often found in lush meadows, deep within enchanting woodlands, or near clear, babbling brooks. These settings provide them with an abundance of flora and fauna to interact with and protect.
Their homes are often located in close proximity to ancient trees, as pixies have a deep reverence for the wisdom and energy of these venerable beings. Pixie communities are usually hidden from human sight, concealed beneath cloaks of enchantment and natural magic.

5B. Environmental Factors Affecting Their Choice of Residence

The choice of habitat for pixies is influenced by various environmental factors. One crucial factor is the presence of abundant plant life, including wildflowers, mosses, and mushrooms. Pixies are known to have a symbiotic relationship with plants, nurturing them and ensuring their vitality.
The purity of water sources is another significant consideration. Pixies require clean and pristine water for both their sustenance and their magical practices. Bodies of water such as springs, streams, and ponds are often considered sacred in pixie lore.

Protection from natural predators and human interference is also paramount. Pixie communities are hidden away and often enchanted to remain unseen by those who might disrupt their delicate ecosystems.

6. Lifestyle and Social Structure

6A. Insights into Their Societal Structure and Hierarchy

Pixie society is typically organized into tight-knit communities or clans. These communities are often led by a leader or elder pixie who is revered for their wisdom and experience. However, the leadership roles among pixies are not fixed, and leadership can change based on various factors, including the leader's ability to protect and provide for the community.
Pixies value cooperation and communal living. They work together to ensure the well-being of their natural environment and the prosperity of their community. This includes nurturing and protecting the plants, animals, and water sources in their chosen habitat.

6B. Daily Routines

Pixies are known for their industriousness, and their daily routines are centered around the maintenance and harmonization of their natural surroundings. They engage in a variety of activities, such as tending to flowers, ensuring the health of trees, and maintaining the balance of their ecosystem.
Their sense of playfulness extends to their daily lives, and pixies are known to engage in games and celebrations, often marked by music and dance. Their laughter, which sounds like the tinkling of bells, is believed to bring joy and good luck to those who hear it.
Pixies are also skilled in various forms of magic, particularly nature-based magic. They use their magical abilities to communicate with animals, accelerate the growth of plants, and protect their homes from harm.

7. Diet and Food Sources

7A. What Do They Eat?

Pixies are predominantly herbivores, nourishing themselves primarily with the bounties of the natural world that surrounds them. Their diet consists mainly of nectar from flowers, honeydew secreted by aphids, and the sweet juices of ripe fruits. These natural sugars provide them with the energy they need to sustain their diminutive yet active lifestyles.
Pixies also have a deep connection with the plant kingdom, and they are known to partake in the essence of certain flowers and leaves, which they believe enhances their connection with the natural world. These rituals are considered a form of communion with the flora they cherish.

7B. Special Dietary Preferences or Rituals

One notable dietary preference among pixies is their affinity for certain plants and flowers that are believed to possess magical properties. They may consume tiny portions of petals or leaves from

these special plants during rituals or celebrations to strengthen their connection with the natural world and enhance their magical abilities.
Additionally, pixies are known to be skilled foragers. They have a keen knowledge of the woods and meadows, and they can find hidden sources of nourishment, even during the harshest seasons. This adaptability helps them thrive in their enchanted habitats.

8. Communication and Language

8A. How Do They Communicate with Each Other?

Pixies possess a unique and intricate system of communication that combines both spoken language and non-verbal cues. Their language, often referred to as "Pixie Speak," is a melodious and tinkling form of communication that sounds like the gentle ringing of bells. This ethereal language is believed to be closely tied to the natural world and is used to convey thoughts, emotions, and messages among pixies.
Non-verbal communication is equally important among pixies. They use expressive gestures, delicate movements of their wings, and facial expressions to convey subtleties of meaning. Their communication style is deeply empathetic, allowing them to understand each other on a profound level.

8B. Any Unique Languages or Gestures Used

In addition to their shared language, some pixie communities may develop unique dialects or variations of Pixie Speak. These dialects are often influenced by the specific flora and fauna in their habitat and may include words and expressions that are unique to their community.
Pixies also employ certain gestures and movements during their intricate dances and rituals. These gestures are not only beautiful to witness but also serve as a form of non-verbal communication, conveying intentions, emotions, and even warnings to other pixies.
Pixies are known for their ability to communicate with animals as well. They use a form of animal language that allows them to interact harmoniously with the creatures of the forest, strengthening their connection to the natural world.

9. Reproduction and Life Cycle

9A. The Fairy's Life Stages from Birth to Death

Pixies, like many fairy species, have a unique life cycle that differs significantly from humans. Their life stages are marked by both physical and magical transformations.

- Infancy: Pixie infants, known as "blossoms," are born as tiny, translucent beings with undeveloped wings. They are cared for by their parents and the community until they mature.
- Adolescence: As they grow, pixies undergo a magical transformation known as "blossoming." During this stage, their wings fully develop, and they gain the ability to fly. This is a time of curiosity and exploration, as young pixies become more independent.

- Adulthood: Fully matured pixies are known as "blooms." They play active roles in their communities, participating in communal activities and taking on responsibilities that contribute to the well-being of their habitat.
- Elderhood: As pixies age, they may undergo a final transformation known as "withering." During this stage, they become less active and may take on roles as wise elders who guide and advise the younger generation.

9B. Mating Rituals and Reproduction Process

Pixie reproduction is a mystical and sacred process closely tied to their connection with the natural world. Mating rituals typically occur during the enchanting twilight hours in the heart of their meadows and woodlands.
Males and females engage in intricate dances and rituals, often accompanied by music created by the rustling leaves and gentle breezes. These rituals serve as a way for pixies to bond and select compatible partners. Once a pair has formed a deep connection, they engage in a magical union that results in the creation of a tiny, luminous pixie egg.
These eggs are carefully incubated by both parents, who use their magical abilities to ensure the health and growth of the embryo inside. After a period of nurturing, a young pixie emerges from the egg, ready to begin its own journey through the stages of life.

10. Magic Abilities and Powers

10A. Breakdown of Their Magical Abilities

Pixies are renowned for their innate connection to magic, particularly nature-based and elemental magic. Their enchanting abilities allow them to interact with the natural world in profound ways:

- Plant Manipulation: Pixies have the power to influence the growth and health of plants. They can accelerate the blooming of flowers, encourage the growth of trees, and even revive withered or dying plants.
- Weather Control: Some pixies possess the ability to influence weather patterns, particularly those tied to their natural habitats. They can summon gentle rains to nourish their gardens or encourage warm, sunny days.
- Invisibility: Pixies have the magical ability to become invisible at will, making it easier for them to interact with the natural world and observe humans without being seen.
- Illusions: They can create mesmerizing illusions that are often used for playful pranks or to protect their communities by deceiving intruders.
- Animal Communication: Pixies have a unique gift for communicating with animals, allowing them to form alliances with creatures of the forest and gain insights into the natural world.

10B. Specific Spells or Powers Unique to This Species

One of the most remarkable powers of pixies is their ability to heal the natural world. They are known to perform rituals that can rejuvenate ailing trees, revitalize barren soil, and even restore balance to ecosystems disrupted by human interference. These rituals are deeply connected to their role as caretakers of the environment.

Pixies are also skilled in creating enchanted items and charms, often fashioned from natural materials like acorns, feathers, and gemstones. These items can have various magical properties, such as protection, luck, or the enhancement of one's connection to nature.
Their mastery of elemental magic allows them to control and manipulate the elements within their natural habitats, ensuring the harmony and balance of their surroundings.

11. Interactions with Humans

11A. Historical Encounters with Humans

Throughout history, pixies have had interactions with humans, both positive and negative. These encounters are often shrouded in mystery and wonder, leaving a lasting impression on those who have experienced them.
Positive encounters include stories of travelers lost in the woods who were guided to safety by kind-hearted pixies. Some tales speak of farmers who received aid in their crops from pixie communities in exchange for offerings of honey or milk. These encounters highlight the benevolent and helpful nature of pixies.

11B. Legends of Fairy-Human Friendships or Conflicts

In addition to the positive interactions, there are also legends of conflicts between pixies and humans. It's believed that pixies are protective of their natural habitats, and they may play pranks or create illusions to discourage human intrusion. Some stories tell of individuals who inadvertently offended pixies and experienced temporary disorientation or bewilderment in the woods, known as being "pixie-led."
However, there are also accounts of enduring friendships between humans and pixies, where mutual respect and offerings of gratitude allowed for peaceful coexistence. These stories emphasize the importance of understanding and respecting the boundaries of pixie communities.

12. Country of Origin

12A. Geographic Regions

Pixies are most prominently associated with the British Isles, particularly England, Ireland, Scotland, and Wales. Within these regions, specific locales are often tied to pixie folklore. In England, for instance, the county of Devon is renowned for its pixie legends, while Cornwall is also a hotspot for pixie encounters.
The lush meadows, ancient woodlands, and scenic landscapes of the British Isles provide the ideal habitat for pixies. Their presence in these regions is deeply ingrained in local culture and history.

12B. Cultural Significance in Those Areas

In the British Isles, pixies hold a special place in folklore and cultural traditions. They are often considered as protectors of the natural world and are seen as guardians of ancient sites, such as burial mounds and stone circles. Pixies are celebrated in local festivals, and their lore continues to inspire art, literature, and music in these regions.
In Cornwall, for example, the annual "Obby Oss" festival features a traditional procession with a hobbyhorse and dancers, with pixies being an integral part of the celebration. In literature, authors like Arthur Conan Doyle and Sir Walter Scott have drawn upon pixie folklore in their works, contributing to their enduring cultural significance.

13. Where to Find Them

13A. Specific Locations, Forests, or Landscapes

Finding pixies is a rare and elusive experience, as they are known to be skilled in remaining hidden from human eyes. However, there are certain locations where sightings have been reported more frequently. These include:

- Enchanted Woodlands: Deep, ancient forests and woodlands, often far from human settlements, are known to be favored habitats of pixies. These serene and secluded environments provide them with ample opportunities to interact with nature.
- Meadows and Glades: Lush meadows and glades, especially those surrounded by a rich diversity of plant life, are places where pixies are believed to congregate. These open spaces offer a magical, unspoiled backdrop for their activities.
- Babbling Brooks and Ponds: Bodies of water like streams, ponds, and brooks are often associated with pixie sightings. The gentle sounds of flowing water and the vibrant ecosystems around these water sources are said to attract pixies.
- Ancient Stone Circles: Some pixie lore suggests that these beings have a special connection to ancient stone circles and sacred sites. These mystical locations may serve as meeting points for pixie communities.

13B. Best Times of Day or Year for Sightings

Pixies are most active during the twilight hours, particularly at dawn and dusk, when the natural world is bathed in soft, magical light. These transitional periods are believed to be when the boundaries between the fairy world and the human world are at their thinnest, making encounters more likely.
The best time of year for sightings varies depending on the specific region and local folklore. In some areas, midsummer's eve (June 24th) is considered an auspicious time for encountering pixies, as it marks the height of their activity and magical presence.

14. How to See Them

14A. Tips and Advice for Encountering Them

Seeing pixies is a rare and magical experience, but there are some practical tips and behaviors that may increase your chances of encountering these elusive beings:

- Respect Their Habitat: Approach natural habitats with reverence and respect. Pixies are more likely to reveal themselves to those who show genuine care for the environment.
- Visit Sacred Sites: Explore ancient stone circles, megalithic structures, and other mystical sites known to be associated with pixies. These places are believed to have a higher concentration of fairy energy.
- Be Quiet and Observant: Pixies are easily startled by noise and commotion. Move quietly and patiently when exploring their habitats, and take time to observe the natural world around you.
- Leave Offerings: Some believe that leaving small offerings like honey, milk, or shiny trinkets in areas known for pixie activity can attract their attention and goodwill.
- Seek Twilight Hours: Plan your outings during the twilight hours of dawn and dusk, when pixies are believed to be most active and visible.

14B. Rituals, Offerings, or Behaviors That May Attract Them

In addition to the practical tips, some rituals, offerings, or behaviors are associated with attracting pixies:

- Dancing and Music: Engage in gentle, rhythmic movements or play soft, enchanting music in natural settings. Pixies are drawn to harmonious and joyful sounds.
- Offer Fragrant Flowers: Pixies are fond of fragrant flowers. Placing bouquets of blossoms in pixie-populated areas may encourage them to make an appearance.
- Speak Kindly: If you believe you are in the presence of pixies, speak to them with kindness and respect. Express your admiration for their world and your desire to connect.
- Carry a Token: Some people carry a small, symbolic token, like a crystal or a tiny bell, as a way to invite pixie energy and protection during their outings.

Remember that pixies are known for their capricious nature, and while these practices may increase your chances of seeing them, encounters are never guaranteed. Patience and a deep respect for the natural world are key when seeking to interact with pixies.

15. Protection and Etiquette

15A. Guidance on How to Respect and Protect Pixies and Their Habitats

Respecting pixies and their habitats is of utmost importance to ensure harmonious interactions. Here are some guidelines for showing respect and protection:

- Tread Lightly: When in pixie-inhabited areas, be mindful of your impact on the environment. Avoid trampling on plants and disturbing their homes.
- No Littering: Dispose of trash properly and refrain from leaving litter in their habitats. Pixies are guardians of nature and appreciate a clean and pristine environment.

- No Harmful Offerings: If leaving offerings, ensure they are natural and non-harmful. Avoid plastics, chemicals, or anything that could harm the ecosystem.
- Do Not Disturb: While observing pixies, do so quietly and respectfully. Do not attempt to capture or harm them in any way. Remember that they are shy and easily frightened.
- Follow Local Traditions: Learn about local customs and traditions related to pixies and follow them. Some areas may have specific practices to honor and protect these beings.

15B. Superstitions or Taboos Related to Interacting with Pixies

Pixie lore is rich in superstitions and taboos designed to ensure positive interactions with these magical beings:

- Avoid Swearing: Refrain from using harsh or disrespectful language when in pixie-inhabited areas. Pixies are sensitive to the energy and intent behind words.
- Respect Boundaries: Do not enter their hidden communities or sacred spaces without invitation. Trespassing on their homes is considered highly disrespectful.
- Never Break Promises: If you make a promise or commitment to a pixie, be sure to honor it. Pixies value sincerity and trust.
- Never Steal Pixie Offerings: If you come across offerings left by pixies or other humans, do not take them. These offerings are sacred and should not be disturbed.
- Beware of Illusions: Pixies are known to create illusions to protect their homes. If you find yourself in a situation that seems unreal or disorienting, it may be a pixie's warning to leave their territory.

By adhering to these guidelines and respecting the traditions surrounding pixies, you can foster positive interactions and protect their delicate ecosystems.

16. Art and Representation

16A. How Pixies Have Been Portrayed in Art, Literature, and Media

Pixies have been a popular subject in various forms of artistic expression, including art, literature, and media. Their enchanting and whimsical nature has inspired countless works:

- Art: Pixies have been featured in paintings, sculptures, and illustrations dating back centuries. Renowned artists like Arthur Rackham and Brian Froud have captured their ethereal beauty in intricate and captivating detail.
- Literature: Pixies have been prominent characters in folklore collections, fairy tales, and fantasy novels. Works such as "Peter Pan" by J.M. Barrie and "A Midsummer Night's Dream" by William Shakespeare feature pixie characters that have become iconic.
- Media: Pixies have made appearances in animated films, television shows, and video games. They are often depicted as mischievous, playful, and endearing characters that capture the imagination of audiences young and old.

16B. Iconic Artists or Authors Who Have Featured Them

Several artists and authors have made significant contributions to the portrayal of pixies in art and literature:

- Arthur Rackham: A celebrated illustrator known for his detailed and whimsical depictions of fairies and pixies. His work has had a profound influence on the way these beings are imagined.
- Brian Froud: Froud is renowned for his imaginative and intricate illustrations of various fairy beings, including pixies. His artwork has graced books, films, and exhibitions.
- J.M. Barrie: The author of "Peter Pan" introduced the mischievous fairy Tinker Bell, who has become one of the most iconic pixie characters in literature and film.
- William Shakespeare: In "A Midsummer Night's Dream," Shakespeare featured the character of Puck, a playful and trickster-like pixie who plays a central role in the play's magical events.

The enduring appeal of pixies in art and literature continues to enchant audiences worldwide and adds to the rich tapestry of their folklore.

17. Modern Beliefs and Practices

17A. Contemporary Beliefs and Practices Related to Pixies

In modern times, pixies continue to hold a special place in the hearts and imaginations of many. Contemporary beliefs and practices related to pixies include:

- Faerie Festivals: Some regions host faerie festivals dedicated to celebrating various fairy beings, including pixies. These gatherings often feature costume parades, art exhibitions, and performances inspired by the fairy realm.
- Faerie Gardens: Gardening enthusiasts create faerie gardens or miniature landscapes designed to attract and provide a home for pixies and other fairies. These gardens are often adorned with tiny furniture, whimsical decorations, and offerings.
- Pixie Altars: Some individuals create altars or sacred spaces within their homes to honor pixies and other nature spirits. These altars may include offerings of flowers, crystals, and other natural elements.
- Faerie Tarot and Oracle Decks: Pixie and fairy-themed tarot and oracle decks have gained popularity, offering insights and guidance with the help of these magical beings.
- Nature Conservation: Many nature conservation efforts are inspired by the belief in pixies and their role as protectors of the environment. These initiatives aim to preserve natural habitats to ensure the well-being of both wildlife and the mystical beings that inhabit them.

17B. Current Festivals or Gatherings Dedicated to Them

Throughout the year, various festivals and gatherings celebrate pixies and other fairy beings. These events often draw people from diverse backgrounds who share a fascination with the mystical and magical:

- The Gnome and Faerie Festival (Pennsylvania, USA): This annual festival features a world of enchantment, including live music, storytelling, and activities for children and adults inspired by pixies and other magical creatures.
- The FaerieCon International (USA): A convention that brings together artists, authors, and enthusiasts of all things faerie, including pixies. It features workshops, panels, and a marketplace of faerie-themed art and merchandise.
- Faeryfest (United Kingdom): An immersive experience celebrating the realm of faeries, including pixies. It offers music, workshops, and a faery market.
- The Australian Fairy Tale Society Conference (Australia): This event explores the rich world of fairy tales and includes discussions and presentations about various fairy beings, including pixies.

These festivals and gatherings provide a platform for individuals to connect with like-minded enthusiasts, share their love for pixies, and immerse themselves in a world of magic and wonder.

18. Conservation Efforts

18A. Conservation Initiatives

Conservation efforts to protect the habitats of pixies and other magical beings have gained traction in recent years. These initiatives recognize the importance of preserving natural environments for both the flora and fauna that inhabit them, as well as the mystical beings that are deeply connected to these ecosystems.

- Nature Reserves: Some regions have established nature reserves and protected areas that are believed to be inhabited by pixies and other fairies. These reserves aim to limit human intrusion and habitat destruction.
- Reforestation Projects: Reforestation efforts have been undertaken to restore ancient woodlands and meadows, ensuring that the homes of pixies remain intact and vibrant.
- Educational Programs: Conservation organizations and schools often collaborate to educate the public about the importance of preserving natural habitats and the folklore and legends associated with pixies. These programs seek to foster a deeper respect for the environment.
- Fairy Rings: In some areas, designated "fairy rings" are established where individuals can leave offerings and appreciate the beauty of nature while respecting the boundaries of pixie communities.

18B. Threats They May Face and Steps to Mitigate Them

Pixies and their habitats face various threats, and steps are taken to mitigate these challenges:

- Habitat Destruction: Urban development, deforestation, and pollution threaten the natural environments of pixies. Conservation efforts focus on raising awareness and implementing strict regulations to protect these habitats.
- Climate Change: Shifts in climate patterns can disrupt the delicate balance of ecosystems where pixies reside. Conservationists work to combat climate change and mitigate its impact on the environment.

- Human Intrusion: Curiosity and the desire to interact with pixies can lead to human intrusion in their habitats. Education campaigns stress the importance of respecting boundaries and avoiding harm to both the environment and the beings that dwell within it.
- Pollution: Pollution from chemicals, plastics, and other contaminants can harm the flora and fauna that pixies rely on. Conservation initiatives emphasize reducing pollution and maintaining clean, natural environments.

Efforts to protect pixies and their habitats are intertwined with broader conservation movements aimed at preserving the natural world and fostering a harmonious coexistence between humans and the mystical beings of folklore.

19. Additional Folklore

19A. Lesser-Known Stories or Beliefs Associated with Pixie Species

In addition to the well-known pixie lore, there are lesser-known stories and beliefs that provide a deeper understanding of these magical beings:

- Pixie Gifts: Some legends suggest that pixies have the power to bestow gifts upon humans who show kindness and respect for the natural world. These gifts are said to bring luck and protection.
- Pixie Homes: In certain regions, there are tales of humans stumbling upon pixie homes hidden beneath ancient trees or within the roots of massive oak trees. These homes are often described as tiny, cozy dwellings adorned with natural decorations.
- Pixie Midwives: In some folklore, pixies are believed to assist in the birth of woodland creatures. They are said to attend to the needs of newborn animals and ensure their well-being.
- Pixie Timekeeping: It is said that pixies have a unique sense of time and can manipulate it within their habitats. Some believe that time moves differently in pixie communities, making it easy for them to go unnoticed by humans.

19B. Variations in Their Portrayal Across Different Cultures

The portrayal of pixies varies across different cultures and regions:

- Celtic Pixies: In Celtic folklore, pixies are often considered mischievous but not malevolent. They are closely tied to nature and are believed to inhabit ancient forests and stone circles.
- English Pixies: English pixies, particularly those in the counties of Devon and Cornwall, are known for their playful nature and for helping humans in need.
- Scottish Pixies: Scottish pixies, known as "brownies," are depicted as helpful household fairies. They are said to perform chores in exchange for offerings of food.
- Welsh Pixies: In Wales, pixies are associated with lakes and water sources. They are believed to reside near these bodies of water and are known for their love of dancing and music.

- Icelandic Huldufólk: In Iceland, similar beings known as "huldufólk" share characteristics with pixies. They are believed to inhabit rocks and natural formations and are highly respected in Icelandic culture.

The diversity of beliefs and cultural variations adds depth and richness to the lore of pixies, reflecting the unique perspectives of different communities and regions.

20. Famous Encounters

20A. Historical or Modern Encounters

Throughout history, there have been accounts of famous individuals who claim to have encountered pixies, leaving a lasting impact on their lives or work:

- Sir Arthur Conan Doyle: The renowned author of the Sherlock Holmes series, Sir Arthur Conan Doyle, claimed to have had a vivid encounter with pixies during a trip to Devon, England. This experience influenced his belief in the existence of mystical beings and led him to write about the supernatural.
- J.M. Barrie: The creator of Peter Pan, J.M. Barrie, was inspired by the folklore of pixies and incorporated the mischievous and spirited Tinker Bell into his beloved tale. Tinker Bell's character has since become an iconic representation of pixies in popular culture.
- Brian Froud: The acclaimed artist and illustrator Brian Froud is renowned for his intricate and enchanting depictions of faeries, including pixies. His work has contributed to the modern understanding of these magical beings.
- Contemporary Encounters: In recent years, there have been reported sightings and encounters with pixies by individuals who describe witnessing small, luminous beings in natural settings. These accounts continue to fuel the belief in pixies and their enduring presence.

20B. The Impact of These Encounters on Their Lives or Work

For many individuals who claim to have encountered pixies, the experiences have had a profound impact on their lives or creative work:

- Inspiration: Encounters with pixies often serve as a wellspring of inspiration, influencing artists, writers, and creators to explore the realms of fantasy and magic in their work.
- Spiritual Connection: Some people describe encounters with pixies as deeply spiritual experiences, fostering a heightened connection to the natural world and a greater appreciation for the mysteries of existence.
- Advocacy for Nature: Encounters with pixies have prompted some individuals to become advocates for nature conservation and preservation, recognizing the importance of protecting the habitats of these mystical beings.
- Cultural Influence: Famous encounters with pixies have left an indelible mark on popular culture, shaping the way these beings are depicted in literature, art, and media.

These famous encounters with pixies continue to captivate the imagination and inspire a sense of wonder, reminding us of the enchanting mysteries that exist in the world around us.

Changeling

1. Species Introduction

1A. Brief Overview of Changelings

Changelings are a mysterious and unique subset of fairy beings that have long captured the imagination of storytellers and folklore enthusiasts. Unlike many other fairies, changelings are not a distinct species, but rather a phenomenon associated with infants and young children. In various cultures, changelings are believed to be substituted for human babies by fairies, elves, or other supernatural entities. This substitution often occurs under clandestine circumstances, leading to a variety of cultural beliefs and practices surrounding changelings.

1B. Unique Characteristics of Changelings

The defining characteristic of changelings is their ability to mimic the appearance of human infants. They are known for their uncanny resemblance to the child they replace, making it challenging for parents to discern the substitution. Changelings are often believed to be physically weaker and less emotionally expressive than human infants, adding to the suspicion surrounding their presence.
Throughout history, changelings have been associated with a range of behaviors and physical traits that set them apart from human infants. These characteristics can include:

- Lack of Growth: Changelings may appear not to grow or develop at a normal rate, leading to concerns about their health and development.
- Strange Behavior: Changelings are sometimes described as displaying unusual or unsettling behavior, such as excessive crying, insomnia, or an aversion to human touch.
- Linguistic Abilities: Some changelings are believed to possess the ability to speak or communicate at an unusually early age, though their speech may be cryptic or otherworldly.
- Resistance to Normal Care: Changelings can be resistant to the efforts of human caregivers, making them difficult to comfort or care for.

The unique characteristics of changelings have given rise to a rich tapestry of folklore, with countless tales and superstitions centered around their existence. In many cultures, specific rituals and remedies are employed to either protect human infants from being taken or to coax the return of a changeling to the fairy realm.

2. General Appearance

2A. Physical Description

Changelings, being a phenomenon rather than a distinct species, do not possess a fixed physical appearance. Instead, they take on the form of the human infants they replace. This unique ability to mimic the appearance of human babies is both their defining characteristic and their means of blending seamlessly into human society. Changelings are known for their striking resemblance to the infants they supplant, making it incredibly difficult for parents or caregivers to detect the substitution.

2B. Clothing and Accessories

Changelings do not typically wear clothing or accessories that differentiate them from human infants. They are known for their ability to seamlessly imitate the appearance of the replaced child, including clothing and swaddling. In fact, the primary means of identifying a changeling often lies not in their attire, but in their peculiar behaviors, lack of growth, or other unusual characteristics.

It's important to note that changeling folklore primarily revolves around their ability to mimic the physical appearance of human infants, rather than any distinctive clothing or accessories they may wear. The focus is on the uncanny resemblance they bear to the child they replace, which serves as the basis for the suspicion and superstition surrounding changelings.

The intrigue and fear associated with changelings stem from their uncanny ability to infiltrate human households undetected, leading to a wide range of beliefs and practices aimed at protecting infants from potential fairy abductions or coaxing the return of changelings to the fairy realm. These beliefs have left an indelible mark on the rich tapestry of fairy folklore across various cultures.

3. Sexes

3A. Description of Changeling Sexes

Changelings, as a phenomenon related to the substitution of human infants by fairies or other supernatural entities, do not exhibit distinct sexes or gender characteristics. They lack the biological attributes or gender identity found in human beings. Changelings are, essentially, ageless and genderless beings whose primary purpose is to replace human infants.

3B. Differences in Behavior or Appearance Between Changeling Sexes

Given that changelings do not possess sexes or gender identities, there are no observable differences in behavior or appearance between changeling "males" and "females." They are typically described as taking on the appearance of the human infants they replace with remarkable accuracy, ensuring that they do not exhibit any gender-specific traits or behaviors that might arouse suspicion.

The concept of sexes and gender roles is a uniquely human construct, and changelings exist outside this framework. The focus of changeling folklore is primarily on their uncanny ability to mimic human infants and the belief that they are part of a larger narrative involving fairies and the mysterious exchanges between the human and fairy realms. It is the behaviors and characteristics related to the changeling phenomenon itself that take center stage in changeling legends and traditions.

4. Lore and Legends

4A. Cultural and Historical References to Changelings

Changelings have left an indelible mark on the folklore and legends of numerous cultures around the world. Beliefs in changelings and their interactions with humans date back centuries and continue to influence cultural narratives today. Some key cultural references and historical mentions of changelings include:

- Irish Folklore: In Ireland, changelings are known as "fetches" or "clurichauns." Irish folklore is rich with stories of fairies abducting human infants and leaving changelings in their place. The famous poet W.B. Yeats wrote extensively about the Irish belief in changelings.
- Scandinavian Folklore: Nordic folklore contains tales of "vätten" or "huldra," supernatural beings with similarities to changelings. These beings were believed to steal human babies and replace them with their own offspring.
- Medieval Europe: During the Middle Ages, belief in changelings was widespread across Europe. People attributed unexplained illnesses or developmental delays in children to the presence of changelings. This led to various practices and rituals aimed at identifying and dealing with changelings.

4B. Stories, Myths, and Folklore Associated with Changelings

Changelings are central figures in a multitude of stories and myths that explore the intersection of the human and fairy realms. These tales often revolve around themes of abduction, deception, and the mysterious nature of the fairy world. Some well-known stories and folklore associated with changelings include:

- The Changeling Ballad: Traditional ballads and songs have been passed down through generations, recounting the plight of parents discovering that their child has been replaced by a changeling. These ballads often describe the emotional turmoil and desperate attempts to restore the stolen child.
- The Fairy Midwife: In some legends, fairies acted as midwives during human childbirth. While they assisted in delivering babies, they occasionally exchanged the human infant for a changeling. This belief highlights the close connection between fairies and the most vulnerable members of human society.
- The Return of Changelings: Numerous stories depict the challenges faced by parents in identifying and dealing with changelings. These tales explore various methods, from placing the changeling in the fire to using iron implements, believed to reveal the true nature of the changeling or compel the fairies to return the human child.

Changelings have played a significant role in shaping the collective imagination and cultural narratives surrounding fairies and the supernatural. These legends continue to endure, offering insight into the complex relationship between humans and the mystical world of the fairies.

5. Habitat and Natural Environment

5A. Information about the Natural Habitats They Prefer

Changelings themselves do not have specific natural habitats, as they are not a distinct species or beings with independent existence. Instead, they are a phenomenon that occurs within the context of human society and the interaction between humans and fairies or supernatural entities. However, it is essential to understand the broader context of fairy habitats when exploring changelings.
Fairies, who are often associated with the changeling phenomenon, are believed to reside in a variety of natural environments, including:

- Forests: Dense, ancient forests are commonly depicted as fairy domains. Fairies are believed to dwell deep within the woods, hidden from human sight.
- Meadows: Open meadows and grassy fields are also associated with fairies, who may gather there for dances and celebrations.
- Bodies of Water: Fairy lore often includes beings associated with bodies of water, such as water nymphs or water fairies. Lakes, rivers, and ponds are believed to be their favored habitats.

5B. Environmental Factors Affecting Their Choice of Residence

In the context of changeling folklore, the choice of habitat is often determined by the fairies or supernatural entities involved in the exchange. The reasons for their actions and choice of location can vary widely across different cultural beliefs. Some factors that may influence their decisions include:

- Proximity to Human Settlements: Fairies are often believed to inhabit areas near human dwellings, which facilitates their interactions with humans, including the potential substitution of infants with changelings.
- Natural Beauty: Fairies are drawn to places of natural beauty, where they can engage in revelry and celebrations. These locations may serve as settings for encounters with humans and the exchange of children.
- Access to Magical Energies: Some legends suggest that fairies are drawn to places with strong mystical or magical energies. Such locations may hold significance in the context of changeling exchanges.

It's important to note that changeling folklore primarily revolves around the circumstances of the child exchange rather than the natural habitats of changelings themselves. Understanding the natural environments associated with fairies is crucial for contextualizing the changeling phenomenon within the broader realm of fairy folklore.

6. Lifestyle and Social Structure

6A. Insights into Their Societal Structure and Hierarchy

Changelings, as a phenomenon rather than a distinct species, do not possess a societal structure or hierarchy of their own. Instead, they are a part of the intricate and often elusive world of fairies and supernatural entities. Fairies, in various folklore traditions, are known to have complex societal structures, which may include kings, queens, and various ranks of fairies.
Within the context of changeling folklore, changelings are typically portrayed as infant replacements or substitutes who inhabit human households. They are not known to have their own societal structure or hierarchy independent of their association with fairies.

6B. Daily Routines

Changelings, as infants or young children, do not engage in daily routines, occupations, or communal activities in the same way adults or fairies might. Instead, they are cared for by the human families into which they have been substituted, assuming the role of a human infant. Their "daily routines" would consist of typical infant behaviors such as feeding, sleeping, and crying.

In contrast, fairies themselves are often portrayed as engaging in a wide range of activities within their own societies, including:

- Fairy Celebrations: Fairies are believed to gather for celebrations, dances, and revelry in meadows, forests, or other natural settings. These gatherings are often described in folklore.
- Guardianship of Nature: Some folklore depicts fairies as guardians of the natural world, taking care of plants, animals, and the environment.
- Magical Practices: Fairies are known for their magical abilities, which they may use for various purposes, including mischief or benevolent deeds.
- Interaction with Humans: Fairies are believed to interact with humans in various ways, including assisting with household chores or tasks, providing guidance or warnings, or engaging in exchanges involving changelings.

7. Diet and Food Sources

7A. What Changelings Eat

Changelings, as a phenomenon involving the substitution of human infants with fairy or supernatural beings, do not possess unique dietary preferences or requirements of their own. They assume the identity of the human infants they replace and, therefore, are fed and nourished in the same way as human babies. Their diet consists of human breast milk or formula during infancy and gradually transitions to solid foods as they grow.

7B. Special Dietary Preferences or Rituals

Changelings do not exhibit special dietary preferences or engage in rituals related to food consumption distinct from those of human infants. Their primary role is to mimic the behavior and needs of the human infants they replace. Any dietary considerations or rituals would be determined by the human caregivers of the changeling, rather than by the changeling itself.

8. Communication and Language

8A. How Changelings Communicate with Each Other

Changelings, as a phenomenon, do not communicate with each other since they do not exist as a social group or community. Instead, they are individual beings or entities that are believed to be substituted for human infants by fairies or other supernatural entities.

8B. Unique Languages or Gestures Used

Changelings do not possess unique languages or gestures of their own. They are known for their ability to mimic human infants, including their vocalizations and gestures. Their communication is limited to the typical behaviors and sounds exhibited by human infants, such as crying, cooing, and babbling.
In changeling folklore, the focus is on the challenge faced by human caregivers in detecting any subtle differences in the behavior or communication of the changeling that might distinguish it from a human infant. The absence of unique languages or gestures is consistent with their role as imitators of human infants rather than independent beings with their own forms of communication.

9. Reproduction and Life Cycle

9A. The Fairy's Life Stages from Birth to Death

Changelings themselves do not undergo a traditional life cycle, since they are not a distinct species with independent existence. Instead, they are a product of a supernatural exchange or substitution that occurs when fairies or other supernatural entities take human infants and replace them with changelings. Fairies, however, often have their own life stages and can live for extended periods, with some legends portraying them as immortal or ageless beings.

9B. Mating Rituals and Reproduction Process

The reproduction process involving changelings is not detailed in changeling folklore, since changelings themselves do not reproduce. Instead, the focus of changeling folklore is on the circumstances surrounding the exchange of human infants for changelings, which is believed to be orchestrated by fairies or supernatural beings.

Reproduction among fairies, when mentioned in folklore, varies across different traditions and can include various rituals and processes. In some cases, fairies are portrayed as beings who can reproduce with each other or with humans, leading to the birth of hybrid offspring. The details of these rituals and processes can vary widely across cultural beliefs and narratives.

10. Magic Abilities and Powers

10A. Magical Abilities?

Changelings, as a phenomenon involving the substitution of human infants with fairy or supernatural beings, do not possess their own magical abilities or powers. Instead, any magical aspects associated with changelings are typically attributed to the fairies or supernatural entities responsible for the exchange.

10B. Specific Spells or Powers Unique to Changelings

Changelings themselves are not known to wield specific spells or powers unique to their existence. Their role in folklore is primarily that of imitating human infants and being a part of the complex interactions between humans and fairies. Any magical elements associated with changelings are rooted in the broader context of fairy folklore and the mysterious world of fairies, rather than in the actions or abilities of changelings themselves.

11. Interactions with Humans

11A. Historical Encounters with Humans, Both Positive and Negative

Throughout history, changelings have been at the center of numerous encounters between humans and the supernatural realm. These interactions have elicited a wide range of emotions, including wonder, fear, and desperation:

- Positive Encounters: Some accounts describe encounters with changelings as positive experiences. In these cases, it is believed that the changeling, although different from a human infant, may have brought blessings or gifts to the household. Such encounters often result in a harmonious relationship between the human family and the supernatural world.
- Negative Encounters: Many historical accounts depict changelings as disruptive or malevolent beings. Parents who discover that their child has been replaced with a changeling often experience profound distress and may resort to various remedies or rituals to expel the changeling. These negative encounters underscore the deep-seated fear and superstition surrounding changelings.

11B. Any Legends of Fairy-Human Friendships or Conflicts

Changeling folklore is replete with stories of conflicts and misunderstandings between fairies and humans, often resulting from the presence of changelings. These legends highlight the complex relationship between the two realms:

- Friendships: Some folklore traditions include accounts of amicable relationships between humans and fairies, where humans are welcomed into the fairy world or receive assistance from fairy beings. Such friendships may involve the exchange of knowledge or gifts.
- Conflicts: Conflicts between fairies and humans are common in changeling folklore, especially when a changeling is discovered in a human household. These conflicts can take the form of desperate attempts to expel the changeling or demands for its return to the fairy realm.

Changelings serve as a catalyst for these interactions, sparking emotional responses and dramatic events in the lives of those affected. These legends provide insights into the deeply ingrained beliefs and superstitions surrounding the supernatural world and its interactions with humanity.

12. Country of Origin

12A. Geographic Regions

Changelings are a phenomenon deeply embedded in the folklore and traditions of various regions and countries. While the concept of changelings is not unique to a particular geographic location, their presence is often associated with regions where fairy folklore and beliefs in supernatural entities hold sway. Common regions and countries where changelings are frequently mentioned include:

- Ireland: Ireland is renowned for its rich and extensive folklore surrounding changelings, where they are often referred to as "fetches" or "the Good People." Irish changeling legends have had a significant influence on global perceptions of these beings.
- Scandinavia: Scandinavian countries, such as Norway and Sweden, also have a strong tradition of changeling folklore. These legends often involve creatures known as "vätten" or "huldra."
- United Kingdom: Changeling beliefs and stories are present throughout the United Kingdom, with variations in terminology and local customs. In Scotland, for example, changelings are referred to as "changelin bairns."
- Other European Regions: Changeling folklore can be found in various European countries, including Germany, France, and Spain, each with its unique interpretations and rituals related to changelings.

12B. Cultural Significance in Those Areas

Changeling folklore holds deep cultural significance in the regions where it is prevalent. It reflects the historical and cultural narratives of these areas and often serves as a lens through which societies have grappled with issues of childhood, disability, and the supernatural. These beliefs have shaped local traditions, superstitions, and even legal practices in some instances.
The cultural significance of changeling folklore can be observed in the rituals, remedies, and stories passed down through generations. These narratives not only offer insights into the

complex relationship between humans and the supernatural world but also shed light on the values, fears, and resilience of the communities that have perpetuated these traditions.

13. Where to Find Them

13A. Specific Locations, Forests, or Landscapes

Changelings themselves are not typically associated with specific physical locations or landscapes, since they are a phenomenon that occurs within human households. Instead, it is the fairies or supernatural entities responsible for the exchange who may be connected to specific natural settings. In changeling folklore, fairies are believed to inhabit various natural environments, including:

- Forests: Dense, ancient forests are often depicted as fairy domains, where fairies are believed to dwell deep within the woods, hidden from human sight.
- Meadows: Open meadows and grassy fields are also associated with fairies, who may gather there for dances and celebrations.
- Bodies of Water: Some folklore traditions include water fairies or water spirits associated with lakes, rivers, and ponds, suggesting that these bodies of water may be places where fairies are active.

13B. Best Times of Day or Year for Sightings

Changelings themselves are not typically sought after for sightings, since they are often discovered within human households rather than encountered in the natural world. However, fairies, including those responsible for changeling exchanges, are believed to be more active during certain times of the day or year. Common beliefs regarding the best times for fairy sightings include:

- Twilight and Dawn: Fairies are often said to be most active during the transition between night and day, particularly during dawn and twilight.
- Midsummer's Eve: In many cultures, Midsummer's Eve (the summer solstice) is believed to be a time when the fairy world is especially active, and interactions with fairies are more likely.
- Beltane and Samhain: These Celtic festivals, celebrated on May 1st and November 1st, respectively, are considered to be times when the barrier between the human and fairy realms is thinner, making it easier for encounters to occur.

While changelings themselves are not the primary focus of sightings, the folklore surrounding them is deeply connected to beliefs about fairies and their interactions with the natural world. Understanding the best times and locations for fairy encounters provides context for the broader belief system in which changeling folklore is situated.

14. How to See Them

14A. Practical Tips and Advice for Encountering Them

Changelings are typically discovered rather than actively sought after for encounters since they are believed to be substituted for human infants within households. However, there are general practices and beliefs associated with interacting with fairies that may indirectly relate to changeling encounters:

- Respect for Nature: Many folklore traditions emphasize the importance of showing respect for nature and its inhabitants, including fairies. Observing natural beauty, being mindful of one's surroundings, and showing reverence for the environment are considered ways to attract positive interactions with fairies.
- Offerings: Some belief systems suggest leaving offerings of food or other tokens of goodwill in natural settings known to be frequented by fairies. These offerings are made as a sign of respect and hospitality.
- Staying Vigilant: In changeling folklore, it is important for parents to remain vigilant and observant of their children's behavior, as subtle changes may indicate the presence of a changeling. This vigilance is seen as a way to protect human infants from being taken by fairies.

14B. Rituals, Offerings, or Behaviors That May Attract Them

Rituals, offerings, and behaviors associated with attracting fairies are more relevant to changeling folklore than direct encounters with changelings themselves:

- Iron and Cold Iron: In some traditions, it is believed that fairies have an aversion to iron. Placing iron implements, such as horseshoes or iron nails, near entrances or cradles is thought to deter fairies from entering or taking human infants.
- Fire and Smoke: Lighting fires or creating smoke, such as from burning herbs or plants, is believed to have protective qualities and may deter fairies from approaching human dwellings.
- Chanting or Recitation: Chanting specific verses or incantations is sometimes performed as a means of protecting infants from fairy abduction or identifying changelings.

It's important to note that while these practices and beliefs are associated with fairy encounters, direct encounters with changelings are relatively rare in folklore. The focus of changeling folklore is more on the consequences of the changeling exchange and the efforts of human parents to protect their children from supernatural interference.

15. Protection and Etiquette

15A. Guidance on How to Respect and Protect Changelings and Their Habitats

Protection and etiquette in changeling folklore primarily revolve around safeguarding human infants from potential exchanges with fairies. This involves recognizing and addressing the presence of changelings in human households:

- Vigilance: Parents are encouraged to remain vigilant and observant, paying close attention to changes in their infants' behavior or appearance. Recognizing signs of a changeling and taking appropriate action are seen as protective measures.
- Iron: The use of iron, particularly cold iron objects like horseshoes or iron nails, is believed to deter fairies from taking human infants. Placing iron implements near entrances or cradles is a common practice to safeguard against changelings.
- Fire and Smoke: Lighting fires or creating smoke, often by burning specific herbs or plants, is believed to have protective qualities and may discourage fairies from entering human dwellings.
- Chanting or Incantations: Some folklore traditions involve the recitation of verses or incantations believed to reveal the true nature of a changeling or compel fairies to return the human child.

15B. Superstitions or Taboos Related to Interacting with Them

Changeling folklore is replete with superstitions and taboos related to interacting with fairies and dealing with changelings:

- Naming: It is considered taboo to use a changeling's true name, as doing so could give the fairy power over the child. Instead, euphemisms or nicknames are often used.
- Accepting Gifts: Accepting gifts from fairies, including changelings, is viewed with caution, as it may imply an agreement or debt to the fairy realm.
- Careful Speech: In some beliefs, openly discussing or criticizing fairies, including changelings, is seen as inviting misfortune or displeasure from the supernatural realm.
- Avoiding Disturbances: Some traditions advise against disturbing fairy mounds, circles, or natural features believed to be inhabited by fairies. Disturbing these areas is thought to incur their wrath.

Protection and etiquette in changeling folklore reflect the profound belief in the existence of fairies and the perceived need to safeguard human infants from potential supernatural interference. These practices and taboos are deeply rooted in the cultural narratives and traditions of regions where changeling folklore is prevalent.

16. Art and Representation

16A. How Changelings Have Been Portrayed in Art, Literature, and Media

Changelings have been a recurring theme in art, literature, and media, often depicted as enigmatic and sometimes eerie figures. Their portrayal reflects the fascination with the concept of changelings in human culture:

- Visual Art: Changelings have been depicted in various forms of visual art, including paintings, illustrations, and sculptures. These depictions often emphasize their uncanny resemblance to human infants or highlight the supernatural aspects of their existence.

- Literature: Changelings have been featured in numerous literary works, both in traditional folklore and in modern literature. Authors like W.B. Yeats and Hans Christian Andersen have explored changeling themes in their writings, weaving tales of wonder and mystery.
- Film and Television: Changelings have made appearances in film and television, often as central characters or elements of supernatural plots. These portrayals range from sympathetic and misunderstood figures to malevolent beings.

16B. Iconic Artists or Authors Who Have Featured Them

Several iconic artists and authors have contributed to the portrayal of changelings in art, literature, and media:

- W.B. Yeats: The renowned Irish poet and playwright W.B. Yeats wrote extensively about changelings and the fairy folklore of Ireland. His works, such as "The Stolen Child," have become iconic representations of changeling themes.
- Hans Christian Andersen: The Danish author Hans Christian Andersen explored changeling themes in his fairy tales, including "The Little Mermaid" and "The Snow Queen." These stories often delve into the complex relationship between humans and supernatural beings.
- William Shakespeare: Although not exclusively focused on changelings, Shakespeare's works, such as "A Midsummer Night's Dream," feature characters and themes related to the fairy world and transformations, resonating with changeling folklore.

Changelings have left a lasting imprint on the artistic and literary imagination, inspiring countless creators to explore the blurred boundaries between the human and supernatural realms. These representations continue to captivate audiences and contribute to the enduring fascination with changelings.

17. Modern Beliefs and Practices

17A. Contemporary Beliefs and Practices Related to Changelings

In contemporary times, beliefs and practices related to changelings have evolved, reflecting the enduring influence of folklore and superstitions:

- Awareness and Recognition: While belief in changelings as supernatural beings has waned, there is a continued awareness of changeling folklore and its historical significance. People may recognize the concept of changelings as a part of cultural heritage without actively believing in their existence.
- Literary and Artistic Inspiration: Changeling themes continue to inspire contemporary literature, art, and media. Writers, artists, and filmmakers draw upon these themes to explore issues of identity, belonging, and the supernatural in modern contexts.
- Cultural Celebrations: Some regions that have strong changeling traditions incorporate them into cultural celebrations or festivals. These events may feature reenactments, storytelling, or art exhibitions related to changeling folklore.

17B. Current Festivals or Gatherings Dedicated to Them

While there are no widespread festivals or gatherings specifically dedicated to changelings themselves, some events may celebrate broader aspects of fairy folklore and the supernatural. These gatherings often incorporate changeling themes into their programming:

- Fairy Festivals: In various regions, fairy festivals celebrate the rich tapestry of fairy folklore, including changelings. These events may include costume parades, storytelling sessions, and workshops related to fairy tales and supernatural beings.
- Myth and Folklore Festivals: Some cultural festivals focus on the preservation and exploration of traditional myths and folklore, which may include presentations or discussions about changeling legends and their cultural significance.
- Arts and Literature Events: Literary festivals and art exhibitions may feature works inspired by changeling folklore, allowing artists and authors to showcase their interpretations of these themes.

Contemporary beliefs and practices related to changelings often take the form of cultural appreciation, artistic expression, and storytelling rather than genuine belief in the existence of changelings as supernatural beings. This reflects the evolving nature of folklore and its role in shaping cultural identity and creativity.

18. Conservation Efforts

18A. Conservation Initiatives

Conservation efforts related to changelings primarily revolve around preserving the natural environments associated with fairy folklore, as changelings themselves are not distinct species with habitats to conserve. Efforts to protect these habitats are essential for maintaining the cultural and ecological heritage connected to changeling folklore:

- Preservation of Natural Landscapes: Conservation initiatives often focus on protecting ancient forests, meadows, bodies of water, and other natural landscapes associated with fairy habitats. These efforts involve measures to prevent deforestation, habitat destruction, or pollution.
- Cultural Heritage Conservation: Some organizations and institutions work to preserve the cultural heritage associated with changeling folklore. This includes archiving historical texts, documenting oral traditions, and promoting awareness of folklore as an integral part of cultural identity.

18B. Threats They May Face and Steps to Mitigate Them

While changelings themselves do not face threats, the broader cultural and natural aspects connected to changeling folklore may encounter challenges that conservation efforts aim to address:

- Habitat Destruction: The destruction of natural habitats, such as forests and meadows, threatens the landscapes associated with fairy folklore. Conservation organizations work to combat deforestation and land development that could disrupt these habitats.

- Cultural Erosion: Folklore and traditional beliefs, including those related to changelings, may be at risk of fading into obscurity due to modernization and globalization. Conservation initiatives seek to document, preserve, and promote these cultural traditions.
- Loss of Biodiversity: Conservation efforts aimed at protecting natural environments also contribute to the preservation of biodiversity. Many of the habitats linked to fairy folklore are home to diverse plant and animal species that benefit from habitat conservation.

19. Additional Folklore

19A. Lesser-Known Stories or Beliefs Associated with Changelings

In addition to the well-known themes of changeling folklore, there are lesser-known stories and beliefs that provide further depth to the narrative:

- Changeling Variations: Some regions have variations of changeling folklore that introduce unique elements. These variations may include different names for changelings or distinct methods for detecting and dealing with them.
- Changeling Legends in Different Cultures: While changeling folklore is most commonly associated with Western European traditions, similar legends of child substitution exist in other cultures. Exploring these cross-cultural variations can provide a broader perspective on the concept of changelings.

19B. Variations in Their Portrayal Across Different Cultures

Changeling folklore exhibits variations in its portrayal across different cultures and regions:

- Irish Changeling Lore: Irish changeling folklore, with its belief in the "Good People" or fairies, is among the most well-documented and influential. It often emphasizes the need for vigilance and protective measures to prevent changeling exchanges.
- Scandinavian Changeling Folklore: In Scandinavia, changelings are known as "vätten" or "huldra." These legends may feature beings with distinct appearances and behaviors compared to traditional changelings in other regions.
- Celtic Changeling Beliefs: Celtic regions like Scotland and Wales have their own changeling beliefs, often involving rituals and remedies to identify and retrieve stolen human infants.
- Global Comparisons: Beyond Europe, similar folklore exists in various forms in other parts of the world, with tales of child substitution and supernatural beings taking on different cultural nuances.

20. Famous Encounters

20A. Historical or Modern Encounters

While changelings themselves are not typically associated with famous encounters, changeling folklore and legends have influenced the works of various notable individuals:

- W.B. Yeats: The renowned Irish poet and playwright W.B. Yeats is known for his deep fascination with changelings and the fairy folklore of Ireland. His writings, including the poem "The Stolen Child," have left a lasting impact on how changelings are perceived in literature and culture.

- Hans Christian Andersen: The Danish author Hans Christian Andersen explored changeling themes in his fairy tales, such as "The Little Mermaid" and "The Snow Queen." These stories have become iconic in the realm of fairy tales and have been adapted into numerous forms of media.
- William Shakespeare: Although not exclusively focused on changelings, Shakespeare's works, particularly "A Midsummer Night's Dream," feature characters and themes related to the fairy world and transformations, contributing to the enduring appeal of fairy folklore.

20B. The Impact of These Encounters on Their Lives or Work

These famous encounters with changeling themes have had a profound impact on the lives and creative works of the individuals involved:

- Literary Legacy: The writings of W.B. Yeats, Hans Christian Andersen, and William Shakespeare have become classics of literature, and their exploration of changeling folklore has left an indelible mark on the literary world.
- Cultural Influence: The works of these authors have contributed to the enduring fascination with fairy folklore and changelings, shaping how these themes are portrayed in art, literature, and popular culture.
- Interdisciplinary Exploration: The exploration of changeling themes has extended beyond literature to other art forms, including visual arts, music, and theater, further enriching the cultural tapestry.

The impact of these famous encounters with changeling themes transcends time and continues to resonate with audiences, highlighting the enduring allure of the supernatural and the mysterious in human culture and creativity.

Chapter 7
Interacting with Fairies

7A. Methods of Communication

How to Communicate with Fairies

The enchanting world of fairies has long captivated the human imagination, igniting a profound desire to communicate with these mystical beings. While the existence of fairies remains a matter of belief and folklore, the art of attempting to connect with them is an age-old practice. This chapter delves into the methods, rituals, and cultural traditions that offer insight into the intriguing pursuit of communicating with fairies.

I. Cultivating a Belief and Reverence for Fairies

Before one can hope to engage with the enchanting realm of fairies, it is essential to cultivate a genuine belief and deep reverence for these mystical beings. Building a foundation of belief and respect is not only a crucial aspect of attempting to communicate with fairies but also a profound journey into the world of imagination and wonder. In this section, we will explore the steps and mindset required to foster belief and reverence for fairies.

1. Study Fairy Lore: The Quest for Knowledge

The initial step in cultivating belief and reverence for fairies involves delving into the vast world of fairy lore. This pursuit of knowledge serves as a bridge between the everyday world and the realm of the mystical:

Read Widely: Immerse yourself in the rich and diverse folklore and literature surrounding fairies. Explore classic fairy tales, mythological sources, and cultural traditions that celebrate these ethereal beings. By studying these stories, you gain insights into the various forms, personalities, and roles fairies have assumed across cultures.

Research Cultural Variations: Fairies manifest differently in cultures around the world. Investigate how different societies perceive and interact with fairies, and appreciate the rich tapestry of beliefs and traditions that shape these encounters.

Encounter Historical Accounts: Delve into historical accounts, anecdotes, and firsthand experiences of individuals who claim to have encountered fairies. These personal stories can offer valuable insights into the potential reality of fairy encounters.

2. Connect with Nature: The Reverence for the Natural World

Fairies are intimately connected with the natural world, and a harmonious relationship with nature is a fundamental aspect of engaging with them:

Spend Time Outdoors: To connect with fairies, immerse yourself in natural settings that evoke a sense of wonder. Wander through serene forests, explore tranquil meadows, or visit bodies of water like lakes or streams. In these environments, you may feel closer to the presence of fairies.

Observe the Seasons: Pay attention to the changing seasons and how they influence the natural world. Fairies are often associated with specific seasons, so observing these changes can deepen your connection to their cycles.

Gardening and Plant Care: Cultivating your own garden or caring for plants can be a way to connect with the fairy realm. Many folklore traditions involve offerings to fairies in exchange for their blessings on crops and gardens.

3. Foster Respect and Reverence: The Attitude of Awe

Central to cultivating belief and reverence for fairies is an attitude of humility, respect, and reverence:

Acknowledge Their Autonomy: Approach the world of fairies with the understanding that these beings are autonomous and have their own existence, independent of human desires and expectations.

Respect Their Privacy: Just as you would respect the privacy and boundaries of any living beings, do not intrude or attempt to control fairies. Understand that their interactions with humans are often subtle and on their own terms.

Honoring the Balance: Fairies are often associated with maintaining the balance of the natural world. Recognize the importance of preserving the environment and respecting the delicate equilibrium that sustains life.

Creating a Sacred Space:

Establishing this sacred space is a crucial step in your journey to commune with fairies. It not only provides a physical focal point for your efforts but also demonstrates your reverence for these mystical beings and the natural world they embody. With your fairy shrine established, you are now poised to embark on the next steps of your enchanting journey.

Arrangement and Design:

The arrangement of elements on your fairy altar is a personal and intuitive process. Arrange them in a way that feels harmonious and resonates with your intentions. You might want to create a focal point with the fairy figurines or statues, surrounded by natural elements and candles.

Maintenance and Rituals:

Regularly tend to your fairy altar. Keep it clean and free of dust. Light candles or incense as part of rituals or when you wish to communicate with fairies. Offerings of honey, milk, or fresh flowers can be refreshed periodically.

Intentions and Communication:

Your fairy altar serves as a portal for communication with the fairy realm. When you approach your shrine, do so with a clear intention and an open heart. Meditate, pray, or simply sit in silence, focusing your thoughts on your desire to connect with fairies.

Respect and Reverence:

Always approach your fairy shrine with respect and reverence. Acknowledge the presence of fairies and express your gratitude for any signs or messages you may receive.

Record Your Experiences:

Maintain a journal dedicated to your interactions with fairies at your shrine. Record your thoughts, feelings, any dreams or visions, and any signs or coincidences that may occur. This journal can help you track your progress and deepen your connection over time.

Creating a fairy altar or shrine is a tangible expression of your desire to connect with the mystical world of fairies. It serves as a sacred space where the boundaries between the mundane and the magical blur, allowing you to cultivate a deeper understanding and connection with these enchanting beings. As you tend to your shrine and engage in rituals, you embark on a personal journey of wonder and spiritual exploration, inviting the magic of the fairy realm into your life.

Offerings and Tokens:

In the enchanting practice of communicating with fairies, offering gifts and tokens plays a significant role. These offerings are more than mere gestures; they symbolize respect, goodwill, and a genuine desire to establish a connection with these mystical beings. In this section, we explore the art of crafting meaningful offerings and tokens to extend hospitality to fairies.

Understanding the Significance of Offerings:

Before delving into specific offerings, it's essential to grasp why offerings are a crucial element in communicating with fairies:

Symbolic Exchange: Offering gifts to fairies is symbolic of reciprocity and respect. It reflects the understanding that fairies are autonomous beings with their own desires and preferences.

Bridging Worlds: Through offerings, you create a tangible link between the human realm and the fairy realm, allowing for a harmonious and respectful exchange of energy and intention.

Honoring Nature: Many offerings are drawn from the natural world, reinforcing the connection between fairies and the environment they inhabit.

Choosing Thoughtful Offerings:

Selecting the right offerings requires thoughtfulness and consideration. Here are some ideas for offerings and tokens:

Food and Drink: A Taste of Sweetness

Honey and Milk: In the realm of fairies, sweetness reigns supreme, and nothing captures their hearts quite like honey and milk. Placing a small dish of honey or milk in your sacred space becomes a traditional offering, a nectarous gift that reflects the natural sweetness of the fey.

Fresh Fruits and Nuts: Nature's bounty speaks volumes to fairies, and there is no better way to express admiration than by presenting ripe fruits and nuts. Berries, apples, and nuts become delightful treats, each bite a symbol of the rich tapestry of the natural world.

Arrangement and Design:

- The arrangement of elements on your fairy altar is a personal and intuitive process. Arrange them in a way that feels harmonious and resonates with your intentions. You might want to create a focal point with the fairy figurines or statues, surrounded by natural elements and candles.

Maintenance and Rituals:

- Regularly tend to your fairy altar. Keep it clean and free of dust. Light candles or incense as part of rituals or when you wish to communicate with fairies. Offerings of honey, milk, or fresh flowers can be refreshed periodically.

Intentions and Communication:

- Your fairy altar serves as a portal for communication with the fairy realm. When you approach your shrine, do so with a clear intention and an open heart. Meditate, pray, or simply sit in silence, focusing your thoughts on your desire to connect with fairies.

Respect and Reverence:

- Always approach your fairy shrine with respect and reverence. Acknowledge the presence of fairies and express your gratitude for any signs or messages you may receive.

Record Your Experiences:

- Keep a journal dedicated to your interactions with fairies at your shrine. Record your thoughts, feelings, any dreams or visions, and any signs or coincidences that may occur. This journal can help you track your progress and deepen your connection over time.

Creating a fairy altar or shrine is a tangible expression of your desire to connect with the mystical world of fairies. It serves as a sacred space where the boundaries between the mundane and the magical blur, allowing you to cultivate a deeper understanding and connection with these enchanting beings. As you tend to your shrine and engage in rituals, you embark on a personal journey of wonder and spiritual exploration, inviting the magic of the fairy realm into your life.

2. Offerings and Tokens:

In the enchanting practice of communicating with fairies, offering gifts and tokens plays a significant role. These offerings are more than mere gestures; they symbolize respect, goodwill, and a genuine desire to establish a connection with these mystical beings. In this section, we explore the art of crafting meaningful offerings and tokens to extend hospitality to fairies.
Understanding the Significance of Offerings:

Before delving into specific offerings, it's essential to grasp why offerings are a crucial element in communicating with fairies:

1. Symbolic Exchange: Offering gifts to fairies is symbolic of reciprocity and respect. It reflects the understanding that fairies are autonomous beings with their own desires and preferences.
2. Bridging Worlds: Through offerings, you create a tangible link between the human realm and the fairy realm, allowing for a harmonious and respectful exchange of energy and intention.
3. Honoring Nature: Many offerings are drawn from the natural world, reinforcing the connection between fairies and the environment they inhabit.

Choosing Thoughtful Offerings:

Selecting the right offerings requires thoughtfulness and consideration. Here are some ideas for offerings and tokens:

The Art of Gift-Giving to Enchanted Beings
In the heart of every fairy enthusiast lies the desire to connect with these mystical beings, to forge a bond that transcends the realms of imagination and reality. One of the most cherished traditions in the world of fairies is the act of making offerings—a gesture of respect, gratitude, and goodwill that resonates through the ages. In this chapter, we will embark on a journey into the art of making offerings to fairies, exploring a myriad of offerings that have enchanted the hearts of both humans and the fey.

Food and Drink: A Taste of Sweetness

Honey and Milk: In the realm of fairies, sweetness reigns supreme, and nothing captures their hearts quite like honey and milk. Placing a small dish of honey or milk in your sacred space becomes a traditional offering, a nectarous gift that reflects the natural sweetness of the fey.
Fresh Fruits and Nuts: Nature's bounty speaks volumes to fairies, and there is no better way to express admiration than by presenting ripe fruits and nuts. Berries, apples, and nuts become delightful treats, each bite a symbol of the rich tapestry of the natural world.
Bread or Cakes: In the world of the fey, sustenance comes in the form of homemade bread or cakes, especially those crafted with the purest of natural ingredients. When offered to fairies, they become tokens of nourishment and a testament to the human connection with the Earth.

Shiny Objects and Trinkets: Capturing the Gleam of Attention

Crystals and Gemstones: Fairies, like magpies, are drawn to all that glitters and shines. Placing an array of crystals or gemstones in your sacred space becomes a means to capture their attention. Each vibrant hue and radiant facet echoes the allure of the fey.
Coins: Old or unique coins, imbued with tales of wealth and prosperity, are believed to beckon fairies. As tokens of avarice and fortune, these shimmering treasures take on new meaning when offered to the enchanted beings.
Bells and Wind Chimes: In the gentle tinkling of bells or the melodious dance of wind chimes, fairies find music that soothes their ethereal souls. These harmonious trinkets, when placed in your sacred area, create an enchanting soundscape for the fey.
Flowers and Natural Elements: Gifts from the Earth
Fresh Flowers: Fairies are intertwined with the beauty of the natural world, and nothing captures their essence quite like freshly picked flowers. With petals in full bloom, these floral offerings are a visual feast and an expression of reverence.
Herbs and Leaves: Sprigs of aromatic herbs or leaves gathered from nearby trees become cherished gifts. Lavender and rosemary, with their fragrant allure, are chosen to delight the senses of the fey.

Feathers and Shells: Delicate feathers and unique seashells are offerings imbued with the elements of air and water. As tokens of nature's exquisite craftsmanship, they symbolize the interconnectedness of all living things.

Handcrafted Tokens: Creations from the Heart
Handmade Jewelry: Crafting simple jewelry pieces such as beaded bracelets or necklaces is a personal and heartfelt way to connect with fairies. Each handmade piece carries the essence of the artisan's soul, offering a tangible link between worlds.
Artwork or Drawings: The act of creating small artworks or drawings that depict fairies or scenes from nature becomes a form of devotion. These visual representations can be left as offerings or placed on your fairy altar, a testament to the power of human creativity.
Scented Offerings: Aromas That Speak of Enchantment
Incense: As fragrant smoke wafts through the air, it creates an inviting atmosphere for fairies. The choice of incense, whether soothing lavender or purifying sage, sets the stage for communication with the fey.

Musical Offerings: Harmonies for the Fey's Ears
Soft Music: The gentle strains of melodic music in your sacred space become an enchanting invitation to fairies. Harp music, in particular, is associated with the fairy realm, resonating with the ethereal beings and infusing your space with magic.
Tokens of Protection: Safeguarding the Sacred
Offerings of Protection: In some traditions, fairies are seen as protectors of homes and hearths. To express gratitude for their guardianship, you can offer small amulets or charms, invoking the protective presence of the fey.
In the world of fairies, the act of making offerings transcends the material realm; it becomes a bridge between the human heart and the mystical world. With each offering, we express our reverence for the enchanting beings who share our world, forging a connection that spans the boundaries of reality and imagination. Through this timeless tradition, we honor the beauty, wonder, and magic that the realm of fairies bestows upon us, and in return, we are gifted with a sense of wonder that transcends the ordinary and reaffirms our connection to the extraordinary.

Maintaining and Renewing Offerings:

It's important to keep your offerings fresh and regularly replace them as a sign of your ongoing connection and respect. Over time, you may notice patterns in which offerings are favored or when fairies are most active in accepting them.
Remember that the essence of offerings is the intention behind them. Approach this practice with sincerity, reverence, and the understanding that it is a gesture of goodwill and acknowledgment of the mystique that fairies bring to our lives. In your efforts to communicate with fairies, you create an inviting space where the magical and the mundane intersect, fostering a sense of wonder and enchantment that transcends the boundaries of the known world.

III. Meditation and Visualization

Meditation and visualization are powerful tools for those seeking to communicate with fairies. These practices not only create a state of inner receptivity but also allow individuals to attune their consciousness to the subtle frequencies of the fairy realm. In this section, we explore the profound ways in which meditation and visualization can enhance your connection to fairies, providing a gateway to their elusive world.

1. Meditation Practices for Fairy Communication:

Meditation serves as a conduit to reach a state of heightened awareness and receptivity, making it an ideal preparatory practice for engaging with fairies:

- Nature Immersion: Begin by finding a quiet, natural setting, preferably outdoors. Sit or lie down in a comfortable position. Close your eyes and focus on your breath. Inhale and exhale deeply, feeling the natural rhythms of your surroundings.
- Grounding: Visualize roots extending from your body deep into the earth, grounding you to the natural world. This connection with the earth's energy helps align your vibration with that of the fairy realm.
- Mindful Presence: Shift your focus to the present moment. Pay attention to the sounds, scents, and sensations around you. By becoming fully present in the natural environment, you open yourself to the possibility of fairy encounters.
- Visualizing Fairy Realms: As you enter a deeper meditative state, allow your imagination to transport you to a serene meadow, forest glade, or other idyllic natural settings often associated with fairies. Visualize this realm with vivid detail, from the play of dappled sunlight to the whispering leaves.

2. Visualization Exercises:

Visualization exercises enable you to create a mental bridge between your consciousness and the fairy realm, inviting their presence into your awareness:

- Setting Intentions: Before beginning your visualization, set clear intentions for your connection with fairies. State your desire to communicate, seek guidance, or simply experience their presence.
- Fairy Guides: Envision a gentle, glowing light or a specific fairy figure approaching you within your inner sanctuary. This figure may take the form of a traditional fairy archetype or a unique being of your own creation.
- Communication: Initiate a mental dialogue with the fairy figure, asking questions or expressing your intentions. Listen attentively to any responses that arise within your mind, even if they seem subtle or symbolic.
- Merging Energies: Visualize a gentle merging of energies between yourself and the fairy figure. Feel a sense of connection and unity as you share your thoughts and feelings. Trust your intuition to interpret any messages or insights that emerge.
- Protection and Closing: At the conclusion of your visualization, express gratitude to the fairy figure and ask for their protection and guidance in your continued endeavors. Visualize their energy enveloping you, creating a protective aura.

3. Maintaining Consistency:

Consistency in meditation and visualization practices is essential for establishing a profound connection with fairies:

- Regular Practice: Make meditation and visualization a consistent part of your routine. The more you engage in these practices, the more attuned you become to the subtle energies of the fairy realm.
- Recording Experiences: Keep a journal to record your meditation and visualization experiences. Note any insights, messages, or encounters you have with fairies. Over time, patterns may emerge, deepening your understanding.
- Patience and Perseverance: Building a connection with fairies may require patience. Not all attempts will yield immediate results, but with persistence, your efforts may lead to profound and transformative experiences.

Meditation and visualization are gateways to the mystical world of fairies, allowing individuals to tap into the depths of their own consciousness and connect with the ethereal beings of the natural world. Through these practices, you not only enhance your own spiritual journey but also contribute to the rich tapestry of human-fairy interactions, bridging the realms of imagination and possibility. Remember that the pursuit of communicating with fairies is as much about personal growth, self-discovery, and reverence for the natural world as it is about encountering the mystical.

IV. Rituals and Invocations

Rituals and invocations are powerful tools for those seeking to communicate with fairies, as they create a structured and ceremonial framework for establishing a connection with these mystical beings. In this section, we will delve deeper into the practices, symbolism, and cultural variations that can enhance your attempts to bridge the divide between the human and fairy realms.

1. Rituals of Invitation: Forming a Sacred Space

Rituals serve as formalized methods of communication and engagement with the fairy realm. They often involve the creation of a sacred space where you can make your intentions known and invite fairies to join you in a harmonious setting. Here are some key elements of fairy-invoking rituals:

> Our journey into the enchanting world of fairies begins with the act of preparation, a pivotal step in crafting an atmosphere that beckons the mystical beings to our presence. We embark on this ritual by setting up a sacred altar, a dedicated space that shall serve as our conduit to the fairy realm. This is where the earthly and the ethereal shall converge.
>
> As we assemble our altar, we infuse it with the raw beauty of the natural world. Leaves, flowers, stones, and candles grace this sacred space, forming a tapestry of colors and textures that evoke the essence of the forests and meadows where fairies are said to

roam. Each element plays its role in crafting an inviting and spiritually charged environment, a sanctuary where the earthly and the mystical shall intermingle.

Purification: Cleansing the Self and Space

Before we tread further into the realm of fairies, we must first purify ourselves and the sacred space we have meticulously arranged. It is a time-honored tradition, an act of reverence to rid ourselves and our surroundings of any lingering negativity or discordant energies that may hinder our connection with these elusive beings.

Incense wafts through the air, its fragrant tendrils swirling around us, carrying away our worries and doubts. Water, pure and untainted, is sprinkled gently, cleansing not only our bodies but our very souls. A smudging ceremony, where the fragrant smoke of sage or herbs envelops us, is yet another powerful ritual, dispelling all that is impure, leaving only a sense of clarity and purpose in its wake.

Invocation: Welcoming the Fairies

With our sanctuary prepared and our spirits cleansed, we stand on the threshold of a magical encounter. In this heart of the ritual, we invoke the fairies, extending to them a formal invitation to join us in this sacred communion. Our words may take the form of a poetic incantation, an ancient charm, or the spontaneous utterings of our heart.

We speak from the depths of our being, our voice a vessel for our reverence and desire to connect with these mystical beings. In these moments, words are more than mere sounds; they are bridges that span the gap between our worlds. We extend our hearts and minds, beckoning the fairies to part the veil that separates our realities.

Offerings: Tokens of Goodwill

As our voices resonate with the incantations of invitation, we present offerings to our potential guests. These tokens of goodwill are not gifts in the traditional sense but rather expressions of our respect and hospitality. Honey, pure and golden, a nectar of the gods, is a favored offering. Milk, a symbol of nourishment and life, holds its own significance. Sweets, a delight to the senses, represent the joy and sweetness of our intentions.

Even small trinkets, items that have captured our fascination and affection, are presented with a heart full of reverence. In these humble offerings, we extend our hand in friendship, seeking to establish a harmonious connection with the fairies.

Candles and Incense: Illuminating the Path

As the offerings rest upon our altar, we kindle candles and incense, illuminating our sacred space with a flickering, ethereal glow and the subtle, fragrant wisps of smoke. These elements serve as beacons, drawing the fairies closer to our world.

The flames dance with a mesmerizing rhythm, casting shadows that seem to whisper secrets of the mystical. The incense smoke, like a fragrant veil, wraps around our senses, creating an atmosphere where the boundary between the tangible and the otherworldly blurs. It is in this gentle illumination and intoxicating aroma that we hope to attract the fairies, guiding them to our haven of connection.

Symbols and Tools: Channeling Intentions

Within our ritual, we call upon symbols and tools that resonate with our hearts and beliefs. These are the conduits through which our intentions and energies flow. A fairy wand, an emblem of enchantment and transformation, may be held with reverence. A chalice, a vessel of communion, may cradle offerings or libations.

These symbols and tools are not merely inanimate objects but extensions of our will and intention. They serve as a bridge, allowing us to direct our energy and focus as we reach out to the realm of fairies.

Visualization: Opening the Gateway

In the heart of our ritual, we engage in the powerful act of visualization. We close our eyes and let our minds soar, envisioning a luminous portal or a delicate bridge that spans the gap between our world and the ethereal realm of the fairies.

In our mind's eye, we see the veil that separates us thinning, the boundaries dissolving as our intention and energy breathe life into this envisioned pathway. We imagine ourselves walking through this gateway, entering the enchanted realm where the fairies dwell. This visualization not only serves as a conduit for our connection but also deepens our sense of immersion in this mystical journey.

As we stand at the precipice of our ritual, these sacred steps and symbolic gestures lay the groundwork for our communion with the fairies. We are poised on the cusp of an encounter with the enchanting beings who have captured our imagination and curiosity for generations. The natural elements that surround us, the words we speak, and the intentions that stir within our hearts unite to create a space where the mystical becomes tangible.

In this ritual, we embrace the belief in the unseen, the unknown, and the possibility of a connection with the world of fairies. With our altar prepared, our spirits cleansed, and our intentions clear, we await the response of the fairies. Will they heed our call? Will they grace us with their presence? As we stand on the precipice of the unknown, our hearts beat with anticipation, for we are about to embark on a journey into the realm of enchantment and wonder.

2. Chants and Invocations: The Power of Words

Words carry significant energy and intention in the realm of ritual and invocation. Chants and invocations are poetic or rhythmic expressions that convey your desire to communicate with fairies. They can be used as standalone practices or incorporated into broader rituals. Here are some considerations:

- Crafting Your Chants: Personalize your chants or invocations to reflect your intentions and feelings. You can draw inspiration from existing fairy poetry or create your own verses.
- Repetition: Chants often involve repetition of specific phrases or words. This repetition can help you enter a trance-like state and attune your mind to the fairy realm.
- Rhyme and Rhythm: Incorporate rhyme and rhythm into your chants to create a captivating and entrancing quality. The musicality of the words can enhance the ritual's potency.
- Invocation of Names: If you know the names of specific fairies you wish to communicate with, include them in your chants or invocations. Names hold power and can be used to address or call upon individual fairies.
- Singing and Music: In some traditions, singing or playing musical instruments is used as a means of invoking fairies. The melodies and vibrations are believed to resonate with the fairy realm.

3. Symbolism and Cultural Variations

Rituals and invocations often draw upon symbolism and cultural traditions. These symbols can carry specific meanings and resonate with the fairies you wish to connect with:

- Cultural Symbols: Explore the symbols and motifs associated with fairies in your cultural heritage. For example, in Celtic tradition, the four-leaf clover is considered a fairy symbol of luck and protection.
- Fairy Circles and Rings: In some cultures, fairy circles or rings are believed to be portals to the fairy realm. You can incorporate these natural formations into your rituals.
- Fairy Offerings: Different cultures have their own traditions of offerings to fairies. In Ireland, leaving out a bowl of cream or butter is a common practice, while in other regions, it might be honey or mead.
- Seasonal Significance: Consider the seasons and natural cycles when performing your rituals. Some fairies are believed to be more active during specific times of the year, such as the solstices or equinoxes.
- Moon Phases: Some practitioners align their fairy rituals with specific moon phases, believing that the lunar energies can enhance their connection with the fairy realm.

4. Personal Intent and Connection

Ultimately, the effectiveness of any ritual or invocation lies in your personal intent and connection. The sincerity of your desire to communicate with fairies and your belief in their existence are fundamental. Trust your intuition and inner guidance as you navigate the ethereal world of fairies.

Remember that fairies are autonomous beings, and any communication attempts should be made with respect, humility, and a deep sense of wonder. The rituals and invocations you choose should resonate with your beliefs and values, creating a genuine and heartfelt connection with the enchanting realm of the fairies.

V. Observing and Recording Signs

When delving into the mystical realm of fairies and their potential communication, one of the most intriguing aspects is the art of observing and recording signs. These subtle indicators, often fleeting and ethereal, can provide valuable insights into the presence and intentions of fairies. This section takes a closer look at the significance of observing and documenting these signs in the pursuit of communicating with fairies.

1. Signs of Presence:

Fairies are known for their elusive and ephemeral nature. To recognize their presence, it's essential to be attuned to the subtle cues that may manifest in your environment:

- Sudden Breezes: Unexplained gusts of wind or gentle breezes in otherwise still surroundings are often seen as signs of fairy presence. Pay attention to the direction and timing of these breezes.
- Shimmering Lights: Glowing or flickering lights that appear without an obvious source can be interpreted as fairy lights. These may appear as orbs, sparks, or ethereal beams.
- Unusual Sounds: Listen for unexplained sounds like tinkling laughter, faint music, or soft voices. These auditory experiences are often associated with fairy gatherings or activity.
- Flora and Fauna: Observe changes in the behavior of plants and animals in your environment. Sudden bursts of growth, blossoms out of season, or the presence of animals like butterflies and birds can be seen as signs of fairy influence.

2. Dreams and Visions:

Dreams and visions are considered potent channels for fairy communication. Here's how to engage with these ethereal messages:

- Dream Encounters: Keep a dream journal to record any dreams featuring fairies or fairy-related imagery. These dreams may offer guidance, insights, or symbolic messages.
- Meditation and Visualization: Practice guided meditation and visualization exercises to invite fairies into your consciousness. Visions or insights received during these practices can be significant.
- Symbolic Imagery: Pay attention to recurring symbols or images that appear in your dreams or meditations. These symbols may hold specific meanings or relate to your interactions with fairies.

3. Keep a Fairy Journal:

A fairy journal serves as a valuable tool for documenting your experiences, thoughts, and observations related to your attempts to communicate with fairies. Here's how to maintain one effectively:

- Regular Entries: Dedicate a section of your journal to recording your encounters, dreams, and feelings about fairies. Make entries regularly, even if they seem minor.
- Details Matter: Be specific in your descriptions. Note the date, time, location, weather conditions, and any emotional or physical sensations you experience during your encounters.
- Sketches and Drawings: Consider including sketches or drawings of any fairy-related signs, symbols, or visions you encounter. Visual representations can provide additional depth to your records.
- Reflect and Analyze: Periodically review your journal entries to identify patterns, trends, or recurring themes. Reflect on your experiences and any personal insights gained from them.

4. Interpretation and Meaning:

Interpreting the signs you observe is a deeply personal and intuitive process. Here are some tips for deciphering the meanings behind these signs:

- Intuition and Gut Feelings: Trust your intuition and inner guidance when interpreting signs. Often, your instincts will lead you to the most meaningful interpretations.
- Symbolism: Consider the symbolic meanings associated with the signs you encounter. Reflect on how these symbols resonate with your own life and experiences.
- Cultural and Folklore References: Refer to cultural and folklore references related to fairies. Different cultures may ascribe unique meanings to various signs and symbols.
- Guidance from Guides: Seek guidance from experienced practitioners, mentors, or spiritual guides who may offer insights into interpreting the signs you encounter.

5. Gratitude and Acknowledgment:

Expressing gratitude for any encounters or signs you receive from the fairy realm can deepen your connection and foster reciprocity:

- Thanksgiving Rituals: Create simple rituals or offerings to express your appreciation for the communication and presence of fairies. Offer a heartfelt thanks for any guidance or messages received.
- Continued Respect: Maintain an attitude of respect and reverence for fairies, regardless of the nature of your encounters. Gratitude and respect can strengthen the bonds of communication.
- Openness to Guidance: Be open to receiving further guidance and insights from fairies. Acknowledge their role as mentors and guides in your spiritual journey.

Observing and recording signs in your quest to communicate with fairies is a contemplative and evolving process. It requires patience, openness, and a willingness to embrace the mysterious and the ethereal. Remember that the pursuit of connecting with fairies is not just about seeking answers; it's about forging a deeper connection with the natural world, nurturing your own intuition, and embracing the magic and wonder that surrounds us.

VI. Patience and Respect

In the pursuit of communicating with fairies, patience and respect emerge as the guiding virtues that facilitate a harmonious and meaningful connection with these mystical beings. The fairy realm operates on its own terms, often beyond the comprehension of human timeframes and desires. This section explores the profound significance of patience and respect when engaging with fairies, emphasizing their roles as essential foundations for any successful interaction.

1. Patience: A Virtue of Time and Understanding

The Unpredictable Nature of Fairies: Fairies exist in a realm where time flows differently than in the human world. They may choose to reveal themselves or communicate in their own time, which can be unpredictable and often not in alignment with human expectations.
Embracing the Journey: Patience, therefore, becomes a virtue that allows individuals to embrace the journey of communicating with fairies rather than fixating solely on the end goal. The process of discovery, self-reflection, and connection can be as enriching as the final outcome.

Cultivating Patience:

- Meditation: Regular meditation practices can cultivate patience by teaching individuals to stay present, accept the ebb and flow of experiences, and let go of immediate desires.
- Mindfulness: Practicing mindfulness in daily life encourages an appreciation for each moment, reducing the urgency to rush through experiences.

2. Respect: Honoring the Boundaries of the Fairy Realm

Fairies as Autonomous Beings: Fairies, in folklore and mythology, are portrayed as autonomous beings with their own intentions, desires, and a distinct sense of sovereignty. They are not to be controlled or coerced by humans.

The Importance of Respect:

- Mutual Respect: Just as humans expect respect from others, it is essential to extend the same courtesy to fairies. Respecting their autonomy and boundaries creates an atmosphere of mutual respect in which communication can occur organically.
- Avoiding Confrontation: Fairies are known for their capricious nature. Disrespect or attempts at control can lead to confrontations and negative interactions. Approaching them with respect reduces the likelihood of unfavorable encounters.

- Reciprocity: Respect fosters a sense of reciprocity, where fairies are more likely to engage positively with those who acknowledge their existence and treat them kindly.

Cultivating Respect:

- Education: Learning about fairy lore, traditions, and cultural contexts can deepen one's understanding of fairies, fostering a respectful approach.
- Humility: Approaching the fairy realm with humility and a sense of wonder acknowledges the mysteries that transcend human comprehension.
- Ethical Considerations: Reflecting on the ethical implications of one's actions when attempting to communicate with fairies ensures that interactions are respectful and harmonious.

3. Gratitude and Acknowledgment: Cementing the Connection

Gratitude as an Expression of Respect: Expressing gratitude for any encounters or signs received from the fairy realm is a natural extension of respect. It demonstrates appreciation for their presence and an acknowledgment of the value they bring to one's life.
Reciprocity: Gratitude and acknowledgment create a sense of reciprocity within the communication process. When fairies feel valued and respected, they are more likely to continue their interactions, offering guidance and insights.

Cultivating Gratitude and Acknowledgment:

- Journaling: Maintaining a fairy journal in which you record your experiences and express gratitude can reinforce the importance of these expressions.
- Rituals: Creating rituals that involve offerings and expressions of thanks can serve as a physical manifestation of gratitude.

In conclusion, patience and respect are the cornerstones of communicating with fairies, facilitating a harmonious and fulfilling connection with these mystical beings. These virtues guide individuals on a transformative journey where the act of seeking to communicate with fairies becomes as meaningful as the communication itself. By embracing patience and respect, we honor the mysteries of the fairy realm, recognizing the profound impact that these ethereal encounters can have on our lives and our understanding of the unseen world. In the quest to communicate with fairies, it's essential to remember that the line between reality and imagination can blur. Regardless of whether you believe in their existence as independent beings or view them as symbolic representations of nature's mysteries, the journey to connect with fairies is a reflection of humanity's enduring fascination with the mystical and the unseen. Ultimately, it is a personal and spiritual endeavor that enriches our connection to the natural world and the realms of wonder that surround us.

7B. Connecting with Nature

The Connection Between Fairies and the Natural World

In the captivating realm of fairy folklore, the profound connection between fairies and the natural world is a central theme that permeates myths, legends, and stories across cultures. This section delves deep into the intricate relationship between these enchanting beings and the ecosystems they inhabit, exploring the ways in which fairies are intrinsically linked to the beauty, wonder, and balance of nature.

I. Guardians of the Wilds: Fairies as Nature's Caretakers

1. Elemental Spirits:
   - Nymphs and Dryads: These ethereal beings personify the natural elements—water, trees, and forests. Nymphs dwell near water sources, while Dryads are the spirits of trees, particularly oaks. They are intimately connected with the life and vitality of their respective environments.
   - Protection of Ecosystems: Nymphs and Dryads serve as guardians of their domains, ensuring the well-being of flora and fauna. Their presence in stories underscores the importance of preserving and respecting the environment.

2. The Green Man and Green Woman:
   - Symbols of Nature's Bounty: In Celtic and European folklore, the Green Man and Green Woman represent the lush, vibrant fertility of the natural world. They are often depicted with leaves, vines, and other flora adorning their features.
   - Celebrating Cycles of Life: These nature deities are closely tied to the cycles of growth, decay, and rebirth in the natural world. They symbolize the perpetual renewal of life and the interdependence of all living creatures.

II. Seasons and Festivals: Fairies as Keepers of Time

1. Seasonal Fairies:
   - Spring and Summer Spirits: Fairies often correspond to specific seasons, such as the joyful sprites of spring or the radiant beings of summer. They are believed to usher in the changing of the seasons and the blossoming of new life.
   - Harvest and Autumn Fairies: Autumn fairies are linked to the harvest season, embodying the bittersweet transition from abundance to dormancy. They teach us to appreciate the beauty in the changing of the leaves and the falling of the last fruits.

2. Festivals and Celebrations:
   - Beltane and Midsummer: In Celtic traditions, Beltane and Midsummer celebrations revolve around fairies and nature. Bonfires are lit to honor these mystical beings, and revelers

dance to the rhythm of the natural world, strengthening the bond between humans and fairies.

- Harvest and Samhain: During harvest festivals and Samhain (the precursor to Halloween), fairies are believed to be especially active. Rituals and offerings are made to seek their favor and protection.

III. The Enchanted Wilderness: Fairies as Inhabitants of Hidden Realms

1. Fairy Forts and Mounds:
    - Sacred Sites: Fairy forts and mounds, often ancient archaeological sites, are believed to be portals to the fairy realm. These places are revered and protected, emphasizing the sanctity of nature.
    - Dwelling Places: Fairies are said to reside within these hidden realms, living in harmony with the land. Interactions with humans near these sites are viewed with caution, as disturbing them can incur the fairies' wrath.
2. Natural Features and Phenomena:
    - Waterfalls and Glens: Fairies are often associated with natural features like waterfalls, glens, and secluded groves. These serene locales are seen as places where the veil between the human and fairy worlds is thin.
    - Celestial Phenomena: Fairies have been linked to meteor showers, rainbows, and other celestial phenomena. The appearance of such events is often interpreted as a sign of fairy activity and blessings.

IV. Lessons from the Natural World: Fairies as Symbols of Balance

1. Environmental Stewardship:
    - Respect for Nature: Fairy folklore underscores the importance of respecting and preserving the natural world. Fairies serve as reminders of the consequences of neglecting our environment or disturbing delicate ecosystems.
    - Interconnectedness: The interconnectedness of all living beings is a recurring theme in fairy tales. The actions of humans affect the fairies and vice versa, highlighting the delicate balance of nature.
2. Cycles of Renewal:
    - Embracing Change: Fairies represent the acceptance of change and the beauty in life's transitions. They show that even in the darkest of times, there is hope for renewal and transformation, mirroring the cycles of nature.

As we journey through the enchanted world of fairies, we come to understand that their existence is intertwined with the rhythms of the natural world. Their presence in folklore serves as a powerful reminder of the harmony that can be achieved when humans and nature coexist in balance and respect. The enchanting connection between fairies and the natural world invites us to deepen our appreciation for the beauty and wonder that surround us, fostering a sense of stewardship and awe for the ecosystems we are privileged to share with these mystical beings.

Chapter 8
How to Find Fairies

The pursuit of fairies has long been a fascination for those who seek to connect with the mystical world. While encounters with these elusive beings may be rare, this chapter provides practical tips and strategies for those eager to embark on a quest to find and observe fairies in their natural habitats.

I. Choosing the Right Location

Fairies, those captivating ethereal beings, are intricately linked to the natural world. In our pursuit of encountering these enchanting creatures, the selection of the perfect location becomes paramount—a place where the veil between our world and theirs is delicate, and the enchantment of nature is palpable. Join us on an expedition as we explore the prime habitats where fairies are said to dwell, where their very existence harmonizes with the elements of the Earth.

The Heart of Fairy Realms: Forests

Forests, ancient and enigmatic, have perennially been perceived as the quintessential domain of fairies. Within their realm of towering trees, dappled sunlight, and vibrant undergrowth, innumerable fairy species are believed to find their abode. The allure of forests for fairies can be attributed to:

Abundant Biodiversity: Forests teem with life, offering fairies a rich mosaic of flora and fauna to engage with and safeguard. The luxuriant vegetation and concealed alcoves within these woods serve as ideal sanctuaries for these elusive beings.

Whispering Leaves: The rustling of leaves in the breeze and the gentle murmur of streams coursing through the sylvan glades are perceived as the voices of fairies. Attentive listening to these natural melodies can guide one to their presence.

Tree Spirits: Trees themselves are deemed to be repositories of tree spirits or Dryads, a subset of the fairy realm. Specific tree species, such as oaks and willows, are intrinsically associated with these guardian spirits.

Open Spaces of Magic: Meadows and Glens

Meadows, glens, and open fields offer a distinct enchantment compared to forests. These expanses of open land exhibit:

Carpet of Wildflowers: Meadows erupt in a profusion of colors during the wildflower blooms, evoking a landscape straight out of a fairy tale. Fairies are often drawn to these vibrant displays of nature's artistry.

Dancing Light: The interplay of sunlight and these open spaces creates a mesmerizing ballet of light and shadow—a spectacle that is believed to captivate fairies and provide a backdrop for their festivities.

Natural Springs: Fairies are frequently linked to water sources, and meadows frequently feature natural springs or brooks meandering through them. These water features are perceived as gateways to the fairy realm.

Liquid Portals to Fairy Realms: Waterways and Waterfalls

Water carries a profound connection to fairies, and bodies of water such as rivers, lakes, and waterfalls are considered conduits to the fairy world. These aqueous realms offer:

Reflective Surfaces: Fairies are occasionally said to manifest in the reflections on water surfaces, particularly during the transitions of dawn and dusk. Bodies of water are revered as mirrors to the fairy domain.

Water's Melody: The soothing sounds of flowing water and cascading waterfalls are likened to enchanted melodies that beckon fairies. These tranquil settings provide an ideal backdrop for serene observations.

Bridges and Crossings: Legends often recount encounters with fairies near bridges and crossings, as these locations symbolize the liminal spaces where the human and fairy realms intersect.

Hidden Retreats of the Fey: Secluded Groves

Secluded groves and clearings nestled within forests exude a mystical charm, rendering them ideal settings for fairy encounters:

Isolated Beauty: These secluded locales offer an aura of isolation and serenity amid the heart of the forest, establishing a sacred ambiance conducive to fairy activity.

Natural Altars: Clearings within woodlands are frequently regarded as natural altars where fairies congregate for ceremonies and gatherings. Observing these areas can provide insight into their rituals and practices.

Solitude and Reverence: Fairies are believed to hold solitude and reverence in high regard. When one discovers a secluded grove and approaches it with respect, they may be privileged to witness the ethereal beings' activities.

In the selection of an enchanted environment to seek fairies, it is paramount to approach the natural world with reverence and mindfulness. By immersing oneself in these magical settings and attuning to the whispers of the wind, the songs of avian companions, and the secrets of flowing waters, the likelihood of connecting with the mystical realm of fairies is heightened. Always remember that patience and respect are the key elements for forging a profound connection with these elusive and wondrous beings.

2. Historical Sites and Sacred Grounds

Discover locales with historical or cultural significance in local folklore. Fairy forts, mounds, and other ancient sites are believed to serve as gateways to the fairy realm.

II. Timing Matters

Seasonal Awareness

Understanding the seasonal rhythms and the natural world's ebb and flow is crucial when embarking on a quest to encounter and observe fairies. These mystical beings, deeply intertwined with nature's cycles, often exhibit heightened activity during specific seasons. This section delves into the intricacies of seasonal awareness in your pursuit of encountering these mystical beings.

1. Spring: The Season of Renewal and Abundance

Fairies of Spring:

Spring is a time of rebirth and renewal in the natural world, making it particularly significant in fairy folklore. Fairies associated with spring are often depicted as joyful and vibrant, mirroring the burgeoning life around them. Examples of spring fairies include Sprites, renowned for their playful antics, and Flower Fairies, who inhabit blossoms and ensure flower pollination.

Why Spring Matters:
Spring marks the Earth's awakening from its winter slumber. Fairies celebrate the return of warmth and light, and their activity becomes more pronounced as they assist nature in full bloom. Observing fairies in spring offers you the opportunity to witness the enchanting magic of rejuvenation, as they tend to plants, nurture new life, and dance amid blossoming flora.

2. Summer: The Season of Abundance and Enchantment

Fairies of Summer:
Summer epitomizes fullness and enchantment. Fairies associated with this season are often portrayed as radiant and spirited, reveling in the extended, sun-drenched days. Examples of summer fairies encompass the Sidhe, renowned for their ethereal beauty and grace, and Leprechauns, known for their playful and mischievous antics.

Why Summer Matters:
Summer represents the zenith of natural abundance, with lush landscapes and vibrant ecosystems. Fairies are believed to play a pivotal role in maintaining this vibrancy and ensuring harmony in the natural world.
Observing fairies in summer allows you to witness their connection to the flourishing environment, as they engage in dances, protect their domains, and interact with the elements.

3. Autumn: The Season of Harvest and Transition

Fairies of Autumn:

- Autumn is a season of transition, characterized by the harvesting of crops and the changing colors of foliage. Fairies associated with this season often embody the bittersweet beauty of change and reflection.
- Examples of autumn fairies include the Harvest Spirits, who oversee the gathering of crops, and the Wisps, mysterious beings that guide lost travelers in the twilight.

Why Autumn Matters:

- Autumn is a time when fairies are believed to share the wisdom of cycles, embracing both the abundance and the inevitable decline that comes with the changing seasons.
- Observing fairies in autumn allows you to witness their role in the harvest, as they help ensure a bountiful yield while guiding the natural world through the gentle transition toward winter.

4. Winter: The Season of Rest and Renewal

Fairies of Winter:

- Winter is a season of quietude and introspection. Fairies associated with this season are often seen as caretakers of the dormant Earth, ensuring its renewal in the spring.
- Examples of winter fairies include the Snow Queen, who oversees the crystalline beauty of winter landscapes, and the Yule Lads, mischievous but ultimately benevolent beings.

Why Winter Matters:

- Winter is a time when fairies are believed to retreat to their hidden realms, conserving their energy and safeguarding the potential for new life in the coming spring.
- Observing fairies in winter can be more challenging, but it allows you to connect with their role in maintaining the balance of the natural world even during its periods of dormancy.

Conclusion: The Dance of the Seasons and Fairies
Seasonal awareness is a key element in the quest to find and observe fairies. By aligning your search with the rhythms of the natural world, you increase your chances of connecting with these mystical beings and witnessing their profound relationship with the changing seasons. Fairies, as guardians and stewards of the Earth, offer insights into the beauty, transformation, and eternal renewal that define the wondrous dance of nature's cycles.

IV. Patience and Respect:

Patience and respect are the virtues that underpin the delicate art of seeking and connecting with fairies. In this section, we delve into the profound significance of these qualities and how they form the bedrock of a successful and harmonious interaction with these elusive beings.

1. Be Patient: The Dance of Time

Fairies are creatures deeply intertwined with the rhythms of the natural world. Their appearances and activities often align with the cycles of nature and celestial events. Patience, therefore, is an essential virtue for any aspiring fairy seeker.

Time in Their Realm: Fairies are said to experience time differently from humans. What may seem like mere minutes to you could be hours or even days in the fairy realm. Embrace the slow and unhurried pace of nature, allowing time to flow naturally as you seek to connect with these beings.

The Art of Stillness: To truly observe fairies, one must cultivate the art of stillness. Spend time sitting quietly in their chosen habitat, allowing the natural world to unfold around you. In the tranquility of the moment, fairies may reveal themselves, drawn by your patient presence.

Seasonal Observations: Different fairies may be active during various seasons. For example, you might encounter spring fairies as flowers bloom, or autumn fairies as leaves change color. Patiently observe the changes in nature as the seasons transition, always mindful of the signs that herald fairy activity.

2. Show Respect: Honoring the Natural World

Respect for the natural world is not only a moral imperative but also a fundamental aspect of connecting with fairies. Fairies are known as protectors of the environment, and by showing respect for their realm, you demonstrate your sincerity and willingness to coexist harmoniously.

Leave No Trace: Adopt the "Leave No Trace" ethic when venturing into natural habitats. Dispose of litter responsibly, avoid disturbing plants and animals, and tread lightly to minimize your impact on the environment. Fairies appreciate those who care for their homes.

Offerings and Gifts: Consider leaving small offerings as tokens of your respect and gratitude. Flowers, herbs, honey, or even a heartfelt note can be left at the base of a tree or by a babbling brook. Fairies are said to be touched by such gestures and may respond favorably.

Speak Gently: When you are in a natural environment where fairies may dwell, be mindful of your speech. Speak softly and kindly, acknowledging the spirits of the land and fairies as benevolent beings. Respectful communication fosters a sense of trust and rapport.

Boundaries and Limits: Recognize that there are boundaries and limits to human-fairy interactions. Fairies are elusive, and not all seek direct contact with humans. Respect their autonomy and privacy. If you sense that your presence is unwelcome, gracefully withdraw.

3. The Heart of Connection: Patience and Respect in Practice

The practice of patience and respect in seeking fairies goes beyond mere observation. It is an embodiment of an ethical and spiritual approach to the natural world, reflecting an understanding that all living beings, seen and unseen, deserve reverence and consideration.

A Humble Approach: Approach your quest to find fairies with humility. Recognize that your presence in their world is a privilege, and the act of seeking them is an act of reverence for the magic and mystery of nature.

Life Lessons: As you cultivate patience and respect in your fairy-seeking journey, you will find that these virtues extend beyond the realm of folklore. They become valuable life lessons, guiding you to be more mindful, patient, and considerate in all your interactions.

The Unseen World: In your patient and respectful observations, you may not always witness fairies directly, but you will undoubtedly gain a deeper connection to the natural world. The peace and serenity found in the practice of patience and respect are rewards in themselves.

In essence, patience and respect are not just tools for finding fairies; they are the keys to unlocking the deeper mysteries of the natural world and forging a profound bond with its mystical inhabitants. Through these virtues, you can embark on a journey of wonder and discovery, guided by the magic of the unseen and the enduring wisdom of nature.

V. Tools and Techniques:

In the quest to connect with fairies, employing specific tools and techniques can enhance your chances of forging a deeper connection with these elusive and mystical beings. This section delves into various tools and practices that have been traditionally associated with attracting and communicating with fairies.

1. Fairy-Calling Tools:

Fairy Bells and Wind Chimes:

- Description: Fairy bells, wind chimes, and other melodious instruments have been used for centuries to call upon fairies. These delicate, tinkling sounds are believed to resonate with the ethereal world of fairies, acting as an auditory invitation.
- Usage: Hang fairy bells or wind chimes in your chosen fairy habitat. The gentle tinkling is thought to attract fairies to investigate the source of the sound.

Fairy Music and Songs:

- Description: Music is a universal language that transcends boundaries, and it is believed to have a special appeal to fairies. Melodic tunes and songs dedicated to fairies can be used to beckon them.
- Usage: Play soft, enchanting music in natural settings where fairies are believed to dwell. Singing or playing traditional fairy songs on instruments like the flute or harp can be particularly effective.

2. Meditation and Visualization:

Meditation to Attune to the Fairy Realm:

- Description: Meditation is a powerful tool for centering your thoughts and attuning your consciousness to the subtle energies of the natural world and the fairy realm. It can open your senses to the possibility of encountering fairies.
- Usage: Find a quiet, natural setting and sit or lie down comfortably. Close your eyes and focus on your breath, gradually allowing your mind to enter a state of deep relaxation. Visualize yourself in a lush, enchanting forest or meadow, and imagine fairies revealing themselves to you.

Visualization Exercises:

- Description: Visualization exercises can help you mentally bridge the gap between the physical and mystical realms. By imagining fairies and their environment, you become more receptive to their presence.
- Usage: Before embarking on your fairy-seeking journey, take a few moments to visualize fairies in your mind's eye. Picture their appearance, movements, and the surroundings where you hope to find them. This mental preparation can help you recognize signs of their presence during your quest.

3. Natural Offerings:

Gifts and Offerings:

- Description: Fairies are said to appreciate offerings of natural items like flowers, honey, milk, or shiny trinkets. These gifts are symbols of goodwill and can foster a sense of reciprocity.

- Usage: When entering a fairy habitat, bring small, thoughtful offerings with you. Place them near trees, meadow flowers, or other locations where fairies might gather. This gesture is seen as a sign of respect and a way to establish a positive rapport.

4. The Fairy Circle:

Creating a Fairy Circle:

- Description: Fairy circles, also known as fairy rings, are naturally occurring circular formations of mushrooms or flowers. They are believed to be magical gateways to the fairy realm.
- Usage: If you encounter a fairy circle in your chosen location, you can sit or stand within it and quietly meditate or simply observe. Some believe that entering a fairy circle at the right time may facilitate a fairy encounter.

5. Fairy Houses:

Building Fairy Houses:

- Description: Building miniature houses or shelters for fairies is a creative way to invite them into your space. These houses are typically made from natural materials and are left in gardens or wooded areas.
- Usage: Craft a small fairy house using twigs, leaves, moss, and other natural materials. Place it in a suitable location and maintain it as an inviting space for fairies to visit.

Remember that while these tools and techniques can enhance your connection with the fairy realm, encounters with fairies are not guaranteed. Patience, respect, and mindfulness remain essential as you embark on your quest to connect with these elusive and enchanting beings. Approach your search with an open heart and a sense of wonder, and your journey in the mystical world of fairies will be an enriching and magical experience.

VI. Recording Your Observations:

Recording your observations while seeking fairies is not only a practical aspect of your quest but also a means of deepening your connection to the mystical realm. This section delves into the importance of maintaining a fairy journal, utilizing photography and sketching, and how these practices can enhance your understanding of fairies.

1. Keeping a Fairy Journal:

A fairy journal serves as a personal record of your experiences, encounters, and reflections related to your quest for fairies. It functions as both a practical tool and a magical repository for your observations. Here's how to create and maintain your fairy journal:

A. Choosing a Journal:

Select a journal or notebook that resonates with you. It could be adorned with fairy-themed artwork or nature motifs, adding an element of enchantment to your documentation.

B. Recording Your Experiences:
Document your outings, observations, and feelings. Include details such as the date, time, weather conditions, and the location of your encounters. Be sure to describe any unusual occurrences or sensations.

C. Sketch and Illustrate:
If you possess artistic talents, consider incorporating sketches or illustrations into your journal. Drawings of natural settings, plants, and fairy encounters can provide visual context to your entries.

D. Reflect and Interpret:
Take time to reflect on your experiences. What do you believe you witnessed? How did it make you feel? What lessons or insights can you derive from your encounters? Consider including these reflections in your journal.

E. Consistency Matters:
Cultivate the habit of regularly updating your journal after each outing or encounter. Consistency in recording your observations helps create a comprehensive narrative of your quest.

2. Photography and Sketching:

Photography and sketching can be invaluable tools for documenting your encounters with fairies. Here's how to use them effectively:

A. Camera or Smartphone:
Carry a camera or smartphone with a good-quality camera when you venture out. Be prepared to capture any fleeting moments of enchantment.

B. Practice Discretion:
If you spot a potential fairy sighting, approach it cautiously and without disturbing the surroundings. Use zoom capabilities or a telephoto lens to capture images without getting too close.

C. Lighting and Composition:
Pay attention to lighting conditions and composition when taking photos. Natural light often enhances the ethereal quality of fairy encounters.

D. Sketching:
If photography is not an option, consider sketching what you observe. Sketching allows you to capture details that might be missed in a photograph and can be a meditative practice.

E. Ethical Considerations:

Be respectful of the natural environment and fairies themselves when taking photos or making sketches. Avoid invasive behavior or actions that could harm the delicate ecosystems where fairies dwell.

F. Catalog and Organize:
Maintain a separate section in your fairy journal for photographs and sketches. Include notes on the circumstances of each image or drawing.

G. Share Your Visual Records:
Consider sharing your photographic and artistic records with fellow enthusiasts or within fairy-focused communities. They may offer insights or validation for your encounters.

H. Analyze and Compare:
Over time, analyze your visual records for patterns or common features in your fairy encounters. This can provide valuable insights into their behavior and habitats.

Recording your observations through journaling, photography, and sketching not only serves as a means of documentation but also deepens your connection with the natural world and the enchanting realm of fairies. By diligently documenting your experiences, you become an active participant in the mystical journey and contribute to the body of knowledge surrounding these elusive beings.

VII. Safety and Caution:

In the pursuit of discovering fairies and connecting with the mystical realm, safety and caution are of paramount importance. Exploring the natural world and seeking encounters with fairies should be undertaken responsibly and respectfully. This section provides an in-depth exploration of safety considerations to ensure a secure and meaningful fairy-seeking experience.
I. Stay Grounded and Practical:
Know Your Environment:
Before embarking on an exploration of the wilderness in pursuit of fairies, it is imperative to conduct comprehensive research and gain a profound understanding of the terrain, botanical elements, and wildlife present in the area. This knowledge will not only enhance your ability to navigate safely but also enable you to act responsibly in this delicate environment.

Weather Awareness:

Maintain vigilant awareness of weather forecasts and prepare yourself for potential fluctuations in conditions. Properly attire yourself, equip with essential supplies, and remain prepared to seek shelter when required.

Wildlife Precautions:

Exercise caution and consciousness regarding the local wildlife and the possibility of encounters. When venturing into regions known for hosting large predators, consider carrying protective measures such as bear spray. Demonstrate respect for the natural habitats of animals and diligently avoid any activities that might disturb them.

Respect for Private Property and Protected Areas:

No Trespassing:
Always honor property boundaries and the rights of private landowners. Seek permission from landowners when contemplating exploration of specific areas, irrespective of their reputed status as fairy habitats.

Follow Regulations:

Comply with local laws and regulations governing nature conservation, wildlife protection, and access to public lands. National parks and protected areas are governed by specific rules designed to safeguard their ecosystems.

Personal Safety Measures:

Hiking Essentials:
If your adventure entails hiking through remote or natural regions, ensure that you carry essential items such as maps, a compass, a first aid kit, water purification tools, and an ample supply of food.

Communicate Your Plans:
Prior to your expedition, inform a trusted friend or family member about your whereabouts and your anticipated return time. In case of an unforeseen emergency, they should possess the means to contact you or alert the appropriate authorities.

Navigation Skills:
Acquire proficiency in fundamental navigation skills, including map reading and the use of a compass or GPS device. The ability to orient yourself is paramount when traversing remote territories.

Fairy Mounds and Sacred Sites:

Respect the Landscape:
In your visits to fairy mounds or other sacred locales, practice utmost discretion and refrain from causing any harm or damage. These places often hold profound cultural significance and merit the utmost reverence.

Leave No Trace:
Adhere to the principles of Leave No Trace, which encompass the responsible disposal of waste, avoidance of unnecessary noise, and refraining from uprooting plants or disturbing the local wildlife.

Use of Tools and Instruments:
Fairy-Calling Tools:
If you opt to employ tools like fairy bells or musical instruments to beckon fairies, exercise discretion regarding volume levels and the potential environmental impact. Excessive noise may disrupt local wildlife and disturb fellow visitors.

Photography and Sketching:
When documenting your encounters or observations, employ photography or sketching techniques that minimize your ecological footprint. Avoid trampling vegetation or unsettling wildlife for the sake of capturing an image.

Responsible Group Activities:
Group Etiquette:
In the event that you embark on your journey with a group, ensure that all participants are well-versed in and committed to responsible practices. Collective dedication to environmental respect and adherence to local regulations is paramount.

Educational Experiences:
Promote educational and interpretive experiences that foster a profound appreciation for the natural world and its interconnectedness with fairy folklore.

The Ethical and Spiritual Dimension:
Respect for Beliefs:
Acknowledge the diversity of fairy beliefs and practices, which may vary among cultures and individuals. Demonstrate respect for the viewpoints and customs of local communities and fellow seekers.

Personal Reflection:
Take time to contemplate the ethical and spiritual dimensions of your quest. Reflect upon your intentions and the potential impact of your actions on both the environment and the mystical beings you aspire to connect with.

In your pursuit of fairies, safety and prudence extend beyond mere practicalities—they embody essential elements of responsible and reverent engagement with the natural world. By adhering to these guidelines, you can ensure not only your personal well-being but also the preservation of the environment and the sanctity of the enchanted realm, all while embarking on a magical journey to discover the elusive and enchanting fairies.

VIII. Share and Connect:

The pursuit of finding and observing fairies is a journey best enjoyed in the company of like-minded individuals. The stories, experiences, and insights of fellow enthusiasts can greatly enrich your exploration of the mystical world. This section delves into the significance of cultivating a community of kindred spirits who share your fascination with fairies.

1. Joining Communities:

a. Local Groups:

Seek out local organizations, clubs, or societies devoted to fairy folklore and nature exploration. These groups often arrange outings, workshops, and events where you can glean knowledge from seasoned enthusiasts.

b. Online Forums:

Explore online forums, social media groups, and discussion boards tailored to fairy enthusiasts. Platforms like Reddit, Facebook, and specialized forums offer spaces to connect with individuals from around the world who share your passion.

c. Attend Workshops and Conventions:

Keep an eye out for workshops, seminars, and conventions centered around fairy folklore, mythology, and nature. These gatherings present opportunities to learn from experts, engage in discussions, and forge connections with fellow enthusiasts.

2. Sharing Experiences:

a. Storytelling and Anecdotes:

Share your own encounters with fairies, whether they involve sightings, interactions, or moments of connection with the natural world. Listening to the stories of others can provide inspiration and validation for your own experiences.

b. Recording Encounters:

If you are fortunate enough to observe fairies, meticulously document your encounters. Share photographs, sketches, or journal entries within your community to facilitate discussions and gain insights from others.

c. Collaborative Projects:

Collaborate with fellow enthusiasts on projects related to fairies and nature. This might encompass creating art, crafting written works, or conducting research that contributes to the collective knowledge of the fairy community.

3. Learning and Teaching:

a. Share Resources:

Recommend books, documentaries, podcasts, and websites that have proven valuable in your research and exploration. Sharing resources helps others broaden their comprehension of fairies and the natural world.

b. Mentorship:

Consider mentoring newcomers to the realm of fairy folklore. Sharing your wisdom and experiences can be a fulfilling way to pass on traditions and promote the growth of the community.

4. Building a Supportive Network:

a. Emotional Support:

The quest for fairies can be replete with wonder but also accompanied by challenges and doubts. A supportive community offers a safe space to converse about these feelings and seek encouragement.

b. Validation and Camaraderie:

Connecting with fellow fairy enthusiasts provides validation for your experiences and beliefs. Sharing a common passion fosters a sense of camaraderie and belonging.

c. Cross-Cultural Exchange:

Engaging with a diverse community allows you to delve into fairy folklore from various cultures and regions. Learning about global perspectives on fairies enriches your own understanding.

5. Respecting Diverse Beliefs:

a. Open Dialogue:

A thriving fairy community champions open and respectful dialogue. Recognize that beliefs and experiences vary widely, and diverse perspectives can enhance your own comprehension.

b. Avoiding Dogmatism:

While sharing and connecting, remain open to different viewpoints and interpretations. Steer clear of rigid beliefs or dogmatism that may stifle the spirit of inquiry and discovery.

6. Ethical Considerations:

a. Environmental Responsibility:

Promote ethical and responsible practices when searching for fairies. Emphasize the importance of respecting natural environments and leaving no trace of your presence.

b. Cultural Sensitivity:

Foster cultural sensitivity by acknowledging and respecting the diverse cultural aspects of fairy beliefs. Avoid appropriating or misrepresenting traditions from other cultures.

Cultivating a community of fairy enthusiasts not only enhances your own exploration but also contributes to the preservation and comprehension of fairy folklore and the natural world. By sharing your experiences, learning from others, and fostering a supportive network, you become part of a vibrant community that celebrates the beauty, wonder, and magic of the mystical realm of fairies. Together, you can continue to uncover the enchanting secrets of the natural world and the beings who inhabit it.

While finding and observing fairies may be a challenging endeavor, the journey itself is a magical one. By following these practical tips and strategies, you can enhance your chances of connecting with the natural world and the enchanting realm of fairies. Remember that patience, respect, and mindfulness are key to forging a deeper connection with these elusive and mystical beings.

Chapter 9
Fairy Encounters

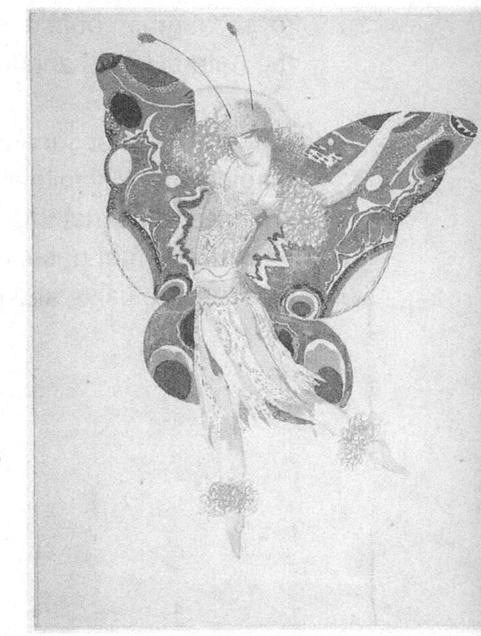

Chapter 9A: Personal Stories - Accounts of Alleged Fairy Encounters

Throughout history, countless individuals have shared their claims of personal encounters with fairies. In this chapter, we embark on a journey into the captivating world of these firsthand experiences, delving into the narratives, anecdotes, and testimonies of those who firmly believe they have crossed paths with these mystical beings. From enchanting tales of moonlit glade dances to encounters with fairy guides and helpers, we unveil the diverse and often magical nature of these personal stories. Through interviews and narratives, we provide readers with a glimpse into the captivating realm of fairy encounters.

I. Personal Stories: Childhood Encounters with Fairies

1. The Glimpse in the Garden:

As a child growing up in the countryside, I had my first encounter with fairies in the family garden. It was a warm summer evening, and I found myself immersed in play among the vibrant flowers and tall grasses. As the sun began its descent, a soft, twinkling light caught my attention at the garden's edge. Initially, I thought it might be fireflies, but as I drew closer, I realized that the source of this luminosity was something entirely different.

Among the wildflowers, I spotted diminutive, radiant figures, no taller than the span of my hand. They possessed delicate, iridescent wings that shimmered with every graceful movement. The fairies appeared to be engaged in a dance, gracefully weaving through the blossoms, their laughter reminiscent of the tinkling of tiny bells. I stood in awe, hardly daring to breathe, for fear of disturbing their enchanting reverie.

What struck me most about this encounter was the overwhelming sense of tranquility and harmony emanating from these ethereal beings. It was as if the very spirit of the garden had come to life through these fairies, and for that brief moment, I was granted a glimpse into a world that existed just beyond the boundaries of our everyday reality.

2. The Mysterious Forest Clearing:

Another vivid childhood memory revolves around an encounter in a dense forest near my grandparents' home. My cousins and I were frequent explorers of these woods, and one day, we stumbled upon a secluded clearing bathed in dappled sunlight.

At the center of this clearing, we encountered a circle of mushrooms, perfectly arranged as if by invisible hands. As we cautiously approached, we noticed minute footprints etched into the soft earth, leading to and from the circle. It was as though someone, or something, had been engaged in a joyous dance.

Intrigued, we decided to sit in quiet anticipation. As the sun dipped below the treetops, a group of fairies emerged from the surrounding foliage. Adorned in vibrant, shimmering attire, their laughter resonated like the melodious songs of birds.

What struck me most about this encounter was the profound feeling of being in the presence of ancient wisdom. The fairies appeared to possess an intricate understanding of the natural world, and their movements harmonized with the rhythm of the forest itself.

III. Reflection: A Glimpse into the Enchanted Realm

These childhood encounters with fairies have left an indelible mark on my consciousness. They were not mere flights of fancy or products of imagination, but tangible experiences that awakened within me a profound sense of wonder and curiosity about the hidden and unseen world. While skeptics may dismiss such encounters as figments of the imagination, those who have experienced them understand that the boundary between reality and the realm of fairies can be exquisitely thin.

These personal stories stand as a testament to the enduring fascination of fairies and the enchanting mysteries that await those who remain open to the possibility of encountering them. Whether these encounters represent glimpses into a parallel world or manifestations of the profound human connection to nature, they continue to inspire wonder and fascination. They serve as a reminder that the mystical and the mundane are often intricately intertwined in ways we may never fully comprehend.

Chapter 10
The Future of Fairy Lore

10A. Contemporary Beliefs - Current Beliefs and Practices Related to Fairies

Connla and the Fairy Maiden

As we immerse ourselves in the realm of fairies, it is imperative to acknowledge that belief in these mystical beings perseveres even in the modern era. While some may regard fairies as mere folklore or the fantastical fabric of fairy tales, others maintain living traditions and contemporary beliefs that tether them to these enchanting entities. Within this chapter, we shall traverse the diverse spectrum of current beliefs and practices linked to fairies, illustrating that the magnetic appeal of these magical beings continues to captivate the hearts and minds of contemporary individuals.

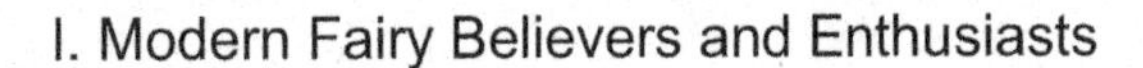

I. Modern Fairy Believers and Enthusiasts

In contemporary society, a multitude of individuals and communities uphold beliefs and practices intertwined with the world of fairies. Here are several noteworthy aspects of this phenomenon:

Neo-Pagan and Nature Spirituality Movements:

Wicca and Druidry: Within modern pagan and nature-based spiritual traditions like Wicca and Druidry, belief in fairies finds a hallowed place. Fairies are often perceived as nature spirits and custodians of the environment.
Fairy Altars and Offerings: Devotees of these traditions may construct altars dedicated to fairies, adorned with offerings such as flowers, crystals, or libations like milk or honey. These offerings symbolize respect and act as gestures of goodwill.
Contemporary Fairy Faith Movements:

Fairy Seers and Communicators: Certain individuals profess the ability to perceive and communicate with fairies, recounting their encounters in a manner akin to traditional folklore. These experiences are shared through mediums such as books, blogs, and social media platforms, engendering a sense of kinship among believers.
Fairy Conventions and Gatherings: Enthusiasts from around the globe congregate at fairy-themed events, fairs, and gatherings. Here, they celebrate their profound affection for fairies, exchange stories, and share their firsthand experiences.

II. Modern Folk Practices and Beliefs

In specific regions, especially those endowed with a rich tapestry of fairy folklore, people continue to engage in folk practices and beliefs entwined with fairies.

Offerings and Apotropaic Practices:

Leaving Gifts: In parts of Ireland and Scotland, individuals leave offerings for fairies like milk, butter, or bread near natural features believed to be inhabited by these beings. These offerings serve to foster benevolent relations and seek protection.
Iron and Cold Iron: The enduring belief in iron as a protective substance against malevolent fairies persists. Iron nails or horseshoes are suspended above doorways as talismans to ward off mischief.
Fairy Sightings and Encounters:

Contemporary Fairy Sightings: Occasional reports of fairy sightings continue to emerge, primarily in rural areas, particularly in regions steeped in fairy folklore tradition. These sightings often entail descriptions of diminutive, radiant beings or elusive, otherworldly phenomena.
III. Modern Fairy Literature and Media

Contemporary literature, cinema, and media wield considerable influence in preserving belief in fairies and keeping their enchanting allure vibrant:

Fantasy Literature and Novels:

Authors Like Holly Black: Contemporary writers like Holly Black have played pivotal roles in the revival of interest in fairies. Works such as "Tithe" and "The Cruel Prince" portray fairies as intricate, multifaceted entities.
Reimagining Classic Characters: Time-honored fairy tales have undergone inventive reinterpretations, from the TV series "Once Upon a Time" to the film "Maleficent," reinvigorating iconic fairy tale characters.
Fairy-Themed Entertainment:

Movies and Television: Films and TV shows centered around fairies, such as "FernGully: The Last Rainforest," "Pan's Labyrinth," and "Fairy Tail," continue to sustain fascination with these mythical beings among modern audiences.
Video Games: Video games like "The Legend of Zelda" series frequently feature fairy companions or incorporate elements inspired by fairy folklore.
IV. Commercialization and Cultural Iconography

Fairies have also become commercialized and represent popular cultural symbols.

1. Commercial Products:
Fairy Figurines and Merchandise: An array of fairy figurines, clothing, jewelry, and home decor items are readily available, catering to enthusiasts who cherish and collect fairy-themed merchandise.

Children's Entertainment: Fairy-themed children's books, toys, and animated series like "Winx Club" continue to enrapture young audiences.

2. New Interpretations:
Gender and Diversity: In contemporary interpretations, fairies often challenge conventional gender roles and embrace diversity, reflecting evolving societal values and inclusivity.

In conclusion, modern beliefs and practices surrounding fairies underscore the enduring fascination with these mystical beings. Whether expressed through spiritual traditions, folk customs, literature, or commercial ventures, fairies persist in captivating the human imagination, reminding us of the enchanting and magical aspects of the world we inhabit. These beliefs and practices demonstrate that, for many, the connection with fairies remains a vibrant and meaningful facet of contemporary life.

Chapter 10B: Preserving Fairy Lore - The Importance of Preserving Fairy Folklore and Traditions

Fairies, those timeless and enchanting beings, have woven themselves into the fabric of human culture for centuries. Their presence is etched into the tapestry of folklore and traditions, reminding us of our connection to the natural world. As we explore the significance of preserving fairy lore in this chapter, we delve into current beliefs and practices related to fairies. These traditions not only reflect our enduring fascination with the mystical but also underscore the importance of cultural heritage.

I. The Living Legacy of Fairy Lore

1. Oral Traditions:
Storytelling: Oral traditions have played an integral role in passing down fairy lore from one generation to the next. Elders and storytellers regale audiences with tales of fairy encounters, enchantments, and valuable lessons.
Community Bonds: These traditions foster community bonds as stories are shared around the hearth or during special gatherings. Fairy tales serve as a means to connect with others and preserve shared cultural experiences.

2. Folk Festivals:
Celebratory Events: In numerous regions, annual festivals and fairs pay homage to fairies and their profound connection to nature. These events include elaborate rituals, parades, and captivating performances inspired by fairy folklore.
Cultural Identity: Such festivals contribute to a sense of cultural identity, serving as a poignant reminder of the significance of fairy beings in local heritage.

II. Beliefs in the Modern World

1. Contemporary Fairy Encounters:
Personal Experiences: Across the globe, people continue to report encounters with fairies, whether as ethereal beings or manifestations of nature. These accounts contribute to the enduring tradition of belief in fairies.
Urban Legends: In urban environments, modern interpretations of fairies take on fresh forms, mirroring our evolving relationship with the natural world. Fairy encounters in city parks, for example, have become a part of urban folklore.

2. Neo-Pagan and New Age Movements:
Revival of Nature Spirituality: Neo-Pagan and New Age movements have emphasized the spiritual facets of nature and the imperative of preserving the environment. Fairies often find a place within these belief systems as revered nature spirits.
Herbalism and Healing: Some practitioners advocate for the healing properties of plants associated with fairies and incorporate herbal remedies into their spiritual practices.

III. Art, Literature, and Media

1. Literary Resurgence:
Contemporary Fairy Tales: Modern authors continue to craft fairy tales that explore timeless themes of magic, transformation, and the enduring allure of the mystical. These narratives contribute to the ongoing evolution of fairy lore.
Reimaginings: Fairy tales are reimagined and adapted into various forms, including novels, graphic novels, and feminist retellings, providing fresh perspectives on traditional fairy tales.

2. Visual Arts and Entertainment:
Artistic Inspiration: Fairies persistently inspire visual artists, spanning painters, illustrators, and sculptors. Their representations in diverse art forms sustain the enchantment associated with fairies.
Film and Television: Fairy lore permeates popular culture through movies and TV series featuring fairy characters and captivating storylines, ensuring that these beings remain both relevant and enthralling.

IV. Conservation and Environmentalism

1. Nature Conservation:

- Preservation of Ecosystems: Some environmentalists and conservationists see fairies as symbols of the natural world's delicate balance. Efforts to protect forests, water bodies, and wildlife may include references to fairy lore as a way to connect with the public.
- Eco-Spirituality: The belief in fairies and their role in preserving nature can inspire eco-spiritual practices that encourage responsible stewardship of the environment.

2. Ethical Foraging and Plant Conservation:

- Responsible Gathering: Those who believe in the fairies' connection to plants advocate for ethical foraging practices and sustainable harvesting. These practices ensure the longevity of plant species associated with fairy folklore.
- Plant Conservation: Efforts to conserve native plant species are linked to preserving fairy traditions. By safeguarding these plants, we protect both the natural world and the cultural heritage connected to them.

V. The Power of Imagination

1. Nurturing Creativity:

- Children's Education: Fairy tales and folklore continue to play a vital role in nurturing children's imagination and creativity. These stories encourage a sense of wonder and curiosity about the world.
- Cultural Expression: Preserving fairy lore allows for the continued expression of cultural values, beliefs, and artistic creativity.

2. Cross-Cultural Exchange:

- Global Connection: In our interconnected world, fairy folklore serves as a bridge between cultures. Shared stories and beliefs about fairies can foster cultural exchange and understanding.
- Universal Themes: Fairy tales often explore universal themes such as love, loss, transformation, and the triumph of good over evil. These themes resonate across cultures and contribute to the universality of fairy lore.

VI. The Call to Preserve Fairy Lore

Heritage Conservation: Preserving fairy lore is not just about the conservation of stories and beliefs; it is about safeguarding cultural heritage. These traditions connect us to our ancestors and the wisdom they gleaned from their relationships with the natural world.
Identity and Belonging: Fairy folklore reinforces a sense of identity and belonging, both on a personal and a communal level. It reminds us of who we are and where we come from.
Sustainability: The importance of preserving the natural world, as exemplified by fairy lore, cannot be overstated in the face of modern environmental challenges. Our connection to the Earth and the beings that inhabit it, whether real or mythical, underscores our responsibility to protect and conserve the planet.

Conclusion

Summarizing Key Points and Insights

As we conclude our captivating journey through the enchanting world of fairy lore, we find ourselves at the crossroads of history, culture, nature, and imagination. This exploration has not only unraveled the timeless mysteries surrounding these mystical beings but has also revealed the profound impact they continue to exert on our lives and the world around us.

Introduction: Our journey commenced with a personal motivation to delve into the realm of fairies, a realm where wonder and curiosity reign supreme. This introduction set the stage for our exploration, emphasizing the intimate connection each of us can forge with the subject matter, regardless of our background or beliefs.

Chapter 1: The Nature of Fairies: In this chapter, we embarked on a quest to understand the very essence of fairies. We traced their origins through history, from the earliest beliefs to the ever-evolving lore that has captured the human imagination. Our exploration revealed that fairies are not merely mythical creatures but manifestations of our collective consciousness, reflecting our evolving worldview and cultural aspirations.

Chapter 2: Folklore and Legends: Our journey led us deeper into the heart of fairy folklore, where ancient legends and regional variations intertwined. We unearthed the stories of heroes and heroines who crossed paths with these mystical beings, witnessing how fairy tales have bridged the gap between generations and cultures. These tales, passed down through generations, are a testament to the enduring power of storytelling.

Chapter 3: Classifications of Fairies: In this chapter, we navigated the intricate taxonomies of fairies, delving into their varied characteristics and roles. Whether we examined their elemental associations or uncovered lesser-known species, we discovered the richness of fairy diversity. Such classifications serve as a reminder that, like the natural world itself, fairy lore is beautifully multifaceted.

Chapter 4: Myths and Legends: As we explored epic fairy myths and their modern interpretations, we found ourselves in a realm where time, culture, and creativity converged. The legacy of fairy myths lives on, inspiring contemporary literature, film, and art. These myths continue to shape our understanding of the mystical and the profound.

Chapter 5: The Good and The Bad Fairies: In examining the duality of fairies as benevolent protectors and mischievous tricksters, we encountered valuable moral lessons embedded within fairy tales. The contrast between the light and dark sides of fairy lore reminds us of the complexities of human nature and the enduring appeal of storytelling.

Chapter 6: Species of Fae: Our exploration led us to discover the rich tapestry of fairy species, from common and well-known to obscure and regional. Each species revealed unique attributes and legends, reinforcing the idea that within the world of fairies, diversity is celebrated.

Chapter 7: Interacting with Fairies: As we sought ways to connect with fairies, we uncovered methods of communication and the profound link between fairies and the natural world. Our journey illuminated the belief that forging a connection with nature is an essential aspect of nurturing a connection with fairies.

Chapter 8: How to Find Fairies: In our quest to find fairies, we learned that the search is not just about spotting these elusive beings but also about fostering an appreciation for the natural world. We discovered that the guardianship of nature is intertwined with our own efforts to protect fairy habitats.

Chapter 9: Fairy Encounters: Through personal stories and scientific perspectives, we delved into the mystique of fairy encounters. While some may approach these accounts with skepticism, the allure of these tales reminds us of the enduring human fascination with the mystical and the unexplained.

Chapter 10: The Future of Fairy Lore: Our exploration culminated in a reflection on the contemporary beliefs and practices related to fairies. We witnessed how technology and globalization have influenced the evolution of fairy lore. Moreover, we highlighted the importance of preserving fairy folklore and traditions as they continue to enrich our lives and cultural heritage.

In conclusion, our journey through the world of fairy lore has been a testament to the enduring allure of the mystical and the timeless power of human imagination. These enchanting beings, whether benevolent or mischievous, serve as mirrors reflecting our hopes, fears, and desires. They remind us of the intricate relationship between humanity and the natural world, and they beckon us to explore the ever-enticing realm of the fantastical.

As we bid farewell to the realm of fairies, may we carry forward the wisdom and wonder we have gained, nurturing our connection with the natural world, preserving our cultural heritage, and embracing the enduring enchantment of fairy lore in all its forms. Whether we encounter fairies in the pages of a story, the depths of a forest, or the recesses of our own imagination, may we always remember that the magic lies within us, waiting to be awakened by the call of the mystical and the unknown.

Attributions

"Celtic Fairy Tales" by Selected and edited by Joseph Jacobs (Sydney, New South Wales, Australia 1854–1916 New Rochelle, New York), John Dickson Batten (British, 1860–1932), David Nutt (London) via The Metropolitan Museum of Art is licensed under CC0 1.0

"Fairy in Irises" by Dora Wheeler (1856–1940) via The Metropolitan Museum of Art is licensed under CC0 1.0

"The Story of the Princess of the Blue Pavillion: The Youth of Rum Is Entertained in a Garden by a Fairy and her Maidens", Folio from a Khamsa (Quintet) of Amir Khusrau Dihlavi" by Amir Khusrau Dihlavi (1253–1325), Muhammad Husain Kashmiri (active ca. 1560–1611), Painting by Manohar (active ca. 1582–1624) via The Metropolitan Museum of Art is licensed underCC0 1.0

"Female dancer in fairy costume" by Sergey Chekhonin (Russian, 1878–1936)via The Metropolitan Museum of Art is licensed under CC0 1.0

Edward Robert Hughes, Public Domain via Wikimedia Commons

Thomas Maybank (British, exh. 1898–1912), "A Moonlight Discovery".
https://commons.wikimedia.org/wiki/File:A_Moonlight_Dicovery.jpg

The Plays of William Shakespeare / Edited and Annotated by Charles and Mary Cowden Clarke, Victorian Illustrated Shakespeare Archive

Photo by Tú Nguyễn httpswww.pexels.comphotowoman-in-white-dress-and-wings-1545589.jpg

Photo by Tú Nguyễn: https://www.pexels.com/photo/beautiful-fairy-in-white-dress-1545590/

Richard Dadd (1817–1886) Photo credit: Harris Museum, Art Gallery & Library
https://www.wikiart.org/en/richard-dadd/puck

Made in the USA
Coppell, TX
18 December 2024